THE NEW REPUBLIC II:
THE QLIPHOTHIC GATES

PART TWO OF A THREE VOLUME TAVISH STEWART
ADVENTURE

K.R.M. Morgan

K.R.M. MORGAN

MADBAGUS BOOKS

Copyright © 2022 by K.R.M. Morgan

ISBN: 978-1-9164472-2-6

Cover design by MadBagus

Footnotes

Based on feedback from readers, in this second Tavish Stewart adventure, I have adopted the use of footnotes to provide the equivalent of an optional "director's cut" version of the story. Those who do not desire such additional information will be able to read the simplified version of the tale and perhaps save the footnotes for any subsequent revisits to the story.

Acknowledgements

The author wishes to acknowledge the help and support from his wife, Maddy, without whom this book would not have been possible.

Social Media

If you enjoy reading this book, please leave a review on social media so others can also discover the adventures of Tavish Stewart.

K.R.M. MORGAN

Summary of the previous book

A series of audacious daytime raids succeed in kidnapping the heirs to the royal bloodlines in every European capital except London. Due to fortuitous timing, antiquarian and Scottish army veteran Tavish Stewart intervenes. However, Stewart's accidental involvement plunges him and his friends into the midst of a sinister plot for global domination by the descendants of one of the most ruthless and evil regimes of all time.

Extract from the closing section of The New Republic: Old Dreams New Nightmares:

"The depth to which these items were buried into the wall indicated to Stewart that whatever was throwing the objects was able to exert considerable force. This supposition was confirmed moments later when, in the full light from the kitchen spots, two of the heavy framed, birchwood, Ercol Shalstone kitchen chairs flew directly in front of where Stewart was standing, smashing full into him and knocking him violently to the floor. The remaining chairs landed violently onto Stewart's prone body before the Scotsman could gather himself back to his feet. These massive blows stunned him to such an extent that he could not respond when he suddenly felt himself being forcibly dragged across the room, picked up some four feet into the air and violently smashed into the wall beside the bed. By now, Stewart was severely dazed. He had been unable to take any evasive action to minimize the full brunt of these latest repeated beatings. All he could do was look up from the floor where he was lying beside the bed, covered in his own blood, and take some small comfort that Sinclair remained oblivious to all the mayhem unfolding around her.

Stewart's brief respite was sadly short-lived as, almost immediately, he heard the ominous noise of the large, wooden Ercol Corso kitchen bench, making a loud scraping sound as it was forcibly dragged at speed across the floor towards him. The heavy bench rose into the air, clearly being readied to repeatedly strike the last vestiges of life from the Scotsman's body.

Gathering himself for one final effort, Stewart looked down at his badly cut arms and hands, where numerous glass and ceramic shards were now deeply embedded in his flesh. His blood-soaked palm rested on one of the stone rubbings that had been smashed from the wall. With what would probably be one of his final thoughts, he noted the grim synchronicity, that the blood-soaked image on the stone rubbing was none other than the Triquetra symbol that had featured so vividly in his recent dream. Bracing himself for the pending deadly impact, Stewart uttered an oath that, should he survive, he would hunt down that bastard Cortez and put an end to his ambitions for his New Republic!"

1   BLOOD PACT

"They are fairies; he that speaks to them shall die." – William Shakespeare.

1st-floor kitchen area,
Stewart's Antiquarians,
18a, New Bond St, Mayfair,
London W1S 2RB

04:08HRS (GMT+1), 9th Sept, Present day

As Stewart completed uttering his blood oath to hunt down Cortez and end his New Republic, a millisecond long, brilliant light was so intense that it whited out the entire room and temporarily blinded the Scotsman. The ferocious flash was followed closely by a deafening roar of thunder, making the whole building shake to its foundations, shattering the glass in the two sash windows at the end of the kitchen and instantly disintegrating the Ercol bench, that was in mid-air flying towards Stewart. The large bench broke into hundreds of small, tinder-sized fragments that scattered to the room's furthest corners.

In hindsight, whenever Stewart would recall this incident, he would always remark that it felt like the lightning and its accompanying thunderclap took place entirely inside the small kitchen, but of course, this is a meteorological impossibility[1].

As Stewart's night vision began to return, the first thing he saw was an indistinct shape, slowly passing alongside his body as he lay on the floor beside the bed. Assuming this was one of the attacking shadow forms, Stewart rolled

---

[1] Assuming, of course, that this *was* a meteorological phenomenon.

sideways, away from the movement, only to partially see a small, hooded figure, around four-foot-tall. This figure appeared to have come through the wall behind the bed based on its location and forward motion. However improbable that possibility might have seemed to Stewart earlier in the evening, his recent experiences in the kitchen had opened his mind considerably to what was possible.

As the Scotsman slowly blinked to try and recover more of his night vision[2], he noted that, in contrast to the shadow entities which had obscured light, this figure emanated a blue glow that illuminated the room with a feeling of warmth. In addition, the foul stench that had filled the air had been replaced with what smelt and felt like a refreshing forest breeze, scented with pine.

Now that Stewart's sight was returning fully, he noticed more details from the strange new figure visiting the kitchen. It had bare feet, with extremely long toes and even longer toenails. It wore a long, green silk gown beneath a full-length, red, hooded robe. One odd detail that struck Stewart was that, although the figure was walking over the broken debris of glass and ceramics, there was no evidence that the figure's bare feet were being cut on the numerous razor-sharp fragments. As Stewart looked more closely to see if there was a trail of blood on the floor where the figure had passed, he suddenly noticed that everything about this visitor was an illusion. The entity's feet were, in fact, not feet but twigs, and the green silk gown was a layered structure of leaves and foliage organised into a shape resembling a dress.

Stewart initially struggled with the realisation but was forced to conclude that the entity that had just materialised must be the same being that had appeared to him in his recent

---

[2] Shutting the eyes can re-sensitize the retina cells (rods) responsible for human night vision.

dream. The presence of this strange visitation was inexplicably linked with a total transformation of the atmosphere within the kitchen. The two shadow figures and the oppressive sense of evil were gone, as was the cold, darkness and the foul stench of decay.

Just as the Scotsman was pulling himself up to check on Sinclair, another unexpected blast of wind blew out what remained of the two sash windows that faced New Bond Street. The foliage that formed the strange visitation gathered itself into a much tighter formation and flew out of the now open windows into the London night.

Sinclair had, by now, regained consciousness and was standing beside her side of the bed. Reaching down, she picked up a few of the oak leaves that were scattered in a long trail towards the now gaping, open sash windows.

"Tavish? A hedge just walked through your kitchen."

"Yes, Cynthia, I believe it just did."

Sinclair looked at the absolute destruction all around her. Literally, every item of furniture, glassware and crockery had been smashed into pieces. Deadly sharp shards of glass and ceramic were deeply embedded into the plaster of the walls, alongside knives, forks and even a few spoons. Before Sinclair could say anything, Stewart interjected,

"You know when you wake up and just hate everything?"

Sinclair laughed,

"Happens to me all the time. But seriously, what the fuck happened here?"

The Scotsman reached down, picking up his now severely scratched and dented Nokia 3310 lying under some of the broken glass and ceramic beside his bed. The display was shattered, but it still worked when Stewart pressed the on button.

"I don't know, but I know someone who will."

Meanwhile, less than a mile away from 18a New Bond Street, at the Wigmore Hall, the four magical adepts were still in their ritual positions for the Yamarāja ceremony.

The adepts and Cortez, who stood beside the Shinto priest, watched the Priestess, sitting cross-legged on the floor, performing a tantric tvikShepa-shakti (astral projection) meditation, during which she passed frequent comments about the progress of the astral attack. Some moments earlier, she had announced that Stewart had exhibited unusual strength of will and had broken free from the hypnotic nerve paralysis she had remotely induced. She had to focus the entire force at her disposal against the Scotsman to finish him before turning her attention on Sinclair, who remained under the influence of the sleep paralysis.

The Priestess's breathing then became more laboured, and thick beads of blood-coloured perspiration began to form on her brow. Suddenly, she pulled her body upright and opened her eyes wide with a loud gasp.

The Shinto priest, Monk and Shaman exchanged looks and turned expectantly at the seated Priestess.

Cortez externalised the shared question,

"Is it done?"

While Cortez and the gathered adepts were eagerly waiting to hear of the Scotsman's demise, less than a mile away, in Mayfair, Tavish Stewart was seated beside Sinclair on the only remaining item of furniture still standing in the kitchen, the folded-out sofa bed. Stewart held his battered Nokia in his right hand as the pair listened to the dialling tone playing from the small, tinny-sounding speaker at the bottom of the cheap handset.

One thousand one hundred miles South West from where Stewart and Sinclair perched on the edge of their folding bed, Father Thomas O'Neill was seated on a long, grey linen window seat, looking out from his upper-storey flat on Vicolo del Giglio, over the Fontana di Piazza Farnese[3]. He wore a pair of grey cotton chinos[4], a thick white cotton "Bridge of Souls" promotional T-shirt, and worn leather moccasins without socks.

When his iPhone began to vibrate on the nearby wooden side table, O'Neill was enjoying his second espresso[5] of the morning, which he drank from a small, white china demitasse[6] cup. His senses were relishing what had turned out to be one of Rome's glorious, early September sunrises, where the temperatures in the capital are delightfully cooler before the oppressive midday heat dominates the city.

The interior of the Jesuit priest's tiny, one-bedroom apartment was entirely given over to tall, wooden bookcases, each nearly ten feet tall, reaching from the wooden floor boards right up to the dark oak beams that framed the ancient ceilings. Every available space seemed crammed with books and manuscripts, primarily devoted to ancient history, archaeology, and theology. Some of the most recent additions to the library were related to a new theme, the human experience of supernatural phenomena.

---

[3] The ornate fountain, located within Piazza Farnese (00186 Rome).

[4] Flint and Tinder, 365 Pant - Tapered

[5] Pellini No. 82 Vivace blend.

[6] An expresso cup.

The only space in the flat not devoted to book storage was occupied by two framed certificates[7] and a single, somewhat blurry photograph[8] showing O'Neill standing beside two other priests. One was a scruffy-looking older man with a shock of greying ginger hair. The other was a supremely elegant-looking younger man with a long, black ponytail and dressed in a superbly fitted, dark wool suit, complete with a magnificent diamond tie pin.

Checking the time on his old battle-scarred Nite field watch, O'Neill put down the book he was reading[9] and picked up the still buzzing iPhone. The caller's identity made him smile, but that expression was quickly lost when he heard what had befallen his friend Stewart.

As O'Neill listened to what had occurred in the small kitchen above the London showroom, he reached for the pen[10] and small notepad[11] resting between the paws of "Ezekiel", Venchencho's ancient, ginger tomcat, who had been soundly sleeping on O'Neill's lap. The old cat's large green eyes jumped open momentarily at the disturbance, perhaps

---

[7] O'Neill's Jesuit ordination from Georgetown University, USA and his doctorate degree in Classics, Ancient History and Archaeology, jointly awarded by Trinity College, Dublin and Columbia University, USA.

[8] Taken by a numismatic dealer, near Vatican City, who had just provided a very finely dressed priest with a leather bag purported to contain thirty silver Roman coins, with a *highly* unsavoury history.

[9] Israel Regardie's "The Art and Meaning of Magic". (2018), New Falcon Publications (US). ISBN-13 : 978-1561845552. One of the numerous texts O'Neill had rescued from the wastebins outside Venchencho's office.

[10] A stainless-steel Fisher Space pen, that had accompanied O'Neill on numerous archaeological digs all over the world.

[11] A Moleskine Classic Ruled Paper Notebook.

wondering if O'Neill was planning a visit to the kitchen before settling back to whatever profound meditative state cats indulge in while on their owner's lap.

As O'Neill made notes about the various alleged paranormal occurrences, he began a series of questions to clarify in his mind what might have caused the phenomena. Did the building have a previous history of haunting? Had any new objects with an esoteric history been brought into the building? Were there any recent building works nearby or any renovations in older parts of the structure? Had any adolescents started staying at the property? And, finally, had anyone recently started any esoteric-related studies, sought advice from an Ouija board, or performed a seance?

Stewart answered in the negative to all of O'Neill's list of "usual suspects" for violent poltergeist phenomena, causing O'Neill to go quiet for a few seconds before admitting that,

"It is very unusual for such persistent, highly directed attacks to occur suddenly. Normally, there is a gradual increase in paranormal activity over weeks. Even in extreme cases, I have not heard of such intense, directed violence towards an individual. Normally, thrown objects miss observers and seem intended more to attract attention than to put people in mortal peril."

Stewart then mentioned his meeting with the group of four ritual magicians during the New Republic event at the Wigmore Hall, followed by the strange appearance of the image of the female magician from the same group, immediately before the poltergeist violence started, adding,

"Thomas, if you don't know what to make of it, I don't suppose there is any chance of consulting Venchencho?"

O'Neill shook his head from a force of habit even though he knew Stewart could not see him.

"Sadly not, he has taken a medical leave of absence. Or at least that is what we have been told. The truth is no one has seen him for some weeks. Everything is being run now by Cardinal Regio, an Italian, who has introduced some quite radical changes, especially in the Deliverance division. He is systematically replacing spiritual interventions with pharmaceuticals."

O'Neill sighed, partially at his inability to help and partially by the Church's new approach to confronting Evil, before continuing,

"Tavish, if you are correct, and you have become targeted by a group of black magicians, then really you need another ritual magician to advise you."

O'Neill consulted his watch,

"It's nearly dawn with you. Daylight should make you relatively safe. I will ask an expert in ceremonial magic to call you later during the day. Her name is Mathers. Madeleine Mathers."

2   AUDIENCE WITH THE QUEEN

Being against Evil doesn't make you good." – Ernest Hemmingway

Wigmore Hall,
36 Wigmore Street,
Marylebone, London W1U 2BP

04.23HRS (GMT+1), 9th Sept, Present day

Meanwhile, at the Wigmore Hall, the three adepts and Cortez stood in silence, awaiting an announcement from the Priestess about the imminent violent end of Stewart and Sinclair. At the Southern end of their ritual space, the Priestess became increasingly agitated, her body visibly shaking, beads of blood sweat flowing copiously from the exposed areas of flesh on her face, arms and legs.

Suddenly, she began screaming, over and over, each scream louder than the last, until she was howling at the top of her voice, repeating a single word,

"Nahin. Nahin! Nahin !!!"

(No. NO! NOOO!)

As the screams reverberated around the courtyard, a brilliant flash of lightning was followed instantaneously by a thunderclap that sounded like a massive bomb had gone off inside the enclosure beside the Wigmore Hall. The unexpected violence shocked Cortez as the glass in the windows facing the courtyard exploded violently, sending flying glass fragments several feet into the paved courtyard space.

Suddenly, a violent wind blew with such ferocity that it made the clothes, hair, and facial skin of those gathered in the courtyard ripple. Cortez staggered backwards a step and reflected that such a violent gale was strange as it was a completely calm evening, filled with thick, damp fog. He could only assume that the weather had suddenly broken or that the next element of the ceremony had begun.

A powerful vertical column of air was drawn down from the sky above them, forming a violent spinning vortex in the centre of the courtyard. Cortez reflected the freak gust must be some kind of rare atmospheric disturbance that was pulling down assorted debris from the sky, high above them. Branches, leaves and soil began to fall from above them and become gathered by the vortex into a single, central point in the middle of the courtyard.

While Cortez focused on his meteorological speculations, the Priestess became increasingly agitated. She sobbed hysterically, clearly terrified of whatever was happening. The other three adepts looked confused, as though they were struggling to accept the evidence of their own eyes.

As the pillar of storm debris accumulated in the courtyard's centre, the wind velocity increased the rotational speed of the spinning vortex. After a few more moments, the clockwise, centrifugal force threw out two large, spherical objects, slightly smaller than soccer balls and what looked to Cortez like an assorted collection of sticks of different lengths and thicknesses. These ejected objects made a clattering and rattling noise as they rolled violently over the stone paving of the courtyard, towards where the Priestess knelt.

These multiple objects ended their short, high-speed journey when they reached the Priestess, coming to a dramatic stop directly in front of her knees. Once they had come to a halt, Cortez could see that the two spherical balls were blood-covered human skulls that had been brutally skinned. There were harsh and deep blade marks visible on what remained of the heads in several places. The assorted sticks, now gathered beside the two skulls, were revealed to be an assortment of gore-covered human bones.

The three adepts stood in shocked silence, looking at the bloody remains that were all that was left of the two reanimated corpses that they had sent against Stewart and Sinclair. Cortez, in contrast, was merely confused, as he was as yet uncertain if this latest development was part of the ritual or some unintended repercussion.

Looking at the Priestess, it was clear that she was in considerable physical and mental pain as, still seated in her meditative pose, she had wrapped her arms around her knees and had started rocking her body gently back and fore, sobbing.

The disintegration of the two reanimated bodies and their associated spectral forms had taken a massive toll on the Priestess. Her face had aged visibly, becoming grey and haunted, as the failure of the ritual had drained the life force from her body.

Eventually, after what seemed an age but was less than a minute, the Priestess looked up at the rotating vortex and screamed in rage. The sound broke the spell that had seemed to fix Cortez's attention upon the gore-covered remains, and now, instead, he followed the direction of the Priestess' gaze. Her terror was directed towards a figure that had started to form from the wind-gathered debris in the courtyard's centre. What had initially been a mass of assorted woodland debris coalesced into a vaguely human silhouette, a cloaked form that looked like a hunched, older woman.

As the light, from the four flickering candles, at the cardinal points around the figure of the elderly woman altered, the image transformed from one that was vaguely human to a variety of other forms. It alternated between looking like bunches of branches and leaves and then changed to other

Things - dark, frightening shapes, full of hideous menace claws, sparkling predatory eyes and fangs. They were the personification of the terrors of every dark solitary night spent in the wilderness and of every small child left alone in the dark.

"What the hell is that?" demanded Cortez.

In a fit of crazed fear, the priestess suddenly rose and, while screaming, charged directly at the mass of rotating debris. With the tantric Yamarāja ritual dagger in her right hand, she commenced a series of wild and uncoordinated attacks directed at the strange shape that had formed before them.

The Priestess cut with the blade in a series of frantic strokes, followed by deep, penetrating stabs, into the centre of the strange figure. The knife strikes were so rapid that it was not until after the attack concluded that it became evident that each cut and thrust made by the ritual blade had immediately acted back upon the Priestess' own body. Deep slashing wounds opened on her face, arms, chest and stomach, each wound haemorrhaging profusely, soaking the already red sari with a brighter, arterial red.

As her blood poured over the paving stones, the Priestess doubled over from a series of vicious wounds that opened up in her stomach. She staggered a few steps, issuing rasping, bubbling noises from her punctured lungs, before finally collapsing to the ground. The blood-soaked ritual dagger rolled across the paving stones away from her now lifeless body.

Cortez stood shell-shocked as he tried to take in the full implication of the vicious destruction of the Priestess.

The Shinto priest yelled,

"You should get out, now!"

18

towards Cortez, as the Monk and Shaman began making pitiful whimpering sounds, clearly terrified at whatever had appeared.

To his credit, Cortez was not so easily frightened.

"Don't just cower there. You are supposed to be some of the world's most senior adepts, Masters of the Dark Arts! Use your Art! Threaten it with endless darkness...."

The Shinto priest looked stunned at the naivety of Cortez's demand,

"Senor, there is no form of darkness that this entity is not already!"

A strange series of sounds began to echo around the courtyard. At first, Cortez could not recognise them as anything more than the random noises made by leaves rustling in a breeze. Then he realised they were forming words. Each syllable made Cortez feel increasingly nauseous and light-headed.

"Mortals. Always imagining that by embracing darkness, they will shine like stars. The truth is, an embrace by darkness always consumes light."

At this pronunciation, the Monk and Shaman rose to their feet. They removed their shoes and ran barefoot across the courtyard, as fast as possible, towards the exit furthest away from the manifestation. Moments later, the Shinto priest bolted behind them, following their example.

Cortez snarled after them,

"You, bloody useless cowards," as he watched the three figures scurrying to the Welbeck Way exit doors at the North of the courtyard.

Upon reaching the doors, the three figures looked back towards the whirling mass in the courtyard's centre and pulled open the double doors with a shared look of relief.

Cortez, who had now given up on the "three masters of the dark arts", turned his attention toward the "whirlwind entity". Having given up on magic, he determined to handle the threat in a more direct and old-fashioned manner.

He drew a classic, gunmetal grey luger[12] from a concealed leather holster[13] inside the left side of his dinner jacket. He aimed the pistol's well-worn sites onto the centre mass of the spinning vortex and gave the rotating *thing* the full benefit of three full-metal jacket rounds from his grandfather's pistol[14].

The deafening report from the rapid, repeated gunshots echoed around the high courtyard walls, and then there was an eery stillness, broken only by the distant traffic noise. Cortez became momentarily blinded during the succession of bright discharge flashes from the old weapon. When his vision returned, he found the mysterious spinning vortex had vanished, along with, Cortez noted, the Priestess' ritual dagger.

Just as Cortez was congratulating himself for successfully dealing with the threat, the relative peace of the courtyard was broken by a series of piercing screams and pitiful sobs

---

[12] A Wehrmacht P08 Pistole Parabellum (9×19mm Parabellum). Yes, you know the one, the classic World War Two German pistol.

[13] A brown, full grain leather, Austrian made, Sheplers, Pistol Shoulder Holster.

[14] The metal bottom edge of the grip on Cortez's pistol bore the faded inscription, Gefreiter (lance corporal) Alois Hiedler, 1914-1920. 1st Company of the List Regiment (Bavarian Reserve Infantry Regiment 16).

emanating from the corridor leading from the Welbeck Way exit.

Wondering if some new threat was about to emerge, Cortez turned and aimed his weapon towards the sounds, just in time to see the bodies of the three fleeing adepts staggering back into the courtyard and falling to the floor. The large, bloody entry and exit wounds on their chests and backs gave clear evidence that they had died from the three bullets that Cortez had just discharged.

Before Cortez could fully react, the spinning vortex of debris re-emerged, this time through the open Welbeck Way double doors where the screams had emanated. It covered the twenty yards from the open doors to the courtyard's centre faster than the human eye could process.

Even Cortez, a man accustomed to acts of extreme violence, was stunned by the brutality of the deaths he had just witnessed,

"Mist[15]! How the fuck did they die?"

"Badly" was the chilling reply, pronounced in a voice that exactly replicated Cortez's own, repeating his directive from earlier that evening, when he had instructed the adepts to end Stewart's life.

For the second time that evening, Cortez demonstrated his fearless nature,

"So, my turn..."

There was a menacing pause like the thing was playing with him.

---

[15] Similar to the English usage "Crap".

"No. I simply repaid in perfect measure what had been discharged into the aether[16] this night, nothing more.

You must face an appropriate mortal response to your actions. One that will follow you relentlessly, destroying all your well-laid plans until, finally, you will welcome death when it comes."

Senor Cortez-Hiedler accepted the ominous threat remarkably calmly as he watched the vortex of wind intensify, pulling the woodland debris up into the air, gradually emptying the courtyard of the strange manifestation, leaving only silence.

After all that he had learned that evening, Cortez suddenly realised what mortal response could endanger his plans. It filled him with an unfamiliar emotion of fear as he quietly uttered the two words,

"Tavish Stewart!"

---

[16] Aether was the fifth element in alchemy and other occult sciences. Believed to be the medium through which invisible influence propagated.

3   THE UNUSUAL SUSPECTS

*"The Way of Mastery is to break all the rules—but you have
to know them perfectly before you can do this; otherwise
you are not in a position to transcend them." - Aleister
Crowley, Magical and Philosophical Commentaries on The
Book of the Law*

*Place du Bourg-de-Four
1204 Genève, Switzerland*

05:12HRS (GMT+2), 9th Sept, present day

One thousand five hundred miles West of where Cortez
stood, an attractive woman in her early forties with high
cheekbones and long auburn hair was seated at a small
table outside one of the stylish cafés that line the historic
Place du Bourg-de-Four, in old Geneva.

Having ordered breakfast, Madeleine Mathers was
savouring a black, French blend coffee as she waited for her
meal to be delivered. The steel-rimmed glasses, which she
usually wore, were folded on the top of the patterned blue
table cloth alongside her phone. In preparation for the long
drive that awaited her, she wore a cream-coloured, Rouje
fleece hoodie over a grey Hermes cotton polo shirt, blue
Levi jeans and a pair of comfortable unbranded flat-soled
shoes. The atmosphere around the French Adept was
permeated by a subtle mix of scents, orange, vanilla and
Egyptian musk, that are the signature of certain classic
French perfumeries[17].

The woman's enjoyment of her first coffee of the morning
was interrupted by her phone's ring tone. She consulted the
time on her Mondaine before picking up her large

---

[17] Probably Guerlain or Hermes.

unbranded android phone. Upon seeing the caller's identity, she frowned and sighed deeply before sliding the answer button on the phone's screen to accept the call.

Fifteen minutes later, Stewart's old Nokia buzzed and danced on the sofabed beside Sinclair and the Scotsman. The two of them had taken turns to monitor the phone while the other hurriedly dressed in the small storeroom at the end of the corridor.

"That was quick. Let's hope we can get some answers."

Sinclair commented as Stewart answered the phone and turned the handset to its rudimentary speakerphone mode.

A female voice with a light Parisian accent came over the small, tiny speaker and queried, in English,

"Good morning. Can I speak to a Tavish Stewart, thanks?"

After a brief set of introductions, Stewart described the events of the evening, including a description of the four people he had met at the reception, whom he suspected were behind the strange phenomena that had occurred.

Mathers recognised the descriptions.

"Yes, I think I know of these four people. May I ask, did you notice if they wore a small flying serpent on their clothing?

Stewart nodded,

"Now you mention it, yes, they did. I remember it because it contrasted with the sideways Z symbols worn by most of the goons at the event."

"The Wolfsangel! That is the symbol of those who promote the worldly interests of the Meri-Isfet."

"Merry Icefit?" Queried Sinclair.

"Mais oui, Yes, the Meri-Isfet call themselves the Beloved of Isfet. These four that you met are second-order adepts from this very ancient society."

Realising that Stewart and Sinclair were unfamiliar with such matters, Mather's explained further,

"The Meri-Isfet or Beloved of Isfet are one of the world's oldest esoteric orders, dedicated to the Egyptian God Apep, the snake deity of darkness and chaos. Such principles of evil were called "izft" in ancient Egypt. Members of this society oppose light, order and truth or Ma'at, as the Ancient Egyptians called such positive principles.

"You are telling us this order has existed since the times of the Pharaohs?" Asked Stewart somewhat incredulously.

Mather's laughed at Stewart's scepticism.

"It does not matter if you believe their history. You have experienced their ability, so believe in that instead."

Stewart nodded his agreement, "Yes, Madeleine. Having experienced what I have, I will remain open-minded."

Sinclair interjected, "I take it you are not a member of this Beloved of Isfet?"

Mather's sounded offended,

"Non, Cynthia, I am what you might call *La Résistancere* (opposition) to these people. We are called the Meri-Maat or Beloved of Maat. The more modern name of our organisation is SPLEE[18]."

Mathers then went on,

"Stewart, when you met these four adepts, were there also three men associating with them?

---

[18] The Society for the preservation of European Esoteric Linages, headquartered in Geneva.

The tallest would have been a dark-haired, athletic type. This man looks in his mid to late thirties but is probably older. He is very wealthy and a world-class polo player. Always très style likes expensive things, always wears a very fine suit.

Next would have been a shorter, middle-aged man. An Italian. He wears wire-rimmed glasses. He is a renowned psychiatrist and holds a senior position at the Vatican.

The final of the three is a younger man, who delights in his Viking origins, a loubard,"

Sinclair mouthed *Hooligan* to Stewart as Mathers continued.

"This one has a shaved head and is covered in tattoos.

These three are the most dangerous of the Meri-Isfet. Their names are Salvador, Regio and Pedersen. All three are third-order initiates; Eighth- and Ninth-degree adepts."

Stewart shook his head,

"No, I only noticed the four characters that I already described. Given the ruthless natures of these people, it is odd that none of them has progressed to even higher degrees."

"Hah!" exclaimed Mathers, "One has, or I should say *had*. Her identity is known to you from recent events."

Stewart had already guessed the name,

"Dr Nissa Ad-Dajjal!"

Sinclair and Stewart exchanged a knowing glance before Stewart continued,

"Explains a lot that I could not previously understand."

Sinclair nodded her agreement before adding,

"Sorry to ask, Madeleine, but what exactly are the second and third orders?"

Mathers paused, clearly wondering how much detail she should provide.

"The hermetic traditions that form the basis of the Western Esoteric Tradition have a symbol, called the *Tree of Life*, that can be used for many instructional purposes to explain the many cross correspondences that exist within the material and nonmaterial worlds. This symbol is most often represented as being composed of ten spheres, or foci, ranging from the most material to the most spiritually refined. From material to spiritual, this progression maps the progress and ability of an initiate as they progress through the tree's ten levels."

Stewart interrupted,

"So, there are ten degrees?"

Mathers agreed,

"Yes, ten degrees. The first four degrees form the first order and are related to the study of the four primary Magical elements. The next three degrees form the second-order and are directed towards increasing practical understanding of magic, the so-called "Adeptus" grades. The third and final order has only three degrees related to the ultimate mastery of Magic and self.

"And you are in this third order of SPLEE?" enquired Stewart.

Mathers laughed nervously, "No, Tavish, I am in the second."

Stewart sounded concerned,

"But I assume that there are others who can deal with those three, most dangerous, third-order masters that you mentioned? Having experienced what second-order initiates did to me last night, it would be good to know that their equals counter the worst of the Meri-Isfet in your SPLEE organisation."

"No. SPLEE does not, and never has, to my knowledge, had any member who lays claim to having crossed the *abyss*, to the third order. I should explain that our most ancient traditions assert that such a progression is not possible while in a mortal, physical body."

Stewart nodded,

"I think I understand, Madeleine. There was, once, a similar concept in martial arts. Students would refuse to progress to a rank higher than their teacher. It was thought to indicate a supreme disrespect to take a grade higher than the person who founded the school you followed. Such principles of modesty and respect vanished in the twentieth century, to be replaced by inflated egos. I assume this was the same with the students of the Meri-Isfet."

"Précisément!" whispered the French voice.

Sinclair then interrupted,

"Forgive my asking, Ms Mathers, but how many SPLEE second-order members are actively countering these Beloved of Isfet?"

There was a long pause, then,

"You must understand, Cynthia, the study is très difficile. It takes decades of devoted practice and considerable ability to make even modest progress. Modern life has so many distractions. The dedication amongst the new generation is.... lacking. There are now only a mere handful of us in the second-order, and most are getting too old to be active or *useful* in any practical form of magic."

"Exactly how many are we talking about who would be able to resist the Beloved of Isfet, Madeleine?" Asked Stewart.

There was another long pause, followed by a sigh.

"Honestly? Just me, Tavish. Just me."

Stewart laughed,

"Well, at least we know where we stand. It sounds like we are in quite a similar situation. You with the Meri-Isfet and Cynthia and I with this New Republic."

"Wolfsangel, Tavish. You should use their real name. Over the centuries, you will find that they have adopted many titles to confuse their enemies and advance their agenda of increasing the sum of suffering while promising radical progress but always bringing misery."

"Whatever they call themselves, tell us more about the four who attacked us last night." Asked Stewart, who was now more determined than ever to learn whatever he could to take the fight to Cortez and his damned New Republic.

"Well, the woman goes by the name Adhira Acharya, although it is anybody's guess if that is her real name. The last time I checked, she had progressed to the fifth degree within the second-order of Meri-Isfet, although she is also the head of her own sect, called the Tama.

It is often the case that the adepts within the Meri-Isfet are heads of their own esoteric lodges or organisations. It is a way for Meri-Isfet to gain influence over more followers. However, most grassroots members are unaware of their organisation's linkage unless they exhibit sufficient magical ability or have some privilege that would be of use.

The Tibetan you described is almost certainly, High Lama Namgyal, from the Kagyupa school. He is the leader of a monastery on the high plateau, whose members are known as the "Brothers of the Shadow". I believe Namgyal has progressed to the sixth degree.

The South American you met is a Machis, or Shaman, from a particularly nasty sect within the Argentinean native Mapuche religion. They practice human sacrifice and cannibalism, especially on small children. I am not sure of his magical rank within Meri-Isfet, but I suspect it would be fifth degree.

The worst of the group you met is Master Kenji, a sixth-degree adept and a full-blown Kannushi[19] at his own temple within the Jishu-Jinja Shrine complex in Kyoto. His temple is renowned for practising some of Japan's darker spiritual pursuits. Including the projection of *Onryō* or vengeful spirits."

"So, you think Onryo was responsible for what happened?" asked Stewart.

"I am not sure, was there anything odd that occurred before the manifestation?"

Stewart initially hesitated, not wishing to sound even crazier, but then continued,

"Well, I know it must sound odd, but, yes, a ball of luminous material appeared, floated to the head of the bed where I was sleeping, and slashed the plasterwork."

"Ah! Tavish, can you send me a picture of what was carved into the wall?"

Stewart complied, using his bashed-up Nokia.

"My phone is not the best, but here we go."

The Scotsman pressed the send button for the media message.

There was a pause, followed by the sound of the French woman typing on her phone, evidently searching through some digitised content, as one could hear the sound of her thumbing through several screens.

Then the French-accented voice returned on the tiny speaker,

---

[19] 神主 - "god master".

"C'est mauvais. Sorry, I mean, it's bad, Stewart. The script is an extract from an ancient tamasic Sanskrit sutra related to the summoning and control of Vizasati Sattva. It is one of the darkest aspects of the Vedic occult arts. The ancients used it to provide protective curses on buildings and objects. It explains the dead bodies often found under and beside ancient sites. But you say these two were already dead when you left them?"

"Yes, very dead." Responded Stewart.

"Then they must have temporarily reanimated their physical bodies before binding them to this new purpose."

"Is that possible?" Sinclair's voice revealed her horror and shock at the possibility.

"Advanced adepts, such as these four, can perform the most unspeakable necromantic acts. Bringing back an immortal spirit from its karmic interlude between lives to kill another person is a fundamental breach of everything sacred. As such, it would be a delight for them." Summarised Mathers.

"And they very nearly succeeded. Thankfully that other *thing* appeared before I was pounded to death under a heavy kitchen bench. Do you have any idea what saved me?" enquired Stewart.

"Without seeing it in person, I can only speculate," said the French adept, "But it sounds to me that when you performed the restoration of the standing stones on your estate and made that rubbing of the symbols carved there, you made an unconscious bond with the entities for whom the standing stones were constructed originally. In that moment of desperation, when your life blood soaked the symbol, you unconsciously invoked these entities with strong intent. Just like a trained Magician consciously does during a ritual."

"And what exactly are these entities that Tavish invoked?" Asked Sinclair.

"They have many names," said Mathers, "different in each region of the world. Some call them Djinn, some regard them as Gods, and others think of them as Devils. In Europe, we know them collectively as the Fae."

Stewart laughed, "Fairies? You mean the small, winged delights from fairy tales?"

Mathers became deadly serious,

"That is a highly romanticised image, created for small children in the nineteenth century. For millennia before our cute modern representations, the Fae were things to be feared and avoided."

"So, this Fae entity is good?" Asked Stewart.

Mathers laughed,

"It is not that simple, Tavish. It saved you because it felt inclined to do so. It could just as easily have ignored your plight or joined in the attack against you. The Fae are notoriously fickle."

Stewart was still trying to get his head around what had happened,

"Would the four adepts be able to destroy this thing?"

Mathers paused, clearly thinking how best to answer,

"These beings are not just magical. Some believe that they *are* magic. All a Magician can do with them is to try and use their manifestation to aid their own goal, much as old-fashioned sailors did with a strong wind. In some cases, Magicians try and make some kind of pact where the entity is the dominant partner. But it would be a very one-sided affair and likely to go badly when the entity becomes bored with the arrangement. Since Black Magicians are invariably bullies, they are also essentially cowards, so my prediction would be that they would run when confronted with a powerful Fae."

"So, the Fae entity would be like a cat with a mouse?" clarified Sinclair.

Mathers laughed, "No, Cynthia, more like a Tiger!"

4   WOLF IN THE FOLD

"Fenrir will walk with its mouth open, its lower jaw skimming the earth and its upper jaw touching the sky, and it would open it wider if there was room. Flames will burst from his eyes and nostrils." - Snorri Sturluson's 13th century Icelandic Prose Edda.

Apartment 17a,
Upper story, Vicolo del Giglio
00186 Rome,
Metropolitan City of Rome, Italy

06:17HRS (GMT+2), 9th Sept, Present day

Father Thomas O'Neill was sleeping, fully clothed, having fallen asleep on his sofa in the early hours of the morning. In his current dream, he was walking through a dense jungle, as he had done during numerous archaeological expeditions in South America. Patches of distant sunlight fell through the tree canopy high above him, dappling the ground and highlighting the vivid colours of the thick detritus that littered the forest floor. Out of long-formed habit, O'Neill focused on the area immediately ahead where he was about to tread. This behaviour was to avoid stumbling over the larger fallen branches and segments of bark that could lie under the accumulated leaves and keep an awareness of the numerous dangerous creatures[20] that often lay hidden in the undergrowth. Pushing his way through the thick foliage made up of innumerable tendrils

---

[20] Such as the Pit Viper and Bushmaster.

34

of jungle creeper[21], O'Neill froze as he heard the distinctive sound of the barking cough from a female Jaguar[22].

The animal was hidden somewhere extremely close by, probably behind the dense leaves of the creepers, as O'Neill could not only smell its rancid breath but he could also feel the warmth from its exhalation flowing over him. He woke with a start to find Venchencho's old cat lying on top of him, breathing directly into his face.

Lifting Ezekiel carefully off him, O'Neill sat upright and, after a brief coughing fit[23] that brought up some foul, smoke-flavoured bits into his mouth, he placed the feline on the floor. Before following the curved, upright tail as it swaggered towards the kitchen, O'Neill was forced to pick several strands of ginger fur from his mouth and try to brush off the cat drool and shedding that had accumulated on his chest over the past hours of unconsciousness. During his walk to the kitchen, O'Neill reflected that he had unfairly assumed that the unkempt appearance of Father Venchencho's vestments had been due to poor hygiene.

He sat at the kitchen table after feeding Ezekiel more of the "fette di pollo cotte" (cooked chicken slices) and tried to make sense of the events of the previous evening as he enjoyed a breakfast comprising of espresso and some warm, jam-filled cornetti[24].

---

[21] Parthenocissus Amazonica climbing vine with thick leaves and tendrils that can smother its host tree.

[22] The female Jaguar (Panthera onca) produces a hoarse barking cough that can sometimes be mistaken for a human.

[23] Those Turkish Royals are famous for it.

[24] Rome's favourite breakfast pastries, cornetti are sweeter than French croissants and come vuoto (plain) or filled with jam.

It had taken O'Neill nearly thirty minutes, and three more Turkish Royals before his nerves calmed sufficiently after his encounter with Sister Christina or whatever had attacked him. Eventually, he left the Tenuta dei Massimi Nature Reserve, returned to the Grande Raccordo Anulare (GRA), and headed north to central Rome. Thankfully, the heavy rain storm had passed by this time, and the hectic rush hour traffic had eased.

Along the way, he pulled into the IP - Pisana Esterna service station. He spent almost half of his monthly disposable income filling up the Mercedes' massive twenty-gallon fuel tank with a seemingly endless amount of extortionately expensive ninety-eight octane fuel. Before leaving the forecourt, he got some badly needed supplies at the garage store before heading to his tiny flat near the Fontana di Piazza Farnese.

Arriving opposite where he lived, he was amazed to find a suitable parking spot large enough for the enormous Mercedes to fit comfortably. He carried Ezekiel from the car and fed him some of the chicken he had been planning to eat before calling his immediate neighbour, Mrs Brambilla, who kept several cats of her own. Explaining his new adoption, he introduced her to Ezekiel, who she insisted on calling,

"Eziekee."

Having completed the introductions, O'Neill "borrowed" some cat litter and a tray to provide Eziekee with a toilet before ferrying all the soaking cardboard boxes from the Mercedes up the four flights of narrow stairs to his flat.

After stacking the wet boxes near the radiators to dry off, he towelled himself and changed into fresh clothes before calling Father Chin Kwon[25]. The latter worked closely with the new Pope and would know about Cardinal Regio and the changes that had come under his leadership. However, Kwon's mobile went to voice mail each time and, upon calling the central Vatican switchboard, he was put through to a surly night response administrator who informed O'Neill that,

"Fr Kwon was on "*indefinite leave*"." And then abruptly hung up.

Undeterred, he next phoned Conrad De Ven[26], the head of Vatican security. De Ven answered quite promptly but refused to talk on the phone when O'Neill mentioned Regio; instead, he insisted on coming round to speak in person.

When De Ven arrived, he looked quite different from how O'Neill remembered him. Gone was the black Armani suit and his elegant demeanour. The sophisticated designer clothes had been replaced by a simple brown leather jacket, unbranded grey polo shirt, faded blue Levi jeans and a pair of scuffed, tan Timberland leather boots. De Ven looked tired and haunted, with dark rings under his eyes. Some days growth of stubble was visible on his face and over his usually immaculately shaved head. The reasons soon became apparent. Removing his brown leather jacket, De Ven sat opposite O'Neill. After Ezekiel joined the former head of Vatican security on the sofa, he started recounting what had caused such a radical change in his circumstances.

---

[25] Fr Kwon had shared O'Neill's recent adventure visiting the Citadel of the Djinn but, due to a rare psychiatric condition, could not recall any of the details and could not corroborate O'Neill's descriptions.

[26] Conrad De Ven had helped O'Neill to gain access to some rare manuscripts within the Vatican library.

"Around a week ago, during a routine inventory check by my staff on the contents of the Vatican Secret Archive, we discovered that the rarest of the esoteric relics were missing. I promptly reported these thefts to Cardinal Regio at a meeting in the Apostolic Palace. Regio appeared genuinely horrified at the loss and asked that I take no further action as he assured me that he would personally deal with the issue. Thomas, in retrospect, I was incredibly naïve.

On the way back from this meeting, the Carabinieri pulled over my car and, in front of my staff, I was cuffed and arrested on suspicion of being responsible for the mysterious death of the Vatican librarian, Ms Dertinz, on the fifth of August. As you will recall, Dertinz had been discovered slumped over her table at the AngryPig Birretta on the Via Tunisi. Despite attempts to resuscitate her, she was pronounced dead an hour later at the Ospedale Santo Spirito Pronto Soccorso Hospital."

O'Neill interrupted De Ven's recollection, "I thought that death had been attributed to the international terrorist, Abdul Issuin?"

De Ven nodded, "Yes. Issuin had been captured on the CCTV within the café seconds before Dertinz collapsed, and it was presumed that he had administered some unknown poison into her drink. However, according to the police investigators, on the day of my arrest, they had received new evidence from an anonymous source that caused me to become the prime suspect instead."

"Sounds like a classic set-up. But they let you out?" O'Neill tried to sound upbeat.

De Ven continued, "Yes, but as my bank accounts were frozen when I was arrested, I had to sell my car as collateral to raise my bail and surrender my passport. Now I may have to wait for the results from an investigation that could take years to complete, given the bureaucracy levels within the Police and Vatican State."

O'Neill wasn't sure what he could say at this point that would not sound trite, but, fortunately, he was rescued from the quandary by Ezekiel, who chose that moment to pull closer to De Ven and head-bump his arm. The cat's gesture caused a grin to form on the otherwise grim countenance of the former Vatican security chief as he rubbed the old cat's forehead before continuing,

"Naturally, on leaving the Central Questura[27] I headed for my office. But when I got there, I found my security pass was no longer valid. The Swiss Guard on duty at the gates gave me a letter stating that I had been summarily relieved of my post and placed on an indefinite suspension without pay by the Pontifical Commission[28]. The staff working for me had not fared much better. Having been accused of stealing the missing holy relics from the Secret Archive, they were dismissed and the entire Vatican Security unit replaced by the private security company, Sichern GmbH, based out of Hamburg, Germany."

"Surely Venchencho can help clear this all up?" asked O'Neill.

"Believe me, I have tried to contact him," Said De Ven, "but no matter when I called, I was informed that he was unavailable."

O'Neill nodded, "I was told exactly the same when I tried to call Kwon."

"Then I think we have to conclude that either Venchencho and Kwon are deliberately avoiding contact with us or...."

---

[27] Police Headquarters of Rome.

[28] Pontifical Commission for the State of Vatican City

O'Neill finished De Ven's thought, "There is something sinister going on at the Vatican."

De Ven agreed, "Sinister is a good description."

O'Neill then briefly described the radical changes at the Deliverance Unit, concluding that he felt that "Cardinal Regio could be behind what is going on."

De Ven's eyes narrowed, "I had come to a similar conclusion, but, Thomas, we need to be very careful as we have no proof. Between us, I have even heard rumours that Regio has diagnosed Chin Kwon and Hugo Venchencho as requiring urgent mental health interventions in his capacity as a psychiatrist. Both are now *guests* at the Sanatorium of St Michael[29] undergoing that infamous WB treatment of Regio's."

At the mention of the WB drug, O'Neill pulled out the small bottle given to him by Regio the previous evening, causing De Ven to snatch the unopened bottle from O'Neill.

"For God's sake, don't take that stuff! I have seen its effects first-hand with my own former deputy. He went from being a strong and independent character to being completely passive and utterly submissive to Regio."

"You think that could be his plan?" mused O'Neill.

"What?" Queried De Ven.

"He instructed me to dose everyone who would normally receive an exorcism." Explained O'Neill.

"You think Regio is trying to create an army of possessed people under his control?" De Ven looked shocked at the idea but could be seen to be gradually accepting it.

---

[29] This infamous clinic is located near San Pietro della Ienca in the Mountains of Abruzzo.

O'Neill nodded. "It would fit with what you discovered if he is also gathering all the most sacred relics of the Church."

De Ven looked at O'Neill, "Thomas, we need to be very careful if you are right. Regio is already one of the most influential people, not just within Vatican City but also internationally. He has formed some kind of society that includes some of Europe's most powerful figures as members."

"You mean the Order of the Concealed Light?"

De Ven nodded. Emboldened by De Ven's acceptance that there could be a darker motive behind the recent changes at the Vatican, O'Neill decided to tell De Ven about his encounter with Regio and Sister Christina the previous evening. De Ven listened in silence and then, after O'Neill had finished, demonstrated his scepticism in the paranormal aspects of O'Neill's account.

"Maybe Christina slipped away behind some cover?" said De Ven, but then seeing that he had offended O'Neill, added, "but it certainly sounds very odd. What on earth could she have been doing with that man in the red Alfa? You are sure they were not il rapporti sessuali (having sex)?"

"I wasn't always a priest, Conrad." said O'Neill indignantly, "But I have never heard of sex so hot that one partner bursts into flames while the other grows eight feet tall and acquires claws."

De Ven laughed. "Ok. If you are *sure* what you saw, I think we should check if Sister Christina has left anything incriminating in that portacabin before it all gets cleaned up."

With that De Ven gently moved the sleeping Ezekiel from his lap, and both men donned their coats before making their way down to the old Mercedes. Ten minutes later, they arrived at the Coach Parking Janiculum, off the Rampa del Sangallo. It was now well past midnight, so the area was totally deserted. The homeless feeding stations had been cleared away, and all that was left to verify O'Neill's story were numerous burnt rubber "doughnut" tire tracks on the wet tarmac, where Sister Christina had raced the Alfa around the coach park. On approaching the further most of the portacabins, not surprisingly, they found the door firmly locked with an "F.lli Facchinetti" branded brass padlock.

O'Neill was not surprised when De Ven pulled out a small black case from his leather jacket containing a set of lock picks[30]. After a careful look around the coach park for CCTV cameras or an unexpected dog walker, De Ven opened the door, and both men stepped inside. Using a sleek-looking aluminium mini flashlight[31] that he placed in his mouth, so both his hands were free, De Ven showed his professional expertise by rapidly performing a systematic search of the small space, returning every item to its original location after a careful examination. Opening one of the tall metal clothes lockers, they found Sister Christina's distinctive red habit and white wimple worn at the Deliverance office earlier that evening.

"Bears out your story." Whispered De Ven as he passed O'Neill the vestments. O'Neill searched the right side of the red habit and removed a distinctive gold-coloured pin depicting a male figure holding a flaming torch above his head.

De Ven raised his eyebrows, "Order of the Concealed Light."

"Based on what I experienced earlier this evening, this is almost certainly Lucifer." Said O'Neill looking at the male figure depicted on the pin.

---

[30] Dangerfield PRAXIS Dual-Gauge Complete Lock Pick Set

[31] A HDS Systems EDC Rotary flashlight.

Meanwhile, De Ven's continued exploration of the locker was rewarded with the discovery of a small wooden box containing three more of the golden "Lucifer" pin badges, alongside some papers that had been folded and left on the top shelf inside the clothes locker. Opening the folded sheets De Ven's torch showed it to be some headed notepaper with the same torch bearer logo and what looked like notes describing lines that needed to be spoken and stage directions for what could have been a play.

"Must be a ritual they were planning." Speculated De Ven.

O'Neil nodded, "Does it say where and when it is due to be performed?"

De Ven nodded, "The venue is listed as Flavian Amphitheatre. Do you know where that is?"

"The Colosseum." Answered O'Neil, "Odd place for a meeting. It's practically a ruin."

De Ven scanned the paper, "Well, it says here there is a rehearsal on the ninth of September at 15:00Hrs."

"That is this coming afternoon." Stated O'Neill as he checked the date on his watch.

De Ven pocketed the stage directions along with the wooden badge box before remarking, "Ok, I think that is all there is to be found. Let's take Christina's clothes and these badges and get the hell out of here before we are discovered."

Unseen by either O'Neill or De Ven, after the pair drove away in Venchencho's old Mercedes, heading for O'Neill's apartment, a single male figure, dressed in an elegant black suit, emerged from the portacabin beside the one that had just been searched. As this mysterious individual walked further from the structure, he became illuminated under one of the massive spotlights of the Janiculum coach park, revealing the figure to be none other than Cardinal Regio, complete with an enigmatic smile on his face.

Simultaneously with Regio's emergence, numerous pairs of headlights came on around the furthest parts of the coach park, where a dozen cars had been concealed in the impenetrable darkness that existed far away from the floodlights. One of these twelve vehicles, a large, black BMW seven series sedan, sped across the empty tarmac and pulled up alongside Regio. The driver exited and opened the rear door for the Cardinal, allowing him to enter the luxurious leather-upholstered interior before heading out of the coach park, closely followed by the other eleven cars. All twelve vehicles that formed this curious midnight convoy were identical in colour and the level of supreme luxury offered to their chauffeur-driven occupants; the only thing that varied was the make of the limousine and the country in which they had been manufactured. Each of the eleven privileged passengers occupied the most senior positions within national governments, global finance, media, technology, engineering and the military.

Making their way in a long convoy along the Grande Raccordo Anulare (GRA), the twelve cars replicated the route taken by O'Neill earlier that evening. Once the convoy reached the outer boundary of the Riserva Naturale della Tenuta dei Massimi[32], the twelve limousines deposited their elite passengers next to a large, black Mercedes minibus[33] and departed, returning to central Rome. The six men and six women were then transported along the unmade country lane that led to the "Le dita di Satana[34]" and, upon

---

[32] The Tenuta dei Massimi Nature Reserve.

[33] A Mercedes-Benz Sprinter 516 minibus.

[34] Satan's Fingers.

reaching their destination, each was provided with a flaming torch and a hooded, long black robe.

Once back at O'Neill's apartment, De Ven took his leave, agreeing to make contact with O'Neill once he had made further discreet enquiries. O'Neill grabbed a few hours of sleep before resuming his regular routine. On exiting his morning shower, O'Neill was pulled back to the present from his recollections of the previous evening. He dressed in a pair of grey cotton chinos, a white cotton promotional T-shirt for his novel and worn leather moccasin slippers. Walking past the stacked boxes recovered from the deliverance offices the previous evening, he noticed a book intriguingly titled "The Art and Meaning of Magic[35]" hanging out of one of the top layers of boxes. Thinking that it could be as good a place as any to start reading through the rescued materials, he picked up the small protruding paperback, poured himself a second espresso and sat on the sofa where he had slept the previous evening. Ezekiel soon joined him, and the pair enjoyed the September morning's sunrise together[36].

The late night and the recent stressful events caught up with O'Neill, and even the two espressos he had consumed could not save him from falling back into a deep sleep on the warm, sun-drenched sofa. He was startled awake by the sound of Ezekiel issuing a loud screeching howl. The ancient ginger cat arched up, his ears flat, just like he had

---

[35] Israel Regardie's "The Art and Meaning of Magic".

[36] Little did either of them know that their tranquillity would be interrupted moments later by a phone call from Tavish Stewart in London, which would require O'Neill to phone the mysterious female adept who had saved him in Geneva two days earlier.

the previous evening when facing the demonic entity. Only this time, Ezekiel stood directly in the flat's hallway beside the entrance, and there were no demons to be seen.

O'Neill was just coming to the conclusion that perhaps the timing of the cat's aggressive behaviour last night was a coincidence when there was a loud rapping knock at the apartment door. Rubbing the sleep from his eyes and staggering across the flat, he pulled open the door to find Cardinal Regio standing outside in the corridor, along with two men dressed in black uniforms who looked very official. Both had the word "Sichern" emblazoned on their chests along with a distinctive logo that looked like a sideways Z character with a bar passing through its centre.

While O'Neill was taking in these details, through the blurry vision of one just woken from a deep sleep, Cardinal Regio stepped imperiously across the threshold; only to immediately retreat as a blur of quickly moving ginger fur grabbed the Cardinal's advancing right leg between both of its front paws, claws extended, and sunk its teeth firmly into Regio's knee.

Regio exclaimed in pain, causing O'Neill to apologise as he pulled the cat from its position, taking large shreds of trouser material trapped in Ezekiel's claws.

"Sorry, your Eminence! I don't know what has gotten into him." O'Neill said as he pushed the furious, hissing ball of fur into the bathroom and firmly shut the door.

"Do your apartment regulations permit pets?" Demanded Regio, holding his right knee and examining a clear, deep bite pattern that was starting to flow with red blood.

"Yes, your Eminence, it does." Stated one of the two men standing behind the Cardinal, reading from a clipboard that he was carrying in his right hand.

Regio hobbled into the cramped hallway and looked aghast as he noticed the stacks of cardboard boxes that partially filled the corridor into O'Neill's living room.

"You took it upon yourself to *steal* these items from Vatican City?" Regio exclaimed in a mix of rage and pain as he was still in shock from the cat bite.

Unexpectedly, the second of the two men, a man called Albrecht, saved O'Neill from his struggle to compose a credible defence, "Your Eminence, technically they were garbage awaiting disposal. They were therefore no longer Vatican property." Regio glared at Albrecht so intensely that the man became flustered, adding, "Strictly speaking anyway."

"Whatever." Shrugged the Cardinal, "But that does not excuse Father O'Neill from failing to attend his newly assigned workplace this morning, as he was explicitly instructed."

O'Neill went to make an excuse, but Regio prevented the response by raising his hand,

"Save me from the pathetic excuses. Actually, I came to find out if Sister Christina was with you." The Cardinal looked quizzically towards the bedroom door as if he fully expected the nun to emerge at any moment after a night of passion.

"She is missing?" asked O'Neill innocently.

Regio's eyes narrowed, "Yes, Father O'Neill, she *is* missing. I expected *you* to meet her this morning at the WB offices to begin treating the patients at the Bambino Gesù psychiatric clinic. In fact, the clinic phoned me," Regio exaggeratedly checked his white-faced, gold dress watch, "thirty minutes ago, querying why no one had arrived to see the patients they had prepared for the visit of the Vatican team." Regio looked sternly at O'Neill. Clearly, the lack of attendance had merely confirmed his assessment of the wayward priest.

"I am sorry, your Eminence, I had a rough night and, well, it must have caught up with me this morning." O'Neil was unsure how convincing he sounded, but he did the best he could.

Regio looked like he had just realised something, "Wait, is that fleabag that attacked me the same cat I had ordered to be destroyed yesterday?!"

O'Neill feigned shock, "No, of course not, your Eminence. I have had "Puss" since I moved to Rome."

The Cardinal's eyes narrowed. He was clearly not convinced but managed to contain his scepticism. Instead of challenging the lie, he decided to put this insubordinate priest to some productive work. He tossed a piece of paper over to O'Neill,

"I have arranged for Albrecht,"

Regio gestured to one of the two security officers standing behind him,

"to escort you to the Bambino Gesù clinic where you will meet a Dr Picard and his patient, Mrs Susan Widee, who I believe is known to you. Since you are already familiar with her case, from that absurd course you were teaching, I thought it appropriate that she should act as your introduction to the WB treatment program. Maybe, just maybe, you will be able to focus enough to stay awake rather than napping your day away."

Regio turned to leave, "Oh, and by the way, Albrecht will make sure you complete your work at the clinic by two pm and bring you back here to change into whatever you have that might pass for formal dress,"

Regio looked distastefully at O'Neill's "Bridge of Souls" T-Shirt, "as you will be filling in for Sister Christina at a rehearsal event this afternoon."

O'Neill looked excited, "You mean a rehearsal for the Order of the Concealed Light?"

Regio gave an enigmatic smile, "As they say, Father O'Neill, be careful what you wish for."

With that, Regio walked away with the security officer carrying the clipboard, leaving O'Neill under the careful scrutiny of Albrecht. O'Neill quickly changed into less casual clothes[37], released Ezekiel from the bathroom and carried him past Albrecht, who took a giant and deliberate step back from the cat as it passed. Thankfully, the neighbour, Mrs Brambilla, kindly agreed to look after "Eziekee" until O'Neill returned. Acknowledging his gratitude to Mrs Brambilla, O'Neill locked his apartment and followed Albrecht to an unmarked, dark blue Volkswagen Passat estate car waiting in the street below.

Forty-seven minutes later, after a hurried drive through central Rome, O'Neill found himself sitting on a grey, two-seater sofa in the elegant offices of Dr James Picard. The office was on the second floor of a beautiful historic building, standing high on the picturesque Gianicolo Hill, overlooking Rome. Whoever had decorated the office had impeccable taste, as the carpet, walls and furnishings were all a perfect blend of stylish colours. The interplay of sunlight against the pastel colours of the furnishings made the atmosphere feel uplifting. O'Neill imagined that it would be an ideal setting for dealing with children suffering from psychiatric disorders.

Although the Bambino Gesù clinic was world-renowned for its focus on providing health care for children, they had agreed to house and treat some specialist adult psychiatric cases at the request of the Vatican; with whom they had a

---

[37] His classical off the peg, black shirt, trousers and jacket with the white dog collar.

long association after being gifted to the Holy See in 1924, before becoming under state control in the mid nineteen eighties.

Seated directly opposite O'Neil, behind a large steel and glass desk, Dr Picard consulted his case notes as the patient, Mrs Widee, was escorted into the large office by a young male orderly. Dr Picard was a young man with dark brown hair and a matching full beard. Under his white lab coat, he was informally dressed in a blue cotton, short-sleeved shirt, cream-coloured chinos and a pair of black Croc surgical clogs.

Susan Widee was an attractive Dutch businesswoman in her late forties from Leidsche Rijn in central Holland. Her case was well known to O'Neill, as she had featured as an example of a potential candidate for exorcism in a lecture series about demonic possession. She looked the same as O'Neill remembered her, except she seemed much more distant, as though she had been heavily sedated. Widee was seated by the orderly onto an oversized, single-seater high-backed chair, to the right of Picard and to the left of O'Neill's sofa. While she was settled in place, O'Neill took a moment to appreciate the glorious panoramic view of the historic capital that was presented through Picard's wide windows.

After the orderly left the room, closing the glass door behind him, Picard made the introductions.

"Susan, this man is Father O'Neill. He is here to discuss your new treatment."

"Hello Susan, we have met before at the PUG[38]. Do you remember?"

---

[38] Pontifical Gregorian University or PUG is one of the leading Roman Catholic ecclesiastical universities.

Widee looked up at O'Neill and nodded but did not say anything. After a moment, she returned her gaze to the floor directly in front of her.

O'Neill tried again to engage with her, "Susan, Dr Picard tells me you have been trying a new treatment for a few weeks now. How is that going?"

There was no response. After an awkward silence, O'Neill looked towards Picard, who stood and walked around his desk to give O'Neill a thick, A4-sized manilla file before sitting next to O'Neill on the sofa. Widee remained silent. Her gaze was fixed on the floor.

O'Neill opened the file and read through the opening page that summarized Widee's condition, which was described as a severe form of multiple personality disorder. The case notes also included some comments in a scrawly handwriting in blue ink that O'Neill recognised as belonging to Hugo Venchencho in his role as Chief Exorcist. Venchencho's notes showed that he believed that certain of Widee's symptoms, including precognitive descriptions of disasters, text mysteriously appearing on walls and blasphemous utterances made in Nabataean dialect Aramaic, all pointed to possession by an "Ulacin", a pre-Islamic form of a discarnate entity called a Djinn. Venchencho had formally written for permission to perform an exorcism, but the death of the previous Pope and recent world events had prevented this request from being actioned.

The attending physicians had dismissed Venchencho's diagnosis, as the case notes outlined the various treatments that had been adopted since his prognosis. The most recent was a daily regime of the German manufactured neuro-inhibitory drug, "WB" or "Wahrnehmungsblock".

Seeing that O'Neill had finished reading the summary, Picard added, "As you can see from the file, Ms Widee has made remarkable progress since the start of the daily WB regime."

"In what way?" Queried O'Neill.

"Her episodes of disassociated behaviour have ceased, and, encouragingly, she has stopped producing the disturbing images that were so frequent in her art therapy.

"Disturbing images? Do you have any examples?" Asked O'Neill, who was curious to see what kinds of images could be classed as "disturbing".

Picard stood and walked back to his desk, picking up an artist's sketch pad with the name S.Widee and a patient id number printed on a sticky label attached to the front cover. Walking back across the room, he handed the pad to O'Neill before sitting again on the sofa.

"You are fortunate in your timing, Father O'Neill, as, following Cardinal Regio's instructions, these materials were all about to be incinerated."

O'Neill opened the A3-sized sketch pad and began turning through the pages that documented each of Widee's art therapy sessions, with the date of the session written at the top of each sheet. The drawings were of a massive grey wolf, portrayed first in simple line diagrams that gradually grew more complex, with the detail focusing on the thick matted fur, huge fangs, long claws and, most disturbing of all, a wild feral look in the animal's face that grew in intensity with each successive drawing in the pad.

Picard tried to explain his own interpretation of Widee's drawings, "Of course, the wolf is a savage force of nature, symbolic of animal forces rising within the repressed psyche."

O'Neill was not convinced. The wolf drawn in the pictures was so detailed and, ridiculous as it might sound, these were clearly representations of the same animal, as the facial features and markings on the coat and muzzle were identical in each image. In the later pictures, the wolf was shown in such a stylised form that they could have been copied from some Anglo-Saxon manuscript and the beast was shown in ever-increasing detail interacting with its surroundings. Breaking free from strands of rope that had restrained it, the creature was tearing down the doors of great wooden halls, attacking human heroes dressed in leather armour. Arrows fired from longbows were shown bouncing harmlessly off the massive beast as it grew ever more prominent in each drawing. As O'Neill continued to scroll through the pad, he saw the enormous canine taking away women and children, devouring them and leaving mountains of bones. These bone piles dwarfed real-world mountains that were drawn so realistically that O'Neill could recognise the distinctive profiles of Mont Blanc, The Matterhorn and Eiger. Towards the final A3 sheets in the pad, the wolf had grown so large from consuming all of humanity that it stood astride the Atlantic Ocean. Its huge forepaws rested on the two continents of America and Europe as it howled into the bleakness of space. Interspersed among these final wolf images were other equally terrifying drawings- some showed boats constructed from human bones and fingernails. These vessels floated on calm seas, devoid of all life. Others clearly showed the destruction of the temples and symbols from the three Abrahamic[39] religions being destroyed, to be replaced by some darker, older worship devoted to the exaltation of a force of evil that sought to consume all of creation in some horrific nightmare. The final image in the pad showed the wolf with its mouth now wide enough to seize the sun and

---

[39] The Jewish, Christian and Islamic faiths.

moon in its fangs, while down below, its massive paws rested on tiny planets filled with leafless trees that were decorated with the dead bodies of humans and animals.

Seeing that O'Neill had finished scrolling through the art therapy drawings, Picard passed over a second A3 pad to O'Neill,

"And these are the drawings that Ms Widee has produced in her art therapy sessions since commencing the WB treatment."

O'Neill opened the cover to see that the dark themes had been replaced with life-drawing compositions; flowers in a vase and sketches of the view from the windows at the clinic down over the city of Rome.

Picard smiled, "As you can see, a complete transformation into producing pictures representing a much healthier, more normal mental state." Picard took back the old A3 sketch pad, "As per Cardinal Regio's instructions, these old drawings and the treatment logs will be destroyed and, since our recent electrograms confirm that Ms Widee's brain patterns are now completely normal, she will be returning to her home within a couple of days."

At that moment, Widee became more animated and spoke for the first time in the entire interview. "Father O'Neill, thank you for coming. It was very good of you to remember me. Please pass on my regards to Father Venchencho for his kindness."

O'Neill went to respond but saw that the brief display of animation from Mrs Widee had disappeared back into whatever depths of her mind contained her consciousness. She resumed her passive gaze, fixated on some point on the carpeted floor in front of her.

Picard smiled and said that since they had finished early and the Vatican driver would not be back for two hours, he would get reception to call O'Neill a taxi to take him back to the city centre. As the doctor left, O'Neill stood and, opening the first sketch pad, began to take a few pictures of the more disturbing drawings with his iPhone. He became so engrossed with this task that he failed to notice Widee's breathing change, as her facial features transformed into that fixed rigour so often associated with demonic possession. Widee stood and, moving in a series of strange, bird-like steps, came close behind and beside O'Neill until her body cast a shadow over the A3 pad, causing O'Neill to turn in surprise. What he saw made an involuntary chill run through his body. As Widee's face looked inhuman, her head tilted to one side and fixed in a terrifying grin. She reached with a claw-like hand to push a ball of crumpled paper into O'Neill's palm as she put a finger to her lips with a conspiratorial "Shhhh!"

A few moments later, having been escorted by Dr Picard's secretary to a waiting taxi, a stunned Thomas O'Neill sat in the back seat of an old, yellow Peugeot e7 cab. O'Neill's face was ashen white as he held the crumpled paper tightly in his hand. Part of him wanted to throw it out of the open car window and ignore whatever insane communication it would contain. Another part of him could not forget the inhuman look that had been temporarily transposed over Widee's features. He knew that contained within the simple ball of paper was the start of another incredible adventure.

Finally, after some minutes of internal debate, he carefully pulled open the crumpled mass of paper. He straightened out the sheet to reveal an even more detailed picture of the fearful wolf; only this one was not killing- somehow, that made it all the more terrifying. Instead, this extremely detailed sketch showed the enormous wolf sitting in front of row after row of soulless human beings, their eye sockets empty, their mouth's hanging open as they stood to attention. An army of followers committed to sharing the

55

wolf's absolute dedication to destruction. Underneath the picture was some writing, roughly scribbled with the intense black of a sketching pencil in what looked to O'Neill to be an ancient form of Aramaic[40]. O'Neill's knowledge of ancient languages was rudimentary, but he roughly translated the text and shuddered.

ܟܘܡܪ ܪܗܘܡ

ܗܘܡ

ܠܗ

(Priest of Rome

Ready

Yourself)

---

[40] Roughly 700-300 BCE. Older than the Nabataean Aramaic Widee normally produced when possessed.

5   KNOW THY ENEMY

Evil is a spiritual being, alive and living, perverted and perverting, weaving its way insidiously into the very fabric of life. - William Goodhart

Stewart's Antiquarians,
18a, New Bond St, Mayfair,
London W1S 2RB

05.15HRS (GMT+1), 9th Sept, Present day

Less than a mile away from where Cortez was trying to come to terms with his recent, preternatural experiences in the Wigmore Hall courtyard, Stewart and Sinclair were sitting side by side on the fold-out bed in the kitchen area above the Antiquarian showroom. Stewart's bashed-up Nokia rested between them, operating on speakerphone, as they continued their discussion with the French adept.

For her part, Madeleine Mathers' breakfast order had been delivered to her table, and she nodded her appreciation to the elderly male waiter. She set her unbranded android phone to speaker mode and placed it beside the grey metal food tray containing four freshly baked pastries, a jug of boiling water, and more delicious fresh ground coffee.

After Mathers' comparison of the Fae with a tiger, Sinclair continued the discussion by enquiring,

"Then the Fae are like demons?"

Mathers exhaled slowly, "No, Cynthia. There is great confusion in the modern world about the non-human species with whom we share this reality. To be honest, TV and movies have made the world of the supernatural into an absurdity. At worst, light entertainment and, at best, a misguided and ill-informed misrepresentation.

For example, they have made open-minded people think that every unexplained event results from demonic influence. The reality is that both Angels and Demons belong to a class of beings that have very little interest in, or interaction with, Humans.

Sinclair sounded surprised, "You make it sound like unseen creatures surround us."

Mathers paused, thinking how best to explain, while she poured the boiling water into the cafetiere, "Look around you, Cynthia, do you see the tiny insects flying past your windows? Can you hear the scurrying mouse behind your skirting boards? Look up at the birds flying high above the roof tops or imagine the numerous microscopic creatures that we know are in your every breath?

The visible, physical world is teeming with life, and so is the nonphysical. It would be absurd to think otherwise. There are as many different types of nonphysical entities as there are types of physical creatures. There are many ways to classify them, but most occult scholars either categorise them by their typical environments or their behaviours. They are a separate class of beings from those in our physical reality, but they are very much of and in this world. However, it would be a mistake to imagine that every unexplained occurrence is produced by one of these invisible beings.

The reality is that most supernatural events are simply misunderstood natural phenomena. For the most part, what serious students term "The Great Art" is merely the application of a forgotten set of techniques that once formed the basis of an advanced civilization that has been long forgotten - other than as a grossly misrepresented myth or a fantastic fiction."

"You cannot mean Atlantis?" exclaimed Stewart as he exchanged a nervous glance with Sinclair. One could see that both of them wondered if they had spent the last few minutes listening to a deluded fantasist.

Stewart decided to double-check, "Isn't Plato's tale of Atlantis just a garbled reflection of an ancient Egyptian account of the volcanic eruption of Thera[41], which triggered the earthquakes and tsunamis that destroyed the civilization on Crete?"

Mathers sighed as she used a small enamel-handled knife to cut open the croissants and spread a strawberry preserve[42] inside the hot, freshly cut pastries. The French Adept was only too aware of any critical person's natural hesitation to the concept of a lost civilization predating our own Neolithic cultures, especially with the sheer number of references in popular culture.

"Tavish, you have had the rare privilege of personally visiting one of the remnants of an even more ancient civilization- that was destroyed nearly eight hundred millennia ago. So you should not dismiss the possibility of humanity rising again to form another in the more recent past. The sanctuary of Agartha you visited in the wastes of the Gobi was created to re-seed humanity with the elements of civilization; writing, mathematics, agriculture, astronomy and the sacred sciences."

Mathers took a bite from one of the croissants and plunged her cafetiere before continuing,

"The problem with any high civilization, even ours, is that its progress relies on having a skilled population, made up of many different specialists, each contributing to a collective whole, but no single individual having the necessary skills to

---

[41] Thera was an ancient city high on the slopes of the Messavouno mountain on the Greek island of Santorini around 1500 BCE

[42] Reflets de France, Strawberry blend.

survive in isolation. When a global catastrophe hits such a civilisation, the complex interdependencies that hold the civilisation together collapse. Water supplies fail, food supplies fail, health care breaks down, and transportation systems cease to function. Rapidly, the social fabric collapses completely and is replaced by the basic laws of survival - dog eats dog. People quickly disperse from cities, and within a few hundred years, nature reclaims what was once streets, buildings and infrastructure."

The French adept paused, taking a sip of coffee from a white ceramic mug, before resuming her explanation,

"This process has been frighteningly familiar throughout human history. Each new civilisation dismisses the possibility that they are just one in a long line of cultures that have risen only to be wiped clean. No one wants to consider that their existence is so extraordinarily fragile.

The civilisation that made the Citadel of the Djinn was from one that we occultists call Lemuria, centred on a landmass located in what we now call the Pacific and Indian Oceans. The later civilisation, that popular culture calls Atlantis, was located in what we now call the Atlantic Ocean."

Stewart interjected, remembering his classics; he quoted Plato "For it is related in our records how once upon a time your State[43] stayed the course of a mighty host, which, starting from a distant point in the Atlantic Ocean, was insolently advancing to attack the whole of Europe, and Asia to boot."

Mathers laughed, "Exactement! Plato introduced the world to the concept of Atlantis in his dialogue Timaeus[44]. But, as

---

[43] Stewart is quoting Plato who is, in turn, quoting what the Egyptian priests were alleged to have told Solon.

[44] Plato wrote Timaeus around 360 BCE.

with everything in life, the truth is much more complex than popular culture or even our modern historians would have you believe. For a start, in the original texts, it was only the central citadel, with its concentric rings, that was called Atlas[45]. Later Greek scholars added the concept of Atlantida[46] to mean the entire island and its supposed ten cities.

Remember, however, that Plato is referencing a second-hand account from centuries before him of how Solon[47] travelled to the Egyptian city of Sais, where a priest[48] of the goddess Neith[49] informed him that nine thousand years earlier, Athens had been in conflict with a great sea power called Atlantis, that was subsequently destroyed in a catastrophe. The catch is that Athens has only been inhabited for five thousand years, so clearly, some timelines were mixed up in the recounting of Solon's story. Ancient Egyptian papyri tell of "Sea Peoples" who terrorised the entire region, but this occurred hundreds of years[50] before Solon visited Egypt, not thousands. Both Egypt and Athens were likely subject to these "Sea Peoples" attacks, and this forms the basis of Athens' repelling the attacker from the sea in Solon's account."

"So, the sinking of Atlantis *is* a myth?" clarified Stewart.

---

[45] Supposedly named after the founder of the city.

[46] Literally meaning "The land of Atlas".

[47] An Athenian statesman who is remembered for his support of democracy (638–558 BC).

[48] The priest's name was reported by Plutarch to be "Sonchis the Saïte".

[49] A goddess of wisdom, birth/creation and fate.

[50] The attacks of the Sea Peoples are dated by historians around 1200–900 BCE

"No, that part of Solon's tale that talks about the sinking of a civilisation is correct, as is roughly the timing. Nine thousand years before the time of Solon's visit to Egypt, esoteric records tell of the sinking of Poseidonis, the last remaining island from the accursed civilisation, in 9564 BCE."

"Why accursed?" queried Stewart, "I thought Plato merely said they became filled with hubris?"

"And if I can add a question of my own," interjected Sinclair, "if it was not called Atlantis, what was this *cursed* civilisation called?".

Mathers paused as she continued eating her breakfast,

"Cynthia's question is the easiest to answer, so I will address that one first. The main thing to realise is that this was an advanced seafaring civilisation, with outposts spread around the globe. The climate and sea levels were vastly different at the time when this civilization was at its height. The entire Northern hemisphere was buried under thick ice fields, some over two miles deep. This massive accumulation of frozen water meant that sea levels were significantly lower than in current times. Consequently, the Mid-Atlantic Ridge, which is currently under the ocean, had the peaks of its mountains exposed well above sea level, appearing as an extended range of islands that almost ran from pole to pole.

The civilization had many names, each from the different parts of the world that interacted with them. The ancient Mayans called them Aztlan. The Southern European peoples remember these lands with Hyperborea, The Fortunate Isles and Thule. Whereas the Celts remember the lands as Hy-Brasil or Tír na nÓg.

More relevant to answering Tavish's question as to why we term them accursed is that in the oldest records of the Egyptians, they refer to their ancestral homeland as being called Sekhet-Aaru and describe it as being located towards the West, in the middle of the ocean. This is significant to our interests because esoteric lore tells that the Egyptian civilisation was seeded by the dispossessed survivors from this advanced civilization as they fled from their destruction."

Stewart interrupted, "Madeleine, you say advanced. How advanced are we talking about?"

"Well, certainly not anywhere near as advanced as popular media would make you believe. In reality, the highest aspects of these people's scientific progress were similar to that enjoyed by Europeans in the eighteenth century[51]."

"You mean how to calculate latitude and longitude?" queried Stewart.

"Yes, exactly, they had mastered maritime navigation[52] to such an extent that they had contact with every habitable part of the globe. Their skills with metallurgy meant that they were equipped with bronze when the rest of the world remained firmly in the Neolithic age."

Sinclair looked perplexed, "Is having Bronze such a big deal?"

Stewart nodded, "It is if you are fighting people who only have sharpened stones as weapons. These Atlanteans must have been an unstoppable force."

Mathers exhaled, "Yes, Tavish, and that was the seed of their demise because, in addition to their progress in the

---

[51] Presumably referring to the work of Tobias Mayer (1755) and Nevil Maskelyne (1766) that resulted in the Nautical Almanac and Astronomical Ephemeris.

[52] Including detailed cartography that provided the basis for the many curious maps of antiquity such as the Piri Reis Map of 1513 and earlier Chinese maps that accurately show the coastline of Antarctica but without the ice fields.

sciences, they also possessed advanced knowledge of esoteric lore."

"They were psychic?" asked Sinclair.

Mathers finished her last pastry before continuing,

"Not exactly, Cynthia; you see, at that time, religion was identical with what we adepts term The Great Art."

"They were Magicians then?" enquired Stewart.

"Oh yes! The study and practice of Magic were fundamental to their day-to-day life, in much the same way that technology is to ours. In the early stages of their civilisation, they followed a sound approach, seeking to use what they knew for healing and returning balance to the natural world around them. Practitioners of the Left- and Right-Hand paths respected each other, and their society was in harmony."

"It sounds like a big *but* is coming." Remarked Stewart.

"Indeed. They reached a stage where they literally had the whole world and its riches under their direction. But power and riches are strange things. For some, it becomes an addiction. For this reason, some of the adepts began to probe aspects of existence that are considered, even by many practitioners of the Left-Hand Path, to be too dangerous to explore."

"Dangerous? In what way?" Asked Sinclair.

Mathers paused, clearly thinking how best to phrase her response, before taking another sip of her strong, black coffee and continuing,

"Contrary to what is taught in most scriptures, ours is not the first creation. In fact, there have been numerous ones before ours, and there will be countless ones after ours ends. Each previous creation had its own set of invisible hierarchies of angelic and demonic beings, just as ours does. These beings' shadows, or remnants, continue after their creation has been dissolved into darkness and reformed into a new creation. It is possible, within certain limits, to make contact with these beings and obtain knowledge that would otherwise remain unknown to mortals. However, opening a connection with the entities from these previous existences mortally damages any living thing that connects with them. Worse than that, each connection tears apart our reality and weakens our creation. Making it less stable and eventually causing its violent destruction. In truth, the sole motivation for these entities to make human contact is the destruction of our entire existence."

"Sounds similar to what we were told about Enochian magic when we were pursuing Ad-Dajjal for the Emerald Tablets." Remarked Stewart.

"Exactly the same, Tavish. In fact, the Meri-Isfet tasked Ad-Dajjal, as their highest-ranking adept, with obtaining the Emerald Tablets so she could access this forbidden knowledge and gain limitless power. A power that she would have used to spawn a new creation filled with nothing but suffering, darkness and despair."

"And it was scary how close she came to succeeding if it had not been for one man's pig-headed determination." Said Sinclair as she patted the rugged Scotsman sitting beside her.

"C'est vrai! (Indeed!). In the same way, nearly twelve thousand years ago, the predecessors of the Meri-Isfet came close to destroying everything. They developed technologies that opened portals to commune with the entities that remain in these previous existences.

"Is there a name for the realms that contain these previous existences and the *things* that dwell there?" enquired Stewart.

"Oui, bien sûr," (Yes, of course), "Those of us who follow the Western Esoteric Tradition of the Jewish Kabbalah call the remains of these previous creations the Hebrew phrase "Sitra Achra", which in English roughly means "The Other Side[53]".

The general term for entities that dwell and remain on "The Other Side" are called "The Qliphoth[54]", which, in English, roughly means shells or husks. Although these entities each have specific identities and names, just like humans."

Stewart interrupted, "Interestingly, those four adepts I met at the Wigmore last night were discussing some forthcoming ritual involving these Qliphoth beings."

"I am not surprised." Responded Mathers. "The Meri-Isfet believe these beings will grant them supreme power and knowledge of the ultimate secret of life. The same old deluded dream has driven the Meri-Isfet for the last 20,000 years. Those who commune at any length with the Qliphoth become obsessed, *literally obsessed*, by a specific entity. The adept, once so affected, loses perspective on the consequences of their actions and becomes addicted to more and more frequent interactions with their obsessing entity."

"How powerful exactly are these Qliphoth entities?" enquired Stewart, as he wondered what they might be facing in the future.

"You must remember that each was once the prime force in their creation. Therefore, each is equal to the entity you encountered inhabiting Father Kwon during your recent adventure." Responded Mathers soberly.

---

[53] Called the "Sitra Achra" 'סטרא אחרא', by Kabbalists.

[54] Qliphoth - קליפות - that literally means "Husks", they are the representation of impure spiritual energies.

"Christ! No wonder the Meri-Isfet fell so easily under their influence." Exclaimed the Scotsman as he recalled some of the phenomena he had seen while accompanying the highly charismatic Kwon.

"Yes, Tavish, the precursors of the Meri-Isfet became so deluded and addicted from their initial contacts with the Qliphoth that they followed their instructions on creating technologies that would permit stronger connections with the "Sitra Achra".

"Technologies? What kind of technologies are we talking about, Madeleine?" enquired Stewart.

Before answering, Mathers finished her coffee and put the empty mug, knife, and cafetiere on the metal tray.

"Based on those few records that remain, they were vast, tube or bell-shaped, rotating machines, called "Wheels[55]" that manipulated space-time[56] sufficiently to tear reality apart and open a temporary gateway to the Sitra Achra. Only one of these infernal contraptions survived the sinking of the last island, Poseidonis, in 9564 BCE, but thankfully it is believed to have been later destroyed. But we do still have crude visual representations in the modern world. Constructed by refugees from the sunken civilization when they fled to the highest ground they could find, fearing more tidal waves and sea level rises.

"You mean Tibetan prayer wheels?!" Said Sinclair with a shocked realisation.

---

[55] Sometimes referenced as "galgalim" גַּלְגַּלִּים (spinning fiery wheels) in the Abrahamic religions.

[56] These devices generated a massive gravitational field (along with other effects) by warping the geometry of the surrounding spacetime.

"Yes, exactly, Cynthia. That is approximately what these accursed machines looked like, but imagine them increased in size by a factor of maybe one hundred and rotating at high speed with strange characters engraved on their sides.

These infernal devices opened the portals to these monsters from the previous creations. Still, in doing so, they also created massive gravitational distortions that caused a vast comet[57] to be dragged from its course, split into enormous fragments[58] and come thundering into our planet. Many of the impacts were in the middle of thick ice fields, and the resulting explosions caused massive glacial meltwater flooding."

"Hence the legend of the global deluge." Concluded Sinclair.

"Exactement!" whispered Mathers.

Stewart, who had been following the discussion closely, was prompted to pose another question. "Madeleine, I now understand why you termed the civilization *sunken* and *accursed*. But, tell me, you said that the Meri-Isfet were after the ultimate secret of life in return for constructing these devices. Did they get it?"

"In a very dark and disturbing way, yes, Tavish, they did. Like all who love power and possessions, the ancestors of the Meri-Isfet inevitably found that the human life span was too short. But rather than embracing love for every moment as one should, they looked for ways to extend their existence. So, Meri-Isfet adepts explored the sacred

---

[57] Allegedly, this comet was originally more than three miles in diameter before the Meri-Isfet's infernal devices altered its normal course around the sun and broke it into a stream of orbiting fragments that smashed into the Earth in a series of impacts spread over tens of thousands of years.

[58] As an example, one of these impacts is alleged to have caused a twenty-mile-wide impact crater in northwest Greenland.

mysteries of life, death and rebirth. They were looking for ways to cheat physical mortality and, more importantly for them, avoid the laws of karma that usually await each individual as punishment or reward, depending on their acts in life. You can imagine the attraction of such a goal for those who are devoted to works of evil to accumulate worldly power and possessions.

Naturally, the Qliphoth encouraged this unnatural fascination. In return for building more wheels, they taught the forbidden art of physical reanimation and spirit transference, called in ancient Sanskrit, "*Trongjug*" or, in Tibetian, which is the only place where the art is still regularly practised[59], it is called "*Sprul-sku*"."

"This is what that fiend, Ad-Dajjal did with Helen, isn't it?" exclaimed Stewart angrily.

"Yes, exactly. As an Ipsissimus[60], she had access to the ultimate secrets of the Meri-Isfet. She was, by all accounts, a mistress of this forbidden art [61], using her skills to enslave numerous people who would serve her unquestioningly and act as alternative host bodies for her immortal principle if and when the need arose.

She subjugated Ms Curren's will and then embedded elements of her immortal essence within Curren[62] . When

---

[59] A secret related to the well documented immediate reincarnations of the Dalai and the Panchen High Lamas.

[60] An esoteric term that literally is the Latin superlative of the term "self". It is the highest initiatory grade possible in the Western Esoteric Tradition, often shown as 10=1 on the Tree of Life.

[61] In Tibetan "Sprul-pa mkyen-pa".

[62] The Silver Cord, or Antahkarana is the thread that passes from the immortal principle to the physical body, giving that target body, life, will and motion. Also often referenced as "The Bridge of

Ad-Dajjal's physical body faced certain death, she could abandon that original body and continue her existence using Curren."

"If I had not heard this from Thomas and Tavish, I would never have believed it was possible." Commented Sinclair.

Mathers mouthed "Convenu." (agreed) in a semi-silent exhalation, which is an almost unique skill of native French speakers, before continuing,

"You have personally experienced the evil that one Trongjug adept can inflict; imagine what seven[63] of them would be like! These ancestors of the Meri-Isfet became a literal plague upon the face of the earth - controlling the minds of critical individuals around the globe. Their rule was utterly ruthless. Immune from the normal limits of physical health, limited lifespan and karmic justice. They indulged themselves in every excess they could imagine.

Encouraged by the Qliphoth, they began to explore the creation of inhuman half-breeds of every description, mixing their human genes with every earthly species until they eventually indulged in the ultimate karmic abomination. Interbreeding with their Qliphoth guides to produce a race of unnatural creatures, half material and half immaterial, who, to the delight of the Qliphoth, ignored the authority of the Meri-Isfet and terrorised the inhabitants of the earth. These *things* were called The Nephilim[64] or *fallen ones*,

---

Souls", hence O'Neill's choice as the title for his book describing their epic adventure.

[63] Called the "apkallu" in the oldest Sumerian myths, these were seven powerful adepts from before the flood.

[64] The Nephilim - נְפִילִים - were mysterious and powerful beings that existed before the flood.

within the Abrahamic traditions and the Quinametzin[65] within the ancient South American lore. These abominations were *the giants* mentioned in every culture's prehistory that terrorised the earth until the global cataclysm wiped them from the face of the globe."

"Sounds like the asteroid strike and resulting surge of glacial meltwater was a blessing if it wiped out these evil people and their creations." Commented Sinclair.

"Sadly, Cynthia, it also destroyed many good things in the process." Replied Mathers, "Like more recent maritime civilisations, all major settlements were located along coastlines. The enormous tsunamis of ice-cold waters swept away those cities, and the rising sea levels caused by the melting ice caps rapidly erased all evidence that the civilization ever existed.

The few people who did survive travelled to higher ground or far inland and made contact with the primitive Neolithic peoples, who were mostly hunter-gatherers. The survivors introduced these nomadic peoples to the principles of agriculture, writing, mathematics, cosmology and, of course, tales of an advanced civilization that was destroyed by the Gods due to its evil acts and arrogance."

"What happened to the Meri-Isfet?" Asked Stewart.

Mathers made another of those uniquely French semi-silent exclamations that signify both understanding and agreement,

"They continued their esoteric order as best they could- they were, of course, greatly reduced by the global cataclysm as were my own order, the Meri-Maat. Both orders established mystery schools around the Nile delta in

---

[65] Quinametzin were enormous creatures that existed prior to a global deluge.

Egypt that were integrated into the exoteric religions of the time. The Meri-Isfet aligned with the worship of the Egyptian God Apep, the deity of darkness and chaos. Since Apep is portrayed as a giant serpent, often with the extended hood of the cobra, fangs bared and about to strike, the Meri-Isfet adopted that as the symbol of their order."

"Hence the striking cobra badges that all four of those creeps were wearing at the Wigmore." Concluded Stewart.

"Correct," Stated Mathers, "Apep was known as the "Enemy of Ra" and also "The Lord of Chaos". The Abrahamic religions know him better, simply as Satan, the principle of Evil[66]."

"Jezi!" Exclaimed Sinclair in shock before regaining her composure and reverting to speaking English, "What about your own order? What is your symbol?"

"Cynthia, our order's symbol is the feather and balance scales representing the Goddess Maat, the Egyptian Goddess of harmony, justice, and truth. Over the centuries, our society has had many names and has spawned numerous subsidiary organisations in different regions, but it has always stood for these same immutable values."

Mathers continued her narrative, "Sadly, the Meri-Isfet has also retained their essential nature, using their knowledge of hidden powers, to pervert and corrupt innocence and inflict suffering wherever and whenever the opportunity presented itself. Fortunately, the interceding millennia created very few civilisations advanced enough to produce the metallurgical compounds and fine engineering tolerances required to attempt to reconstruct the infernal "Wheels" that had caused the global deluge. So, the Meri-Isfet focused instead on attempting to obtain the Emerald

---

[66] Evil was termed "Isfet" by the ancient Egyptians.

Tablets. Every few generations, when the desert revealed the lost city of Agartha, the Meri-Isfet tried to gain possession of the Holy Table hidden there. They almost succeeded on several occasions.

In more recent times, the conflict between the two orders has become more openly manifested. At the beginning of the twentieth century, the Wolfsangel gained sufficient worldly power that they took control of many nations in North Africa, Asia and the Middle East that held significant ancient esoteric relics. The Meri-Isfet then misused these powerful relics to disturb the world's stability, plunging its people into two global wars. Each war was intended to destabilise the existing social structures sufficiently that a new world order could be established, based on Evil.

By the late nineteen twenties, Meri-Isfet lodges in Berlin and Munich had identified highly skilled, deep trance mediums who could, under the mesmeric influence of senior adepts, open a limited, one-way communication with the Qliphoth. These mediums seldom survived more than one session, their bodies and minds rapidly becoming corrupted. However, human life and suffering have no value to the Meri-Isfet, and the spiritualist churches had many talented mediums at that time, so finding replacements was not a challenge.

Through these communications, the Meri-Isfet received detailed instructions for the design of advanced technology, military strategy and, more worryingly, since manufacturing tolerances and engineering had become sufficiently advanced, schematics for the construction of new Wheels to open gateways to the Sitra Achra.

Under the guidance of the Qliphoth, the Meri-Isfet used their agents in the Wolfsangel to commence a series of aggressive invasions that quickly overwhelmed the nations of Europe.

The allies fighting this oppression became so overwhelmed that it was not clear if they would succeed, so the Meri-Maat was forced to openly use its network of affiliated lodges throughout the European mainland to support resistance movements and assist minorities in avoiding genocide and help allied soldiers avoid capture and torture. As a result, the Society's lodges, and their members, suffered terrible consequences. Lodges were raided, and their accumulated records and priceless esoteric libraries were seized by the agents of the Wolfsangel to be handed to the Meri-Isfet. By the end of the second world war, my order was very nearly destroyed. Very few active members escaped torture and execution. My grandparents were heads of the Paris Lodge at the time and were captured, tortured and finally executed. By the end of the war, only our Geneve Lodge remained."

"I am sorry," said Stewart, "Sounds like your order members and close family were exceptionally brave."

"Héros, mais ça devait être" (Heroes, but it had to be), whispered the French adept, who was deeply moved by recounting the narrative.

"What is the current situation between the two orders?" Asked Sinclair as she walked to the kitchen and began looking for any surviving drinking glasses so she could quench her thirst.

Mathers continued, "At the end of the second world war, the Meri-Isfet was also in a desperate situation. The number of senior adepts was greatly reduced, their lodges were destroyed, and those members who did survive were forced to go into hiding. However, as society embraced its newly won freedoms, the pursuit of self-interest, hedonistic pleasures and new age philosophies made for an easy recruiting ground for the Meri-Isfet; their numbers proliferated as people wholeheartedly embraced Crowley's philosophy of "*do what thou wilt be the whole of the law.*[67]

In contrast, a philosophy of truth, balance and altruistic self-discipline became increasingly unattractive to successive generations. Finally, we reached a stage where the number of new students within the Meri-Maat has ceased. Given that the Meri-Isfet seem poised to resume their attempts at world domination, we could badly use more support."

"Well, you have two new allies!" affirmed Stewart.

Mathers laughed. "And I could not wish for two better partners. But I think we are all in for testing times in the coming days."

"Why so?" Asked Sinclair, who was now standing beside the seated Stewart, holding a tall glass of water.

Mathers paused, gathering her thoughts, before explaining, "For the past six months, I have been following a series of disturbing paranormal occurrences that have been reported at different locations throughout France, Spain, Italy, Germany and Switzerland. At the most recent of these events, in Geneva, I encountered our mutual friend, Fr Thomas O'Neill."

Stewart nodded, "One of the good guys."

Mathers giggled, "He certainly means well. But he is a little green. Green is the term, yes?"

Now it was Stewart's turn to laugh, "Yes. I can imagine he has much to learn, but that is true of us as well, Madeleine."

"Naturellement." (Naturally.) The French adept continued,

"The phenomena at each of these sites have genuinely terrified all those who have experienced them. Some have

---

[67] Aleister Crowley's famous esoteric instruction.

gone insane, while others have been driven to take their own lives. When I examined each of the events, I found the same thing. At first glance, they all look to be the results of very dark rituals that strongly resemble an ancient Scandinavian form of shamanistic magic called, Seiðr. However, the residual energies at each location show clear evidence of the use of advanced ceremonial ritual magic, specifically the advanced rituals of the Meri-Isfet. Given the use of the elements of Seiðr to disguise the true essence of these rituals, I believe them to be the work of Oscar Pedersen or Magister "Oskar IronHeart", as he prefers to be called. One of the three senior adepts of the Meri-Isfet that I mentioned to you earlier."

"What do you think Pedersen is up to?" Asked Stewart.

"I am not sure; it is almost like he is trying to draw attention to his actions. I am in the process of following some rumours that Pedersen has established a Meri-Isfet temple on a private island fortress that has been constructed on Lake Skadar, near the Montenegrin and Albanian border."

"Is that where you are now?" Asked Sinclair.

"No, but with luck, I should arrive there tomorrow."

"Be careful, Madeleine. As I found out tonight, these bastards are ruthless."

The French adept exhaled, "Yes, but we need to know what they are doing. What about you two?"

Stewart looked at Sinclair, who nodded her agreement as she sipped her water. "We will locate Cortez, as he is the key to the kidnapping of the heirs to the European royal families. Any idea why they have done this?"

"All I can tell you is that the Wolfsangel only exist to promote the worldly interests of the Meri-Isfet, so in some way, the kidnappings must be related to the current goals of Meri-Isfet."

"Agreed, but do you have any clue as to those current goals?"

"Nothing definite." Mathers paused, clearly wondering again how much to share, "There is a rumour that the three senior adepts of the Meri-Isfet are making preparations to reopen the gateways to the Sitra Achra."

The shocked silence in Stewart's kitchen was only broken by the sound of Sinclair's drinking glass dropping from her hands and shattering on the wooden floor.

6   MYTHS AND MONSTERS

"I will tell you of, dark days and hidden things, concerning the ends of the earth and the death of the gods. Listen, and you will learn." – Neil Gaiman, Norse Mythology (2017), Ragnarok: The Final Destiny of the Gods

Oppio Caffè
Via delle Terme di Tito, 72,
00184 Roma RM, Italy

12:23HRS (GMT+2), 9th September, present day

As the badly dented yellow Peugeot e7 taxi van descended the narrow two-lane winding road that led away from the Gesù clinic to the ancient city of Rome, Father Thomas O'Neill held the crumpled paper, with its disturbing image, tightly in his hands. It was as if he feared it would be snatched from them by some invisible force out of the cab's open windows. His mind raced, wondering what, if anything, he could or should do about this warning.

"First things first." O'Neill remarked to himself, in an attempt to slow his racing mind, as he dialled the number for Cardinal Regio's driver, Albrecht, that he read from the back of the "Sichern" business card that he had from the Vatican driver after being dropped at the clinic earlier that morning.

It took a while, but eventually, the call was answered with a gruff, "Sì?" (Yes?)

Speaking in English, as a way to get some feeling of control over the situation, O'Neill informed Albrecht,

"I have finished early at Gesù and will make my own way to meet Regio at the Colosseum."

Albrecht sounded disinterested, clearly more absorbed in the loud discussions that could be heard in the background on his end of the line. Ending the call, O'Neill pushed the used Sichern business card into one of the numerous tears in the transparent plastic seat cover, which only partially protected passengers from the numerous deep, black oil stains visible on the original rear seat upholstery. He then took a deep, calming breath and gazed out of the window at the passing villas that rushed past on either side of the long tree-lined roads that are so frequent in the suburbs of Rome.

Twenty minutes later, the small, yellow van pulled over on the Via Nicola Salvi side road opposite the imposing ruin of the Colosseum. Through its rear sliding door, O'Neill exited the rear of the e7, paid the driver, and headed to one of the outside tables at the Oppio Caffè.

O'Neill's watch said it was 12:23HRS, still early for lunch by Italian standards, so he had no problem getting one of the six metal folding tables laid out under the café's wide awnings. Sitting at the table nearest to the entrance, hoping that the service would be better there, he looked across the constant stream of traffic rushing along the busy Piazza del Colosseo at what was regarded as one of the seven wonders of the modern world.

Since he was still feeling slightly nauseous from his traumatic experience at the clinic, O'Neill ordered a light lunch of a Caprese Salad[68] with pesto sauce, followed by a small bowl of minestrone and rye bread. After finishing, he asked the young waitress for a cappuccino. At the same time, he looked guiltily at his iPhone, resting on the colourful, blue check oilcloth table covers, trying to get over his deep discomfort at calling Madeleine Mathers for a second time in the same day.

---

[68] A fresh mozzarella cheese and tomato salad.

A minute later, and 230 miles North of where O'Neill was sitting in Rome, a generic, silver-coloured android phone began to emit a distinctive ring tone[69] as it rested on a café table top, not too dissimilar to O'Neill's. But rather than gazing at the historical glory of the Roman Amphitheatre, the view from this café table was of a large square lined with the Medieval & Renaissance buildings of the central Piazza[70] in the historic city of Bologna, filled with street-side cafes and busking musicians.

The vibrating android device was lying beside a classic black, open-faced motorcycle helmet[71] and a pair of dark sunglasses[72] resting next to the remains of a light lunch[73] that stood on a plain, white ceramic plate[74]. Nearby, a young, bearded man dressed in an 18th-century costume played a solo violin, filling the Piazza with the energetic cords from the Spring Concerti. The air was filled with the scents of numerous delicious meals served; pasta, fish, seared meat and garlic.

Some ten feet away from the cafe stood the propped frame of a large black, classically proportioned motorcycle[75] that,

---

[69] Mathers had by now assigned O'Neill his own specific ringtone: Tubular Bells, by Mike Oldfield. The theme from the 1973 movie, The Exorcist.

[70] Piazza Maggiore, Bologna.

[71] A Kangol Colt helmet.

[72] Classic Ray-Ban Original Wayfarers

[73] Fresh fruit and natural yogurt along with a bottle of water to minimise the astral and elemental loading on the French Adept's body.

[74] By Astier de Villatte ceramics.

[75] A tuned and modified, Triumph Bonneville with a 1.2 litre engine developing over 110 HP.

at first glance, looked like it was straight from the nineteen fifties. That is until you looked closer and saw that its classic exterior was, in fact, an illusion, for this large motor bike was equipped with the latest specifications developed by Triumph at its Hinckley factory in the UK. Given the numerous difficulties of finding parking for the VW van in central Bologna, Mathers had parked outside the city's centre and used her bike to travel into the centre for a civilised lunch before continuing her long drive in the van.

Mathers was wearing a T-Shirt decorated with the famous vintage art nouveau poster "Tournée du Chat Noir" (Tour of the Black Cat) by the renowned artist Théophile Alexandre Steinlen[76], under a long-sleeved, dark grey hooded sweatshirt baring the heavily faded[77] red text "Sorbonne Universite"[78] across its chest, and a pair of worn, blue Baukjen jeans. On her feet were a pair of grey, Giesswein, merino runners.

She was contemplating the possibility of encountering the Meri-Isfet when the phone's sound disturbed her thoughts. Recognising the distinctive ring tone, she raised one eyebrow and answered,

"Thomas! Calling twice in one day, should I be flattered or worried?"

---

[76] The poster originally advertised the tour of a 19th-century French cabaret "Le Chat Noir"

[77] Mathers must have had fond memories of her studies evidenced by the numerous patches and repairs that decorated the well-used hooded top.

[78] Mathers, M. "Influences philosophiques de la tradition ésotérique occidentale" Maître de Philosophie, Paris Université. The French Adept's graduation thesis.

"Am I disturbing you?" enquired a nervous-sounding Irish-American voice that was partially hidden by the sound of Vivaldi on the nearby violin.

"No, in fact, your timing was parfait (perfect) as I had finished eating and was preparing to continue on my travels."

O'Neill began to summarise his meeting with Cardinal Regio the previous evening when Mather's abruptly interrupted him.

"Cardinal Regio? Is this the same man who is also a psychiatre? (Psychiatrist)"

"Yes, he was quite renowned, I believe, before he found God."

"Dieu!? This man has nothing to do with God, at least as you would understand God. He is complètement Mal (completely Evil). You must stay away from him, please, I beg you."

"Madeleine, believe me, I already have first-hand experience of his evil nature," said O'Neill as he described his encounter with Sister Christina the previous evening at Satan's Fingers.

Mathers commented, in Latin, without interrupting, as O'Neill told of how a man had been lured away and then sacrificed in some bizarre ceremony by the demonic form.

"Congregata de anima condemnabitur[79]." (gathering of a damned soul)

When he finished describing Christina's transformation and the exorcism, O'Neill fully expected Mathers to react in the same way that De Ven had done, by dismissing the demonic

[79] The formal Latin description for the collection of the souls of the dammed in the 15th century "Liber incantationum, exorcismorum et fascinationum variorum" in the Bavarian State Library, Munich.

transformation and eventual disappearance, but not only did she believe him, she congratulated him.

"Enfin, vous avez découvert votre vraie volonté!" (At last, you have discovered your True Will!)

"I will not have to worry so much about you." Teased the French adept, clearly thinking this was why O'Neill had called her.

However, instead of drawing the conversation to a close, O'Neill described Regio's changes to the Deliverance program, his theft of the relics from the Vatican secret archive and finally, the introduction of the WB drug program to replace exorcism. Before O'Neill could explain about his meeting with Mrs Widee that morning, Mathers interjected.

"Thomas, believe me when I say what you are describing is all too familiar a pattern for Regio and his organisation. They want to be the only ones with access to esoteric forces and knowledge, so they can be unopposed when they unleash their destructive evil!"

O'Neill nodded, even though he was sitting alone at the café table in Rome, "My friend, Conrad De Ven, came to that very same conclusion. But what I wanted to ask you about was some highly curious drawings made by one of the possessed patients I visited this morning as part of Regio's modified deliverance program."

Mathers listened as O'Neill described Widee's art therapy sketches before commenting to herself,

"Signes et presages." (signs and omens) and then asking,

"Do you have any of these images you can send me?"

"Thought you would never ask!" laughed a very relieved O'Neill.

O'Neill began sending email after email with the images. As Mathers started viewing them on her phone, she recited what sounded to O'Neill like a poem.

"In giant-wrath does the serpent writhe;

O'er the waves he twists, and the tawny eagle

Gnaws corpses screaming; Naglfar is loose.

O'er the sea from the north, there sails a ship

With the people of Hel, at the helm stands Loki;

After the wolf, do wild men follow[80]"

When O'Neill sent the last image, Mathers exhaled a

"Oui..." (Yes) before explaining,

"Thomas, I am convinced that the wolf in these images is known as Fenrir or, more correctly, Fenrisúlfr[81]. It is from the darkest elements of Norse mythology that describe how the world will come to an end in an event called the "Twilight of the Gods[82]".

"Do the sagas say how the end will come about?"

"Oh yes, they describe Ragnarök in some detail. The world remains safe so long as Fenrir remains bound by some vaguely described magical binding."

"Sounds like there is a big but coming?"

---

[80] Mathers is quoting from the Icelandic "Codex Regius" thought to have been written during the 13th century, based on the most terrifying of the Scandinavian sagas related to the end of days.

[81] Fenrir is also known as Hróðvitnir and Vánagandr, or Vanargand.

[82] Ragnarök or Ragnarøkkr, literally "Fate of the Gods" or "Twilight of the Gods".

Mathers Laughed nervously, "Yes, you are correct. In the sagas, the beast is helped by some unspecified force of evil to break free, and it runs berserk, bringing down all of creation, including the Gods themselves."

"Just a wolf causes the end of the world?" the incredulous O'Neill asked.

"Well, it is no ordinary creature, and it does not act alone. In the sagas, Fenrir has two siblings, the Jörmungandr, an enormous serpent that constricts the globe and a female being called Hel, who presides over the realm that gives us the Hell, that is so familiar to your religion. These three monsters were the offspring from a mating between the trickster God Loki and a giantess called Angrboða."

O'Neill scrolled through the images he had just sent to the French Adept,

"And what about the horrific boat made from what look like human bones and nails?"

"That is also part of the Norse prophecy about the end of days. The boat is called the Naglfar[83]. It is made from the fingernails and toenails of the dead. During the final stages of Ragnarök, the Naglfar boat sails bringing hordes of monsters to the place of the final battle, called Vígríðr, to kill the Gods."

"Sounds like all hell is let loose."

"Literally, since one of the figures leads Hell."

"Can I ask a silly question?"

"They are never silly questions when they come from you, Thomas," Mathers said teasingly.

---

[83] The boat is also known as the Naglfari, "Nail Farer".

"Fenrir is clearly not literally a giant wolf, so do we have any idea what it is?"

"No, only that it is symbolic of some entity devoted to destruction that can be released by the conscious actions of those devoted to chaos." Mathers thought of the Meri-Isfet as she made the remark and wondered if O'Neill's pictures were a warning intended for her.

"What will Fenrir do when it is loose?"

"The correct question is, Thomas, what won't Fenrir do when it gets loose!"

Mathers went on,

"You must keep your acquisition of Venchencho's things secret as if Regio finds out; it may put your life at risk. Regio is not just dangerous in the spiritual realm. He is also utterly ruthless in his daily life."

O'Neill grimaced but decided to say nothing about Regio's visit to his apartment that morning. Instead, he volunteered that Regio had invited him to attend a rehearsal of an Ordo Lucis Occultos ceremony that afternoon.

"Clearly an absurdly dangerous trap!" exclaimed Mathers.

"You mean dark forces?"

"Almost certainly dark forces, but you face other perils in this situation. I mean, if you attend, they will certainly kill you."

Five hours earlier, and 1,100 miles North West of the table outside the Oppio Caffè, from where O'Neill would phone the French adept, stood the famous One Hyde Park complex. Originally built in 2009 by Laing O'Rourke, the Candy brothers designed the lavish interiors as the ultimate central London address. Within the building was one of the most luxurious, five-bedroom penthouse apartments.

In addition to Arab Sheikhs, Russian Oligarchs and Global Hedge Fund owners, this was also the residence[84] of the British Home Secretary. Sir Reginald Twiffers was having what he would probably remember as the single best day of his life. It had started with the phone unexpectedly ringing, disturbing him from one of those deep, dreamless periods of sleep that invariably followed a late night with conspicuous overconsumption of Moët & Chandon[85] and the finest Colombian cocaine.

Raising his rumpled face from the heavily scented[86] hundred thread Egyptian Cotton[87] pillow and pulling aside his monogrammed bedding[88], he sat upright. He waited for that momentary swimming nausea that always accompanies an evening of overindulgence to pass.

---

[84] The apartment was on a "semi-permanent loan" from certain Eastern European organisations as a gesture of their gratitude for reducing police numbers, redirecting law enforcement priorities away from serious & violent crime to focus instead on social media insults and, of course, substantial changes to the Criminal Justice System, so that the odds of a successful criminal prosecution for serious crimes were close to those of winning the lottery jackpot, several times in succession.

[85] A leading brand of French champagne.

[86] A specially blended mix of rosemary and lavender by Dunhill of London, "to ease away troublesome worries and promote a restful sleep". Ideal for those *rare* moments when a politician has a troubled conscience.

[87] Sferra Milos Seamist hand made in the Alpine foothills in the North of Italy.

[88] Porthault Jours de Paris. Handmade near the lavender fields of Rieux-en-Cambrésis, the historic seat of the textile industry in northern France.

He then turned on the bedside light[89] before glancing at the face on his diamond-encrusted, 18kt yellow gold Rolex Day-Date[90]. He noted that it was nearly four hours before his accustomed time to be woken, with a freshly brewed pot of Da-Hong Pao[91] by his gentleman's gentleman, James.

As the buttonless ultra-secure red phone[92] continued its incessant intrusion, Twiffers slowly pulled on his silk dressing gown[93]. He contemplated the convoluted revenge that he would inflict on the unfortunate individual who had made the error of calling him at the god-forsaken hour of seven am.

When he finally lifted the handset, it was with an acid-filled,

"Yes, pray do tell me, who has died?"

However, the sourness etched into the Home Secretary's face was rapidly replaced by a smile only rivalled by the Cheshire Cat[94]. The voice on the other end of the line was The Cabinet Secretary, informing him that Mrs Susan

---

[89] Handmade to order by Officina Luce. This particular lamp was originally made for Muammar Muhammad Abu Minyar al-Gaddafi and was "acquired" from his palace shortly after Libya and its numerous oil fields were "liberated" by Western forces.

[90] One of the many gifts bestowed on him by a grateful Middle Eastern monarch for helping to smooth over certain "human rights irregularities".

[91] This tea is harvested from special 300-year-old tea plants grown in the Wuyi Mountains, Fujian Province.

[92] Such dedicated private lines are exclusively for serving senior cabinet ministers.

[93] A bespoke Verona silk dressing gown by Versace.

[94] From Lewis Carroll's "Alice's Adventures in Wonderland."

Merriweather had unexpectedly withdrawn from public life overnight to spend more time with her family[95].

In the several microseconds that followed this announcement, Twiffers started to worry about how a change of Prime Minster might affect the numerous financial interests he had developed while being Home Secretary. Then his world transformed as he was informed that the party chairman[96], under advisement by senior members of the Party, had used extraordinary executive powers to appoint Twiffers as the acting prime minister.

Assuming he accepted the nomination, he was expected to visit Buckingham Palace at ten am that morning to formalise the new appointment and then attend a meeting at Number Ten with the senior Downing Street staff at his earliest convenience to begin selecting the members of his new Cabinet.

As Twiffers hung up after the call, he sat down on the edge of the bed[97], thinking that his day could not possibly improve. However, he was proven wrong, as moments later, his reverie was interrupted by a knock on his bedroom door. It was James, dressed in his usual black blazer and grey trousers, informing him that,

---

[95] Presumably inside the Merriweather family cemetery.

[96] You just *think* you know which political party Twiffers serves but the truth is that the party is never named because all the political parties and politicians are equally corrupt, self-serving and disingenuous, at least in this book. Admittedly, given the age and size of the Universe it is *possible* that there is or has been an honest politician in the infinite set of possible politicians.

[97] A Hastens Vividus bed acquired from Saddam Hussein Abd al-Majid al-Tikriti's summer palace in Bagdad when Western forces "liberated" the city and Iraq's numerous oil fields.

"There was a lady to see him, and yes, she did appear to have an appointment."

Before Twiffers could pass any comment, a short older woman with collar-length grey hair and black, framed glasses with thick, tinted lenses that would once have been described as "beer bottle spectacles" ambled into his bedroom- the strange woman was carrying a small, linen roll bag covered in calligraphy that looked Chinese, at least to the Acting Prime Minister's inexperienced eye.   Twiffers was completely taken aback by this woman's nerve. After thirty years of marriage, even his wife no longer dared such an intrusion! What could have possessed James to permit this creature into his inner sanctum? Twiffers pondered.

"What... what *is* the meaning of this untimely imposition? I would *never* have made an appointment this early!" exclaimed Twiffers - although, in truth, he was struggling to achieve his usual levels of bitterness due to his continuing elation from his recent good news.

The woman looked to be in her seventies, with a deep tan that only highlighted the numerous wrinkles on her face. She was wearing a light grey silk suit, with a tangzhuang jacket[98] and matching grey silk, ankle-length skirt. On her feet were a pair of flat-heeled Tai Chi shoes in matching grey coloured linen, and, oddly, since it was a warm day, her hands were concealed inside grey silk gloves.

The woman turned and instructed James,

"Thank you, James, that will be all." She spoke with a strong German accent but with a trace of another inflexion that

---

[98] The Tangzhuang jacket (唐裝) is a Chinese style jacket with a straight collar. It is based on the design of the riding jacket once worn by Manchu horsemen.

Twiffers could not quite place.   After the butler had left, the woman retraced her steps back to the door and locked it.

"I say, who the hell do you think you are!?" demanded Twiffers, rapidly regaining his customary caustic nature.

The woman turned and walked calmly towards the Acting Prime Minister until she stood some three feet away, directly in front of where he was seated on the side of his bed.

"Mr Cortez sent me to *cement* your relationship."

Now she was closer, Twiffers recognized some Chinese inflexion amongst the stronger German accent and a strong scent of Patchouli oil.

"What on earth do you mean?" Twiffers reflected that he *might* have been much more receptive if Cortez had sent one of the young, dark-haired, female "companions" who so often populated his social gatherings as "hostesses". But he could not imagine anything that *this* woman could offer that could interest him, let alone influence him; now he was, he reminded himself with considerable pride, Prime Minister.

While the Twiffers was distracted by his self-absorbed vanity, the older woman opened the long fabric roll bag onto the side of the bed, next to where Twiffers was sitting in his silk Versace dressing gown.

The first item to emerge from the roll was a small, sterling silver box, around the size of a large box of matches. The top was adorned with a short silver straw, fitted by two sets of clasps shaped to look like elephant trunks to the top of the container[99].

Twiffer's eyes sparkled with desire as he recognised the box as similar to the ones handed around at some of Cortez's gatherings at the South American club. As his grasping

---

[99] A visual pun related to snorting the contents, presumably.

fingers reached eagerly for the container, the woman briskly patted his hand away,

"Not yet, have patience."

"I say, you can't tell *me* what to do....." Twiffers' angry outburst ended as abruptly as it had started. The woman removed one of her silk gloves, held Twiffers' extended left hand in her un-gloved right hand, and began to manipulate the thick flesh between his thumb and forefinger deftly.

Twiffers gasped and began to breathe more slowly his eyelids fluttering; as his parasympathetic nervous system and etheric body experienced the expert administration of the very weakest[100] of the mythical བདེ་བ ཉེ་འབྲེལ (pleasure connections). This manipulation is one of the many techniques that form a part of the forbidden Tibetan esoteric arts of ལས་ཕྱག་གྲྭ, more commonly known in the lore of occult literature, as the "Las Kyi Phyag Rgya".

Legend tells that these techniques once formed legitimate elements of medicine, spiritual contemplation and the martial arts before becoming consolidated by the infamous tenth-century sage, བླ་མ་ སྦྲུལ Bla Ma Sbrul[101] into a system of physical and astral, sexual energy manipulation.

The older woman looked at the stunned Twiffers and placed his outstretched hand back on his lap. As the sixty-five-year-old Acting Prime Minster sat, slack-jawed in a state of

---

[100] The ancient heretical Tibetan text དེ་བ ཁྲི་ འབུམ "the book of ten thousand pleasures" defines seven levels or degrees of sexual pleasure that can be achieved using their techniques. Normal human beings suffer extreme cardiac trauma with anything more than first level techniques, unless they are habitual extreme stimulant users, such as Columbian drug cartel members, rap singers and, of course, members of the British Parliament, allegedly.

[101] Literally, Master Serpent.

clear ecstasy, the woman continued, calmly emptying the remaining contents of the roll bag onto the bed.

By the time she had finished, she had unpacked a shoebox-sized, rectangular, wooden container engraved with numerous Tibetan inscriptions, all related to the infamous LHP (Left Hand Path) Grand Lama, Bla Ma Sbrul. Inside the box was a mixture of objects, bottles of oils, dark-coloured ash, and a selection of crystals, arranged in an order that reflected their colours and primary vibratory rates within the Vedic sciences.

Having unpacked six of the crystals and placed them carefully on the bedspread, in the order of the human chakras[102], the woman removed her left glove, picked up the Acting Prime Minister's right hand, inhaled and, while intoning a vowel-rich mantra[103], gently blew on his fingers. This act sent a pulse of three of the five[104] charged forms of vyāna[105] contained within the breath. Twiffers' body began to shake, and a fine layer of perspiration formed on his face. He gasped,

"I feel young again like I did when I was sixteen,"

his sentence trailed off as he entered a profound altered state of consciousness. While Twiffers' mind floated in a blissful state known as "Mya Ngan Las 'das Pa" (ཨུ་ངན་ལས་འདས་པ[106]), the woman removed his dressing gown and then his silk Fendi pyjamas; exposing the flaccid, pale body

---

[102] Muladhara; Svadhisthana; Manipura; Anahata; Vishuddhi and Ajna, respectively.

[103] The mantra, D-Maaarrr (ངར), forms part of the forbidden Tibetan tantric lore. You should forget you saw it here.

[104] Nine are mentioned in some of the oldest Vedic texts.

[105] A specific form of prana involved with the circulation of energy.

[106] The lowest of the seven levels of sexual bliss.

of someone whose idea of exercise for the past forty years had been pushing his way past the queues to the Members Bar at the House of Commons.

Noting that the requisite layer of perspiration had formed on the skin, the woman began to place the six crystals she had carefully prepared onto specific points on Twiffers' body. The faceted stones stuck easily to the older man's sweaty flesh. They scintillated as they established a powerful connection with the seven tantric centres of sacred sexual energy[107] that, unlike the better-known chakra system, are embedded in the etheric bodies rather than being interlinked between the physical and non-physical, like the exoteric yoga chakras.

It must be understood that such para-sexual techniques were never developed for simple sexual gratification. However, sadly, this has become the goal of nearly all modern ritual sex magick. The reality is that, too often, sex magick is simply an excuse for older "adepts" to grossly abuse the trusting nature of younger spiritual aspirants- to allow them to achieve sexual gratification that would otherwise be unlikely with younger or better-looking partners.

The true nature of the techniques of subtle energy manipulation included within the forbidden art of Tibetan Las Kyi Phyag Rgya[108] allows the adept to not only understand the effects of subtle energies on human consciousness but also, eventually, to transcend the material and lower etheric realms and gain a mastery of the higher immortal principles. Although, admittedly, such a mastery

---

[107] Dakini; Rakini; Lakini; Kakini; Shakini and Hakini, respectively.

[108] Known as "Maithuna" (मैथुन) in ancient Hindu Vedic sources and Kappuringu (カップリング) in the ancient Japanese sexual magick techniques of Tachikawa-ryu.

often can take more than one lifetime[109] to complete, and such perseverance and determination are extremely rare, especially within contemporary society.

The elderly woman had devoted numerous lifetimes achieving her current level of expertise. The adept currently inhabited a body had been born the only child of a couple of German embassy officials who had died in a tragic car accident on one of the winding mountain passes so frequent in the Tibetan highlands. At the age of six, the orphaned young girl, who had been christened, Ingerid Faber-Nietz, was adopted as the principal attendant for the elderly Head Lama, Bla Ma Sbrul the twenty-sixth, at the infamous Karmamudra Monastery[110]. She rapidly became the old Lama's favourite and showed exceptional talent in manipulating subtle energies. When the old Lama died unexpectedly, he assumed her body as the next physical vehicle[111] in his endless cycle of earthly incarnations.

So, at the age of thirteen, Ingerid Faber-Nietz, became Grand Lama Bla Ma Sbrul the twenty-seventh and ruled the monastery for the next twenty years. During this period, the secret teachings and techniques of the Las Kyi Phyag Rgya remained largely unknown to the outside world, except for the odd traveller who had completed decades of Tantric initiations in India or Japan and came seeking the very highest teachings.

In the late nineteen eighties, the West started getting more accepting of alternative paths of spiritual practice, and so it

---

[109] Soul transference is well established within the magick of Tibetan high lamas.

[110] Located high on the Qinghai-Tibet Plateau.

[111] Fans of the spiritual teachings of the High Lamas prefer to gloss over what happens to the original souls who get "bumped" from their bodies to make way for older souls who are skipping death.

was that the Grand Lama, Bla Ma Sbrul attended an exposition in Berlin, where she displayed some elementary techniques of Tibetan tantra. What she demonstrated were the simplest exoteric principles of her school. They would have been dismissed as child's play in Tibet. Still, to the naïve western audience, they were a revelation - beyond anything being practised by even the most advanced Tantric Yogis and senior adepts of Sex Magick. Thinking that an occidental woman would be more open in sharing the inner secrets of sex tantra than the Tibetan masters, she was recruited as a member of one of the oldest exoteric sex magick temples in Europe.

However, the members of this temple rapidly discovered their error because this woman demonstrated a Magickal ability that vastly exceeded those of the current heads of the order; causing the members to have no choice but to elect her as Imperatrix of the Penetrali Secreto[112] - the oldest of the European Sex Magickal orders, located in a discrete, red brick, three-storey town-house, in the Charlottenburg district of Berlin.

News of this adept's powers spread and eventually caused her to be approached by the world's oldest and most potent order devoted to Left-Hand Path[113] Magick, the Meri-Isfet. The beloved of Isfet was not (just) interested in experiencing the sublime heights of sexual ecstasy; such experiences are regarded as mere distractions by serious students of the LHP. Instead, they understood that these unique abilities could be useful to their own goals of bringing darkness,

---

[112] Formed in Berlin by Polish aristocrat and adventurer, Count Otto Von Ferkov, in 1892. The "Penetrali Secreto" claimed, like many similar organisations created around the same time to teach the inner secrets of all other occult orders.

[113] Vāmācāra (वामाचार) is a Sanskrit term meaning "left-handed attainment".

chaos and suffering to the modern world - goals that, once explained to Grand Lama, Bla Ma Sbrul, she embraced fully.

Apart from the ultimate goal of spiritual enlightenment, the forbidden techniques of Las Kyi Phyag Rgya have an additional effect; addiction to the induced erotic delight as it supersedes any other earthly pleasure. Once having experienced this artificially induced para-sexual state of excitement, every individual becomes unconsciously devoted to the mentor who introduced them to this state of ecstasy. For this reason, Grand Lama, Bla Ma Sbrul, had been systematically visiting senior politicians across all the European capitals to *initiate* them into the delights of Las Kyi Phyag Rgya. It must be understood that age, gender, or sexual orientation made no difference to the Grand Lama. Such superficial differences become supremely irrelevant to someone who has lived twenty-seven lifetimes.

Although Senior Cortez was instrumental in selecting the targets, the Grand Lama's goal was not to assist Cortez but was instead to guarantee that when the time came, all the European leaders would act as one in supporting and undertaking actions that would help the long-term goal of the Meri-Isfet.

The Grand Lama of the Karmamudra monastery, who was so easily manipulating the sexual energies within the ageing body of the Acting Prime Minister, brought the *initiation* to its concluding stage. One where she would guide the Right Honourable Reginald Twiffers, MP, to unimaginable levels of sexual ecstasy.

She pulled a red silk bag from the ornately carved wooden container and released the drawstring, carefully removing a bottle of human ash, a red skull-cup, a small drum[114], flaying knife, thighbone trumpet, and a peculiar-looking variant of

---

[114] A damaru (ཌ་མ་རུ) is a small two-headed drum.

the classic skull-topped tantric staff[115] carved from human bone.

She then opened one of the small glass bottles, poured a handful of the specially formulated oils into her hands, and then began applying the oil over the sweat on Twiffers' body. The acting prime minister's ageing body responded by beginning to shake violently, so much so that the Grand Lama had to intervene to rapidly calm the older man's physiological reactions with a series of pressure point applications on Twiffers' chest, and shoulders and back. With the sixty-five-year-old body more stable, the Grand Lama stood, undid the row of buttons on her dress, and stepped out of it, revealing her naked body, complete with a large, hooded cobra tattooed in red ink onto the centre of her back.

Pouring more of the sacred oil into her hands, she massaged it over her body and guided the stupefied Twiffers to her oil-soaked torso, absorbing the first doses of the special unguent into his mouth. The acting Prime Minster began to gurgle like a delighted infant.

Eventually, The Grand Lama gently pulled Twiffers' face from her chest and, holding his head between her hands, confirmed that the Prime Minister's pupils were fully dilated.

For the first time in the entire encounter, the Grand Lama smiled as she removed her wig and revealed the classic shaven head of a Tibetan monk. She gently guided the dazed Twiffers to his knees on the floor in front of her; as she assumed the formal seated posture associated with Ambhala, the Tibetan sexual deity and began to anoint her

---

[115] This staff is called a khatvanga. In the sexual tantric practices of Tibet, the staff is smaller than its Indian namesake and the small carved skull head on the top of the staff is more phallic in shape than those in traditional Indian tantra.

skull-topped tantric staff with the special oils and the ashes derived from cremated human remains.

Some hours later, Sir Reginald Twiffers was woken from a dreamless sleep by a loud knocking on his bedroom door and the sound of James' voice,

"Sir Reginald? As the High Lama instructed, I have left you undisturbed after your meditation session, but I thought I should remind you that your limousine to The Palace will be here in less than twenty minutes."

Grunting an acknowledgement, Twiffers pulled his cold, bruised and aching body up from the hardwood floor. Sitting up, he noticed a strange coppery, acidic taste in his mouth and was forced to pluck some tiny, dark curly hairs from his tongue. Looking down at his naked body, he was horrified to discover that his groin area was covered in a sticky, slimy mixture of aromatic oil and ash that stung every part of his genitals. This dark grey goo looked similar to the remnants from a cigarette, but instead of smelling of burnt tobacco, the residue covering his most sensitive parts emitted an odour like badly burnt steak mixed with ammonia.

Staggering to his feet, he lurched unsteadily towards the en-suite bathroom as his oil-covered feet slipped on the hardwood floor. After the first couple of steps, he was forced to stop, his face fixed into a wincing grimace because of searing pain from his backside. Gingerly reaching between his two buttock cheeks, he discovered a small, rough-edged object that, when examined closely and wiped clean of ash, looked like a fragment of a broken bone[116], one side of which had been carved into a human skull.

---

[116] Don't worry the High Lama has an extensive supply of khatvanga.

7 THE DEEP FAKE SOCIETY

"The powers that be no longer have to stifle information. They can now overload us with so much of it, there's no way to know what's factual or not. The ability to be an informed public is only going to worsen with advancing deep fake technology. Incriminating audio and video will hold even less weight than it already does. A government doesn't have to lie to its people or censor its enemies when no one believes a thing to begin with. We're entering the Post-Information Age." - J. Andrew Schrecker

Beyond Facts, INC,
London Office,
48th Floor, One Canada Square,
Canary Wharf, London E14 5AB

09:21HRS (GMT+1), 9th Sept, present day

After the disturbing pronouncement by the *whirlwind entity* during its departure, Cortez stood for several minutes, silent and shell shocked, looking at the gore and bone fragments scattered around the courtyard. His usual icy calm had been disturbed. His face drained of its colour, and, most uncharacteristically, his hands shook. He knew he had to respond aggressively or risk losing the momentum of his planned global revolution.

Exiting the courtyard through the Eastern main entrance that led into the reception area of the Wigmore Hall, he found members of his close protection detail waiting for him, along with one of his many personal assistants. The numerous guests who had assembled to hear Cortez had vacated the building shortly after his speech had been interrupted, so he was alone with his staff. After instructing that the courtyard be cleared and thoroughly cleaned,

Cortez walked through the reception area behind the drinks bar and helped himself to a very large brandy[117].

Picking up one of the courtesy Craven A cigarettes from behind the bar, he fumbled through his jacket pockets for his gold Dunhill lighter and took a deep drag, waiting for the calming kick from the nicotine. Cortez usually only smoked his beloved, Montecristos[118], but he was in a hurry for a nicotine fix. As he gulped the drink from a large snifter[119] glass, his eyes settled on a gold-embossed business card promoting a company called, Beyond Facts, "*let your vision become their dream*", which had come from his left jacket pocket, while searching for the lighter. As Cortez recalled his earlier brief meeting with the card's owner, his mind settled on a strategy to deal with Stewart to pre-empt all possible future action by the Scotsman. Once his plans were clarified in his mind, he found his hands stopped shaking. He walked calmly to the Wigmore's front entrance, where he was escorted by six, armed bodyguards to the luxury of the leather-bound sanctuary that was the rear of his black Mercedes-Maybach S 600 Guard[120] stretch limousine. Once seated safely within the cocoon of luxury, Cortez began to feel increasingly focused, listening to a perfect rendition of Mozart's serenade number thirteen, played by the Berlin Philharmonic, through numerous embedded, Definitive Technology speakers.

Seventeen minutes later, the Maybach pulled up at the curb side of a brick-fronted, Edwardian townhouse on Dean Ryle Street, flanked by two black Mercedes G-wagons containing

---

[117] Remy Martin Louis 13 Cognac.

[118] Montecristo Linea 1935 Leyenda.

[119] The balloon or bulb classic glass design that enhances the aeration of the spirit.

[120] Includes VR10 rated protection for bullet and bomb proofing

his ever-present security detail. Even at the absurdly late (or early) hour, many of his staff were waiting for his arrival home. Two smartly dressed butlers took his dinner jacket and walked with him across the marble entrance hall floor to the twin golden doors of a German-made, GEDA, blast-proof elevator. Moments later, Cortez was standing in his spacious dressing room, wearing a grey, Thai silk Armani dressing gown while waiting for his hot bath. Although he had not slept for over twenty-four hours and had endured a traumatic evening, his resolution to deal with Stewart filled him with renewed energy.

He luxuriated in the depths of his white, Italian marble, sunken jacuzzi, soaking in the thick, fragrant bubbles from an exclusively blended mix of Epsom salts and magnesium flakes[121]. As he lay in the bath, Cortez dictated notes to one of his aides, instructing them to send specific sets of source files in preparation for a breakfast meeting with the European head of Beyond Facts, who he had met at the Wigmore Hall the previous evening. Upon emerging from the bath, Cortez resumed wearing his Armani dressing gown as he sat in a red leather barber's chair[122] for his daily ritual of a hot towel cutthroat shave and a restyling of his long, silver hair.

Twenty minutes later, Cortez was sitting back inside his Maybach, escorted by the two G wagons containing his security detail, heading through the busy London streets towards the glass and steel skyscrapers that make up Canary Wharf. The Argentian wore a grey, wool and silk, bespoke tailored, Hugo Boss three-piece suit, a Dior, white, Egyptian cotton shirt, his signature, bolo, leather neck tie[123]

---

[121] Created by Hoffmann-La Roche in Basel, Switzerland.

[122] A hand made Chelmsford professional barber's chair.

[123] Complete with Wolfsangel slide decoration.

and a pair of tan leather brogues[124]. The rich leather smell inside the Maybach was complimented by the bergamot, orange and lemon scents from Cortez's Farina cologne[125].

His three-vehicle, motorized entourage halted outside César Pelli's distinctive pyramid topped, glass and steel building at One Canada Square. Upon exiting the Maybach, Cortez was met at a discreet entrance behind several small, potted conifer trees by a dark-suited security officer. The security officer scanned the digital immunisation and identity pass on Cortez's Siemens phone and gestured for the Argentinian to enter a private, glass-fronted, high-speed elevator that opened upon verification of his identity and current immunisation status. As the two transparent doors closed and the lift progressed up the 770 feet to the forty-eighth-floor offices of "Beyond Facts", Cortez was treated to a spectacular view over the skyline of the British capital.

When, after thirty seconds, the elevator finally came to a stop, the twin doors facing into the building opened, revealing an opaque glass wall, fronted by a brushed steel reception desk, above which was etched the black text,

Beyond Facts, INC

New York, London, Berlin, Moscow, Beijing, San Francisco

"Shaping opinions, influencing change."

Beyond the reception area, Cortez could see a large, open-plan office with a high[126] ceiling, filled with a variety of comfortable seating but very few tables and no desks whatsoever. The few tables he could see were occupied by

---

[124] James Taylor & Son of London.

[125] Mäurer & Wirtz, Farina's 4711 Eau de Cologne,

[126] 9 feet high.

designer drinks dispensers and assorted expensive and exotic snacks. Servitors, dressed in grey, cotton, full-length Barista overalls and matching caps with a Beyond Facts badge, stood at these refreshment stations, providing complimentary unlimited access to a wide range of high-end brand names.

The entire[127] forty-eighth floor was dedicated to office space and was, as far as Cortez could see, occupied by less than thirty people in total. All the staff he could see appeared to be in their late teens or very early twenties, and all had a similar, androgynous look, with pale complexions and short, slicked-back hair. Except for those working serving the refreshments, these individuals were older, in their thirties and forties.

Another striking thing was that everyone was wearing identical glasses and the young staff seemed to be working like mime artists, performing their typing action in mid-air in front of wherever they were seated. For a moment, Cortez wondered if the staff were all short-sighted but then realised that the glasses were providing some augmented view that must have included a virtual keyboard and screen.

Approaching the reception desk, Cortez found a set of glasses, similar to those being worn by all the staff, wrapped in cellophane. Inside the clear wrapping, along with the pair of glasses, was a single piece of small, white paper with his name and the simple instruction,

Wear Me

"Welcome to Wonderland[128]."

---

[127] Roughly 280 square yards.

[128] Cortez is making a reference to the 1865 classic story, "Alice's Adventures in Wonderland" by Lewis Carroll.

Commented Cortez, tearing open the clear packaging and putting on the black frames. Almost immediately, he was presented with a welcome in text and sound, fed through small speakers embedded in the temple tips of the glasses, followed by directions on how he should proceed to his meeting with Aspen, Executive Vice President, Europe.

Alongside the large, yellow, moving arrow that floated in the air four feet in front of his eye level, there was an animated countdown timer for when his appointment was scheduled to begin. It currently showed that he was six minutes and forty seconds early.

Deciding to take advantage of the nearby table serving drinks, he approached and requested the Barista to mix him a Cortado[129]. Sipping from the medium glass, Cortez remarked,

"Nicely brewed. Thanks. Rare to find a good barista."

The dark-haired man smiled,

"Glad you enjoyed it; Beyond Facts is very generous in providing opportunities for retirees."

Cortez looked surprised, "But you can only be thirty?"

"Thirty-two, Sir. But, in the creative industries, that is well," The barista paused, "*Past it,* I think, is the kindest way of expressing it."

He laughed, "In fact, most people around here think twenty-five is "past it" in the disruptive age."

Cortez noted that the augmented reality countdown timer displayed in front of him reminded him that his breakfast

---

[129] Two ristretto shots topped with warm milk. In case you are not a coffee connoisseur, like Cortez, Ristretto is a more highly concentrated espresso. Cortez probably needs the additional caffeine after a sleepless night.

meeting was about to begin. Nodding his thanks, he followed the floating yellow arrow towards a set of virtually rendered, opaque glass walls with the name "Aspen" that appeared to be engraved on the glass. Taking a moment to look over his augmented reality lenses, Cortez could see that although the entire office space was open plan, the augmented reality vision showed a series of opaque glass walls around a few selected members of staff.

As the countdown alarm completed its task, the opaque glass in front of him disappeared, allowing Cortez to see a figure seated on a white chair.

Approaching this figure, he enquired,

"Ms Aspen?"

"Just Aspen," came the response, as a female figure, with shoulder-length dark hair looked up from her work in her virtual reality workspace.

Aspen was in her late twenties but was trying to look like a teenager, as she was dressed in a loose linen shirt, baggy denim trousers and black lace-up canvas basketball trainers with white linen laces.

Since Cortez had requested a breakfast meeting, Aspen's ample and usually empty office space had been temporarily equipped with two large tables with white linen table clothes. The food and drinks were laid out on one table, while the second table had been prepared with two high-backed, white wooden chairs, set facing each other across the table width. Sets of wooden plates, ceramic cups and polished steel cutlery were laid out neatly in front of each seat.

As Aspen and Cortez helped themselves to the food, Cortez noted the discrete labels on each tray, showing the restaurants that had prepared each dish. Most were from a nearby favourite, The Ivy, but other restaurant names were less familiar to the Argentinian.

Believing that one can learn much about a person from what they eat, Cortez carefully noted Aspen's selection of avocados on lightly toasted whole wheat, artisan bread and a ROOT blend smoothie. She ate at a slow and deliberate pace, focusing on her client.

Cortez's staff had requested a cooked breakfast of scrambled eggs on whole-wheat toast, a rare lomo steak[130], mushrooms and a black, Dromedario[131] brand coffee. The request was intended to test how exactly his order would be followed, and, to Cortez's surprise, the meat was Argentinian prime beef, cut correctly and cooked to perfection. One sip of his coffee told him all he needed to know. These were people who researched meticulously and implemented things perfectly. Ideal partners.

As the two ate their respective meals, they discussed the work that Cortez had commissioned.

Aspen began, "Thank you for the down payment and the media," she tapped the air in front of her, "since we received your files early this morning, our Shanghai lab has already been working on making a first pass on the requested revisions and modifications."

Cortez's glasses displayed two sets of video streams, side by side. One showed the original, genuine footage of the failed kidnapping attempt by Fourth Republic operatives in Chelsea the previous morning. The second feed showed an alternative playback. A reality where the Fourth Republic operatives were unarmed, and Tavish Stewart was the merciless aggressor, executing harmless protestors as they

---

[130] An Argentinian term for a filet mignon.

[131] An exclusive Spanish coffee house.

tried to show banners to the passing Royals and the Royal Protection officers who tried to intervene.

Cortez beamed, "Excellent, truly excellent."

Aspen smiled,

"Thank you. Senor Cortez. Our video manipulations are acknowledged as being among the best. When combined with our targeted social media campaigns, they are over ninety per cent effective in mobilizing significant emotional and behavioural reactions in over twenty per cent of the general population. Do you understand how our targeted social media campaigns operate?"

"Only what you briefly outlined last night." Replied the Argentinian.

"Then we should perhaps quickly explain the background to our methodologies for influencing social change. We design highly compelling alternative narratives and use a combination of influencers and social media bots to project the alternative narrative to our target demographics."

Aspen could see that Cortez was becoming lost in the jargon, so she altered her approach.

"Maybe things will become clearer if we briefly discuss the history behind our techniques. The first thing to realise is that the US intelligence agencies are closely aligned with all the big American tech companies. After the fall of the Berlin Wall, the Cold War ended, and the Western Intelligence communities began to search for an alternative focus. Without any clear enemy, that attention naturally turned toward their own populations.

Advances in technology meant that computers became increasingly common in the home as well as in the workplace. Therefore, it was only natural to develop ways to monitor the activities of ordinary people as they used these systems. By the late 1990s, social media had become the ultimate surveillance tool. The intelligence community were amazed at how much personal data users would voluntarily supply to social media platforms. As these technologies became more and more popular, there came a realisation that it was not just a tool to monitor but was also, potentially, a way to access and control the population. However, to fully realise that goal, social media needed to become mobile, so considerable investment was made to encourage smartphone development.

By 2010 phones had, for the first time, become ubiquitous. Even the poorest people in the most remote regions on earth had a phone and could, for the first time, be in constant communication with each other and, more importantly for our story, with social media.

The fundamentals of what we do at Beyond Facts are derived from a covert Western Intelligence project from early 2009 that explored if manipulated social media could play a role in mass social influence. The target was the oppressive regimes in North Africa. PSYOP[132] specialists within DARPA[133] and the CIA designed scenarios that would inflame existing social tensions. Then, they began feeding targeted individuals using numerous fictitious social media accounts populated by skilled agent provocateurs. These targetted individuals had social media profiles which indicated disillusionment with their nation's existing regime. These disillusioned people were fed specially constructed dialogues, documents and images deliberately designed to encourage and spread dissent. The impact of these targeted messages was amplified by bots that repeated the

---

[132] Covert operations to convey manipulated information to audiences to influence their emotions, objective reasoning and behaviour.

[133] Defense Advanced Research Projects Agency.

messages and gave the appearance that large numbers of people supported the dissident views.

"bots?" queried Cortez.

"Short for robots, but these are not physical, but rather software." Clarified Aspen, before continuing,

"The Americans hoped to use the technique to spark revolutions, which it did. However, they also naively expected the revolutions to transform the Arab nations into mini-American capitalist democracies and give American corporations access to exploit North Africa's rich natural resources.

What happened instead was extraordinary violence and chaos. The places that had been targeted descended into a mayhem that only ended when replacement hard-line governments seized power."

"Typical CIA optimism," commented Cortez, "Just like the Hungarian uprising of nineteen fifty-six and the failed Cuban invasion of nineteen sixty-one."

"Exactly," nodded Aspen.

"Please, do continue," prompted Cortez.

"Although the goals of seeding the spread of liberal democracies in North Africa failed, using social media to influence the thoughts, emotions and actions of large groups of people was a success. This success led to a business model where populations can be influenced for anything from purchasing a specific brand of trainers to instilling a particular idea in a target demographic.

"Why aren't Governments using it?" Asked Cortez, who was thinking of how the method might be used to advance his own political agenda and deal with Stewart.

Aspen laughed, "Oh, they are... The Russians and Chinese are our best customers spreading destabilising misinformation. As for the Western Governments, the cost, combined with the fear of how their populations would react to finding how they were being manipulated, discourages them. One only has to recall the fuss about the Facebook emotional contagion experiments[134] in 2013 to know why democratic governments are cautious.

For the most part, Western leaders have opted for the alternative strategy, which is deliberate information overload in the press, TV, and internet, with numerous conflicting scenarios. The population never knows what is true and are kept so afraid of what might happen that they tolerate the status quo."

Aspen looked directly at Cortez,

"I trust that fear of discovery will not be a barrier for you, Mr Cortez?"

Cortez smiled and sipped his strong, black coffee, "No. Ms.... Sorry, Aspen."

"Just to clarify, the goal of your campaign is,"

Cortez interrupted before Aspen's sentence was completed, "To destroy this man,"

He retrieved some papers from inside his jacket and, unfolding them, handed Aspen a two-page, A4-sized dossier with a photograph of Stewart in the top right-hand corner. Aspen took the dossier and summarised the contents.

"Sir Tavish Stewart, VC. Highly decorated military veteran. Owner, Stewart's Antiquarians, here in our beloved Mayfair, owns an ancestral estate in Scotland. He has all the

---

[134] Adam D. I. Kramer, Jamie E. Guillory, and Jeffrey T. Hancock. "Experimental evidence of massive-scale emotional contagion through social networks" Proceedings of the National Academy of Sciences (PNAS) June 17, 2014 111 (24) 8788-8790.

trappings of privilege, so manufacturing a strong public dislike towards him will be easy. Plus, he is a boomer - our target demographics particularly distrust them."

"Boomer?" enquired Cortez.

"Those born between the end of the second world war and the mid-1960s are called the Baby Boomers, as they represent a dramatic post-war increase in population. They are also the generation who formed much of our modern world. So, highly successful Boomers are seen by large segments of contemporary society as greedy, uncaring and responsible for numerous environmental and social inequalities.

What makes modern society unique is that increasing numbers of people have never known a world without pervasive technology, so they have absolute trust in technological progress. Consequently, they desire to have the latest information and remain constantly connected to their peers through social media connections. For these people, identity and self-worth are formed and maintained by their presence on social media.

Not only do they dislike and distrust authority figures, who are typically successful individuals from the boomer generation, but they are also constantly searching for new moral causes that they can participate in so they can document their involvement on their own social media feeds, showing their awareness of emerging social injustices. This trait allows us to successfully spread our message and influence their thoughts, emotions, and behaviour.

Cortez looked at the large poster images of the company's "key influencers" that were being projected onto his virtual display. Predictably, there were a few sports celebrities and music entertainers. For the most part, they were just good-looking people having a designer, nonstop party lifestyle in exotic places and always with expensive branded products in clear sight. The only thing that seemed to unite them was that no one looked like they had ever worked for a living. The accompanying "influence charts" showed dramatic increases in sales directly related to the product placements in the "key influencers" images.

Cortez could not understand how such individuals could influence anyone, let alone be regarded as role models. Prompting the Argentinian to ask,

"How can so many people be so easily manipulated?"

Aspen smiled, "A combination of factors has shaped modern society into becoming the perfect targets for our behavioural and cognitive influence.

To a large extent, their social status and concepts of self-worth are directly related to their projected image on social media. They are highly influenced by posts, likes or comments made by individuals who are highly regarded within their peer groups as "social influencers"- especially for comments made by such "social influencers" on an individual's own social media profile. This predisposition makes our target demographics extremely reliant on constant positive reinforcement. Consequently, they are often quite fragile, mentally and emotionally volatile. Traits that make them ideally primed for our interventions.

The second factor is that these target demographics believe that they are victims of numerous social injustices that deprive them of the possessions, status and achievements that should, by right, be theirs. These beliefs are largely due to their educational experience. When many of this group were young, education changed its emphasis and moved away from a focus on vocational skills acquisition. Instead, it concentrated on increasing social awareness, highlighting injustices that occurred in recent social history. Many educators also believed that the exclusive goal of education should be to make the experience emotionally rewarding.

Since many theorists proposed that telling a learner they were wrong harmed their natural inquisitive nature, they introduced a philosophy of avoiding negative feedback. Each person was encouraged to believe that they were special and could achieve anything. In retrospect, this approach reinforced a belief in large segments of society that they were entitled to get whatever they wanted.

Combined with this change in primary and secondary schools, there was a massive expansion of higher education. Governments believed that if everyone attended post-secondary education, the result would be a population filled with innovative geniuses who would advance society. Sadly, the reality is a population with many highly dissatisfied individuals who believe that the older generations have, and are, actively denying them the recognition and lifestyles they deserve.

You see, universities and colleges are almost exclusively run by people with strong liberal views who are typically opposed to those in authority, who they view as constantly underfunding and undervaluing the contributions of the education sector. The result is that these institutions almost exclusively hire people with liberal ideologies who distrust authority.

This ideological bias has increasingly formed the basis of higher education for the past decades. The courses that so many people have completed were designed and delivered by individuals who felt undervalued by society and taught their students to distrust traditional authority figures. This distrust was inculcated by course materials that highlighted the numerous abuses of power that have taken place during the recent history of most developed nations. The result is that an increasing number of people distrust authority and implicitly believe that the only hope for society to address social injustice is by disrupting the existing forms of practically every aspect of modern life. They implicitly distrust all existing power structures, so they are predisposed to believe the misinformation transmitted by those they admire and emulate.

This scenario is the basis of our business model: Through carefully manipulated texts, pictures, memes and videos, we provide these people with fictitious injustices that need to be addressed - through messages given explicitly and implicitly by our influencers and the millions of bots who appear to show massive support for whatever idea we are promoting."

Aspen paused to check that Cortez had followed her detailed explanation of the business model that would apply to his case,

"By the way, I see you are not using our usual narratives for discrediting an individual of abuse or sexual deviance?"

"No," responded Cortez, "I want something definite. Something targeted to strip him of everything that makes him who he is – his titles, wealth, possessions, friends, and business. Leaving him with nothing, so he is utterly broken."

The Argentinian handed Aspen a folded paper sheet from his jacket pocket. As she was unfamiliar with such primitive media transmission, Aspen hesitated but took the summary.

She read through it and smiled,

"Delightful alternative narrative. Creating the deep fake audio and video that are necessary evidence will take us some hours. But we can start the rumours circulating from some of our key social influencers immediately."

"Will the mainstream media be a problem?" Asked Cortez.

Aspen laughed, "No, not at all. The entire newspaper business model is based on outsourced freelancers, and most of the key ones belong to us anyway. As for the rest, they will follow whatever is leading social media at that moment.

"Now, we can quickly go through some of our optional extras, if we may?"

Aspen began filling in a form that appeared suspended in mid-air in front of Cortez.

"Did you want violence included with any protests? We outsource, of course, to minimise the risk of liability. But having the odd police officer brutalised and shop fronts kicked in gains much more news coverage. And, once our agents instigate the violence, the rest of the crowd inevitably learn to follow their examples very quickly."

Cortez nodded, and Aspen ticked a box on the virtual paper before proceeding to the next option.

"For a modest additional fee, we can add having the odd car being burnt and road blocks constructed. Many of our French clients are especially fond of these extras with our contracts."

Cortez smiled, swiping with his hand to enable all the tick boxes, pre-empting any further questions

"Aspen, let's go for the *full service*."

8 ORDO LUCIS OCCULTOS

*"To deny the possibility, nay, the actual existence of
witchcraft and sorcery, is at once flatly to contradict the
revealed word of God in various passages both of the Old
and New Testament..." - William Blackstone*

*Flavian Amphitheatre (Colosseum)
Piazza del Colosseo, 1, 00184 Roma RM, Italy*

14:45HRS (GMT+2), 9th September, present day

After ending his phone conversation with the French Adept,
Father Thomas O'Neill ordered another espresso. Due to the
stressful events of the day and the lack of sleep the previous
night, he suddenly felt mentally and physically exhausted.

As the waitress started to clear his table, O'Neill snatched a
bread stick and asked for a piccolo[135] of the house red[136]. A
few moments later, passers-by and the young waitress
smiled as they saw the lone priest pray by himself and, in
turn, raise the bread stick above his head, then the tiny
bottle. He then crossed himself, took a small bite from the
bread roll, unscrewed the bottle, and took a sip before
retightening the top and placing the partially consumed
bread and wine into his left and right jacket pockets[137].

After the dire warning from Mathers about the mortal risk of
attending Regio's rehearsal that afternoon, O'Neill called De

---

[135] A small one glass bottle of wine, usually around 6.5 fluid
ounces.

[136] Almost certainly a local wine from the Sangiovese grape,
referred to as a "Chianti" by Dr. Hannibal Lecter.

[137] O'Neill is clearly expecting the worst from his coming encounter
with Cardinal Regio. He has just placed his soul in a "state of
grace".

Ven, so at least someone would know where he was going. But the calls all went unanswered, each one going to De Ven's voice mail.

While O'Neill left his friend a detailed message about Regio's invitation, he noticed six identical blue Volkswagen Passat estate cars, with prominent "Sichern" branding on their sides, pull up alongside the Colosseum. They deposited around twenty security personnel out onto the pavement and three sinister-looking Doberman Pinscher dogs with clipped ears and tails. The dogs were led off by three handlers into the Colosseum complex and were soon out of O'Neill's sight.

All of the men and women who had emerged from the Passat cars were dressed as if expecting a serious confrontation to erupt. They wore black paramilitary uniforms and were heavily armed with what looked to O'Neill's inexperienced eye, to be machine guns similar to those he had seen carried by police at railways and airports.

The tough-looking men and women who had emerged from the Sichern vehicles started taking stacks of red plastic traffic bollards from the rear of the Passat estate cars and systematically closing off one of the two lanes on the Piazza del Colosseo road. By the end of their efforts, the traffic flowed considerably more slowly, with the inevitable beeping of car horns and obscene hand gestures from the inconvenienced Italian drivers.

Minutes later, a procession of large, black executive limousines arrived. Each car passed into the coned-off area and then over the pavement, through a large double gate into the cobblestone area inside the perimeter wire fence of the Colosseum grounds. Cardinal Regio emerged from the lead car, which looked like the same BMW 7 he had used the previous evening. These executive vehicles clearly enjoyed diplomatic status based on the numerous flags that adorned their fronts, including Regio's, which sported the

119

distinctive yellow and white Vatican flag. In amongst the row of black limousines being guided to their respective parking spaces by the Sichern operatives, O'Neill noticed an exception, a bright red, classic 1960s sports car[138]. The driver was a tall, athletic man with the looks of a professional male model, dark flowing hair, a deep tan and an exquisitely cut suit. Even from a distance of fifty yards, O'Neill had an instinctive dislike for him. He was simply too good to be true, and O'Neill was sure that, had Ezekiel been present, the old tomcat would have been exhibiting his classic response to evil.

Whoever this good-looking man was, he was treated with great deference by the gathering group of VIPs as they exited the ever-growing number of high-class vehicles assembling outside the Colosseum. The man who had been driving the red sports car made a big show of embracing Regio and kissing him on both cheeks.

The other guests were a mix of males and females, all over forty, clearly very successful, wearing classic business attire. Based on how they interacted, they all knew each other very well and looked like they were enjoying the chance to meet again. There was also an element of expectation in their attitude - the way they looked at Regio and the sports car driver did not look to O'Neill like a group about to attend a rehearsal. It was much more like the expectation from spectators before a major title fight. As the last of the limousines drew into line and parked, a white Volkswagen transporter van arrived. A single female occupant was escorted by two Sichern staff from the transporter over to the Colosseum entrance. The gait and walk of the woman looked lifeless, but there was something about her that

---

[138] O'Neill is not a car enthusiast, so he did not recognise this red 1964 Ferrari 250 GT Lusso. One of the most coveted and expensive sports cars in existence.

looked familiar to O'Neill. However, the distance was too far for him to make any guess as to her identity.

O'Neill checked his watch, and since it was 14.50HRS, he left a tip for the waitress and walked across the two roads over to the Colosseum, getting a few frustrated horn honks and gestures from drivers on the congested Piazza del Colosseo road. He was waived through the armed guards at the gate by Regio, who welcomed him warmly,

"Father O'Neill, I am so delighted that you could join us this afternoon."

Regio was dressed in his customary dark suit with a dog collar and made a big show of being the perfect host, offering to take O'Neill on a tour of the ancient site before the rehearsal began. As the pair walked together up the slope into the entrance to the site, they were joined by a tall, powerfully built, middle-aged man with long grey hair tied into a classic Japanese top knot. Regio introduced the man as "Kenjo-san", who was the head of the twenty strong Sichern protection team assigned to keeping the event private and secure.

Regio beamed as he continued his introductions,

"Kenjo-San is an exceptional man, Father O'Neill. He served twenty-one years in the Tokushusakusengun[139] before forming his unit within Sichern. He hand-picked the men working today from Tier One units worldwide[140].

The acronym meant nothing to O'Neill, but clearly, he was meant to be impressed, as evidenced by the giant smile on Kenzo-San's face. But that emotion rapidly faded when the

---

[139] The Tokushusakusengun (特殊作戦群) or Special Forces Group is Japan's Self-Defence Force counter-terrorist unit. Similar to the USA's Delta Force.

[140] Tier One is the highest designation within "special forces" units.

modern samurai's gaze fell on O'Neill, who he continued to look at with the disdain familiar to every nerd when they are found wanting by the school athletics coach. Regio appeared not to notice the distaste on Kenzo's face.

"You may think it strange that a Japanese national would be leading such a unit, but, as you know, the Germans and the Japanese have a history of close cooperation."

"With the Italians too." Commented O'Neill.

Regio looked a little disconcerted by this comment but shrugged it off and, turning away, led the three men further into the labyrinth of columns that filled the interior of the ancient structure, giving O'Neill the chance to get a closer look at the enigmatic Kenzo-San.

In addition to the same black polymer hand gun carried by the other Sichern operatives, Kenjo-san had a long, Japanese sword that he carried tucked into a black silk band around his waist. Unlike many of the other Japanese swords that O'Neill had seen in museums and public displays, this sword's scabbard was a simple black metal covered with dents and a highly distinctive row of deep score marks instead of adornments. O'Neill could see that the weapon had suffered many decades, if not centuries, of hard use.

As they walked into the ruin complex, it was clear that some special preparations had been made for the rehearsal. A wooden stairway had been installed to provide access to the lower level. Using this stairway, Regio led O'Neill and Kenzo-San down to what had once been the basement for the arena.

As the small group passed numerous thick columns, there was a constant radio chatter in German that could be heard indistinctly from the earpiece and throat microphone attached to Kenjo-San's neck and ear.

Regio looked back towards O'Neill and saw the priest glancing at the series of over twenty deep score marks that had been made into the sword's sheath, just close to the exposed sword hilt.

"Ah, I see you have noticed Kenzo-San's tally of the occasions that fate and circumstance have combined to permit him an opportunity to use his family's sword for its intended purpose."

"You mean killing?" O'Neill sounded shocked, "Surely the combat potential of a sword has long been rendered obsolete by the gun?"

The face of Kenzo-san transformed into an expression of anger, and he spoke, for the first time,

"At close quarters, a blade is often faster than a gun and more honourable. A gun is a coward's weapon."

O'Neill nodded and moved closer to Regio, who appeared unaware of O'Neill's discomfort. The Cardinal turned towards O'Neill,

"This lower level was used to prepare the gladiators and store the many animals used in the major spectacles."

Regio sounded like a tour guide as he pointed to the collapsed segments of outer walls that seemed more visible from the lower perspective.

"Most of the structural damage you can see on the Southern side occurred during the great earthquake of 1349. Those collapsed walls were built on less stable alluvial terrain. Still, we must not mourn the loss because most of the Rome we know today would not have existed without that collapse, as the tumbled stones were used to build palaces, churches, and other medieval buildings."

Enjoying the antiquity that surrounded him, O'Neill rubbed his hand against one of the massive blocks of travertine limestone, forming a twelve-foot square column that would have once helped support the arena floor above them. It was now just an open space to the blue September afternoon sun high above them.

Regio noted O'Neill's gaze,

"Yes, above us would have been around fifty thousand spectators cheering their favourite gladiators."

Kenzo-San grunted, "Nobler times that understood the need of real men to test each other in deadly combat."

Regio patted the samurai's massive shoulders, "You must forgive Kenzo-San, Father O'Neill. Our modern society is too gentle for his warrior nature. Come, I have something you will find interesting,"

Regio led the three men around a series of columns near the end of the lower area into what appeared to be a dead end. A raised wooden stage had been set up, exhibiting a diorama of gladiator equipment and beyond the stage was an underground stairway exposed under a series of raised flagstones.

"I did not know this was here!" exclaimed O'Neill.

Regio smiled, clearly enjoying his moment of superiority over the archaeologist.

"It is not public knowledge, but as my special guest, I will let you see everything this afternoon."

"Everything?" Asked the suspicious O'Neill.

Regio laughed, "Yes, Father O'Neill. Nothing will be hidden from you today."

O'Neill looked carefully at the Cardinal as, for some reason, he was reminded of Regio's comment from the morning to "be careful what one wishes for".

The Cardinal continued with his geniality. Even if it was an act, O'Neill was keen to use this opportunity to find out everything he could about what Regio was doing with his secret order. Fortunately, Regio seemed unaware of O'Neill's suspicions.

"After the recent violent destruction of all the world's consecrated sites devoted to organised religion[141], we had to find and repurpose suitable locations for our devotions. Thankfully, my order has sufficient funds to locate and acquire sites that have fallen into ruin or disuse, like this one."

At the bottom of the subterranean stairway, O'Neill found himself standing in a long hallway, some forty feet wide, fifteen feet high, and well over two hundred feet long. It was noticeably colder and darker down in this lower level, the lack of direct sunlight having an immediate impact. There was also that slightly musty smell in the air that one often encounters in confined underground spaces.

O'Neill looked around him. The walls, ceilings and floor were formed out of blocks made from travertine limestone, volcanic rock and Roman concrete. Pairs of flaming torches stood at regular intervals along the room's length, providing a basic illumination and causing sinister-looking shadows to be cast in the furthest corners. The stone walls, floors and high ceiling magnified the sound of their footfalls, and when they spoke, their voices reverberated within the confined space with a slight echo.

Looking along the vast underground corridor, O'Neill could see that further ahead, there were stone structures that protruded from the walls on either side of the hallway,

---

[141] As part of Ad-Dajjal's dark Magickal rites, she broke one of the first seals of creation. Destroying the pillars of faith.

narrowing the passageway to about fifteen feet in width at its narrowest points.

There were numerous carvings and statues on the walls through which the three men were walking. Christian symbols were alongside older pagan idols from the ancient Roman religions. There was a Chi-Rho[142], alongside a human-sized statue of Mars, the God of war, portrayed as a powerfully built male, wearing a distinctive Roman helmet and carrying a spear.

Alongside Mars, there was what O'Neill recognised as Morta, the Roman Goddess of death—portrayed as a female skeleton, wearing a shroud and carrying a long knife to reap the living[143]. Finally, next to some wall graffiti of a fish[144] was Pluto, the Roman lord of the underworld[145].

Regio noted O'Neill's fascination with the Pagan deities,

"Yes, Father O'Neill, there are numerous images related to centuries of worship here."

As they continued to advance along the corridor, they came upon a stone altar and more Christian symbols, including IHS[146] and a Cross.

"I didn't know there was a church here?" exclaimed O'Neill as he crossed himself.

---

[142] Chi Rho is one of the earliest forms of Christian symbol. Created by superimposing the first two letters of ΧΡΙΣΤΟΣ (Christos) so that the vertical stroke of the Rho intersects the centre of the Chi.

[143] Thought by many to be the inspiration for the modern image of the Grim Reaper.

[144] Another early Christian symbol based on scripture ("I shall make thee fishers of men").

[145] The so called Chthonic ("subterranean") realms.

[146] Jesus, spelt "ΙΗΣΟΥΣ" in Greek capitals, has the abbreviation IHS.

"Yes, in the late 6th century, a small chapel was built into the arena's structure. I find that such sacred spaces[147] help considerably with certain rites." Explained Regio.

As they continued, O'Neill noticed that many of the flagstones were, in fact, gravestones, prompting him to ask,

"Consecrated ground?"

Regio looked curiously at O'Neill, "You are quite observant. Yes, the arena was converted into a cemetery at one time, but earlier Christian practices were much less fussy about the official nature of what was consecrated."

By this time, they had reached the sets of structures that O'Neill had seen when they first arrived in the lower level that jutted out and reduced the width of the passageway. Up close, they could be seen as cells, with iron bars on the doors and chains on the walls, along with some hideous-looking instruments of torture.

"A prison?!" O'Neill sounded genuinely shocked.

Regio nodded.

"At the start of the thirteenth century, the Frangipani family took over the Colosseum and fortified it as a castle, complete with the dungeons and torture equipment. That use lasted for a couple of hundred years until, in the fourteenth century, a religious order moved in, and they continued to inhabit the area until the late eighteenth century.

By the middle of the eighteenth century, the Pope[148] consecrated the structure, installing the Stations of the

---

[147] Consecrated grounds are filled with hidden energies that can be used for good and, of course, evil.

[148] Pope Benedict XIV consecrated the site in 1747.

Cross[149] and dedicating the building to the Passion of Christ - because of the number of Christian Martyrs who died on the site. So, as you can see, Father O'Neill, my order has merely returned the space to more devotional purposes."

O'Neill nodded. "What does the order of the concealed light do exactly, Cardinal?"

Regio seemed to find the question amusing,

"Many things, Father O'Neill. As you saw yourself last night, one of them is taking in the homeless and starving and providing them with badly needed food."

O'Neill started as he realised that his activities last night had been seen and were known. The question now was; did they also know about his confrontation with Sister Christina? O'Neill decided that was unlikely, as otherwise, why would Regio invite him here and provide this tour. Whatever the answer, O'Neill had to bluff it out and try and find out as much as he could. Hopefully, De Ven would have gotten his message by now and be headed here to rescue him if things suddenly went badly wrong.

"Yes, I did notice some of the homeless were being given medicines as well as food." Stated O'Neill, trying to sound much more fearless than he felt.

"Indeed, there is no crime in doing that, is there, Father O'Neill?" Regio countered.

"No, of course not. But I did notice the WB logo on some of the medicines being given." Said O'Neill.

Regio began to look more and more like a cat building up to playing with a mouse that he had found.

---

[149] The Stations of the Cross are a series of fourteen devotions that commemorate the events in the last day of Jesus Christ's life as a human being.

"My, you do have sharp eyes. Indeed, as I am sure you know, many homeless people suffer from severe psychiatric disorders, and we do our best to treat them, freely, of course."

O'Neill pondered on the implications of Regio's responses. If De Ven was correct about how WB affected people, one had to ask what became of the zombified homeless.

By this time, they had passed beyond the narrower section of the corridor containing the dungeon cells that the Frangipani family had built. They came to a broader area, some forty-five feet square, where two other passageways joined into the one more significant corridor that O'Neill had been traversing. The location was filled with a growing mass of people as they filed out of the two passageways on the main corridor's left and right-hand sides.

Ahead of the group of around thirty people was a set of three trestle tables set up directly in front of a high, circular stone archway, some twenty feet wide and twelve feet tall. This arch marked the end of the long two-hundred-foot passageway Regio had brought them along over the past few minutes.

Standing behind the row of tables were a group of five people, each dressed in identical, full-length grey hooded robes. Two of them were carrying the same machine guns that O'Neill had first noticed when he observed the Sichern operatives arriving at the Colosseum earlier.

The five robed attendants checked people's names from a list and then searched through a series of clothes racks set to the left of the trestle tables. As O'Neill watched, the five attendants efficiently located each person's robe and provided each one with a large, transparent plastic box, like those provided at airport security screening. Each person then undressed, entirely without any pretence of modesty, placing their belongings into the boxes, and they were then given a ticket in exchange for handing over their effects. The boxes were sealed with a plastic lid and stacked on the right-hand side of the tables. It was a well-planned operation that had been completed before on numerous occasions, as everyone seemed very familiar with the entire procedure.

Most of the group were provided with black robes, fewer with red ones. Only Regio and the elegantly dressed man, who had emerged from the red Ferrari, were given highly distinctive purple robes. All of the assembled people, including Regio, were unashamedly naked under their robes and proceeded towards the large archway after they had changed into their ceremonial dress.

O'Neill noticed that those wearing black robes deferred to those in red, while Regio and the other man in their purple robes were treated like royalty. The black robes were decorated with red silk embroidery on their backs, with the same golden lucifer symbol he had seen on the badge worn by Sister Christina the previous evening. The back of the red robes had similar delicate embroidery in a silver thread - but, instead of the man with a flaming torch, the back of these red robes was adorned by the striking snake symbol that O'Neill had seen tattooed onto Sister Christina's back. The same striking snake appeared on the backs of the two purple robes, except the embroidery was in a delicate golden thread.

It soon became apparent that O'Neill was the only person who was not being issued with a robe,

"Don't I get a costume?" enquired O'Neill, wondering what the omission might mean, if anything.

Regio waved his hand in a dismissive gesture,

"No need, Father O'Neill. After all, you are our guest." The emphasis on the word guest sounded like it contained a veiled threat. O'Neill began to hope that De Ven would soon turn up so he could escape whatever fate was planned for him.

The Cardinal then motioned O'Neill to follow him through the large stone archway. Unlike the corridor, which had smelt vaguely stale, the air wafting through this portico was heavy with a musky and intoxicating scent of henbane, opium and other exotic flora that have been developed over the millennia to raise consciousness and reduce the inhibitions of the rational mind.

Passing through the archway, they entered into a massive hall area over two hundred feet long and eighty feet wide with a twenty-foot-high ceiling.

Spotlights on the walls illuminated inverted pentagram symbols - but as O'Neill's eyes adjusted to the lower light levels in the hall, he saw that these five-sided figures resulted from small projectors beaming the image of the inverted pentacles on the walls.

What light there was came from sets of flaming torches set into the walls and from a group of four large pillars that surrounded a massive black statue of a goat-headed creature that dominated the centre of the enormous space. Each of the flames emitted the thick, heady incense that O'Neill had noticed as he walked through the entrance. He was acutely aware that his senses were rapidly becoming intoxicated by whatever substances were contained in the thick smoke that filled the air. Already, he noticed his mind was working more slowly, and it seemed to take an age for him finally recognise the image portrayed in the central goat sculpture and exclaim,

"The Goat of Mendes!"

Regio sighed, "Your lack of knowledge disappoints, Father O'Neill. Many mistakenly think that the Dark One would manifest as a goat or satyr. But that is because goats had a reputation for lustful behaviour that was regarded as unhealthy and sinful in unenlightened times. After the work of Freud, Kinsey, Johnson and Westheimer, we now understand that there is nothing sinful in healthy sexual expression. Other misguided writers and thinkers from earlier times linked the pre-Christian gods of Pan and the Egyptian ram-headed god with the Dark One. Note that such ignorant people even confused a Goat with a Ram when citing Banebdjedet, the ancient God of Mendes."

"Then what is that statue doing here? Was it left over from the previous occupation of this site?"

Regio looked amused at O'Neill's attempt to find an innocent explanation for the enormous goat-headed statue that had a dominating position in the ceremonial hall.

"No, Father O'Neill, we have included this representation of Levi's[150] Baphomet, as it fits the expectations of many of our outer order members, who seek confirmation that they have found an organisation that conforms to society's stereotypical iconography. The true nature of the inner order will elude these simpletons."

O'Neill was startled that Regio had just implicitly admitted that this meeting was, if not Satanic, certainly not orthodox Christian.

"If these people are such a burden, why do you include them?"

Regio looked at the twenty figures in their black robes, who were now gathering in a semicircle around the centre of the hall,

"They are a source of influence over the world from the positions many of them hold in senior appointments and, to be entirely honest, their financial donations help fund

---

[150] The 19th century French occultist and ritual magician Eliphas Levi.

events such as this." Regio gestured to the massive hall around them.

"And exotic cars, like that Ferrari I saw at the entrance?" O'Neill decided to see where these disclosures were leading.

Regio ignored the pointed comment and continued,

"Occasionally, as you will see tonight, they can also make other more significant contributions to our rituals."

Regio then went back to talking about the statue – pointing towards it with an expansive gesture,

"The nineteenth-century occultist Eliphas Levi sketched an image of a fictitious Templar idol, Baphomet, in one of his books[151] and, like much else contained in his writings, created an erroneous link between the supposed blasphemy of the Templar knights with a Satyr-like deity from Mendes. Numerous occultists have subsequently repeated this mistake.

Many simpletons," He gestured to the black-robed followers, "Believe it is the Dark One, so we give them that pleasure. The more enlightened take its meaning in other ways."

"What other meanings could that thing have?" asked O'Neill, clearly horrified that anyone was being encouraged to worship the image of a goat-headed creature with pendulous female breasts and hooved hands and feet.

Regio calmly continued with his explanation as if he was discussing the weather that afternoon,

"As a representation of the harmony that can exist within all things and, of course, the astral light. A universal medium that permeates the universe and, if understood properly,

---

[151] Dogme et Rituel de la Haute Magie (1855)

permits certain manipulations of that universal medium to effect change."

O'Neill recognised the implied reference to some of the basic principles of Magic he had been reading in Regardie's[152] book that morning, "In accordance with the will."

Regio gave a sarcastic slow clap,

"Very good, Father, you have clearly been learning something from those old books of Venchenco's that you stole. Shame it is too late to help you."

Regio smiled as two grey-robed male attendants arrived on either side of O'Neill. Suddenly all pretence of pleasantness was gone from Regio.

"Now, Father O'Neill, if you will be seated."

O'Neill felt needle-like sharp points pushing into his body. Looking down and to his side, he saw that each of the two attendants held long steel daggers aligned at his spine and heart. They efficiently frisked O'Neill, taking his iPhone and beloved MX10 watch, stamping violently on both items, smashing them on the flagstone floor. The two men dismissed the broken bread stick and a small half-empty bottle of wine, casting them to the floor. They then forced O'Neill into a single, oversized wooden chair that looked and felt like it dated from when this area must have been part of the dungeon for the Frangipani's castle.

O'Neill's arms, legs and neck were firmly tied down with leather straps attached to the chair arms and chair back. Before his neck was made immobile, O'Neill saw that the ancient chair had been riveted into the stone floor and

---

[152] Francis Israel Regardie was an English occultist and ceremonial magician who brought the Golden Dawn Magical system to greater public awareness.

aligned to the goat-headed statue in the midline of the massive, smoke-filled hall.

Once O'Neill was immobile, Regio snapped his fingers, and someone or something approached from behind where the Priest was seated. O'Neill could not see who it was, but its approach sounded like a horse's hooves on a cobbled street. The approaching figure cast an unnaturally long shadow over the floor in front of O'Neill - the flickering lights from the flaming torches making the shape appear grotesquely malformed.

The scale of the shadow, when compared with those of the two men standing on either side of O'Neill, made this figure appear unbelievably tall. The chair's back and sides were too high to permit O'Neill to see anything behind him, but the shadow showed that this incredibly tall figure was carrying something - something that was thrown harshly to the flagstone floor in front of where O'Neill was seated.

It took a moment for O'Neill to realise that the thing that had been thrown was a human being. Whoever it was, they were covered in blood. Their face was black and blue, like a swollen football. The poor soul thought O'Neill. They looked to be dead or very close to death. With a start, O'Neill recognised the blood-soaked, brown leather jacket and jeans as belonging to Conrad De Ven.

Seeing the startled recognition on O'Neill's face, Regio gestured to the bloody body on the floor,

"Last night, you both expressed a desire to see what we do, so I extended my invitation to Mr De Ven. We collected him shortly after I left you this morning, and we had a delightful time with him. Extraordinarily brave, he never broke down once, regardless of what was done to him. I admire that in a person. So rare these days."

Regio spoke like he was discussing a passing event, not a brutal murder.

"What have you done to him?" demanded O'Neill.

Regio feigned interest in De Ven's prone body.

"I fear that some of our members sometimes get carried away with their devotion to the order."

9 THE FALL

"Some men fall from grace. Some are pushed." - Jim Butcher

Stewart's Antiquarians,
18a, New Bond St, Mayfair,
London W1S 2RB

08:00HRS (GMT+1), 9th Sept, Present day.

The sound of the pealing church bells from the morning service at St George's[153] found both Sinclair and Stewart awake, fully dressed and standing in front of the showroom's long wooden serving counter, near the front shop entrance, looking out over New Bond Street. The shop was filled with the delightful smell of freshly brewed coffee as the pair enjoyed a light, cooked breakfast from 45 Jermyn Street[154] that Sinclair had ordered while Stewart was shaving in the upstairs bathroom. Sinclair took the initiative since the showroom's upstairs kitchen had been completely wrecked after the previous night's astral attack.

After finishing their early morning phone conversation with the French Magician, they plugged in Stewart's old Nokia to recharge and made an effort to clear up the office and kitchen area mess. Almost everything in the space had been destroyed - computers, tables, chairs, and kitchen utensils and equipment. Sinclair could see Stewart's mind assessing the cost of the damage. She knew that, due to the

---

[153] An eighteenth-century Anglican church located in Hanover Square, within a hundred yards of Stewart's showroom in New Bond Street.

[154] One of Mayfair's finest restaurants, known to serve one of London's best breakfasts, including a home delivery service that is especially useful for those occasions when you have been up all night combatting the forces of evil. Trust me, I know.

Government's refusal to return his seized assets and the loss of his showrooms in Rome and Istanbul, the Scotsman was struggling financially, especially as he was continuing to provide financial support to Sek's family in Istanbul[155]. That evening's destruction of the office equipment and digital records was an additional loss he did not need. Even though she was aching severely from the physical injuries she sustained during the previous day, she helped sweep the floors. Stewart carried the heavy broken furniture down to the street and placed them in the rear of the City of Westminster garbage collection van left parked opposite the showroom by Cortez's accomplices last evening.

By the time they had restored some order to the office and kitchen, it was nearly seven o'clock, so they took turns using the small bathroom to wash and prepare for the coming day. Sinclair had the few clothes she had grabbed when leaving her apartment, so she wore a plain, white linen Stewart's Antiquarian's T-Shirt, worn over a pair of faded, blue Levi 501 jeans and a pair of blue Crocs flat shoes. Stewart's financial situation meant he was also very limited in wardrobe choices. He opted to wear a blue, short-sleeved, Charles Tyrwhitt, sea cotton shirt over a pair of Incotex, light khaki chinos, and worn, tan leather, Chatham, deck shoes with crepe soles.

While Stewart shaved and washed, Sinclair had used the showroom phone to place a food order using her NCB[156] card[157]. The food was delivered to the showroom just as

---

[155] Mohammed Sek was still recovering from injuries sustained from his escape from the depths of the ocean as Ad-Dajjal's ship, the Tiamat, sank.

[156] National Commercial Bank Jamaica

[157] Sinclair's private bank account (not her government issued card).

Stewart completed brewing two large mugs[158] of Jamaica Blue Mountain[159] in the showroom's Braun coffee maker[160]. Stewart unpacked two meals from their insulated wrapping as Sinclair enjoyed the rich jasmine and peach flavours that always reminded her so vividly of her tropical home. Sinclair's breakfast started with fresh fruit, Dorset yoghurt and charcuterie[161], followed by Buckwheat Pancakes, Seasonal Berries and Coconut Yoghurt. While in contrast, Stewart had Scotch porridge with honey followed by scrambled eggs with smoked, wild salmon.

Their enjoyment of these fortifying meals was short-lived, as Stewart's consumption of the succulent, pink, perfectly cooked salmon was interrupted by the distinctive ring tone of his old Nokia. The gruff cockney accent on the other end of the line was Jacob, one of the senior servitors at Helen Curren's apartment building, announcing that there had been, as he put it, "an incident". Stewart put the battered phone into speaker mode and placed it on the wooden counter between himself and Sinclair, asking,

"What kind of an incident, Jacob?"

Although Jacob was a tough character, who ran an amateur boxing club in Hackney that Stewart often frequented for exercise when he was in town, he was deeply shocked by whatever had occurred as it took him a moment to gather his thoughts.

---

[158] Mugs with the distinctive Bridge of Souls logo, of course.

[159] Specifically ordered by Stewart from Whittard of Chelsea to remind Sinclair of her home. The stock was kept in the shop safe for special occasions.

[160] A Braun BrewSense Drip – purchased in the golden days when Stewart was more financially secure.

[161] Cold meats.

"Tavish, some bastards have taken Ms Curren!"

Stewart tried to understand,

"When and how, Jacob? Your building is as secure as Fort Knox!"

Jacob began to calm down and explained,

"Ok, where to begin? At first light this morning, a white Ford transit pulled into Cadogan[162] and parked outside our entrance. Alan, who was the night doorman, assumed it was an early delivery for one of the residents, so he opened the doors, only to have six, heavily armed men dressed in black military fatigues burst from the rear of the van into the entrance of the building. They bundled Alan to the floor and, while they held him down, stuck a wad of wet material in his face that must have been soaked in chloroform or something as Alan was away with the fairies[163] when I arrived just before six. Having checked the CCTV, I can see these bastards left with Ms Curren just ten minutes before I arrived."

Sinclair interjected, "Chloroform has fallen from use, more likely to be Halothane. It sounds like these people were pros who knew the staff schedules and timed this with precision."

"Cortez!" Snarled Stewart as Jacob continued,

"On finding Alan unconscious in the hallway, I called an ambulance, and it was then I heard Mr Sonnet shouting from somewhere upstairs. So, I went up the steps, as the old service lift is always broken, and I found Mr Sonnet sitting, slumped in the doorway to Ms Curren's flat, a blood-soaked pistol in his right hand. His bare chest was

---

[162] Cadogan Square, in the heart of Knightsbridge.

[163] Unconscious

peppered in red gouges that were seeping blood over the floor. I have seen some bad cuts in the ring, Tavish, but nothing like these wounds."

"The bastards shot him to take Helen?" exclaimed an incredulous Stewart.

Sinclair reached over and squeezed the Scotsman's shoulder while asking into the mobile, "Is Jeff ok?"

Jacob was as annoyed as Stewart. You could hear the anger in his thick cockney accent.

"They shot him five or more times, Miss, but he took two of the fuckers down. Their bodies were lying in the flat hallway where there had been a gunfight."

Stewart growled, "Jeff is good, but six against one in an unexpected early morning attack will never be a fair fight. You said you had called an ambulance?"

Jacob confirmed he had, "The ambulance arrived within ten minutes. They were very good. They put Mr Sonnet on an oxygen mask and a drip. Took him away to the Royal London Hospital."

"The Major Trauma Centre. The best place in the UK for treating gunshots." Stated Sinclair.

"Where he is currently undergoing surgery." Confirmed Jacob.

"Did Jeff, sorry, Mr Sonnet say anything about these attackers?"

"Oh yes, in fact, he insisted that I call you and tell you," There was a pause and the sound of papers being consulted where Jacob had taken down some notes before the cockney voice continued,

"Before he was taken away, Mr Sonnet told me that six men had kicked down the wooden front door to Ms Curren's flat at around five-forty AM, waking both Ms Curren and Mr Sonnet. Mr Sonnet said he had told Ms Curren to lie in the steel bathtub while he attempted to hold the attackers off from the bedroom with his gun[164]. After emptying all eight rounds, he took down two of them, but the remaining men overwhelmed him. They shot him while he was pinned to the floor and left him for dead, while they took the unconscious Ms Curren away with them."

"Cold-hearted bastards," snarled the Scotsman. "Is there anything else, Jacob? Anything at all that might help me find who did this and get Helen back?"

There was the sound of more papers being consulted, and then,

"Yes, here we are. Mr Sonnet said the attackers had Glocks if that means anything to you?"

"Probably 17s, same as the ones used by the Fourth Republic thugs yesterday." Commented Sinclair quietly so as not to interrupt.

"Did Sonnet get any idea where they were taking her?" Asked Stewart.

"Umm. Yes, hang on, it's here somewhere." there were the sounds of more papers being consulted. "Mr Sonnet said the men were talking in German and were under some kind of deadline to get Ms Curren to some rendezvous in Rome at 15HRS."

---

[164] Sonnet's service pistol from his time working with the British Secret Intelligence Service. In a private joke to himself Sonnet opted to carry a Walther PKK (Polizeipistole Kriminal). A stainless-steel pistol with an eight-round magazine chambered for the .32 ACP round.

"Italy? What the fuck could be in Italy?" commented Sinclair to Stewart, who shrugged. But clearly, Jacob thought Sinclair was addressing him as he replied.

"I have no idea, Miss. But it was definitely Rome."

"Thanks, Jacob. If anyone needs us, we are heading to the Royal London Hospital." Concluded Stewart before hanging up and immediately dialling for a taxi[165].

Exiting the showroom, Stewart and Sinclair were surprised to find New Bond Street filled with young people, some standing and vaping, others riding e-scooters up and down, while still more posed for selfies with Stewart's showroom as their backdrop. All these young people were transfixed, watching something on their costly smartphones. These crowds were so intense that the black TX4 hackney carriage had to use its horn to get through them. Inside the cab, Stewart and Sinclair were so preoccupied with what had happened to Curren and the shooting of Sonnet that they did not remark on the crowds. Both knew that there had been some interest from the major Hollywood Studios in making a movie based on O'Neill's book and assumed that things had progressed to the point that the London showroom had become a tourist landmark.

Thirty minutes later, after heading along the A11, they arrived at Whitechapel Road and disembarked at the red-fronted, two-storey main entrance of the hospital. After walking into the door to the accident and emergency (A&E) unit, they followed the signage to the Major Trauma Centre (MTC). As is often the case in British hospitals, the A&E unit was chaotic, filled with sad and desperate people. The overworked medical staff struggled to cope with the sheer number of people needing help, with everything from a cut

---

[165] The London Cab Company is on Stewart's mobile directory, speed dial.

finger to gang-related stabbings and, as had happened to their friend, multiple gunshot wounds (GSW).

The air was full of a mixture of distinct odours, predominantly disinfectant, but as they walked through the space, numerous other smells accompanied them - everything from powerful cologne worn by one of the male nurses to the less pleasant scent of dirt and sweat. The sounds that filled the air were as varied as the scents, everything from quiet talking and babies' cries to the screams and shouts of the patients suffering some agonising pain.

Sinclair and Stewart queued for an hour to talk with the receptionist, where they asked to speak to one of the doctors treating Mr Jeffery Sonnet, who had been brought in with GSW. The receptionist typed their details into a dirty-looking Dell computer screen before asking them to sit and wait in one of the rows of red, plastic benches set out in a long, narrow passageway that connected the A&E unit with the rest of the main hospital. To provide some distraction for the numerous people sitting in this area, the hospital administrators had positioned a series of cheap, low-resolution monitors on the wall pillars along the length of the corridor. The morning news summary began as Sinclair and Stewart sat on a bench next to a small, skeletally thin young man with thick greasy hair and numerous needle tract marks on his arms.

The lead story was the resignation of Prime Minister Susan Merriweather, who had, apparently, suddenly decided to retire from public life to spend more time with her family.

"Did not see that coming", commented the grubby man next to them.

"Neither did she," said Sinclair, remembering Merriweather's startled face as she lay dead on the plastic sheeting in the Wigmore Hall courtyard.

The stranger looked towards Sinclair and Stewart, noticing the bruising and cuts on their faces; he remarked, "What the fuck happened to you?"

Stewart leant over and said conspiratorially to the stranger, "The sad truth is we got roughed up by some nasty men."

"You and your missus should learn a Kung Fu or something, innit?" Exclaimed their tiny companion authoritatively.

The ring tone on Stewart's Nokia sounded at that moment, and the Scotsman pulled out the old battered phone and got up and walked outside to converse with whoever had called. The nosey bystander pulled a face that showed his utter disgust for anyone who would own such an old phone and turned back to the TV, where the news reader's coverage continued.

"After the declaration by Downing Street of Merriweather's resignation early this morning, Sir Reginald Twiffers and opposition leader Sir Johnathan Premble announced that they had formed a national unity coalition. Twiffers will serve as Prime Minister, and the former opposition leader, Premble, has assumed the role of Foreign Secretary. Lord Jeremy Kenner, formerly Defence Secretary, has become the Home Secretary in this new style of unified government. A complete unknown, a Mr Cortez, has been made the Chairman of the new merged national unity party in a surprise move. Mr Cortez is a relative newcomer to UK politics. He was involved in leading a highly successful breakaway independence movement in his home country of Argentina. When reporters asked about the new party's focus, Mr Cortez said it would be the first of what he hoped would be a European-wide political movement based on the principles of a Socialist Workers Party."

Sinclair was absorbing this news when Stewart returned, looking like some piece of a puzzle had fitted into place. He sat beside Sinclair, who prompted him with,

"And?"

"That was Conrad De Ven."

"From the Vatican in Rome? That's too much of a coincidence." Stated Sinclair.

The nosey man sitting near them on the bench sighed loudly as if they were disturbing some vital work as he watched adverts for soap powder that had interrupted the news coverage.

"Yes, especially when he told me that he and Thomas had discovered that there will be some big, black magic ceremony taking place this afternoon." Stewart whispered, "With bloody great demons, at least according to what O'Neill told De Ven."

"In Rome?" whispered Sinclair back.

"Yes, the Colosseum, to be precise."

"That must be where they are taking Helen." Speculated Sinclair.

"Yes, and that fits with what Mathers told us about the Meri-Isfet's plans to try and get Ad-Dajjal back. That bitch was inside Helen when she got the chop. So, my guess is that they will plan to use Helen in their damned ceremony," agreed the Scotsman.

"T, you have to go and stop them. There is nothing you can achieve by staying here, and I will do whatever I can for Jeff."

The Scotsman was just reluctantly agreeing with Sinclair when a tired-looking doctor, with black rings under his eyes from too many back-to-back twelve-hour shifts, approached them. His name badge proclaimed that this exhausted young man was Dr Adhik Kaam-Karana, the acting[166] registrar for the MTC.

"Mr and Mrs Stewart?" enquired the registrar.

Stewart and Sinclair ignored the error about their relationship status.

"Any news?" asked Stewart.

The registrar consulted some notes before answering, "Mr Sonnet was admitted to us at 06.43 with multiple gunshot wounds from what we estimate to be six, 9mm, hollow point projectiles. These caused considerable cavitation at the impact sites and significant tissue damage from the penetrating track injuries that resulted in massive blood loss. Your friend went into cardiac arrest in the ambulance before being admitted, but thankfully, the paramedics could resuscitate him."

"Will he be, ok?" demanded a grave-looking Sinclair.

The registrar looked again at his notes, "Your friend is in a critical condition and is undergoing surgery to try and stem massive internal bleeding and tissue damage. We will have a better idea of his long-term prognosis after the surgery is completed, and we can assess his progress in ICU. The next forty-eight hours will be crucial."

The doctor looked at the two of them before continuing,

"Mr Sonnet's surgery is likely to take another six to eight hours before he stabilises enough to be moved to the ICU. I would suggest you both go home. If you give the receptionist your phone number, we will call you when there

---

[166] Acting positions are an excellent way to save costs and gain control over people. People in such positions cannot disagree with their management as they will immediately lose the temporary promotion and be guaranteed never to get any further substantive promotion.

147

is any change. I am sorry that I do not have any better news at the moment."

10 OLD FRIENDS

"When you meet with your old friends, you recollect some of the finest moments of your life and find yourself in a joy that has no comparison." - Syed Badiuzzaman

The Silver[167] Club,
St James's Square,
St. James's, London SW1Y 4LE

14:57HRS (GMT+1), 9th September, Present day

In one of the rooms on the upper floors of one of London's most exclusive private members' clubs, Senor Cortez sat, enjoying his afternoon Italian blended coffee[168] from a white porcelain cup[169]. It was one of those little routines that he felt gave life that extra degree of meaning, along with hand-rolled Havana cigars, fine clothes and drinking vintage cognac. The air in the opulently furnished room was filled with the mix of aromas from the freshly brewed coffee and recently applied leather polish.

The mid-afternoon sun flowed through the tall sash windows of the elegant brick-built Edwardian townhouse, illuminating the finely polished wooden floors and the faded and frayed tarot[170] cards being dealt out onto a small mahogany card table, set out in front of where Cortez was sitting on his brown leather two-seater chesterfield.

---

[167] A subtle pun based on the Latin for Silver, argentum. A term the Spanish used in reference to the land we now call Argentina.

[168] Passalacqua Cremador Espresso. Famed for its rich flavour and low levels of acidity.

[169] By the classic German ceramic manufacturer Könitz Porzellan.

[170] An original set of the 1909 Rider-Waite-Smith deck.

The deck was being handled by a striking-looking woman with cascading long, blonde hair who, based on her dress and jewellery, had Viking heritage or pretended to have such a heritage. In between the sound of the rosewood mantel clock[171] chiming three and the muffled traffic sounds from the nearby St James Square, Cortez authoritatively declared,

"Begin."

The seer[172], who was one of many[173] that Cortez had acquired to provide additional acumen for his mission to reassert the Fourth Republic back into its European fatherland, nodded and dealt the first Tarot card[174], placing the King of Swords on the table.

The woman raised her eyebrows,

"The cards see a ruthless man of extraordinary martial talents."

Cortez nodded, clearly unimpressed. "We have an abundance of such men. What of him?"

The woman drew the next card, The Tower[175].

"He brings violence and change."

---

[171] Made by master German clock maker Lenzkirch, circa 1870.

[172] A person who is gifted with the ability to foresee the future, by natural talent, practice or formal training.

[173] The turnover for prognosticators is higher for those who give unfavourable readings.

[174] Since the unsatisfactory reading with the ancient blood runes, during the raid on Sinclair's apartment Cortez has clearly become open to less Nordic divination techniques.

[175] By some coincidence, The Tower seems to get drawn in many Tarot readings that are related to Sir Tavish Stewart.

Cortez took another sip of his coffee, commenting,

"Such men often do. Where will this man act first?"

The woman laid down the next card, The Hierophant.

"The cards indicate it will be near the Pope."

Cortez appeared more interested,

"Rome. Well, better he is directed there than here in London. Will his actions affect my plans?"

The answer to Cortez's question came in the form of the Nine of Swords. The woman interpreted,

"The Lord of Cruelty[176]. Yes, this man's actions will bring your cause much sorrow."

Cortez frowned, "Draw another card. What else do I need to know about this man?"

The woman drew Death. She looked at the other cards for a moment before continuing,

"The death card does not always signify death but, in this context, that is exactly what it means."

Cortez sighed, "Always Death. The question is mine or this man's?"

The seer looked at Cortez,

"Senor, this man, he brings death to everyone...."

Cortez spat out his mouthful of coffee, "Stewart!"

Nine hundred miles South East from the opulent surroundings of the Silver Club, an elegantly dressed, middle-aged man with piercing grey eyes that contrasted with his blue, sea cotton shirt stood waiting outside an

---

[176] Another name for the Nine of Swords.

anonymous-looking mirrored glass door. Located less than a mile North West of the Papal Palace in Rome, the shop entrance was on the ground floor of an imposing seven-story granite structure that was built in 1931. The only indication of the nature of the business conducted within was from a discrete trident[177] symbol that was the most recent of the logos associated with the world-famous gun-making company, Beretta, over its five-hundred-year history.

The man seeking admittance to Armeria Frinchillucci[178] stood six feet two inches tall and weighed a lean and fit two hundred pounds. The short dark hair on his head and jaw showed signs of grey, but he exuded that rare charisma of a classic man of action, who was more than capable of handling himself and others, should the need arise.

The mirrored entrance door opened, and Stewart was met by a sour-faced young man in his twenties, wearing a Juventus sweatshirt, a pair of blue[179] Prada jeans that were

---

[177] The motto associated with the Beretta trident is "Dare In Brocca" or "hit the target". The encircled arrows represent the three shots fired by a battleship as it engages with an enemy vessel. The left arrow represents the first warning shot, fired at the stern. The right most arrow represents the second warning shot, fired at the bow. The central arrow represents the final round fired, aimed at the main body of the ship.

[178] Located on Via Barberini, Armeria Frinchillucci is one of Italy's most renowned Gunsmiths, founded in 1871.

[179] Made in a "replica" sweat shop in Bangladesh.

missing their knees, white[180] Nike trainers and sporting a massive steel[181] Panerai dive watch. He demanded,

"Sì?"

Before Stewart could respond, the young man was gently pulled aside by an older man in his seventies, with short white hair, round steel glasses and wearing a set of traditional blue overalls. The older man waived the Juventus supporter away with a,

"Va bene Paul, conosco questo cliente." (That is ok Paul, I know this customer.)

Paul moved to the back of the shop and stood watching, clearly unhappy about being overruled by the older man who, it turned out, was his uncle.

The older man's face lit up seeing Stewart, and after embracing the Scotsman, he gestured for him to enter into a large room filled with guns of every description on the walls and in glass cabinets located some four feet in front of each of the locked wall racks. The air smelt of fresh oil and the other carcinogenic substances that enable gun mechanisms to function smoothly. If the older man noticed the bruises on the Scotsman's face and the dark lines under his eyes, he was too discreet to mention them.

"Sir Stewart, sempre un piacere. Che tipo di caccia fai oggi?" (Sir Stewart, always a pleasure. What kind of hunting are you doing today?)

---

[180] Made by child labour in a fake Nike production facility in Vietnam.

[181] Manufactured by one of the numerous PARNIS factories in China (homage watch makers).

The Scotsman started looking at a range of 9mm pistols from German, American, and Italian manufacturers in the glass cabinets in front of him.

"Most probably creatures weighing around eighty kilos."

The elderly gunsmith smiled and responded in English, "The kind that shoots back, I assume?"

Stewart nodded, "But they are not what I need help with, as I already have experience in how to deal with them."

The gunsmith winked at Stewart, "With some success," the old man crossed himself, "long may it continue."

"Today, I may be facing something quite different, and for that, I need your help, Giuseppe."

The elderly shopkeeper looked intrigued and led Stewart to the rear of the shop, where there were rows of high-powered shooting rifles. The gunsmith began to unlock a rifle rack containing three classic hunting weapons that Stewart recognised well[182].

"All excellent rifles, but from what I have been told of the creature I am hunting, I may need more stopping power."

The young man, who had been standing to one side, sniggered.

"Idiota, non sa niente di fucili !" (Idiot, does not know anything about rifles!) as he looked with total disdain toward Stewart and walked out to the back of the shop.

Stewart and the elderly gunsmith ignored the snide comment, both clearly having great respect for each other's respective expertise.

---

[182] The Marlin 336, Ruger Mini-14 and a Winchester Model 70, respectively.

"How big are we talking about here, Tavish?" Asked the gunsmith.

The Scotsman used his hands to vaguely define the enormous demonic entity De Ven had described as having confronted O'Neill.

"How about the Benelli M4?[183]" Offered the gunsmith,

Stewart looked sceptical, "Is there anything a bit smaller and easier to carry, with even more stopping power?"

Now the old gunsmith's eyes went wide. He thought for a moment before walking to one of the long drawers beneath the wall displays. "We may have just the thing."

Unlocking the drawer, the gunsmith pulled out a black shotgun pistol with a short, eleven-inch barrel. Announcing,

"The Fabarm Martial Pistol.[184]" as he handed the gun to Stewart, who looked over the weapon as the gunsmith described its features and the fact that this weapon had already been cleaned and checked by the elderly gunsmith himself. As the Scotsman rapidly disassembled and then reassembled the gun, the gunsmith continued,

"Cal.12 Magnum, with an excellent shot pattern at fifty yards."

Stewart looked impressed and enquired,

"Capacity?"

---

[183] The M4 is the standard issue shotgun for the US Marine Corps. This 12-gauge shotgun has an 18.5-inch barrel, a muzzle velocity of 1,340 ft/s and delivers 1,200-foot pounds of muzzle energy.

[184] The Martial Pistol was developed by Fabarm for the Swiss Government with the remit to be able to deal with heavily armed and armoured terrorists.

"Four plus one," The old man responded, "will you be needing a holster?"

Stewart nodded while still examining the short, black gun.

The gunsmith pulled out what looked like a set of dog harnesses,

"It's American[185], but a comfortable wear for a long day's hunting."

"Hopefully, not too long a day." Countered the Scotsman as he took the harness and fitted it to his waist and thigh.

"Indeed, but it is quick and easy to draw." Commented the gunsmith.

Stewart put the short shotgun pistol in the holster and tried a few draws before nodding his appreciation, asking,

"Ammunition?"

"Buckshot[186] or slug? I usually suggest buckshot, as it does have the advantage of not passing through targets and causing unintended injury." Suggested the gunsmith.

Stewart agreed with the assessment but said, "In this case, definitely slugs. I am not worried about unintended injury."

"Very well. What kind of mass does your target have?" queried the old gunsmith.

"Could be quite large," answered Stewart, as he thought of the supernatural creature that had attacked O'Neill.

"Bear?" Asked the gunsmith, reaching for some cardboard boxes containing twelve-gauge slugs.

---

[185] In the dim light of the shop, it looks like a shockwave shotgun thigh holster.

[186] Buckshot is comprised of numerous small projectiles within a single round. In contrast, a slug is a single, larger projectile.

"Larger." Answered Stewart. The gunsmith moved further along the boxes to more powerful and heavier gauged rounds.

"Elephant?" The older man asked, looking towards the Scotsman, to check he was not the victim of a practical joke.

Stewart used both hands to gesture that it was larger than an elephant.

The old gunsmith raised his eyebrows again and looked sceptically at the Scotsman before remarking,

"That's a hell of a creature you are hunting."

"Literally, a hell of a creature." Replied Stewart without a trace of humour.

The older man looked at Stewart and, seeing that he was being serious, commented,

"Maybe you need an exorcist, not a gun."

"Normally, I would agree, Giuseppe, but in this case, first I have to save the exorcist." Said the Scotsman.

The older man crossed himself before passing over a red cardboard box with a distinctive Brenneke[187] label.

"Then might I suggest these?"

Stewart looked at the box and read the label, "Magnum Crush?"

The old gunsmith nodded, "Only available in twelve-gauge, three-inch chambering. Weighs 666[188] grains and delivers nearly 4,000 foot-pounds of force. The reason for its name, Magnum Crush, is self-evident."

---

[187] Inventors of the shotgun slug in 1897.

[188] Given the satanic association with 666 this is literally, one hell of a round.

"Sounds just what I was looking for." Stated the Scotsman with deadly seriousness.

"How many boxes, Sir Stewart?" asked the gunsmith pulling out the remainder of his supply.

"Five should be enough."

The gunsmith raised his eyebrows again as he placed the five red boxes on the glass countertop.

Stewart moved the boxes into a single stack before asking,

"Is there a suitable ammunition belt?"

The gunsmith nodded, "Might I recommend the Teales[189]?" while he opened another of the wide wooden drawers beneath the wall gun racks and pulled out a long leather ammunition belt.

Stewart nodded his thanks as he began opening the ammunition boxes and loading the shotgun slugs into the rings on the long belt.

Walking towards the till, Stewart saw a full-length, white, waxed cotton trench coat and checked the price label. The old gunsmith noticed,

"Second hand... but it is a Canali[190] , and the length is perfect for discretely carrying the Fabarm."

"Just what I was thinking," agreed Stewart, picking the coat from where it was hanging before adding, "Thanks for your help, Giuseppe."

---

[189] The Teales 12 Bore Premium Leather Cartridge Belt carries 25 rounds.

[190] Made in Italy since 1934, Canali is an icon of Italian craftsmanship.

The old gunsmith nodded before ringing up the total on the till. "Shall I charge these to your usual account?"

Stewart shook his head, "No, today I will be paying with these," and counted out a series of gold sovereign coins[191].

The gunsmith smiled,

"Always a pleasure. Good hunting, Sir Stewart!"

The old man waited until the Scotsman had left, with the showroom door locking securely behind him, before walking into the back of the shop, where Paul, the young assistant, was playing the worldwide gaming sensation "Maelstrom Attack!" on his large screen Samsung smartphone. Giuseppe smiled. The young lad was very gifted at the game and had reached "the Gordon Square incident", where players tried to fight off a group of three, heavily armed special forces troops using just an antique large bore shotgun.

Standing outside the shop doorway, Stewart used his mobile to call TAXI 3811[192]. Eight minutes later, he entered a white Toyota Corolla taxi and switched a new disposable sim card[193] into his old Nokia as they drove off along Via Barberini.

Back at the subterranean temple beneath the Colosseum, the source of the incredibly tall shadow that had been cast

---

[191] Stewart is clearly raiding the last of his British forces "escape and evasion" belts. These were issued to operatives for use under extreme circumstances to "buy" their way out of trouble. The belts contained twenty solid gold sovereign coins.

[192] Stewart always preferred to use TAXI 3811 Roma Italia when in the ancient capital. They were reliable and the cabs were cleaner than some of the "dustbins" that circulated the streets.

[193] A TIM Viaggio Pass sim. Purchased at Rome airport.

on the floor passed around O'Neill's chair and came into his view. Surprisingly, it was a woman of average height, dressed in a red nun's habit with a white wimple that he recognised with cold and terrifying certainty, indicated only one thing. De Ven had been right when he said that Sister Christina had slipped away, unseen, from the exorcism scene last night. O'Neill wondered if perhaps the entire demonic transformation had been an illusion. The attractive female form in the red ecclesiastical habit waved away the two men who had been holding knives at O'Neill's vital areas with a dismissive,

"You may leave us now. I can handle the *good* Father."

Her voice retained that silky, seductive tone that had so confused O'Neill at the deliverance meeting the previous evening.

The two attendants walked forward, advancing to stand alongside a semi-circle of twenty wooden stools set up around the centre of the temple. Having reached their designated spot, the two attendants guided a long procession of black-robed participants into the twenty seats.

In addition to these twenty black-robed members, a smaller group of twelve adepts, wearing red robes, processed past to gather in a circular formation closer to the hall's centre. It was noticeable that everyone assembled was expectantly facing towards where the hideous goat-headed statue was standing.

Finally, the Ferrari driver, who was dressed in purple robes, similar to those worn by Regio, passed by and took his place, standing directly in front of the disgusting statue. Some thirty feet back from the sculpture, the chair where O'Neill was restrained was in such darkness that even the occasional backwards glance would not have revealed the restrained priest in the old wooden torture device.

Once all the members had assembled and were facing the representation of Baphomet, the figure of Sister Christina transformed from her human form and all doubts about the reality of last night's exorcism vanished from O'Neill's mind.

The terrifyingly tall figure he had confronted at the Satan's Fingers site loomed closer. O'Neill's face was subjected again to the terrible stench that he recalled only too well from last night's exorcism.

Regio chuckled, "Surely you did not think I would not *retrieve*[194] her? She is an *essential* help to me, and she was so very keen to meet you again. Weren't you, Sister?"

With its long fangs, the twisted reptilian face grinned as it brushed close to O'Neill's left cheek in a parody of affection. Then Regio gave a friendly goodbye wave as though he was leaving a lunch party,

"Now, forgive me, Father, I have a ceremony to perform, one I am sure you will find *educational*. I won't spoil the surprise, but you may be reunited with yet another old friend if we are successful. Indeed, it is only the anticipation that this person may wish to *thank you* that is keeping you alive, for now."

He laughed, "In the meantime, I will leave you in the *tender* care of Sister Christina."

He then turned to the hideous figure that was looming over the seated priest,

"Christina, after the ceremony, put both bodies in the Tiber."

Regio then strode away to join the Ferrari driver, standing beneath the bronze image of the sabbatical goat. Both senior adepts were dressed in identical purple robes,

---

[194] The purpose of the midnight gathering at Satan's Fingers.

adorned with a golden embroidered serpent's head on the centre of their backs.

Christina wheezed an acknowledgement to Regio's parting instruction and passed in front of O'Neill, where he could see that the creature was severely malformed. There were deep scars and tears in her reptilian torso, some of which went clean through her body, inflicted from the holy water O'Neill had cast over her. Clearly, Regio's resurrection ceremony could not heal everything. The leering snout pushed itself into O'Neill's face. The stench was so overpowering from the creature's maw that O'Neill wished he had some of Venchencho's Turkish Royals as he tried to imagine the pungent tobacco that had functioned so well in dispelling the odour the previous evening.

"Regio says I am not to kill you *yet*, or even to strike you, as apparently, I got carried away with your friend." The monster gestured with one of its three-clawed hands to the bloody body on the floor, "but I am to make sure you cannot try any of your silly prayers that might spoil the great work, so...."

She reached out with the other of her scaly talons, which should have been her right hand, and rubbed O'Neill's face in another parody of tenderness before pushing harshly into the sides of his mouth. There were a series of loud cracks accompanied by searing pain. O'Neill suddenly found copious amounts of blood and broken teeth fragments in his mouth, causing him to gag and forcing him to spit the bloody mess out onto the floor beside him.

Not content with these horrendous injuries, the monstrous creature placed its scimitar-like claws around O'Neill's chest and compressed his rib cage until she heard the cracking sounds of numerous fractures, which made her face break into a smile or what O'Neill summarised must pass for one.

"There, that should stop you, now be a good boy and sit back and enjoy the show."

She stood to his left side as he continued spitting blood and tooth fragments onto the stone floor; his mouth was now so misshapen with swelling and his lungs so congested with rising blood that he struggled to breathe, let alone speak. Every rasping, bubbling breath was agony. While he was gasping, he could feel three claw-like fingers wrapped around his head and throat in case he tried to make any intervention in whatever perverse ceremony was about to unfold.

11 LET THE GAMES BEGIN

"Those who are about to die, salute you." – proclamation made by gladiators in the arena.

The Colosseum
Piazza del Colosseo, 1, 00184 Roma RM,
Italy

15:25HRS (GMT+2), 9th September, present day

Outside the Northern side of the Colosseum, a white Toyota Corolla taxi edged its way through the heavily congested traffic to reach the curbside. A man dressed in a full-length, white Canali cotton trench coat exited the car. The long coat was unbuttoned, revealing a blue cotton shirt, khaki chinos and rubber-soled[195] deck shoes.

The elegantly dressed man paid the driver and quickly checked on a battered Nokia phone before walking towards the six-foot-high wire mesh fence that surrounded the cobbled parking area around the ancient amphitheatre. The coach park was filled with nearly thirty high-end limousines, their immaculate bodywork gleaming in the reflected afternoon sunshine. The afternoon air was thick with the smell of exhaust fumes, and already there was evidence of black specks of pollution laying on the bodywork of the lighter-coloured cars.

Scanning carefully to check the area was empty, Tavish Stewart completed a textbook vault that took him swiftly over the high fence and let him rapidly move across the cobbled area, over to the high circular walls of the Colosseum. He walked quickly and quietly around the

---

[195] Although Crepe is not as stylish or classic as a leather sole, for silence and grip it is unsurpassed.

structure's circumference, being surprised to find the entire front area free of people. Usually, professional chauffeurs would not leave a group of thirty expensive limousines or a classic red Ferrari unattended. Stewart began to feel that familiar sensation that he had encountered so many times before during military operations deep behind enemy lines that something was badly wrong. An ambush of some kind almost always accompanied these feelings. The Scotsman wondered if perhaps he should have brought more people to this particular party.

Approaching closer to the entrance ramp of the structure, he could see that, across the cobblestones, the two-wire entrance gates had been shut with a thick chained padlock. A single, blue Volkswagen Passat estate, with Sichern branding on the side doors and rear hatchback, was parked outside the secure gateway. The Scotsman muttered something under his breath as he noted that under the Sichern branding on the side of the blue Passat was the text "A proud member of the Wolfsangel Group."

Although the traffic noise from the Piazza del Colosseo was considerable, Stewart heard sounds like whimpering coming from inside the Colosseum complex. Making his way silently up the ramp, Stewart could see into the atrium of the ancient structure. There were covered passageways to his right and left that circled the open central area and were originally accessways for the spectators. Stewart quickly scanned these corridors and, after finding them empty, proceeded to the edge of the central area.

The iron railings, which normally keep visitors safe while viewing what was once the underground structure of the amphitheatre, had been temporarily removed, and a set of wide wooden steps had been installed down to the hypogeum[196]. Checking if he was being observed, the Scotsman silently descended the stairs and began walking towards the pitiful cries.

The main features of the structure were several large rectangular columns, around fifteen feet long and six feet wide, made out of a light-coloured limestone. The columns must, at one time, have acted as supports for a stone floor above, but that floor was long gone, and now there was just a clear blue September sky above.

Standing in and to the left of the open space between the columns was a figure who was facing away from Stewart. This man wore a black paramilitary uniform, with Sichern branding printed on the centre of his back and the lapels of his jacket. This Sichern operative was around six feet tall, in his twenties, with a blond crew cut. The sides of his face and his uniform were spattered with blood from where he was mercilessly beating an older and smaller man with an extendable steel baton around twenty-one inches long and heavily stained with blood.

The elderly victim was on his knees, whimpering like an injured animal. His face was grossly disfigured by enormous, bloody welts and his hands, arms and legs oddly displaced, where the bones had been shattered under repeated strikes from the baton.

Lying just beyond this pathetic figure were several other bodies, maybe as many as twenty in all, piled on top of one another and littering the floor. They were still and lifeless but covered in the same vicious, bloody welts; some had multiple bullet wounds in the arms and legs, showing a prolonged and sadistic death. Many of these corpses' broken, impossible postures showed the same systematic

---

[196] The hypogeum was originally a subterranean network beneath the combat arena where gladiators and animals were held.

beating inflicted on the older man. Based on the clothing of the bodies and the current victim, these people must have been the drivers and bodyguards from the numerous parked executive cars outside. Stewart had served in multiple peacekeeping operations in some of the most vicious regimes on earth but had seldom seen such an exhibition of pointless sadism.

Further back from where the beating was taking place, there were intermittent sounds of a firefight. The Scotsman recognised the exchanges as being between light submachineguns and, replying to them, small calibre hand guns, probably 9mm or smaller. Such a mismatched confrontation strongly favours the machine guns and is never a fair fight. Stewart assumed that at least some of the drivers had been armed bodyguards and were making a stand against the systematic killing being conducted here today.

When Stewart had arrived at "Leonardo da Vinci[197]" on his crowded EasyJet flight that morning, he had purchased a Lonely Planet city map of Rome. He had anticipated using it as a prop to play at being a stupid tourist, looking for directions, to gain access to the Colosseum. However, events had superseded that intended use, so instead, the Scotsman walked up to the blood-spattered, baton-wielding Sichern operative and interrupted him in mid-preparatory swing, with a cultured Scottish accent typical of Edinburgh natives.

"If you don't mind me interrupting, but your technique is all wrong."

The man turned in disbelief to see a smartly dressed middle-aged man with short-cropped dark greying hair, carrying a Lonely Planet guide in his right hand and,

---

[197] Rome–Fiumicino International Airport "Leonardo da Vinci".

incongruously for such a warm and sunny day, wearing a full-length raincoat.

Up closer, Stewart noted that, in addition to the steel baton, this operative was carrying a sub-compact pistol of German design and, standing propped against the nearby column well away from where the beatings had been taking place, a submachinegun.

Stewart pointed to the pistol, "Nice choice of sidearm. I have always admired the design of the P30SK[198]. I see you have opted for the smaller ten-round magazine."

The operative glanced down at his side while Stewart continued, pointing to the machine gun propped against the nearby column. "Say, isn't that an MP7[199]? I don't see many of those. Most organisations opt for the lighter MP5. But I think that is a short-sighted choice as the proprietary rounds have vastly superior penetration, especially against CRISAT[200]."

The guard frowned and looked at this stranger with growing disbelief. Before he could say anything, Stewart continued, "But, as I said, I just wanted to let you know that your baton technique is sloppy."

"Sloppy?! I will show you fucking sloppy. You can join these other losers." The man talked with a strong northern European accent as he gestured to the pile of corpses in front of the battered elderly driver before advancing on

---

[198] The Heckler & Koch (HK) P30SK is a sub-compact pistol chambered for 9mm with 10-round magazines.

[199] HK MP7 uses a propriety 4.6x30mm round from a 20-round magazine and can fire at 950 rounds per minute. It is the preferred weapon of many elite commando units since it can penetrate standard NATO CRISAT body armour at 200 yards.

200 Collaborative Research Into Small Arms Technology (CRISAT) define the body armour standards for NATO.

Stewart and preparing a head-height swing with the blood-soaked steel baton in his right hand.

Stewart advanced towards the blow, effortlessly catching the operative's right elbow with his left hand, effectively halting the striking motion of the baton, while simultaneously ramming the rolled-up Lonely Planet map into his attacker's face, in a spot under the nose and above the top lip.

The operative doubled up, pulling his left hand to his face as blood flowed from the man's nose. He snarled, "You cunt!"

Stewart did not wait for the next attack. Instead, he swung the rolled-up lonely planet map down and over the bridge of the man's nose, avoiding the left hand that covered the man's mouth. The man stumbled backwards, dropping his baton, placing both hands over his face and mumbling through his now blood-soaked fingers, "What the fuck?!"

Now the attacker's hands were covering his face, Stewart jabbed the rolled-up map into the man's windpipe, hard enough to bend the paper. The attacker began gasping, and Stewart stepped around the man as he straightened the rolled-up paper and struck behind the man's left knee, hard onto the rear strapping of his protective knee pads. The man fell to his knees, ineffectively gasping through a smashed trachea as blood flowed from his eyes, nose and mouth. Finally, Stewart used the rolled-up map to nudge the back of the man's neck gently, so he fell face forward onto the ground, dead.

Before discarding the now bloodied and crumpled map, Stewart glanced at the quote emblazoned on the back cover of the Lonely Planet booklet, "*your essential companion*", remarking,

"Truly invaluable."

The Scotsman quickly moved over to the older man, who had been given such a terrible beating by the Sichern operative but found no pulse. Clearly, the beating had been too much for him. The Scotsman closed the older man's frightened eyes and was just standing when a couple of rounds ricocheted from the column wall in front of him, the double report echoing all around the ancient structure.

Stewart rolled sideways and came to his feet, looking straight into the barrel of a pistol of identical design to the one he had been admiring with the baton-carrying operative. Except this one was just about to be fired, as Stewart could see the finger assuming the pressure on the trigger and the somewhat crazed manic grin that was displayed on this young man's face. Clearly, this man enjoyed murdering innocent people just as much as the baton wielder. Instinctively, Stewart moved his body right and backwards, away from the gun's intended trajectory. Simultaneously, he grasped the pistol barrel with his left hand and struck powerfully, up and forward, with his right hand, executing a classic Ju-jitsu palm heel strike to the attacker's chin. Stewart's technique was done with such force that the man would have fallen back to the floor if the Scotsman had not been holding the assailant's gun arm. Instead, the attacker's head was tilted backwards, well beyond its natural range of motion. There was a loud cracking noise from the man's neck, and his body immediately began to collapse to the floor. However, Stewart sensed movement in his peripheral vision and grabbed the attacker under the arms, supporting the body so that it remained upright, just as two more operatives appeared from around one of the columns some thirty feet ahead and raised their MP7 machine guns.

Moments later, the body in Stewart's arms began to shake violently as several high-velocity rounds slammed into the ceramic body armour plates on the back of the dead gunman. Thankfully, Stewart had not let go of the 9mm in his hand and peeked over the dead man's left shoulder; the Scotsman made two instinctive shots with his left hand from under the dead man's right arm pit. The first shot hit one of the two shooters in the centre of the forehead. The second shot was less impressive but just as deadly, hitting the femoral artery in the groin of the second shooter. The first man instantly fell dead on the floor from his head wound. The second man made two wild discharges with his MP7 before collapsing in a growing pool of his blood. Now able to take a more considered shot, Stewart's 9mm barked once more, achieving a clean head shot and ending the man's agonising death.

The sound of the running gun battle between the bodyguards and the professionally equipped killers taking place some distance ahead terminated with a blaze of semi-automatic fire - signifying the end of the brave stand by the limousine bodyguards. A strange silence descended over the ancient ruin.

Stewart was about to advance toward the source of the most recent bursts of automatic fire[201] when he was interrupted by a shadow moving on the floor in his peripheral vision. Turning towards the motion, the Scotsman seamlessly transferred the pistol to his right hand and scanned the area for threats. Unlike in the movies, Stewart did not assume the classic double-handed triangular aim. Instead, he opted for the much older and more classic pistol aim over his bent left arm[202]. By Stewart's estimation, the weight of the P30SK indicated only

---

[201] Advancing towards the sound of a gunfight is considered madness by some and standard operating procedure (SOP) by others.

[202] The bent arm aiming technique makes it much more difficult to disarm the shooter.

a single round was left in the ten-round clip. Normally, he would have removed the magazine to check, but any dead time without the ability to make an instant response would literally become dead time under the current circumstances.

Then, from behind one of the massive columns appeared a figure dressed in a grey robe, which he was in the act of removing as he emerged. Under the grey mantle, the man was wearing the same black suit as Stewart had seen on the dead drivers and bodyguards. This man was older than the others that the Scotsman had just faced, maybe in his late thirties or early forties, with a few deep scars on his face and thinning red hair that he wore long in a classic 1980s style mullet. He had been watching the various confrontations over the past few minutes as he clapped slowly while walking towards the Scotsman,

"Bravo, nice to see some fighting spirit for a change." The man spoke with a thick Australian accent.

"That's close enough." Stated Stewart coldly as the man came within twelve feet.

"Relax, *mate*, I am on your side," the ginger-haired man said reassuringly, still coming closer.

"I was with the other drivers. We were invited in for coffee by those scallywags, and then the buggers started killing everyone!"

"Why didn't they kill you?" Asked Stewart, pointing his pistol directly at the advancing man's forehead, not trusting him.

"Well, I needed a leak and went behind that pillar," The man pointed back to the pillar from where he emerged. Noticeably, Stewart's eyes never left the centre point of the man's chest, where the Scotsman's peripheral vision would instantly pick up any movement from the stranger's hands or feet.

"When the shooting started, I decided to lay low. Then I saw you, mate, and decided it was safe to come out."

"You have come close enough, *mate*," declared the Scotsman firmly. There was something just not right about this newcomer. Stewart noticed the distinctive sideways Z-shaped badge on the man's left lapel just as the Australian launched into a powerful roundhouse kick with his right leg. The Australian gleefully exclaimed, "I will enjoy fucking you up ugly, you pommie bastard[203]!"

Stewart stepped sideways, keeping the pistol he had acquired in his right hand. He gathered the incoming kicking leg with a scooping motion of his left arm, which then flowed into a circular clockwise motion that pulled the extended leg simultaneously forwards and sideways. While the Australian was wildly off balance, Stewart delivered a downwards blow with his right elbow onto the knee of the extended kicking leg, causing a sickening cracking noise as the knee joints[204] fractured. Then, the Scotsman swept the attacker to the floor, continuing the circular pulling motion. Finishing the Takenouchi-ryū[205] counter to a roundhouse kick[206], Stewart retained the ankle of the attacking leg in the grasp of his left hand and used it to guide his own thrusting kick down into the man's groin.

---

[203] Australian term for a person of British heritage. Like all insults directed against the British this is regarded as perfectly acceptable in all cultures worldwide.

[204] The patellofemoral articulation, patellar groove and two tibiofemoral articulations, respectively.

[205] Takenouchi-ryū jujitsu is one of the oldest forms of Japanese Martial Art.

[206] The round house kick is called Mawashi Geri within Japanese forms of Karate.

The man lay on the ground screaming but, to his credit or stupidity, didn't give up his aggression, pulling a modified[207] Glock 17 HK pistol from inside his jacket and drawing it on Stewart, declaring,

"Time for death, motherfucker!"

"Your choice, *mate.*"

Remarked the Scotsman coldly as he reluctantly put his last 9mm round into the head of the man with the pistol that had remained in Stewart's right hand throughout the short confrontation. The sound of the single shot seemed to echo endlessly around the tall columns.

Walking away from the Australian's body, Stewart passed by the bodies of the four dead Sichern operatives who had attacked him, only pausing to search for any remaining magazines from the dead bodies that he could use to reload his pistol. There were none. Stewart reflected grimly that these bastards had used them all, systematically wounding the drivers, before baton man had slowly beaten them to death. The Scotsman checked the MP7s and found a similar story. Unlike the movies, in real life, bullets are quickly used up, especially when using a machine gun in the semi-automatic mode during a firefight.

The Scotsman continued through the rows of wide columns, towards where he had heard the sound of the prolonged firefight, hoping he would find another handgun. In a push, he would use an MP7, but the current situation was classic close quarter combat (CQC), and in confined spaces, like these ruins, a long-barrelled carbine could be more of a liability than an asset.

---

[207] Modified with the same biometric sensors that were used in the attack on Sinclair's apartment.

Stewart encountered a tangled mass of four dead, blood-soaked bodies at the next intersection of columns, all dressed in black business suits. Clearly, these were the armed bodyguards who had put up such a brave resistance against the murderous and better-equipped Sichern operatives. The bodyguards had almost made it as far as a stairway down to a lower level, revealed by removing several large flagstones. This descending stairway was a temporary feature, as the flagstones that had been removed were propped against the edge of a large wooden stage set in front of the opening in the floor, some twenty feet ahead. Two dead, black Doberman dogs were lying beside the bodyguard's bodies, both killed by head wounds from the pistols in the dead men's hands. Deep, blood-soaked canine bite marks were in evidence on the necks and ripped trouser material of the crutch areas on two of the dead bodyguards[208].

Further away from the dead bodyguards, closer to the raised wooden stage and the exposed stairway, were two dead Sichern operatives, both with massive traumas to their heads, from what looked like 9mm pistol rounds. Based on the number of torn, bullet-sized dark tears on the two men's chests, their body armour had made their heads the only viable target.

Since he already knew that the bodyguards would have used up their ammunition, Stewart knelt and searched the two dead Sichern operatives, keeping his peripheral vision scanning around him for any movement. All the Sichern equipment was very high-end and certainly not what one would expect to be provided to security guards. Their choice of weaponry and ammunition indicated to Stewart's experienced eyes that these young men were serving

---

[208] Military canines are trained to attack the throat and groin of human prey.

175

members of an EU special forces unit, gaining "experience of the private sector[209]". After a few moments, Stewart found the only remaining viable assets, two so-called flash bangs[210], which he placed into the deep pockets of his blood-splattered Canali.

Standing up, the Scotsman noticed that to reach the stairwell, he had to pass through a historical exhibition dedicated to the activities that had taken place in the Roman arena in its heyday. The floor area had been raised by five feet and covered with a thick plywood stage. Additional plywood sections had been erected as six-foot-high walls, showing dioramas of what were thought to be typical arena scenes. Stepping up into this exhibition area, Stewart walked carefully and silently, thankful that he had worn crepe soles. There were two exhibits. One was devoted to the animals that had been forced to perform here. The other depicted the people who lived and died for the amusement of the rulers and to distract their populations.

In the animal exhibit, two propped open trap doors were constructed on the plywood floor to show how animals would have been held before being released into the arena to attack armed and unarmed human targets. A small table had been set up near one of the trap doors, and a copper bowl had been left on it, filled with a disgusting-smelling semi-yellow liquid. The bowl was labelled as "Urine: European Brown Bear". The Scotsman pulled a repulsed face

---

[209] Such "secondments" to private contractors are popular with the serving special forces operatives as typically they are very well paid and much less demanding and dangerous than their usual mission briefs.

[210] A ThyssenKrupp branded variant of the US m84 grenade that produces a blinding flash of seven megacandela and a bang greater than one hundred and seventy decibels.

from the foul odour as he read that large African predators were often reluctant to attack human beings unless they were made to smell like their natural prey.

"Cannot say it would encourage me."

Commented Stewart as he moved rapidly into the next part of the exhibition, which presented a series of life-size human figures, showing the dress and weapons of the gladiators. The Scotsman was just appraising the differences between the Retiarius, with his net[211] and trident[212] and the Secutor, with his sword[213] and dagger, when a loud growling sound came from behind him. Turning towards the noise, Stewart saw a black Doberman attack dog advancing slowly towards him. Some ten feet behind the animal stood the K9[214] handler, dressed in the usual black Sichern uniform, issuing a repeated command.

"Rykke.. rykke.." (advance, advance)

With each word, the dog took a couple of paces closer to Stewart, growling and baring its teeth. Based on the cruel grin on the handler's face, he was looking forward to issuing the final attack command and seeing the animal tear at the Scotsman's groin or neck.

Stewart reacted as the handler cried, "dræbe!" (kill), causing the dog to leap towards the Scotsman. While the Doberman was in mid-flight, Stewart grabbed the Retiarius' weighted net and cast it over the form of the flying dog. Keeping hold of the netting, he hurled the net and dog down into the nearest open trap door. Based on the sounds that then issued from beneath the raised wooden flooring,

---

[211] The Rete was a weighted net.

[212] The Fuscina was a trident.

[213] The classic Roman sword was called the Gladius.

[214] K9 = Canine or trained dog.

the Doberman had quickly escaped from the netting and was becoming increasingly agitated in the semi-darkness beneath, barking, growling and leaping at the open trap doors.

The frustration must have been contagious; as the K9 handler advanced closer to Stewart, pulling his MP7 up from where it was hanging on his chest and looking down, he selected semi-automatic firing of the weapon[215]. Stewart used the operative's momentary lack of attention to grab the bowl of bear urine from the table with his left hand, casting the contents over the K9 handler. The Sichern operative snarled and raised his MP7, intent on filling the Scotsman with high-velocity rounds at point-blank range. There is an excellent reason that all advanced weapons training advises against getting within eight feet of a trained martial artist. Stewart grasped the end of the MP7 and, before it could be fired, used it in a perfect example of a jōjutsu[216] throw, where the stick or, in this case, a gun is used to magnify the force of the throwing technique.

It has been said that striking martial artists hit their opponents with parts of their bodies, whereas the throwing martial artists hit their opponents with the planet Earth. The urine-drenched dog handler flew through the nearby open trap door and almost immediately had his motion abruptly terminated by the limestone blocks of the floor under the wooden stage[217]. The shock of the impact caused the two

---

[215] Short rapid bursts of fire, usually three rounds at a time.

[216] Jōjutsu is the art of using a short cane, either in defensive blocks, offensive strikes or as an extension of the throwing techniques.

[217] Measurements of the force generated by a fourth-degree black belt Judoka throw have been recorded at two hundred Newtons (45 pounds-force). With the increased angular momentum from the 26-inch long MP7 Stewart generated just over four hundred

trap doors to fall shut with a loud clap that reverberated throughout the ruins and cast the area under the wooden platform into darkness. In the enclosed space, the Doberman sniffed the air, recognising the pungent scent of one of its ancestral adversaries. Although the dog could not see the bear, he could hear it groaning and moving in the darkness.

Above this slowly unfolding drama, Stewart walked back to the gladiator diorama. He took the Gladius sword and its leather scabbard from the display, along with a six-inch-long dagger[218]. While he immediately placed the knife in his coat pocket, he spent more time appreciating the sword's almost perfect weight[219] and balance. After testing its razor-sharp double-edged blade[220] on some hairs on the back of his hand, he returned the Gladius to its scabbard and attached the sheath to the leather belt on his trousers. He thought to himself that at least he now had something suitable for close-quarter combat[221].

There were increasing groaning and growling noises coming from beneath the floorboards that exploded into sounds of a frantic scuffle terminated by a gurgling scream. As the

---

Newtons of force (around 90 Pounds-force). This is unlikely to be a deadly impact but would stun most individuals.

[218] This dagger was known as a Pugio and was primarily a stabbing weapon, although its balance permitted a skilled user to throw it as well.

[219] Two pounds

[220] A twenty-two-inch long and two-inch-wide blade. The sword was twenty-seven inches in total length including the leather-bound hilt.

[221] Certainly not as good as a 9mm pistol but it was constantly refined over nearly six hundred years of intensive use so, within its intended scope of use, it is as close to perfection as you can get.

Scotsman walked towards the end of the wooden exhibition area, towards the large set of descending stairs, he remarked to the growling Doberman, "Good boy."

12 PUBLIC ENEMY

"Power is not a means, it is an end. One does not establish a dictatorship in order to safeguard a revolution; one makes the revolution in order to establish the dictatorship." –
George Orwell.

Stewarts Antiquarians,
18a, New Bond St, Mayfair,
London W1S 2RB

14:23HRS (GMT+1), 9th Sept, Present day

The classic, black London hackney carriage progressed slowly through the increasingly heavy traffic that snaked along the A11 as it headed back from Whitechapel Street to New Bond Street.   Sitting on the grey vinyl-covered back seats of the TX4, Dame Cynthia Sinclair reflected on Cortez's remarkable rise to power and the resources and detailed planning work required. She had faced many deadly opponents in her long career, but she had to acknowledge that Cortez was proving to be the most dangerous. It took a lot more than just money to rapidly achieve such levels of influence, especially in the complex political landscape of the United Kingdom.

Cortez's comments on the news that morning about having ambitions for a European political movement indicated that he was working on a grander plan than just ruling the United Kingdom. Given such an ambition, Sinclair found the naming of his new political movement, the Socialist Workers Party, had a chilling resonance with the

Nationalsozialistische Deutsche Arbeiterpartei[222] of 1930s Germany.

As Sinclair had seen at his speech last evening at the Wigmore Hall, the Argentinian had a powerful, charismatic influence over his audience. The massive crowds that she had seen on the news broadcast outside Downing Street had cheered loudly when the new Prime Minister, Twiffers, had announced that Cortez had assumed the role of Chairman of the new coalition's national unity party. Such a response showed that the public had forgotten entirely that only the previous day, Cortez had orchestrated armed terrorists to try and kidnap the heir to the British throne and had successfully abducted the heirs to eight other nations. Whatever propaganda machine the Argentinian had set up was highly effective. Sinclair was reminded of one of Stalin's infamous quotes, "We don't let our people have guns. Why should we let them have ideas?"

Before leaving the Royal London, where their friend would be undergoing surgery for the rest of the day, Sinclair had purchased a cheap, blue Nokia 105 and a prepaid Tesco sim card from the hospital shop. After her work and personal mobiles had been confiscated by MI5 the previous day, she needed some way to remain in contact with Stewart and get updates from the Royal London on Sonnet's condition.

Using her NCB card and the new phone, she had purchased Stewart an EasyJet e-ticket to Rome and had drawn out three hundred pounds from a hole in the wall[223]. Funds that would cover Stewart's cab to the airport and whatever money remained could be changed into Euros at Gatwick before his flight. The leather belt that the Scotsman always

---

[222] National Socialist German Workers Party, better known as the NAZI party.

[223] ATM - Automated Teller Machine.

wore contained a supply of gold coins sown into the fabric, so she knew that in the worst case, he would be able to acquire whatever additional items he might need using his connections once in Rome. She then called two taxis, one for Stewart and the other for herself, intending to return to the New Bond Street showroom to wait for an update on Sonnet's surgery - as her apartment would remain unavailable until the investigation into yesterday's events was completed.

Once her taxi had settled into traffic, Sinclair used her new phone to check her private voice mail. Lev Bachrach, her Russian counterpart in the espionage game, had called just after midnight, saying that he had been unexpectedly recalled to Moscow to answer some questions and warning Sinclair that, in his words, "Something is rotten in the state of Denmark".

This ominous message was followed by two further voice mails; both made just after eight am. The first was from Sinclair's secretary, Julian, informing her that the investigation into the alleged wrongdoings, initiated by the Home Secretary yesterday, had resumed with added vigour since Twiffers' elevation to Prime Minister. Sinclair's suspension had been reactivated and made permanent. Further, she was required to surrender immediately at the nearest police station to be interviewed by Presumed Innocence, who was now in charge of all investigations related to the cold-blooded murder of innocent representatives of South American civil rights group "La Cuarta República".

"Fuck that!" commented Sinclair under her breath as she deleted the message and moved to the final and third voice mail. It was from her mentor in the FCO, Sir Fredrick Richards.

Richards sounded uncharacteristically upset,

891020111091288812989868888888

"Sin, my dear. Just to update you that I have been removed from my PPS role at the FCO as of immediate effect. Found out when I went into the office this morning at seven-thirty. Twiffers' braggarts had emptied my office and put my things in a cardboard box. A Lidl box at that! Bloody cheek - that is not how such things should be done after over forty years of service. But there you are, that is the modern world. Anyway, watch yourself, Sin. Twiffers is a rotter and has his sights set on you; now, he is unchallenged. I am off to Great Scotland Yard[224] for a stiffener[225] before informing the good lady[226] that she will be seeing a lot more of me."

Sinclair became lost in thought for some minutes. There was no doubt that Twiffers had an agenda against Sinclair, but the situation was made worse by the knowledge that the puppet master controlling the new government was someone like Cortez. Sinclair was not afraid of Twiffers, she had been handling prejudiced people like him since she was a teenager in Jamaica, but Cortez was a different and much more dangerous creature.

As the black hackney carriage made its way slowly back along the A11 to Stewart's showroom, Sinclair noted that, even by London standards, the roads were unusually busy. Most of the vehicles that surrounded the taxi were large coaches, but there were also minibuses, other taxis and private vehicles. The only thing that united them was that every single vehicle was packed to capacity. Likewise, the pavements were filled with people of every age and every demographic; clearly, all of them were headed in the same direction with a unified purpose.

---

[224] The address of the Civil Service Club, located between Whitehall and Northumberland Avenue.

[225] A strong drink.

[226] Slang term for Wife.

"Any idea what's going on?" Sinclair asked the cabbie.

In shock, the driver looked back at Sinclair, "You mean you don't know? Given where you asked to go, I assumed you were one of them."

"One of who?" enquired the perplexed Sinclair.

"There will be a mass rally and protest outside that address you provided." Stated the cabbie as though it was as well accepted as a national holiday.

"What, 18a New Bond St?" Sinclair was becoming concerned. The attack on Sonnet and the abduction of Curren had completely occupied her mind, so she had not been paying attention to current affairs; apart from the brief news flash about Twiffers becoming Prime Minister, everything else had felt irrelevant. Now she was wondering what she could have missed.

The cabbie quickly looked at the face of his passenger in his rear-view mirror and, after deciding that this woman was genuine in her ignorance, continued,

"18a New Bond Street? Yeah, that's the place. Some fancy toff is finally going to face the consequences of his actions. About bloody time, if you ask me. These privileged types always think they can exploit everyone else."

To avoid the worst of the congestion, the driver pulled down some side streets but everywhere was abnormally busy. Finally, they arrived at Piccadilly Circus, where the traffic had come to a complete stand still due to the sheer mass of people gathered. Over a hundred thousand people must have been crammed tightly together, marching and singing.

"This is as far as I can take you, Luv," declared the taxi driver.

Sinclair looked at the meter, which had run up over two hundred pounds due to the slow-moving traffic and was about to pay; when turning around from his driving position, the cabbie took his first good look at his passenger, asking,

"Are you going to wear that T-Shirt?"

Sinclair looked down at the loose-fitting Stewart's Antiquarians T-Shirt that she had put on the first thing that morning and had subsequently forgotten as she became so engrossed in the unfolding events.

The cabbie raised his eyebrows, "Have you not been watching the news?"

He passed Sinclair five folded morning newspapers through a gap in the Perspex screen. The coffee stains on many of the front pages indicated that the driver read them during breaks while waiting for his next fare.

The Telegraph headline asked, "Was Stewart the mastermind behind the UNITY and Maelstrom movements?" followed by an editorial titled "Evidence shows Stewart orchestrated one of the biggest conspiracies of modern history."

The Guardian led with, "Titled Scottish landowner fabricated Ad-Dajjal, Maelstrom and UNITY to extort trillions from world's population."

The Daily Mail's headlines were more pointed, "Mass Murderer living amongst us in London! Sir Tavish Stewart responsible for the death of a quarter of the world's population."

The Mirror's headline was simple, "Worse than the NAZIS!! Crimes against humanity! The death penalty is the ONLY answer to these right-wing fascists!"

In contrast, The Sun led with a picture of a scantily clad model and the headline "England striker had a six-hour orgy with Las Vegas hooker. Shock horror exclusive photos."

Most of the papers carried pictures of Stewart[227] but, more worryingly, also photos of Sinclair, Sonnet and Curren. It was alleged that the four of them had used state-of-the-art computer-generated imagery (CGI) techniques to create Ad-Dajjal and her henchman, the world's most feared international terror mastermind, Issac bin Abdul Issuin. Thankfully, the cabbie had not linked the elegant images of a Dame Cynthia Sinclair printed on the newspaper front pages with the bruised and informally dressed woman in dark sunglasses sitting in the rear of his cab.

"This is all complete bullshit!" Stated Sinclair as she carefully folded the papers to make sure the incriminating photographs were out of sight before passing the newspapers back to the driver.

"The British papers usually are," conceded the driver, "But in this case, the video evidence looks pretty conclusive."

The cabbie pointed to the massive[228], ultra-high-definition, curved screen that wrapped around the building high above them in Piccadilly Circus, which Sinclair had not even noticed due to the mass of shouting people who were swarming past the black cab.

Interspersed between advertisements for expensive blended Whiskey[229] and mass-produced perfumes with pretentious names were segments of world news. The current video stream showed the infamous scene of Dr Nissa Ad-Dajjal standing on a podium in Istanbul harbour, accepting the

---

[227] Apart from The Sun, which focused on the extensive photo shoot with the Vegas hooker and gave substantial hints about the identity of the millionaire football star.

[228] Sixty feet high by one hundred- and forty-eight-feet wide LED display.

[229] As Tavish Stewart would advise, with respect to blended Whiskey, just don't.

submission of numerous nations to her rule in exchange for the promise of a vaccine to end the red death plague. The familiar video segment had been duplicated into two simultaneous videos, side by side, one showing the scene as everyone remembered it and the second showing the same clip but supposedly without the digital editing. In this second scene, Ad-Dajjal had a different face and body. The face and body of Helen Curren!

"What the fuck?!" exclaimed Sinclair as she did a double-take. The images looked so convincing that even she would have been fooled if she did not know better.

"Told you," Smirked the cabbie, "keep watching."

The next video was an equally famous scene, supposedly taken from a CCTV security system, that showed the hawk-faced terror mastermind, Abdul Issuin, brutally executing some Turkish Police officers during a Maelstrom raid on the Turkish Prime Minister's office. In this clip, again, the screen had been split, this time clearly showing the face and body of Sir Tavish Stewart as the real identity of the terror mastermind.

Sinclair's mind reeled with the implications of what was being shown. If people genuinely believed that Stewart was behind the recent global massacre and attempt to enslave the world, no wonder there were mass protests. While Ad-Dajjal and Abdul Issuin had both been presumed dead, there was no living person to be held to account for the evil that had been done. Giving the world the identity of someone who was alive and could be brought to justice would result in the biggest witch hunt in history. Emotions would be running so high that there would be no way that Stewart would be able to expect a fair trial.

While Sinclair was considering the terrifying brilliance of this subterfuge, the giant video screen switched to the final clip. It showed the interior of a control room on the bridge of an enormous luxury yacht, The Tiamat. Ad-Dajjal and Abdul Issuin could be seen sitting beside each other, manipulating some controls on a panel to override the weapons systems on an American warship, to release dozens of armoured MQ-8 Fire Scout[230] drones that were marked with sinister biohazard symbols and the words "3B mix[231]". On the duplicated, unedited version of the playback, Curren and Stewart could be seen instead of Ad-Dajjal and Abdul Issuin and heard laughing about the trillions of dollars they would be able to extort from the world as the red death spread through the global population.

"Christ almighty." Whispered Sinclair.

"Now you can see why you should not wear that T-Shirt out there!" exclaimed the driver as he pointed towards a chanting group who had just passed by them, shouting something about burning the fascist bastards. He continued,

"Given the size of the fare," he pointed to the meter, "Take this." he passed back an old Dire Straits "Brothers in Arms" sweat shirt that had been resting on the seat beside him. It was much too large for Sinclair but served well to cover up the T-Shirt that would have caused her to be torn to pieces by the angry crowd. Sinclair gratefully accepted the sweat shirt and paid the fare. She pulled on the oversized sweat shirt and then exited the cab and looked around to get her bearings.

---

[230] Made by Northrop Grumman, the MQ-8 Fire Scout is an unmanned autonomous helicopter used for reconnaissance and the delivery of other weapons systems.

[231] An airborne bioweapon with a triple mix of genetically modified Pneumonic/Bubonic Plague, Haemorrhagic Hanta virus and Anthrax, in optimised droplet and particle dispersion formats.

As Sinclair became engulfed in the swarming crowd, back inside the cab, the driver pulled up a black Bosch, encrypted two-way radio and announced,

"Sigma drei hier. Das Ziel hat das Taxi verlassen und hat ein Sweatshirt in einer Notlage mit Ortungsgerät."

(Sigma three here. Target has left the taxi and has a Dire Straits sweatshirt with the tracking device.)

A voice replied over the radio,

"Bestätigt. Sigma drei."

(Confirmed. Sigma three.)

Originally, Sinclair had intended to go to Stewart's showroom in New Bond Street, but the release of the deep fake videos had radically transformed the situation. Previously, she had recognised that Cortez was a very dangerous opponent, but she and Stewart had vastly underestimated the man. The attack on Helen Curren and the shooting of Sonnet that had seemed so important was just a distraction. It was a distraction that allowed a social media disinformation campaign to gain so much traction that it had now taken on a life of its own and was probably unstoppable.

Sinclair also recognised that she was being manipulated and was almost certainly precisely where Cortez wanted her to be. She had to admit that, as a campaign, it was all being done extraordinarily well. Having tried and failed twice to kill them, the Argentinian had switched tactics. Clearly, the goal of the current plan was not the immediate termination of Stewart and his associates but rather the destruction of their reputations before a rabid crowd demanded their public, state-sanctioned execution because there was no doubt in Sinclair's mind that nothing but the death penalty awaited Stewart and Curren after these broadcasts.

The only positive was that she had not been personally included in the deep fake. All she faced at the moment was the prospect of an enquiry into her operating in the UK, in violation of the mandate of the secret intelligence service to only operate on foreign soil. Such a violation could lead to a termination of employment but not the death penalty.

The sheer mass of people filling Piccadilly Circus and swarming towards New Bond Street meant it was impossible to move in any other direction than towards the Antiquarian showroom. The only options available to Sinclair were to either be taken up Regents Street or along Piccadilly. She could see that in response to the angry mob, all the shop fronts in Regents Street had been boarded up, so there would be no opportunities to dive into a shop and make an escape. Sinclair quickly decided that the route along Piccadilly would take her up the entire length of New Bond Street and that there might be a designer showroom that was still open where she could take refuge or exit through the rear.

Having started to push her way into the fast-flowing river of people heading down Piccadilly, Sinclair noticed her "tails[232]" for the first time. As far as covert operatives went, they exhibited exceptional tradecraft; however, as was often the case, their shoes gave them away. No matter how good an agent's disguise or how often they change that disguise, few have the time to change their shoes, especially in the middle of a mass of fast-moving people. The male and female agents, who were currently tailing Sinclair, all had the same distinctive black leather Magnum[233] combat boots. With a flawless irregularity, they switched places. Good tradecraft always involved avoidance of any pattern of

---

[232] Tails are professional agents tasked to follow another person, usually another spy.

[233] Magnum Viper Pro 8.0

behaviour that was regular or predictable because human beings are hard-wired to notice such patterns. These Magnum wearing "tails" showed the same levels of professionalism and ability that Sinclair had noted in the Wolfsangel team who had invaded her apartment the previous day. If they were Wolfsangel, she knew they were extremely dangerous and would have already killed Sinclair if that was their intention. Since she was still alive, they clearly had another objective than her termination. She began to keep as close an eye on them as they were on her. She noted that there were six agents who, after spending a random amount of time close to Sinclair's left and right sides, would peel away and vanish into the crowd of people where they were provided with a change of coat, hat or glasses so that they could switch back into close proximity to their target. As Sinclair continued her professional assessment of her surroundings, she noticed a couple of much less competent figures who were also observing her. These two young males were overweight and dressed in ill-fitting, uncomfortable-looking, brown polyester two-piece suits that could not have stood out more clearly in the mass of casually dressed people. These two agents were loitering around the junction between Piccadilly and New Bond Street. Clearly, Five[234] had also put out some spotters for Sinclair. However, any chance of getting close to them and offering herself for arrest to escape whatever scheme Wolfsangel had planned was out of the question as the river of people flowed so quickly up New Bond Street that Sinclair was past the two MI5 agents within seconds.

Sinclair's original intention of escaping into one of the many designer boutiques that lined New Bond Street was rapidly dismissed. Every shop front had been boarded up with thick plywood, and the police had placed interlinked metal crowd control barriers along both sides of the street for the

---

[234] MI5

entire length of the road.   A series of large signs, set up at intervals along New Bond Street, indicated that the Metropolitan Police had set up a funnel so that the protesters would each get their moment to exhibit their rage in front of Stewart's showroom before passing on through a one-way system. This one-way funnelled towards a coordinated exit on Oxford Street that guided the crowd towards Marble Arch and then into Hyde Park. Several signs indicated that Chairman Cortez would address the people in Hyde Park at four pm.

As they approached closer to Stewart's showroom, there was a carnival atmosphere with music, dancing and posing for selfies. Where all the other shops had been boarded up for their protection and provided with a metal barrier, Stewart's had been left unprotected.

Fragments of the armoured glass from the showroom's window glittered like diamonds over the pavement. Looters had covered the street with smaller items from inside the shop - while larger items had been gathered into bonfires that caused plumes of smoke to rise high into the London skyline.   Groups of people sat nearby the bonfires, some drinking alcohol and others openly shooting up heroin. The few Police officers who were present were joining in the dancing and drinking, some even laughing as they borrowed cans of spray paint and joined in defacing what remained of the shopfront.

Every few minutes, one of the many TV crews would shout for "action", and the seated people would rise and shout abuse and chant at the smashed-up shop before stopping the moment the TV crew said "cut". Most people passing by the shopfront took the time to pose for a selfie before moving on towards Hyde Park, where they were promised free alcohol and a range of fast food, compliments of Chairman Cortez.   As Sinclair walked closer to the smashed-up shop front, she was glad that Stewart could not witness how his hard work had been so rapidly destroyed. Spray painted in large capital letters were a set of slogans

#CLOSESTEWART

#JUSTICEFORBILLIONS

#RETURNTHETRILLIONS

Just as Sinclair approached the showroom, a figure emerged from Stewart's showroom. The woman was the same height and build as Sinclair and wore a Dire Straits "Brothers in Arms" sweatshirt, blue Levi jeans and oversized dark sunglasses. The TV crews came forward and focused their cameras on the woman, alongside shouts of

"It's the Sinclair bitch!"

As several crowd members approached this woman, she pulled out a gun, which Sinclair recognised as her beloved Beretta Raffica pistol confiscated by MI5 yesterday. Before anyone could react, the woman opened fire on the crowd, the police and the TV crews. As bodies fell into a bloody mess, the woman turned back into the smashed shop front and disappeared. Sinclair moved to follow her, only to find herself surrounded by heavily armed police officers from the Metropolitan Police's SO15[235]

Dame Cynthia Sinclair muttered, "Well played", before raising her hands above her head as she waited to be cuffed. Her arrest was closely filmed by those TV crews who had miraculously survived the high-velocity gunfire.

---

[235] The Met's counter-terrorism unit, called Counter Terrorism Command (CTC) or SO15. The SO stands for Special Operations.

13 DAMNED IF YOU DO

"Hell is Empty
All the Devils are Here!" - William Shakespeare.

The Colosseum
Piazza del Colosseo, 1, 00184 Roma RM,
Italy

15:35 HRS (GMT+2), 9th September, present day

Meanwhile, in the underground temple beneath the Colosseum, Father Thomas O'Neill felt the rough, scaly skin and three sharp claws grasped firmly around his throat suddenly transform into the smooth and soft form of a human hand. Either Sister Christina felt that O'Neill had accepted his fate or, more likely, she was concerned if one of the black-robed acolytes, seated some twenty feet ahead, might catch an accidental sighting of her demonic form. O'Neill had not given up. He had faith that God, in His infinite wisdom, had some plan for him but hoped that plan did not involve joining his friend De Ven floating down the Tiber. Instead of dwelling on such negative thoughts, O'Neill decided to focus on looking around him. Maybe he could learn something that he could use to his advantage to stop these evil people.

The ancient stone floor in front of O'Neill was marked out with two large concentric circles made of some kind of metal cast into the stone floor. These metal circles were around thirty feet in diameter at their outer circumference. Inside the innermost circle, a large metal triangle had also been cast into the stone flooring. Such detailed work would have taken considerable time and effort, not something one would do if the venue was only intended for temporary use, realised O'Neill.

The light from the flickering torches was inconsistent, so although O'Neill could see that there were numerous words inset into both the circles and the perimeter of the triangle, it was not possible to read them. However, he could see enough to tell that the writing was in several different languages. He thought he recognised Hebrew, Assyrian cuneiform, Sanskrit and squiggles that looked similar to the symbols Venchencho's magical books had described as spirit sigils or signatures.

Curiously, numerous grooves were cut into the floor, starting where the acolytes sat and leading in a series of zig-zag lines into the two concentric circles. These grooved lines looked as if they would drain and direct a flow of fluids.

In the centre of the triangle was an oversized wooden chair with chains embedded into its frame that linked to some machinery on the high ceiling, some twenty feet above them. O'Neill surmised that these chains were used to raise and lower the chair as required. This strange seating arrangement had been placed directly in front of a large, empty circular wooden container designed to hold some form of liquid.

Looking further around the large hall, O'Neill could see that images were being projected onto the walls in the main cardinal directions, North, South, East and West. Unfortunately, O'Neill was so disorientated from his injuries that he could not tell which direction he was facing while tied to his chair. To O'Neill's right side[236], the banner had a white background overlaid by a golden cross, with a blue and red hexagram. To O'Neill's left was a projection of a

---

[236] O'Neill does not know it but he is facing North, so the banner to his right is in the East, where the sun rises.

black background with a white triangle and a red cross[237]. He could not see behind him due to the high back on his chair and his restraints. In front of him, the hideous goat statue obscured whatever banner might have been projected there.

As the exorcist grew more accustomed to the thick, choking black incense smoke that filled the air, he noticed marked differences where different types of attendees were standing or sitting. The majority were wearing black robes with the flame carrier symbol embroidered on the centre of their robe backs. A select few, around twelve in total, gathered in the centre of the circle – were wearing red robes with a silver hooded striking snake on their backs.

Separate from these two groups were two other figures, both men, one of whom was Regio, leading the ceremony. These two men stood in front of the Baphomet statue and wore finer purple robes. Finally, standing in the middle of the twelve red-robed acolytes near the wooden chair, a solitary hooded figure dressed in a white robe swayed as they stood.

At some unseen signal, everyone began to vibrate a deep resonating sound that O'Neill could not recognise as a word, but it must have been intended to raise the room's vibratory energy as the flames danced much higher on the four torches that surrounded the centre of the room. The group then began to chant, led by the Ferrari driving man standing beside Regio, in what O'Neill believed must have been some sinister variant of the Lord's Prayer. Although O'Neill could not speak, he silently prayed the more

---

[237] Golden Dawn magicians or followers of esoteric lore will recognise these as modified versions of the banners of the East and West respectively.

traditional Pater Noster while the obscene variant was loudly proclaimed around him.

"Magna Bestia" (Great beast)

"Noster Accipere Tributa" (Accept our tributes)

"Deorum De Tenebris" (Gods of darkness)

"Ligatis Pedibus Nostris" (Bind our wills)

"Ad Communem Vobis Fore" (To your desires)

At that point in the blasphemous litany, each of the twenty lesser grade members, with the flaming torch symbol on the backs of their black robes, took turns to step forward and describe some recent activity in which they had betrayed a trust, violated or harmed an animal or, in some cases, another human being. With each disgusting description, chants of delight rose up from the assembled group.

"Quoniam suavis ac tenebras !" (Exalt the darkness!)

On reflection, the confessions were relatively minor, and O'Neill decided that if these were the extent of the group's evil doings, the world was pretty safe. He had heard far worse at confession. After the entire group had made their declarations, there was a pregnant silence as a live, red rooster was brought, clucking and flapping its wings, into the circle, by one of the grey-robed attendants.

With grand ceremony, Regio cut its throat with a long-curved dagger, casting the poor animal's blood over the hooved feet of the goat-headed statue, exclaiming,

"Omnis Creatura Pati !" (Let all creatures suffer!)

At first, O'Neill thought nothing was happening, but then out of the corner of his eye, he was aware that the figure of the goat moved its hooves and then raised them above its horned head in a grand gesture, causing a massive cheer from the gathered group.

O'Neill's rational mind tried to make sense of the moving statue and was somewhat relieved when Sister Christina, still in her human form, lent forward and whispered,

"Animatronics, these simpletons like a show they can understand, something mildly shocking but nothing too upsetting for their sensitive natures. We even have vegetarians among *this* group."

Then the crowd grew silent as one of the two seniors, who arrived in the Red Ferrari, addressed the group.

"Brothers and Sisters, welcome!"

Two of the twelve adepts in the circle's centre pulled the white robe from the swaying figure standing in their midst, revealing a naked woman with collar-length brown hair, who O'Neill suddenly recognised as Helen Curren. She must have been drugged as she did not attempt to resist when she was led by two of the other red-robed adepts towards the central chair, where she allowed herself to be tied with leather straps into the wooden seat by her hands and feet. As O'Neill struggled vainly to free himself from his bonds and help Curren, Sister Christina tapped the side of his head, causing the priest to lose consciousness momentarily. When O'Neill awoke, it was to see Curren sitting motionless in the chair.

Located close in front of where she was restrained was the large empty wooden container - its sides were covered in strange symbols that O'Neill could not see clearly in the poor light.

At a prearranged signal, Sister Christina left O'Neill's side. Assuming her most attractive human female form, she looked back at O'Neill and smiled as she pulled up the robe of her habit and withdrew a long stiletto blade that momentarily glinted in the flickering torchlight and then was instantly hidden in the long sleeve of her gown.

Sister Christina walked to each of the seated, black-robed acolytes and paused with each, kneeling beside them before rising and moving to the next. She looked like she was sharing some confidence with each person. By the time she had completed the circuit around the seated members, the robed figures that she had visited earlier began collapsing to the stone floor beside their chairs.

In the flickering light from the flaming torches, O'Neill could see that the fallen figures nearest to him had a dark pool of black ink flowing from where their bodies were lying. As the seconds ticked by, it became clear to O'Neill that the black robes were becoming soaked, especially around the neck and groin. With a start, O'Neill realised that the black ink was blood, blood that was flowing into the curious groove arrangements on the floor that O'Neill had noticed earlier.

As this river of blood began to fill the numerous channels in the floor, the outer edge of the metal circle that surrounded and enclosed the centre of the hall started to edge lower via some unseen mechanism. This movement was slow at first but rapidly increased in its speed of downward movement until the metal circle, which O'Neill recognised as the classic protective Magical circle so often portrayed in the esoteric literature, ended up some six feet deeper than the surrounding floor. The increased depth caused the rivulets of blood to merge into five cascading streams that poured over the edges of the sheer drop to the lower level in their clearly designed blood grooves. As the lifeblood from the twenty victims flowed down these grooves, they formed the points of an inverted pentagram.

Simultaneously, with the descent of the whole area within the central magic circle, the hideous statue of the goat sank into the floor behind Regio and the Ferrari driving adept.

Baphomet was replaced by a large, rectangular frame, covered with a black cloth that must have been intended to be removed at some later stage of the ceremony, as no less than three spotlights highlighted the covered rectangular shape.

The projectors casting the images of inverted pentagrams on the walls were dimmed and replaced by new images of classical gods of darkness, some of which O'Neill recognised. The Egyptian god Seth was represented as a composite figure with a canine body, slanting eyes, square-tipped ears, a forked tail, and a long, curved, pointed snout. The Greek god Typhon was a monstrous serpentine giant. While Morta, the goddess of death, was represented as a skeletal female with glowing red eyes that shone from under her hooded gown, with a curved, sharp knife grasped in her bony fingers. Similarly, the lighting that had illuminated the North, South, East and West banners became replaced by a single giant golden flying serpent on the North-facing stone wall. O'Neill recognised the representation as the ancient Greek god Ἄποφις, better known as Apep, the ancient Egyptian deity who embodied chaos.

Now that the black-robed acolytes' bodies were lying prone on the floor, dying or dead, and the central section of the ceremonial space had become lower, O'Neill had an unobstructed view of poor Helen Curren. She was strapped into the iron chair in the centre of the inner evocation triangle. Curren's eyes were open, but clearly, she was unaware of her surroundings or her predicament.

O'Neill began a silent prayer in a moment of desperation, begging Christ to intercede to stop this ceremony. Whatever dark plan these people had in mind, it had already cost the lives of twenty of their followers, and O'Neill did not doubt that they intended something equally bad for Curren.

Just as O'Neill finished his heartfelt plea for divine intervention, he heard the distant sound of gunfire, causing the priest to begin to hope that some miracle was occurring. However, these hopes were dashed when Regio announced,

"No cause for alarm, Brethren. We have more than sufficient protection to prevent even a small army from interrupting our ceremony. Kenzo-San has special forces operatives providing our security tonight. We will continue!"

Some six hundred feet to the South and one storey up from where Cardinal Regio was making his placatory announcement, Sir Tavish Stewart had reached the top of the stairway leading to the lower level. On reaching this point, he had to drop to the ground. The air around him was filled with bursts of MP7 rounds, flying wildly in all directions and causing the distinctive whining-whizzing sound that was so universally disliked by all infantry soldiers.

Stewart's face grimaced as he fumbled in the pockets of his Canali and, finding what he was looking for, threw down both of his flash-bangs. The Scotsman immediately wrapped his hands around his head, covering his ears and shutting his eyes, before there was a deafening explosion and blinding flash of light. Stewart quickly rose and hurried down the steps, taking them two and three rows at a time. At the bottom, he found himself in a long dark tunnel filled with the thick acrid smoke from the grenades. The twin stun grenade blasts had extinguished whatever lights had existed in the chamber, leaving minimal visibility.

Suddenly, Stewart sensed a figure charging at him from the right, intending to drive the Scotsman's body hard into the left sidewall. Stewart avoided the charge by rolling to the left and coming to a standing position, with his back to the stone tunnel wall. Peering through the darkness, he found himself surrounded by three men who, emboldened by facing someone who looked like an unarmed opponent due to his long coat, decided they would have some sadistic fun creating a slow and painful death for the newcomer.

Standing to Stewart's left, the nearest man dashed towards him, brandishing a vicious-looking black combat knife that the Scotsman recognised as the customised variant of the Eickhorn[238] combat knife he had first seen at Sinclair's apartment the previous day.

To avoid the wide, throat-high, slashing strike, Stewart rolled forwards and sideways, returning to a standing posture, now with his back to the stairway. At first, the three attackers thought their victim intended to escape up the stairs, but then he drew a short thick bladed weapon in his right hand. Being more used to modern sabres and the classic Japanese katana, the three men assumed this was just a long knife.

The nearest of the three men snarled and launched into a lunge that would have stuck his seven-inch blade deep into Stewart's stomach. The blow would not have proved immediately fatal. Instead, it would have caused a slow, debilitating injury, weakening the victim for the other two men to add their own brutal attacks.

The Scotsman blocked this central body stab with his left hand while slicing down on the attacking arm with his Gladius. The attacker's arm severed cleanly and fell to the ground, leaving the maimed man screaming and holding on to the bloody stump.

While the badly injured man slumped to the floor sobbing, Stewart faced the second of the attackers who charged towards him, with his KM2000 held in a reverse grip and slashing the blade wildly in arcs as he advanced. Stewart switched the Gladius to his left hand, waited until the attacker's blade had completed one of its long swinging

---

[238] KM2000

arcs and moved closer to the assailant, grabbing the elbow of the attacking knife arm with his right hand, pushing it close to the attacker's body before launching his counter-attack- thrusting the ancient Gladius in a classic technique that would have been familiar to thousands of Roman legion soldiers.

The front of the attacker's uniform suddenly turned crimson, blood pouring from his mouth, as the Scotsman's blade penetrated clean through the ceramic body armour chest plate and extended some two inches out of the man's back. As the man slumped to the ground, Stewart struggled to remove his blade from the dead man's body. After seeing how the other two men had faired against the strange civilian, the third man pulled his pistol and carefully, because of the poor light, drew the weapon's simple iron sights[239] on the outline of the stranger's distinctive white raincoat.

Stewart knew, unless he could do something drastic, his life expectancy was measured in mere tenths of a second. Time seemed to slow down for the Scotsman. In desperation, he reached into his waistband and, using the force involved in dropping his body to his right knee, threw the ancient pugio dagger in a classic overhead motion completed with all his might and over thirty years of martial arts experience. Before the gunman could complete his shot, a leather-bound hilt became embedded in the middle of the bridge of the man's nose, perfectly equidistant between his eyes, at a slight downward angle. The remaining six inches of pugio blade were buried inside the shooter's skull, penetrating through the frontal cortexes, severing the corpus callosum,

---

[239] The traditional set of markers on the top of a gun barrel that, when set correctly, allow specific aiming from a calibrated weapon.

top of the brain stem and the cerebellum- killing the man instantaneously[240].

As the gunman's body fell sideways to the floor, Stewart rose from his kneeling position and walked back toward the two other bodies. The Scotsman pulled free the belt from the waist on his Canali and, kneeling beside the unconscious form of his first attacker, tied the belt tightly around the severed arm as a tourniquet. Unlike his murderous assailants, Stewart took no pleasure in killing or inflicting pain and would avoid it whenever possible, although his current situation and the levels of testosterone exhibited by these special forces men were making that option impractical.

Stewart walked back to the second attacker and, after some considerable effort, managed to pull the Gladius free from where it had become embedded in the deformed front and rear ceramic plates of the man's body armour. He went to retrieve the pugio but, seeing the fountain of blood that was pulsing from around the hilt, decided against it, declaring,

"Bloody bad business."

As he wiped the blood-soaked Gladius blade on the sleeve of his Canali, the Scotsman walked further down the wide, dark tunnel only to find himself facing a single opponent who had been watching him deal with the last three attackers. Stewart noted that gathered some ten yards behind the single figure ahead of him were a group of four Sichern operatives, armed with MP7 carbines, making sure the Scotsman had to face whatever was coming from this

---

[240] The term *killed instantaneously* is subject to considerable variation. In this specific case of stabbing through the brain, severing the top of the brain stem and destroying the hind brain, most meaningful nervous activity would be terminated.

lone figure. These four men stood beside two flaming torches set into the walls on either side of the passageway. These two lights cast an eerie flickering glow that created an ominous atmosphere that was made worse by a piercing scream from within a darkened archway some distance behind the four shooters.

The solitary figure that stood directly in the Scotsman's path nodded to Stewart and, putting his pistol on the floor, drew a long, classic Japanese Katana[241] sword, and issued a clear challenge.

"My yōtō[242] Muramasa[243] against your Gladius! To the death!"

The Scotsman was unfazed by the dark reputation of Kenzo-San's sword. He did not believe in the numerous legends associated with the yōtō. In his experience, martial skill was the primary determinator in the outcome of most conflicts. Besides, based on Stewart's recent encounters with the preternatural, people who needed to boast about supernatural powers seldom really had them.

Holding the ancient roman sword with a relaxed grip in his right hand, the Scotsman stood still, carefully watching this would-be modern samurai. The proposed match was hardly a fair one. The twenty-seven-inch blade of the Katana had a superior reach to Stewart's twenty-one-inch, classic Gladius, but forcing an unfair fight was hardly a surprise given the

---

[241] The katana, (kata=side na=edge) is the name of the larger sword carried by samurai. They also carried a smaller blade called the wakizashi.

[242] A yōtō (妖刀) is a so called "cursed katana".

[243] His family sword, the Kenzo-Muramasa was made by legendary swordsmith Sengo Muramasa (千子村正) in the early 16th century. The date engraved on the blade actually specifies the 13th day of the 10th month of Eishō 10. That is 10th November 1513.

way the Sichern operatives had behaved with the unarmed drivers and lightly armed bodyguards. Although Stewart's Gladius had two razor-sharp edges to its blade, it had been primarily designed as a stabbing weapon, thrust from behind the relative safety of a wall of shields. In contrast, although the Japanese Katana had a razor-sharp point and could be used to stab an opponent, it was primarily designed for use in a slicing cutting attack. The two weapons were, therefore, radically different in design and intended purpose. Given the significant difference in blade length, Stewart knew that if he were to stand any chance in the coming clash, he would need to ensure a single and very close contact between the two men.

For his part, Kenzo-san held his beloved family sword with both hands high and to his right side and proceeded to advance on Stewart in a series of short steps, clearly expecting the Scotsman to either run away or charge blindly at him.

The small group of men behind the sword-bearing man were clearly in awe of the advancing samurai as they began a chant that started quietly but quickly gathered in speed and volume.

"Kenzo-San!

Kenzo-San!

Kenzo-San!"

In what looked like an abnormal response to any inexperienced observer, Stewart, when faced by the advancing armed samurai, assumed a kneeling position- the classic Suwari waza[244] of ancient Takenouchi-ryū jujitsu. The Gladius blade was placed on the floor in front of his wide, kneeling position.

---

[244] An ancient samurai seated position for combat.

Kenzo-san's eyes narrowed as his opponent knelt. Either this man was very sure of himself, or he had accepted his fate. On reflection, it was undoubtedly the latter of the two alternatives. Like all modern opponents, this coward was avoiding conflict. Still, in a matter of moments, he would be adding yet another notch on his scabbard, and the day would not have been a complete waste of his time; although he had been badly disappointed with the performance of the so-called *special forces* personnel he had been assigned for today's babysitting duties.

Kenzo-San would have far preferred if this kneeling stranger had shown some courage and made a fight of it with him, but he was just another coward. The samurai advanced closer and closer. At a point, some ten feet in front of the seated Stewart, Kenzo-san screamed a Kiai[245]- as he raised his blade above his head, initiating the famed and deadly Shomen uchi vertical strike[246] that would split the seated Scotsman cleanly in two down the centre line of his body.

Just as it looked like Stewart had accepted his fate to die by the hand of the charging Kenzo-san, he launched into his counter. He rose from the kneeling position in a blindingly fast movement and picked up the Gladius. Faster than the human eye could see, both men's bodies passed each other, their clashing blades issuing a harsh metallic grating noise that caused a series of sparks to fly into the air. Both men's bodies carried on their forward motion for a couple of paces, and then, slowly, the body of Kenzo-San fell to its

---

[245] 気合 Is a shout that is intended to emphasize the force and focus behind a martial technique. Some also propose that, at advanced levels of practice, the technique can project a psychic energy against a target, allegedly capable of killing birds in trees.

[246] Although frequently shown in the movies, this move is, in reality, extremely difficult to complete correctly as the rounded shape of the top of the human skull deflects strikes.

knees and then front down to the floor, blood gushing from the top of his torso.

Some four paces away from the dead body, further down the wide corridor, Stewart's left hand held Kenzo-San's lifeless head by its chonmage[247]. The Scotsman wiped the blade of his Gladius on his already blood-soaked coat and tossed the severed head down the corridor towards the four men, who had assumed a shocked silence as they gawped at the head of their leader rolling towards them.

Two of the Sichern operatives began to fire their MP7s, but their aim was disrupted by a sudden and extremely violent earth tremor that shook the passageway and caused Kenzo-San's dismembered head to commence rolling again. Armour piercing rounds began to slam into the stairs further behind Stewart and the stone floor beside him, ricocheting wildly in the confined space, having missed the Scotsman by mere inches. Stewart rolled sideways, picked up Kenzo-san's P30SK pistol, and took refuge inside the entrance of an ancient prison cell built into the side of the passageway. Stewart discharged four rounds from around the corner of the cell wall towards the shooters as covering fire before risking putting his head around the doorway and taking proper aim. The Scotsman's P30 barked twice, and both of the men who had been firing their MP7s at Stewart fell to the ground from lethal wounds to their heads.

Having seen what this stranger could do with his bare hands, a sword and finally, a gun, the two remaining Sichern operatives did not care to remain. They both dropped their MP7s, turned and ran, leaving Stewart to emerge from the dungeon cell and advance behind them towards the large stone entrance way at the end of the long passage.

---

[247] (丁髷) is a form of Japanese traditional topknot.

14 RESURRECTION

"The texts are unanimous on one point: the dead do not like being summoned back." - Claude Lecouteux

The Colosseum
Piazza del Colosseo, 1, 00184 Roma RM,
Italy

15:45 HRS (GMT+2), 9th September, present day

While Stewart stood in the dark corridor, awaiting his tense confrontation with the modern samurai, Kenzo-San, the other senior adept standing next to Regio in his purple robe, walked down a series of steps into the sunken, blood-soaked, magick circle.

The twelve red-robed adepts who stood in a circular formation inside the recessed area waited as the blood of the twenty black-robed acolytes flowed around them in a series of shrinking concentric grooves in the floor that overflowed and soaked their bare feet. These rivulets of lifeblood headed ever closer to the circle's centre point, where the iron chair and empty wooden vat were located.

The Ferrari driving senior adept addressed the group, standing proudly beside the centre of the circle,

"Fraters and Sorors, it has been two dark phases[248] since the passing of our former high priestess! I welcome you to this ceremony to mark the second cycle of fourteen days since her passing when her spirit can be liberated from Bardo[249]

---

[248] Moon phases.

[249] An esoteric term from the "Tibetan Book of the Dead" for a limbo like state between life and death, where the immortal principle has not yet fully passed from physical incarnation.

and return to us on the terrestrial plane. With only three high members of the Meri-Isfet remaining in physical incarnation, I, Frater Amans in Virtute[250] have been nominated to lead our evocation today."

There was a nod of acknowledgement between Regio and the Ferrari driver before they began whatever was planned next. All of the adepts, including Cardinal Regio, who remained outside the sunken magical circle, turned to face North- towards the covered picture frame beside Regio.

In unison, the assembled adepts raised their arms above their heads in a diagonal direction of forty-five degrees from the horizontal. They brought their feet together, so their bodies formed an inverted triangle, denoting that matter and desire dominate the spirit.

Then they began to perform a series of movements and intonations in an entirely synchronised manner[251]. Each of the adepts took a steel dagger concealed in their robes into their right hands and bowed their heads towards the North (signifying the place that never gets the sun). They then bent over and, after dipping their hands into the blood-soaked floor, said,

"Ego sum omnium rerum quae" (I am all that matters)

They then placed their hands on their groin (staining their robes), saying,

"Sententiae meae tam multae." (my desires)

---

[250] "Lover of power". You probably have already recognised the world-famous playboy and polo player, Señor Edwardo Salvador.

[251] Although O'Neill did not recognise them, these movements and evocations form the so called, "Tri-Qliphothic Meditation" that is one of the core practices of the Meri-Isfet and is a darker alternative to the "Qabalistic Cross" seen within the outer orders of the Western Esoteric Tradition.

They then touched their stomachs (again leaving a blood stain) and said,

"Mea Gula." (my gluttony)

Next, they placed their left hands over their hearts (with minor blood staining), saying,

"Voluntatem." (my will)

Then, having completed this proclamation and celebration of self-centred gratification, they clasped their hands before their stomachs, repeating the affirmation,

"Semper." (always)

Finally, they took their daggers in both their hands and, pointing the tip towards the ground, again closed the strange performance by proclaiming,

"Sic Erunt!" (So it will be!)

After this opening ritual was completed, the red-robed adepts sheathed their blades and linked arms, forming a small human circle around the centre point of the recessed area. The purple-robed Frater Amans in Virtute began the classic and very ancient form of magickal banishing known within the Meri-Isfet as the "Ritual of the Inverted Man" or RIM.

The outer orders[252] often base their banishing rituals on the Golden Dawn's Lesser Banishing Ritual of the Pentagram[253]

---

[252] Outer orders are not privy to the history or the secrets held by the two primary hidden inner orders, the Meri-Isfet and the Meri-Maat, respectively. In almost all cases the membership of such outer orders are completely unaware of the existence of the inner orders, often regarding them as mythical "secret masters" and assigning them as living in remote mountain retreats.

[253] The components of the Qabalistic Cross were derived by Samuel Liddell MacGregor Mathers (one of the Golden Dawn founders) from the works of 19th century French occultist Eliphas

(LBRP). In contrast, the inner orders base their ritual procedures on much older sources. The RIM banishing is derived from the pre-Sumerian magickal text known as "the formulation of the inverted man[254]".

Whereas the more mainstream LBRP banishes specific astral energies from a sacred space, using an elemental association traced within an upright pentagram, the RIM ceremony dispenses with elemental energies and instead summons the primal forces of chaos to fill the sacred space. Such a magickal operation is extremely dangerous for the immortal principles of all present, but adepts of the Meri-Isfet are not concerned about such consequences, as they are already committed to maximising chaos and suffering.

As O'Neill watched, Frater Amans in Virtute took his ritual dagger in his right hand and drew an upside-down human figure[255] in front of him in each cardinal direction, starting from the North and proceeding anti-clockwise around the sunken blood-soaked circle until he faced North once again. At each stop in this procession around the cardinal

---

Levi. While the language of the LBRP text originated as a traditional Jewish children's bedtime prayer.

[254] Mention of the RIM ritual can be found in an Akkadian text describing the performance of, what was even then regarded as an ancient, kišpū, ritual. Purported to have been recorded by the Sumerian magician, Maabû-Māddiin-šunni, it is described in the 3000-year-old British Museum, cuneiform tablet 4 23R.

[255] Within the Magical lore, a five-pointed star is used as a representation of the human form. When a human being stands with their arms straight out horizontally with their legs spread wide, they resemble a pentagram. In the upright position, such a five-pointed star (or human) is the symbol of the spirit or intellect governing matter (order, creation). When the star is depicted in its inverted form it represents matter or the senses dominating spirit (disorder, chaos), the basis of the so called, LHP.

directions, the purple-robed senior adept loudly vibrated one of four names[256], making O'Neill's blood run cold.

"SATN!

"LUCFR!"

"BLEZB!"

"Al-SHTN!"

Whereas the traditional, outer order ritual methods banish all evil and unwelcome spirits, this RIM ceremony has the opposite effect. Instead of making a clean sacred space into which other forces can be invited, this ceremony banishes all positive energies from the area. It replaces them with energies devoted only to the darkest desolation, suffering and destruction.

Sitting some feet away from the unfolding ceremony, O'Neill felt sudden deep despair fill his entire being with utter hopelessness. This emotion was accompanied by a stench that eclipsed even the odour he had experienced from Sister Christina.

While O'Neill found himself uncontrollably sobbing from the dark emotions that filled his mind, Frater Amans in Virtute began to repeat his anti-clockwise perambulations, but this time he evoked the dark guardian entities[257] to protect the

---

[256] These vowel filled evocations are for Satan, Lucifer, Beelzebub, and Al-Shaytan, respectively. This is in contrast to the usual rituals used in the outer orders, even ones who believe they are performing LHP magick which use upright pentagram shapes and the more traditional Golden Dawn names of God, (YHVH, ADNI, AHIH and AGLA). Obviously, when a LHP magician uses Christian god names and upright pentagram traces it is illogical.

[257] In contrast to the outer orders (even LHP) who use the traditional archangel names from the Golden Dawn: Raphael, Gabriel, Michael and Uriel.

area from any good or beneficial energies that might be directed to try and intervene.

"Stat ante me, Angele magne Nigrum." (Before me stands, Samael the Black. The Accuser)

"Stat post me, Belphegor." (Behind me stands, Belphegor. Lord of the Dead)

"In dextra manu mea stat: Astharoth." (At my right-hand stands, Astaroth. From the Flood)

"Sinistram manum, stat apud me Lamia." (At my left-hand stands, Lilith, Night Spectre)

"Versa est mihi incendit!" (Before me burns the inverted man!)

"Nigra retro obscurato sole!" (Behind me is obscured by the black sun!)

As these evocations ended, Sister Christina emitted a series of cries that sounded to O'Neill like ecstasy, as sets of dark shadows began flitting in and out of existence, dancing around the inner edges of the sunken magickal circle. O'Neill wondered if these images could be video projections, as he already knew this group were not beyond light and sound tricks, but as the flitting shades coalesced into more physical forms, the shadows manifested what looked like long flowing arms that shook the torch stands around the edge of the ritual space, as they reached out from within the containing circle.

The stench that had started to fill the air intensified into that sickly, gagging aroma, a noxious mixture of decay and excrement, so familiar to anyone who has been forced to come into contact with a body that has been allowed to decay for several months within a confined area.

O'Neill continued to feel emotions of overwhelming despair as an icy cold breeze began to flow through the whole hall. The intensity of the air movement increased, guttering several of the flaming torches, knocking over some of the stools and, finally, blowing off the fabric cover from the large rectangular picture frame standing above the pit, revealing an extraordinarily detailed painting. The picture was of a raven-haired beauty dressed in purple Meri-Isfet Magus robes with a golden flying serpent symbol on the right front side of her regalia. The image, once unveiled, dominated the space inside the large temple. O'Neill coughed violently, bringing up copious amounts of his blood. He made an involuntary painful deep inhalation when he recognised the picture as none other than the infamous Dr Nissa Ad-Dajjal. Finally, O'Neill understood the intent of this diabolical ceremony, these fiends intended to resurrect Ad-Dajjal from her eternal prison!

Frater Amans in Virtute raised his arms above his head and shouted since the atmosphere inside the hall was gusting strongly like a gale-force wind at sea.

"Etiam tenebrarum dominis exaudi me!" (Lords of Darkness, hear me!)

(There was another violent gust of wind)

"Soror Lupus et Exitium transierunt gradus et dignitatis, quae intelliguntur qui ab illa, non tenuit normalis fines provocat." (Sister Lupus et Exitium passed to levels of advancement that mean that she is not held by normal bounds of mortality.)

After a short pause, he continued,

"Inventi sumus convenienti" (We have found a suitable vessel.)

At that moment, the purple-robed adept bowed towards Curren, who was immobile, still strapped to her chair and by some prearranged signal, the chains attached to the chair began to raise the seat into the air.   The red-robed adepts in the recessed circle started to chant as Curren was raised five feet into the air above the wooden vat.

"Accipere nostra commutatione." (Accept our exchange)

"Animam pro anima viginti unius animae." (a soul for a soul, twenty souls for one)

"Accipere nostra commutatione." (Accept our exchange)

Frater Amans in Virtute continued his proclamation,

"Unde habemus aquam Soror Lupus et Exitium requiescit in patenti prensus Aegaeo." (We have water from where our Sister rests in the Aegean sea!)

From where he was seated, above the sunken pit, O'Neill could see that water had begun to flow into the wooden vat beneath where Curren was suspended.

The purpled robed, Frater Amans in Virtute, continued,

"Spiritus aquae vocavi te." (Spirits of this water, I summon you)

O'Neill could see the water within the wooden container bubble, rapidly becoming like a boiling cauldron. The light from the remaining four torches dimmed further and cast weird shadows that danced anti-clockwise around the large hall.

The Ferrari driving senior adept then continued what was some form of resurrection litany,

"Objectum e qu dilecto nostro navem, in Tiamat" (Items from our beloved's ship, the Tiamat.)

One of the red-robed adepts placed an orange flotation device[258] into the bubbling waters inside the wooden vat. The purple-robed adept continued,

"Dilectis nostris items portavit." (Items our beloved has worn.)

Another red-robed follower placed a stained and dirty white Chanel jacket into the waters.

At this moment, O'Neill could feel the atmosphere in the hall become even colder, his breath forming steam with each sob from the overwhelming despair that seemed to fill every aspect of his being. Through his tears, the Exorcist could see Curren becoming more agitated, visibly shivering, either with pain or cold; it was not clear which. Copious amounts of steam began to rise from the churning waters in the wooden vat beneath her, making it increasingly difficult for O'Neill to see what was happening.

What O'Neill could see was that the purple-robed adept had advanced towards Curren and, with his dagger, cut deeply into her lower left calf, causing blood to drip into the bubbling vat of Aegean Sea water below her.

Frater Amans in Virtute then lifted a golden chalice above his head, declaring,

"Soror Lupus et Exitium transfer calicem istum vermiculum mortuos visibiliter apparendo Istanbul advocavit. Similiter noster accipere commutationem!"

(Our Sister filled this crimson cup and summoned the dead to visible appearance in Istanbul. In a similar fashion, accept our exchange!)

---

[258] Yes, well remembered, it *is* the same floatation device purchased from Stewart's London store.

The purple-robed senior adept then placed the chalice under Curren's bleeding leg and began to fill the cup that he then poured into the bubbling waters within the wooden vat, instantly turning the liquid into a deep penetrating black.

He then took a step back, and all the gathered adepts knelt as strange shapes began to emerge from the churning waters. Through the gathering steam that rose from the wooden vat, it looked to O'Neill like spectral skeletal fingers had risen from the black liquid and were grasping something that slowly emerged from the waters. The circling winds bellowed through the sunken magick circle, temporarily clearing the mist and revealing the semi-transparent image of a wooden table emerging from the waters. This spectral table was covered in strange Sanskrit characters and, strapped to the centre of the table, was the outline of a female form, dressed in the remains of a tight-fitting red suit.

Curren rose higher in her chair, clearly defying gravity so much that she would have risen higher had she not been so firmly strapped down. Then she began to scream, generating a noise that transcended any sound that O'Neill had ever heard. The kneeling adepts, including Frater Amans in Virtute and Regio, who was outside the circle, covered their ears and fell to the floor. Suddenly, there was a violent earth tremor that shook the entire structure of the Colosseum. O'Neill's chair shuddered, and two of the four tall, flaming torches that had illuminated the hall's centre fell over, extinguishing their flames.

As the tremor subsided, the wooden table, with its attached female figure that had emerged from the bubbling vat, slowly descended into the dark waters. Curren's terrifying scream ended, and the violent wind circling inside the hall ceased. The hideous odour that had nearly suffocated the Catholic Priest subsided, and the temperature slowly returned to normal, dispelling the mist gathered above the wooden vat. The waters inside the wooden container stopped churning and gradually returned to their normal colour.

Curren was unconscious, still strapped into her chair, but the shock of the earth tremor had released the chains that suspended it in the air and dropped the seat down into the wooden vat of water. The purple robes of Frater Amans in Virtute remained standing beside the wooden container, where he had been leading the ceremony, but his body had been transformed. The dashing good looks of the six-foot-tall, Ferrari driving, international playboy had been replaced by a four-foot-tall mound of a brown semi-liquid substance[259] that sparkled slightly in the flickering torch light. Regio, who was wiping dried blood from the corners of his eyes, snapped his fingers and Sister Christina, still in her female human form, bounded over from where she had been standing beside O'Neill and leapt down into the sunken pit, in a feat of acrobatic skills that would once have astounded the Catholic Priest before his exorcism experience but was now predictable.

While Regio and Christina were focused on the fate of Frater Amans in Virtute, the red-robed adepts were getting up from the floor inside the sunken magick circle, where they had been thrown during the seismic event. Ignoring the caked blood on their faces and the fate of the purple-robed adept who had been leading them, they were instead all fixated on the picture of Ad-Dajjal. The portrait had been transformed from a portrayal of the infamous raven-haired beauty to a broken skeleton, surrounded by darkness with a vast, six-winged figure visible behind her, holding a flaming sword emblazed with Enochian symbols. Ironically, the

---

[259] "But his wife looked back from behind him, and she became a pillar of salt." Genesis 19:26

symbolic transformation of the picture made more sense to Father Thomas O'Neill than it did to any of the adepts who had performed this diabolical ceremony, as he alone had first-hand experience of exactly what had happened to Dr Nissa Ad-Dajjal at the infamous Citadel of the Djinn.

Regio either had not noticed the picture or had anticipated such a result, as he was only interested in what had happened to his fellow senior adept. Looking down expectantly at Sister Christina, who was examining the rapidly dissolving figure, he demanded,

"Well? What has befallen our beloved Frater?"

Before Christina could respond, the silence inside the ritual hall was shattered by the sound of nearby gunfire, followed by two of the Sichern security operatives coming through the main entrance, and running at full speed. They ran along the entire length of the ritual hall towards an exit that must have been concealed somewhere at the Northern, furthest end.

Regio snarled at them, "What is the meaning of this dereliction of duty?"

None of the men responded. They were terrified of something following them because they focused only on running at full speed and getting away as quickly as possible.

The shadow of a lone figure was then cast onto the floor from the entrance as someone strode slowly and confidently into the temple through the entrance archway. O'Neill's restraints made it difficult to turn and see who had entered, so he had instead to rely on how the others reacted.

Regio looked towards the newcomer and then expectantly behind him, demanding,

"Where is Kenzo-San?"

A cultured Scottish accent replied,

"Lost his head, back there" Stewart nodded behind him, towards the temple entrance that led to the long corridor he had just left.

"You must be the meddling Scotsman. I was warned you would try and intervene," sneered Regio.

"Warned by your boss Cortez?" Countered Stewart. The Scotsman was playing for time as his eyes adjusted to the smoke-filled gloom inside the long hall. Noticing O'Neill in his chair, he approached the restrained priest with Kenzo-San's pistol in his right hand, covering the group of Meri-Isfet devotees.

Regio laughed, "My dear Stewart, you have it all reversed. Cortez serves us. He is merely a distraction to keep idiots like you in the outside world occupied while we can conduct our business."

Stewart knelt beside the body of De Ven and, while still covering the group with the gun, used his left hand to check for a pulse on the neck of the former head of Vatican Security. The Scotsman then stood and again, using just his left hand, while his right hand directed the 9mm, untied the restraints on O'Neill. He then responded,

"You mean business, like abducting women from their beds, strapping priests to chairs and torturing an unarmed man to death?" Stewart gestured towards De Ven's dead body, "Hardly the pinnacle of the dark arts, is it?"

Regio's face twitched in anger, "What would an antique dealer know about the dark arts?"

Stewart decided to continue pressing this man, as his ego was his weakness.

"Enough to deal with Ad-Dajjal."

The Scotsman nodded towards the broken skeleton portrayed in the picture that was illuminated beside the purple-robed Regio.

"And, more than you do, judging by the outcome of your efforts here today,"

Stewart looked pointedly at the twenty corpses scattered around him and the bloody faces on all the red-robed adepts standing in the recessed circle,

"You are all as incompetent and bat shit crazy as Ad-Dajjal."

Regio's face almost became the same colour as his robes as he snarled,

"Christina, deal with this insolent swine! We are all Meri-Isfet here, so show your true nature."

The nun, who had been standing next to the dissolving remains of Frater Amans in Virtute, suddenly began to transform, becoming the hideous monster O'Neill had encountered at his exorcism the previous evening. She leapt out of the sunken circle in a single bound, grinning with her hideous reptilian snout, and began advancing towards the Scotsman, who remarked,

"Bet you don't get many scrolls on Tinder."

O'Neill tried to warn Stewart that the pistol in his right hand would not work against this monstrosity, but his broken teeth and swollen mouth prevented coherent communication. In the end, he just grabbed the 9mm, shaking his head.

Regio laughed, "You should listen to the good Father. That peashooter will do you no good against a true infernal manifestation."

"Thankfully, I came prepared." Replied Stewart, calmly putting the pistol in his pocket as he brushed aside his Canali and drew the Fabarm. He cycled the gun's pump-action, braced himself against O'Neill's chair and aimed the shotgun from his hip.

"I am so going to enjoy..." Christina's sentence was never completed as Stewart emptied five rounds from the shotgun into the monstrosity- opening dinner plate-sized holes in the creature's body and repeatedly knocking it to the floor, but the abomination rose again and advanced each time. The deafening noise of the shotgun discharges reverberated around the enclosed space, and the air around the Scotsman became thick with gun smoke and the smell of cordite.

The sight of the demon being physically thrown backwards and disfigured unnerved Regio and the other adepts. They rapidly left the hall using the same exit that the two fleeing Sichern operatives had used. The Scotsman and Exorcist were too busy dealing with Sister Christina to pay the fleeing adepts much attention.

Within two minutes, Stewart reached the final five Magnum Crush rounds from his Teales ammunition belt. He racked his brains for some other tactic that he could try against this invulnerable adversary while O'Neill frantically scrambled around on the floor beside where he had been restrained. The Exorcist finally retrieved a small, half-empty bottle of red wine that he offered to the Scotsman. Stewart looked at the wine bottle with some disbelief before remarking,

"Thanks, Thomas, but I would prefer a single Malt."

In frustration, O'Neill grabbed the last Magnum Crush cartridge, poured the red wine's remnants over the shell casing, and then handed it back to the Scotsman. Stewart's eyes narrowed in understanding as he loaded the final round into the Fabarm.

O'Neill made the sign of the cross over the shotgun, and Stewart pulled the weapon to his shoulder and took careful aim, waiting until Christina was literally within feet of the two men. Then he pulled the trigger, aiming directly into the demon's face. The transubstantiated blood of Jesus Christ in O'Neill's sacramental wine removed the supernatural elements from the confrontation, rendering Christina into a normal, albeit enormous, reptilian creature. The 666-grain round impacted the beast's maw with four-thousand-foot pounds of force, disintegrating the head and spraying shards of reptilian flesh over most of the walls in the massive hall.

However, Stewart and O'Neill's joy was short-lived as, turning towards the sunken magick circle, they saw the entire area was empty. The Scotsman grimaced,

"Those bastards have taken Helen!"

15 LETTING OFF STEAM

"To hell with circumstances; I create opportunities." – Bruce Lee

Уулзварт hostel (Crossroads hostel),
On the great Gobi plateau,
Outer Mongolia,

00:15HRS (GMT+8), 10th Sept, Present day

The three jet black military transport helicopters flew without any onboard lighting in a close linear formation over the desolate, moonlit surface of the Gobi Desert at over two hundred knots[260]. The aircraft's sophisticated automated electronic navigation systems[261], guided by China's propriety BeiDou encrypted military satellite navigation network[262], gave these three aircraft unrivalled, millimetre-scale navigation accuracy. This technology enabled them to maintain their operational cruising speed thirty feet above the ground, automatically adjusting their height to accommodate ground-based obstacles. The two pilots in the space ship like cockpit flew with night vision systems that transformed visible and invisible light spectrums into a clear and vivid 360-degree view of the terrain. While advanced AI[263] systems automatically

---

[260] Over two hundred and thirty miles per hour.

[261] Reverse engineered from the classified DARPA next generation PAVE Precision Avionics Vectoring Equipment program.

[262] The Chinese BeiDou satellite navigation system is separate from America's GPS, Russia's GLONASS or Europe's Galileo systems.

[263] Artificial Intelligence systems reverse engineered from plans obtained from DARPA "Smart Sight Program".

identified and categorised any possible targets around them.

The Harbin Z-20 helicopter is a reverse-engineered clone of the US military's run silent, stealth Blackhawk but with a more angular tail-to-fuselage joint frame and additional blade rotors. It has a greater lift, cabin capacity, and endurance than the original Blackhawk. The aircraft's angular profile and specialised shielding make the aircraft invisible to all forms of ground and air-based radar surveillance systems. Thanks to a system of coordinated external cameras and projectors mounted around the aircraft, that beam live ground and sky images onto the helicopter's fuselage surfaces, the aircraft is also practically invisible to ground and air-based sight tracking. If these technological advantages were not enough, the additional rotor blades, powered by the Chinese-designed and manufactured WZ-10 turboshaft engine[264], enable the aircraft to hover and fly in near silence[265].

Inside each helicopter were members of the PLA 's elite counter-terrorist special forces, troops from the Chengdu Special Forces Unit, "Falcon" in Beijing. These extraordinarily fit and powerful men sat impatiently, strapped into rows of side-facing seats, their faces blackened with camouflage paint, their scalps visible through their number one crew cuts and their foreheads covered with thick, black linen, head bands adorned with the white Chinese characters,

"高山低頭，海水讓路". (The mountain bows, the ocean gives way)

---

[264] Providing over 1,600 kW (2,100 HP)

[265] Emitting less than forty decibels, the sound of a domestic cooling fan running at a slow speed.

Some of these tough men chewed gum[266] , but most chain-smoked, freely passing around cigarettes from packs with a distinctive white crane on their wrappers[267].

Sitting next to the open doors was their unit commander, Huan Su-Fin, a large and powerful man in his early forties. His short-cropped, iron-grey hair showed well-defined jaw muscles as he smoked a Cuban Montecristo No.4 cigar and pointed the helicopter's six-barrelled, belt-fed, rotary breeched Hua Qing minigun at the rapidly moving ground passing beneath the open sliding doors to the military transport helicopter.

Each Falcon operative carried highly specialised weapons. Their sidearm was the QSW-06, equipped with a twenty-round magazine containing 5.8mm armour piercing rounds. This weapon was not just designed to penetrate helmet steel but also to do so in almost complete silence, hence its name, "Wēishēng Shǒu Qiāng", literally 'Minimal noise, hand gun'. Western commandos are almost always equipped with the 9mm Heckler and Koch MP5 submachine gun. These commandos used the Chinese-designed QCW-05, which uses the same 5.8mm armour-piercing rounds as the QSW-06 pistol and, like that pistol, is designed to fire in near silence.

Some of the primary assault group who rode in the second of the three helicopters would be inserted via the hostel's rooftop. These men carried the HD66 pistol, which allows its operator to fire at targets around a corner without being exposed to the possibility of return fire. In addition to carrying this distinctive corner gun, these primary assault

---

[266] Probably Wrigley's Doublemint Chewing Gum, which is the most popular brand in China.

[267] The Baisha (白沙) brand has a white crane on the pack. It is favoured by PLA troops.

team members were distinguished from the other Falcon commandos, who all wore black face camouflage and headbands, by wearing fire retardant balaclavas and full-face gas masks to protect them from the effects of CS[268] gas and flash-bang grenades.

Each man's thoughts were directed towards their mission, to identify and neutralize what had been categorised as a clear and present danger to Chinese national security, namely, the re-emergence of the world's most feared international terror mastermind, Issac bin Abdul Issuin. Their target was believed to be responsible for releasing a biological agent that resulted in the deaths of over one billion Chinese citizens. Every man in the Falcon force knew the personal loss of family members from the actions of their target for tonight's mission. There would be no mercy shown to the individual known throughout global elite special forces as *"the most dangerous man in the world"*.

In addition to their orders to terminate this man, each member of the elite assault team secretly wanted to prove themselves against their intended target and lay claim to the global recognition associated with assuming his title. The income from product endorsements paid by combat gaming platforms and weapons groups on social media would provide an escape from the harsh and often short life of an elite combat soldier in the PLA. So, although their orders clearly stated they were to find and eliminate their target, privately, each team member craved the kill to be their personal honour and theirs alone.

---

[268] 2-chlorobenzalmalononitrile is a cyanocarbon that causes violent reactions in the airways and exposed mucus membranes, temporarily incapacitating exposed persons. The initials C and S are derived from the names of the American developers Ben Corson and Roger Stoughton.

Thirty miles away from the three helicopters that were speeding over the Gobi Desert towards the hostel, *the most dangerous man in the world* lay in a simple bunk bed. After the exertions and physical trauma of the past days, he was exhausted. Lying prone on his back, he looked to an external observer like he was resting in a deep sleep. In fact, he was in a specialised meditative state called Nidra[269]. Normally, advanced yogic practitioners train for decades to enter such an exalted state while seeking the blissful state of Samadhi[270]. However, in Adbul Issuin's case, he was using this altered state of consciousness to focus his body's resources exclusively on regenerating tissue.

Before commencing his meditation, he recalled the months of daily practice he had endured in a freezing cold tenement along Leningradsky Prospekt[271] that had perpetually smelt of cabbage soup and damp washing whenever he climbed the two hundred and forty steps up the graffiti-filled stairway to his teacher's residence. The spartan apartment at the top of the stairwell was home to a small, white-haired man in his sixties, known only as "Qui". The KGB provided this orange-robed adept of Five Rites Tibetan yoga to enable their most elite operatives to acquire selected yogic skills, giving them a significant operational advantage in the field. One of these more unusual abilities was the capacity to significantly reduce the time needed for recovery from illness and injury.

---

[269] Yoga Nidra (Sanskrit: योग निद्रा). One of the deepest forms of meditation where the practitioner retains consciousness.

[270] Samādhi (Sanskrit: समाधि). The eighth and final limb identified in the Yoga Sutras of Patanjali. A state of super consciousness, where the practitioner experiences the unity of their consciousness with the cosmic.

[271] A suburb of Moscow, reached via the Zamoskvoretskaya line of the Moscow Metro.

However, on this occasion, the hawk-faced man's deep healing meditation was abruptly interrupted by a distinctive noise that most people would never even have noticed, let alone identified - but he recognised as the suppressed rotor blades from a stealth helicopter. Silently rising, like some predatory animal, he walked silently to the right-most of the two windows in his hostel room and, keeping his body in the shadow to the right side of the window frame so that he would remain unseen, he gazed out.

The window itself was deeply inset into the exterior walls, which were over three feet thick and made of specialised thermal materials to help cope with the severe cold that was so frequent in the Mongolian wastelands. Buried deep inside the insulation was a network of titanium pipes that had super-heated water pumped through them to help the insulation resist what could be some of the coldest conditions on earth. The extraordinary cold of the Gobi had required the designers of the crossroads mining hostel to insulate the building beyond Siberian standards by including a special oil fuelled boiler system that circulated this super pressurised, hot water throughout the structure of the building. These heated pipes were hidden from view in most of the building on safety grounds. The only exceptions were in the kitchen, laundry, and communal bathing facilities. Where these pipes were exposed, numerous safety signs showed graphic warnings of the 200-degree[272] Fahrenheit heated water and the need to mix the outflow with copious amounts of cold water before use for cooking, laundry or ablutions.

The hawk-faced man's highly experienced eyes rapidly adjusted to the darkness outside his window. He saw three indistinct, shimmering shapes hovering around twenty feet

---

[272] The boiling point of water at the 5,200 feet elevation of the Crossroads hostel.

above the ground, some six hundred yards away from the Southern side of the hostel, holding in a static formation relative to each other. To most casual observers, these aircraft would have been invisible, but to a man like Abdul Issuin, they might as well have been illuminated and covered in high visibility paint. To his expert eyes, it was clear that these aircraft were utilizing some advanced form of electronic invisibility camouflage. His assessment was based on the tell tail blurring around the edges of their outlines as airborne sand particles disrupted the projected images on their fuselages.

At first, he thought the three aircraft were American Blackhawks, but he rapidly detected the additional fifth rotor blade, and he realised these stealth helicopters were of Chinese design and sure to be carrying insertion teams sent for his capture or, more probably, termination. Referring to his comprehensive knowledge of the Chinese military, he anticipated that the PLA would probably have sent members of their elite Falcon counter-terrorism special forces (SF). Clearly, whoever had initiated this operation was taking him very seriously. In the milliseconds it took him to realise that the web cam on the old computer he had used that afternoon was probably the cause of his discovery, he began to prepare his response to cope with three SF insertion teams.

As he took in the complete environment outside the hostel, aside from the three helicopters, he saw that towards the Eastern side of the building, all the other residents at the hostel had been assembled and were now gathered, two hundred yards away from the main structure. They were closely supervised by the hostel staff and around six police officers. The expert eyes of the assassin identified the latter by their very high peaked caps, so prevalent in uniforms from the former communist states. The hostel staff and the civilian police were all busy making sure that the fifty guests, who had been herded from their rooms in the middle of the night to stand in the cold darkness, remained silent and well away from the windows on the South side of the hostel where Abdul Issuin was residing. That meant the hostel would be empty, maximising the number of locations that he could hide- but this also indicated that he should anticipate what was termed in special forces jargon, "a hard entry" by the three Falcon teams when they eventually stormed the building.

Interestingly, the international assassin categorised the stealth helicopters exclusively as potential transportation methods rather than as a threat that needed elimination. Accordingly, none of the dozen possible plans being formulated in his mind included the destruction of the aircraft. Unfortunately, for the members of the Falcon SF team, that was not the case for the fifteen men who were about to launch an attack on the hostel.

Taking one final look at the preparations of the PLA commandos, he could see that one of the helicopters had separated from the other two and was heading towards the South side of the hostel, where Abdul Issuin was standing. He could make out the outlines of four men hanging from the sliding doors on either side of the aircraft in readiness for insertion onto the building's roof. The partially lit contours of these four operatives were highly distinctive to the experienced eyes of the hawk-faced man. Their bulky backpacks and sets of large cylinders attached to their arms indicated to Abdul Issuin that the initial roof top insertion would be utilising so-called 徘徊的蜜蜂 (Hovering Bee[273]) technology. This was a clandestine copy of the US Military's

---

[273] The "Hovering Bee" jet suit exceeds the 12,000-foot altitude ceiling and 800 mph speed limits of the US original. When Western corporations outsource all the key component manufacturing to China, making copies becomes child's play.

Gravity Industries' Jet Suit that had been obtained through one of the many successful "honey trap[274]" operations of the Chinese intelligence agency[275] on US soil.

Behind them, the two other aircraft had landed. One Falcon team had exited their helicopter and set up a perimeter two hundred yards away from the hostel building. In contrast, the other team advanced towards the hostel, intending to storm the entrances and ground floor windows. The hawk-faced assassin expected the combined assault to begin with flash bangs[276], immediately followed by SC-2 lachrymatory/smoke grenades, before the "hard entry" started in earnest.

But oddly, all three Falcon groups held off their imminent attack. Abdul Issuin saw that the perimeter group were setting up a large satellite dish, around thirteen feet in diameter, which they were aiming towards the hostel. The hawk-faced man reacted by rapidly pulling the thin, steel sprung mattress from his bed, wrapping it around himself and rolling under the metal frame of his cot bed. Seconds later, the air throughout the hostel became filled with a powerful electrical static charge. This electrical field caused the hairs on the hawk-faced man's body to become agitated as the classified Chinese NNEMP[277] weapon, known as Wú

---

[274] The Chinese have found Western diplomats to be extraordinarily susceptible to the attentions of an attractive Chinese suitor.

[275] The Intelligence Bureau of the Joint Staff of the Central Military Commission – what used to be called "the 2nd Bureau". The military intelligence arm of the PLA who run the majority of covert foreign operatives.

[276] A stun grenade used to temporarily disorientate an enemy.

[277] Non-nuclear electromagnetic pulse

yān long or "Smokeless Dragon[278]", was directed at the hostel. Electrical devices throughout the building abruptly failed, wall clocks stopped, cooking appliances burst into flames, rodents suffered first-degree fur burns, and the kitchen cockroaches folded into twisted shapes as their exoskeletons deformed[279].

The moment he felt the static charge end, Abdul Issuin emerged from under the wire frame bed, removed the thin mattress, which had acted as an improvised Faraday cage, from around his body and began his special preparation for his guests. He partially broke the frame on his room's only chair so its wooden struts were exposed and carefully placed what remained of the seat by the left window. Next, he cautiously broke the room's glass table and placed the table frame near the right window, so large shards of glass were exposed. His next action was to systematically pour the contents of the two "безудержный як" (Rampant Yak[280]) branded vodka bottles he had purchased at the gas station over the carpet and curtains near the windows and doors. Finally, he placed the empty glass vodka bottles and glasses on their sides near the room entrance before closing the door and walking calmly and silently down the long third-floor corridor and entering the communal washroom.

---

[278] Wú yān long - 无烟龙. An Electro Magnetic Pulse (EMP) weapon, reverse engineered from the classified DARPA electronic disruption project.

[279] Interestingly, the seventy-five-year-old Waffen-SS issued "Laco" mechanical watch on the wrist of the assassin remained completely unaffected, having been designed and specified to be immune to the effects of EMP.

[280] безудержный як or "Rampent Yak" vodka is a locally distilled 190 proof spirit, said to taste like antifreeze and drain cleaner and is probably an effective substitute for both liquids.

The hawk-faced assassin had long since completed an assessment of the entire hostel for possible escape routes and hiding places, as he did automatically in any new environment. His evaluation of the current situation indicated he stood the best chance of evading and then overcoming the fifteen men from the three Falcon SF teams by concealing himself for the time being.

The thirty-foot square communal washing facility smelt strongly of chlorine from its recent end-of-day cleansing. The floor and wall surfaces were covered in utilitarian grey ceramic tiles. The room had one sizeable multi-person bath, near the double swing entrance doors, before the row of ten toilet stalls and a bank of showers. The tiled wall at the end of the room had a row of small window bricks that provided the only dim light in the large room after the EMP had destroyed the building's electrical systems.

Within seconds of entering the washroom, the hawk-faced assassin had used the knife he had acquired during breakfast to remove the bath panel and had hidden inside the service space. He then replaced the front panel so there was no trace of his presence. In the darkness, he waited, with the long steel SS dagger, handwritten log book and the seventy-five-year-old Walther pistol he had collected from the cave.

Simultaneously with the concealment of the hawk-faced assassin, the "hovering bee" equipped assault team members who had landed on the building's roof commenced their "hard entry" into Abdul Issuin's room. The window glass exploded with a series of flash-bang grenades that immediately ignited the vapour from the 190-proof "Rampant Yak" vodka, causing the carpets and curtains to erupt into flames and produce a thick smoke which, combined with the three SC-2 smoke grenades that rapidly followed, made visibility in the room practically zero.

The first two commandos, who swung into the hostel room from ropes suspended from the roof, became immediately impaled on the chair struts and the large shards of glass that had been placed near the windows. As the third and fourth members of the roof assault team stormed through the room's door, they encountered a wall of superheated flames when their forced door entry radically increased the oxygen supply to the fire. Within moments they were engulfed in a fire storm that raged inside the confined space of the hostel room. Following standard operating procedure to extinguish flames on the body, the two operatives rolled onto the hostel room's floor only to find themselves cut to ribbons on the large shards of glass that littered the flaming carpet.

Back in the dark crawl space inside the bathtub service area, Abdul Issuin could hear the sounds of grenade detonations, along with screams of pain and calls for urgent medical assistance from a male voice, talking into a hand-held two-way radio. Then he heard the sound of the second assault team, systematically working its way through the building up from the lower floors, with a series of loud percussions from flash-bang grenades, followed by shouts in an unfamiliar language as rooms were systematically declared "Míngquè" (clear).

Minutes later, he heard a single person enter the washroom. This individual walked with a heavy gait, indicating a large and powerful man wearing specialised assault boots. The footsteps walked past the bath unit and systematically inspected the toilet stalls. Abdul Issuin waited in silence and timed his exit from the bathtub panel to coincide with when he estimated that the searching commando would have reached the final three toilet stalls.

The grey-haired Falcon unit commander, Huan Su-Fin, was experienced enough to have developed that sixth sense about threats that often saves the lives of the world's top warriors. So it was that Su-Fin turned around just as the hawk-faced assassin emerged from the bath, and the two men faced each other across the width of the room.

As the leader of the Falcon assault teams, Su-Fin had opted not to wear the tight-fitting balaclava and gas mask - instead, he had hung them on his utility belt. He had also decided not to participate in the dangerous work of systematically checking the rooms inside the hostel. Room clearance, using flashbangs left permanent hearing damage, and even the best fitting masks did not eliminate all the toxic CS gas. Su-Fin had seen enough top calibre men become old before their time from too much exposure to these SF occupational hazards. He preferred to supervise, and, as was the case here, he would often be rewarded by checking things outside of the routine.

Su-Fin grinned as he spat out the smouldering remains of his Montecristo No.4 and stubbed out the glowing Cuban cigar with his right boot. Here, in front of him, was "*the most dangerous man in the world*" but not looking as fit or capable as one would suppose from his illustrious title. Based on the discharges seeping from numerous cuts on his arms and legs, which showed as dark stains on his sleeves and trousers, time and circumstance had caught up with this man. Su-Fin also noticed a severe wound on the lower left side of his target's abdomen, which had reopened from the exertions of cramming his body into the small crawl space inside the bathtub.

Seven hundred miles to the East, the four command-and-control officers supervising the Falcon operation in the underground bunker at the Chengdu Special Forces Unit in Beijing began to confer with each other excitedly. Their evident excitement caused their grey-haired and corpulent supervisor, Jip Keing, to stop reading his newspaper[281], rise from his desk and walk over to his staff. Like most supervisors, who have risen to a managerial role within corrupt environments, Keing was a career incompetent who ruthlessly managed his team. He harshly disciplined anyone who showed ability or integrity[282] and promoted only those who, like himself, were dishonest, open to bribes and gratuitously deferential towards anyone higher in authority.

Standing behind the excited command and control operators, Keing began comparing the live broadcast picture from Su-Fin's body-cam to the grainy image they had from Abdul Issuin's use of the internet café the previous evening. It was the same man. The old-fashioned and ill-fitting European expedition clothing and the distinctive hawk-like features were identical. The supervisor ran to the red phone on his desk and immediately called his supervisor, launching a series of late-night phone calls that eventually reached Zhongnanhai[283], located in the former imperial garden in the Imperial City.

Back in the communal washing facility of the Crossroads hostel, Su-Fin regarded the hawk-faced man standing before him. Based on his injuries, Su-Fin could see that the wounded man in front of him was nowhere near as dangerous as he had been before his joss (luck) turned sour. One could almost feel sorry for him, but business was business, and he would kill this stranger, wounded or not,

---

[281] PLA Daily (Jiefangjun Bao). The official daily newspaper of the People's Liberation Army.

[282] To the incompetent person, NOTHING is more threating than a competent, hard-working person.

[283] Central headquarters for the Chinese Communist Party (CCP) and the State Council (Central government) of China, respectively.

and take the riches and fame that came with the reputation of such a kill. Assessing the capabilities of the wounded assassin Su-Fin came to a decision. Yes, shooting this man would bring some recognition, but, he speculated, there would be far greater recognition if the kill was made through hand-to-hand combat.

Meanwhile, Abdul Issuin watched and waited for his opponent to make his move, all the while imperceivably closing the distance between the two men by tiny incremental steps every time his opponent blinked. The grey-haired Falcon operative was approximately the same height as the hawk-faced assassin but with a slightly heavier build. In the milliseconds it took for the hawk-faced man to assess that he and this commando were approximately the same sizes, a plan of action was formed. It was a plan that could provide a means to escape and a return to the cave to retrieve the gold mentioned in the journal he had been reading. Abdul Issuin returned to observing his opponent, who stood some twelve feet away and held a Chinese-designed QCW-05 sub-machine gun, aimed casually towards the assassin's midsection. The QCW-05 fired over nine hundred rounds a minute with a fifty-round magazine but was calibrated for distances of between sixty and four hundred yards. At close quarters, like these, its accuracy would be erratic, especially allowing for the recoil. It looked wicked, but, in reality, it was not an ideal weapon inside a confined and fully tiled space such as this. There would be more risk of injury from the ricochets and tile fragments than from the firearm itself, provided one could quickly get inside its twenty-inch barrel length.

Just as the hawk-faced assassin was closing into an effective distance, where he could disarm his opponent, the grey-haired Falcon operative made the surprising move of turning off the body-cam attached to his chest, dropping his sub machine gun and slowly unclipping his weapon belt, kicking both weapons away from him on the tiled floor. He then removed his heavy body armour[284] before assuming a classic unarmed combat offensive posture and gesturing with his left palm for Abdul Issuin to attack him.

Back in the underground bunker at the Chengdu Special Forces Unit in Beijing, there was a mix of disbelief, frustration and blind fury that Su-Fin had not followed his standing order to terminate his target on sight. Instead, he intended to indulge himself in some testosterone-inspired death match. The control room supervisor snatched the communications device and yelled abuse into the microphone, but the only response was static. It could only be concluded that Su-Fin had removed his throat mic and earpiece simultaneously as he disconnected his body cam. The supervisor began to loosen his tie and collar, knowing he and his family would face the most terrible consequences should the Falcon mission fail to terminate *the most dangerous man in the world*.

While the corpulent control room supervisor suffered an attack of hypertension, *the most dangerous man in the world* was blessing his good fortune. He had considered if he should use his ancient Walther pistol to kill his unarmed opponent and dismissed the idea. After eighty years sitting in a damp cave, Abdul Issuin estimated a forty-six per cent chance of the bullets[285] misfiring and a twelve per cent chance of them failing to discharge at all. The other consideration was that the sound of an unsuppressed 9mm round discharging in the confined space of the tiled

---

[284] The weight of full body armour with ceramic plates makes rapid movement much harder.

[285] The Böhmische Waffenfabrik 9mm rounds were manufactured in occupied Czechoslovakia by a factory in Prague exclusively devoted to munitions for the SS.

washroom would reverberate throughout the building and bring members of the second Falcon insertion team. So, uncharacteristically he reciprocated the commando's action and placed his ancient luger pistol on the floor. The hawk-faced assassin then took a long stride back and looked carefully at the grey-haired Chinese commando. The man was either insane or had an extraordinarily high opinion of himself. The latter of the two alternatives was proven moments later when the commando loudly announced,

"White Crane"

Before commencing a series of bird-like arm and leg movements that launched the Chinese commando's body towards Abdul Issuin, who effectively blocked the pecking and sweeping movements but was forced to retreat some steps backwards as he felt his wounds complaining about every violent block. The Chinese commando smiled as he noticed his opponent was breathing more heavily before announcing,

"Tiger,"

and launched his next attack, which imitated the lightning-fast swipes and claw-like strikes of the giant feline, which lends this style its name. Again, Abdul Issuin was forced to move backwards by the power and ferocity of the attacks. For the first time in the fight, a strike connected with his already injured left side, causing Abdul Issuin to stumble momentarily before countering with a reverse punch that caught the Chinese commando fairly on the nose, making him stumble backwards and end the attack. Wiping the blood from his face, Su-Fin nodded to Abdul Issuin, to acknowledge the quality of the strike before announcing,

"Houquan," (monkey)

and launching his next attack on the assassin. This time the Chinese commando's body assumed a very low position that allowed him to sweep Abdul Issuin's legs away from him, and, for a moment, it looked like the Chinese commando would launch a killing strike on the rear of the hawk-faced assassin's neck. But, at the last moment, Su-Fin found himself impaled on a vicious Krav Maga defensive back kick that struck the Chinese commando in his solar plexus, lifting him into the air and landing him on his back near the end of the long washroom.

As both men raised themselves painfully from the tiled floor, Su-Fin decided he would end this ill-advised challenge. It was time to utilise the deadliest techniques developed from the centuries of evolution within the Chinese martial arts. He shook himself and adopted the distinctive swaying stance of the most deadly and esoteric of the traditional Chinese martial arts before announcing,

"Praying Mantis"

Tang Lang (Praying Mantis Fist), is said to have been created by the ancient sage Wang Lang (王朗), at the request of Abbot Fu Yu (福裕) of the famous Shaolin monastery in the thirteenth century, to give Shaolin monks an ultimate defence against other rival martial forms. The art's most distinctive feature is the infamous mantis hook, made from three fingers, that directs the force of blows in a whip-like manner. The "tángláng gōu" or mantis hook can also attack critical points, such as the groin, eyes or, in more advanced forms, secret acupuncture meridians- including the legendary "dim mak" (death touch[286]) pressure points that many say were responsible for the mysterious deaths of many famous martial artists, who died under enigmatic circumstances.

---

[286] Part of the Mi Shou or secret hands techniques. Although many martial artists are familiar with the legend of the "dim mak" (literally: 'press artery') few know the real nature of its techniques.

As the hawk-faced assassin watched his opponent advance slowly towards him, performing the classic movement that made the attacking hands look just like the swiping pincers of the insect from which the style took its name, he knew that a "Mi Shou" (secret hands) strike from this ancient style could be extraordinarily dangerous, making an innocuous-looking blow produce an instantly incapacitating injury, followed by slow and painful death. Given the numerous wounds that already existed on his body from the three previous exchanges with this skilled martial artist, he knew he needed to be extraordinarily careful.

Su-Fin stopped his advance and gestured with the fingers of his right hand that he wanted Abdul Issuin to attack him. In response, the hawk-faced man reached for a thick, coarse, white cotton towel from a nearby shower rail that the Chinese commando anticipated would be used as a weapon and so taunted him,

"Tell me the name of the style you will use with that towel..."

In an unexpected blur of movement, which exhibited a preternatural speed which had been noticeably absent from all of the previous techniques executed by Abdul Issuin, the hawk-faced assassin wrapped the thick towel around the superheated titanium pipe at his head height and, pulling down with his full body weight, heaved the pipe free from its fittings. The severed pipe unleashed a stream of 200-degree plus Fahrenheit heated water at the Chinese commando, who could only flail his hands helplessly in response, screaming, while the skin on his face and hands dissolved. The unexpected ferocity of the torrent of super-heated water caused the Chinese commando to retreat rapidly, ending up with his back against the grey tiled end wall of the washroom.

At the exact moment that Su-Fin's body impacted against the rear of the shower room, Abdul Issuin pulled down even harder on the pipe, while still holding it through the thick towel, breaking an eight feet long section of titanium pipe free and ramming it deep into and through the chest of the Chinese commando, leaving his opponent impaled to the broken tiled wall, like a pinned insect[287] on a butterfly collector's board. The hawk-faced man grunted in grim satisfaction at the result of his improvised technique,

"I call that scalding water, broken pipe".

---

[287] Presumably a praying mantis.

16 WHEELS WITHIN WHEELS

"The workmanship of the wheels looked like the gleam of beryl, and all had the same likeness. Their workmanship looked like a wheel within a wheel." - Ezekiel 1:16.

Godinje (Годиње) village,
Municipality of Bar,
Montenegro, near the Albanian border.

12:22HRS (GMT+2), 10th Sept, Present day

A thick, chocolate-coloured dust cloud rose into the clear blue midday sky, high above a narrow dirt road that snaked away into the distance. The roadside grasses, which had once been lush and green, now assumed a yellow hue, dried and dead, lying on their sides after what had been an exceptionally long, dry central European summer. The air was filled with that distinctive smell of dried vegetation and the faint odour of ozone from an unseen expanse of water from somewhere in the far distance.

The hours of driving along these narrow dirt tracks had accumulated thick layers of brown powder-like dust over the entire bodywork, obscuring the distinctive green paintwork on the lower sections of the old, split windscreen Volkswagen camper van. The white canvas coverall protector for the large black motorcycle, strapped on the rear-mounted carrying rack, was now a khaki colour from the covering of dried dirt disturbed from the unmade road surface by the old van's narrow, fifteen-inch diameter Michelin tyres.

Arriving at the top of a steep hill that looked down onto a small hamlet of cream-coloured houses crammed close to the rocky hillside, the minivan driver paused from her progress to take in the view that could have come from the Middle Ages. Beyond the traditional square-shaped stone farmhouses, with their terracotta roof tiles, was an area of lush, toad green vineyards that eventually led to Lake Skadar's expanse of water.

Before beginning the drive down into the tiny hamlet, the auburn-haired driver recalled her preparations in Geneva for the intense days of travel she had just completed to reach this beautiful and idyllic setting. Mathers had to remind herself that, if her briefing was correct, this was a place that hid a monstrous secret.

After the meeting at the SPLEE lodge on the eighth of September, Mathers had spent the night in an ancient apartment that adjoined the society buildings at Place du Bourg-de-Four. The French adept enjoyed a luxurious bath in a classic iron and enamel bathtub manufactured just before the second world war at the Aquas factory, just North of Lyon. She then phoned Albert, the mechanic at the Volkswagen garage in central Geneva, informing him of a change of plan. Instead of the originally scheduled return to Paris that evening, she was now going on a much longer journey down into Eastern Europe. Mathers asked that, if Albert could complete the necessary work in time, she would like to pick up her beloved VW the following morning.

Mathers spent the night serenaded by the cooing of the doves from the Lodge's traditional coop[288], located on the building's rooftop, after which she rose at 05.06, two hours before dawn[289]. After washing and dressing, Mathers had a

---

[288] Originally used for sending messages, the coops and their birds were now more of an historical artefact than a working communication system.

[289] Sunrise is at 07.09 HRS in Geneva on the 9th of September.

breakfast of freshly baked bread rolls, apricot jam, and two cups of dark French blend coffee at one of the cafes surrounding Place du Bourg-de-Four's central plaza. She then took a yellow and white[290] Coopérative de Taxi to promenade du Lac, near Lake Geneva.

The Garage VW Geneve, SA, was just opening. Albert was expecting Mathers as he put down his coffee cup and quickly updated the French Adept on the work he had completed on the van and motorcycle, so they would be ready for what Mathers had described on the phone as an intercontinental road trip. The 1600cc air-cooled engine had been fully serviced, the tyres and windscreen wipers replaced, a new cooking gas bottle had been supplied, and fresh drinking water and food supplies. It was clear from these details that Albert must have been working late into the night to be ready. He had even found a small tracking device someone had secreted onto the van's rear-mounted motorcycle. After showing it to Mathers, he winked mischievously as he placed the device on the underside of the Coopérative de Taxi parked on the garage forecourt while the cab driver enjoyed a cigarette in the morning sunshine beside the large lake.

After settling up the bill with Albert and thanking him profusely, Mathers headed out of Geneva on the A40 highway that wound its way into the Alps and would eventually take the old caravanette over the Swiss border into France. As the altitude increased, the weather deteriorated. The clouds turned into a drizzle that quickly turned into heavy rain that comprehensively tested the new windscreen wiper blades on the split windscreen. As the temperature plunged below zero, the heavy rain turned to sleet and then finally snow, which gathered on the road and caused the narrow, old-fashioned tyres to struggle to get

---

[290] Mercedes A class

any traction. The old heater inside the van could only keep the front windshield clear of condensation, and Mathers was forced to pull onto the hard shoulder to change into her motorcycle leathers with a thick winter parka over the top. After exiting the van to fit snow socks on all four tyres, she resumed a long, slow slog through the thick layers of ice and slush that had gathered on the high alpine road. In less than two hours, Mathers had crossed the French and the Italian borders on the N205 before entering the T1 Mont Blanc tunnel down from the mountains into Northern Italy, where, thankfully, the climate returned to temperatures more suited to the old camper van. Having removed the snow socks from the tyres and her extra layers of clothing, Mathers focused on covering the miles on the excellent Italian highways, passing through Turin, Milan and Bologna through to Rimini. Twenty hours of hard-driving brought the old VW to the Eastern port of Ancona, where she boarded the car ferry to Zadar on Croatia's Dalmatian coast.

The French adept managed to catch a badly needed six hours of sleep inside her VW. After a quick sink wash on the ferry, Mathers disembarked and enjoyed an early morning breakfast of fruit, natural yoghurt and fresh bread, washed down with a strong black coffee that she purchased from the few market stalls that were in the process of opening to catch the incoming ferry from Italy. The French Adept indulged in some people watching as the market slowly opened, sipping the bitter, strong coffee so popular in Eastern Europe, while she sat on a low stone wall outside the ninth-century St Donatus church. After finishing her breakfast, she drove the old VW down the E65 through Benkovac, Skradin and Split, where the E65 became the M6 that headed to Niksic. She passed without incident through the border checkpoint between Croatia and Montenegro with her French passport. The French Adept paused in Podgorica to get some local guide books and fresh supplies before heading on the P16 for the final stretch of the long journey to Godinje.

Having completed a gruelling thirty-six hours of travel, it was just after midday that Madeleine Mathers' ancient Garmin GPS finally announced that they had reached the outskirts of the tiny hamlet called Godinje (Годиње). She headed down a single-track dirt road that looked down over a slope that was covered in a mass of green vineyards leading towards a huge lake that looked like an inland sea. The narrow road was signposted as heading towards the town's centre, so she thought it was unusual that she did not encounter any people. The houses were mostly traditional, stone-built structures, with thick, red, curved ceramic tiles on their rooves. The outhouses and some other facilities showed evidence of more modern methods of construction being made out of breeze blocks and concrete with corrugated metal roofing.

Initially, Mathers assumed that the population must be occupied with work in the local industry that she knew, from her cursory reading of the local guide books, was predominately agricultural. When her VW finally arrived at the market square, she was surprised to find a group of twenty men and women. These twenty people were being directed by three men in the task of unloading a wooden crate, around forty inches square, from the back of a huge Ural-4320 military truck[291] with Russian number plates. The three young men wore matching black overalls and carried gunmetal grey PYa pistols[292] on their webbing belts. As

---

[291] A Ural-4320 is a Russian general purpose off-road 6×6 vehicle, capable of carrying 13,200 lb loads.

[292] The 9mm MP-443 Grach or PYa, for "Pistolet Yarygina" ("Yarygin Pistol") is the Russian standard military-issue side arm. It carries an 18 round magazine of semi-armour-piercing bullets with a tempered steel core.

they marched around the six-wheeled truck, supervising the crate's removal, they barked Russian commands at the assembled group that made the whole situation feel rather brutal. Maybe it was simply Mathers' unfamiliarity with the local customs- but it looked and sounded like the locals were being forced to unload the crate rather than undertaking a task they willingly accepted. As Mathers pulled up and exited her VW van, she was surprised by how the large group of able and strong-looking locals struggled to move such a small crate. Even using four powerful-looking Russian-made Kirovets tractors[293] fitted with lifting rigs, the crate was barely being moved. When it eventually got lifted from the rear of the huge truck, it caused the big diesel, YaMZ-240 B engines on the four tractors to strain and fill the air in the market square with thick, choking black smoke. As the four tractors slowly moved the crate from the truck's rear, it passed closer to Mathers. She could not help but read the Cyrillic text printed on the side of the wooden packing, "Государственный Эрмитаж", which, due to the distinctive logo embossed next to the text, the French Adept recognised as The State Hermitage Museum in Saint Petersburg, Russia. Other markings on the side of the crate indicated that the object, whatever it was, had come from the "Зимний дворец" (the Winter Palace), but, unfortunately, the French Adept's poor knowledge of Russian prohibited her from gleaning this additional information.

As the unloading proceeded, Mathers backed away into one of the shop entrances as the whole procedure looked to her to be quite unstable. Her assessment proved correct when, just as the crate was mere inches from the ground, one corner slipped free from the rig, and the item crashed onto the stone cobbles of the small square. Although the crate was only small, the impact made the ground shake quite

---

[293] The K-700 is a 13-tonne tractor manufactured by Kirovets in St Petersburg.

noticeably, and there were loud shouts from the three men supervising. As the three Russian men came round to examine the crate, their anger intensified when they saw that the wooden sides of the box had shattered under the impact, and the object inside had partially rolled out onto the ground.

Unable to resist her curiosity about the item, Mathers approached closer, risking the obvious displeasure of the three, armed men, who appeared horrified but, Mathers noted, it was not so much the damage to the crate that displeased them. Instead, it was the public exposure of what had been concealed inside the container. The object that had rolled out of the fractured wooden frame of the packing box was considerably smaller than the crate dimensions suggested. The rest of the space inside the crate had been packed with sawdust which now blew into the air. These airborne particles were not as benign as they looked because the three men supervising the unloading pulled on particle filtration masks and goggles[294].

Mathers decided she would take one quick look at the item before retreating to the relative safety inside her VW van. The revealed object had a dark green semi-metallic colour and was comprised of a pair of cylinder-shaped objects, inset inside one another. It was around ten inches long and five inches in diameter. There were fittings on the top and bottom of the object where it could be suspended and, one presumed, rotated. Although, given the extraordinary weight of the object, the fittings to hold it would have to be unusually rigid and strong. The sides of the dark green cylinders were deeply engraved with a script that looked like Sanskrit but was much, much older than any Vedic

---

[294] The three Russians are clearly assuming that the deadly reputation associated with the device is due to the emission of radiation. This assumption is incorrect.

literature. Additional writing had been added over the curved surfaces in Cyrillic and German using what looked like white chalk. With a horrified shock, the French Adept realised she was looking at one of the occult world's most legendary items of dark magick- the infamous *St Petersburg Qliphothic Wheel.* Or as it was known by those dark magickal adepts who had used it in the early years of the twentieth century, in St Petersburg, "the Trubka" (трубка) or Tube.

Long thought by occult historians within SPLEE to have been lost or destroyed at the end of the second world war, the Trubka was known to have been captured by a specialised unit[295] of SS officers in 1941 during the siege of Leningrad (St Petersburg). The device had been obtained to help resolve difficulties encountered by the Meri-Isfet in constructing their own much larger Qliphothic wheel device[296] that, it was promised, would provide the ultimate Wunderwaffe and assure the Nazis supreme victory and global domination. Indeed, many occult historians within SPLEE had postulated that Hitler's otherwise questionable decision to invade Russia and open the Eastern Front was primarily to obtain this legendary object to produce the

---

[295] The Ahnenerbe operated as an occult research unit under the direct mandate of Heinrich Himmler, the Reichsführer of the Schutzstaffel (SS).

[296] In 1941 this Meri-Isfet project to create a large "wheel" had the SS code name "Charite Anlage" (Charite facility) and was located in a basement beneath Charity Hospital in Berlin, to minimise the risk of damage from allied bombers. However, because of the numerous terminal illnesses associated with close proximity to the device, the project was moved from Berlin to a series of underground facilities in Poland. Due to high mortality rates nearby concentration camp prisoners were used as workers on the project.

ultimate wonder weapon that promised to overcome the losses he was suffering from the Western Allies.

The origins of the Meri-Isfet's attempts to create their own large "Qliphothic Wheel" can be traced to the early 1930s when Thule Society occultists[297], who were aligned with the extreme far-right goals of the Nationalsozialistische Deutsche Arbeiterpartei (Nazi party), began to open communication channels with members of the Meri-Isfet lodge in Berlin. The Meri-Isfet could see the potential of this collaboration and began to provide detailed instructions that would lead eventually to the formation of an extreme political ideology, expansionist military strategies and elements of forgotten technologies, to allow the Nazis to rapidly achieve technological superiority over the nations of the world. Knowing that a country that controlled the world would have almost unlimited resources, the Meri-Isfet encouraged the idea of Wunderwaffen with the leaders of the Nazi party and, included amongst numerous other projects, their goal of recreating the Qliphothic Wheels of their antediluvian predecessors.

This project, known to the modern conspiracy theorists as "Die Glocke" (The Bell) had, mercifully, failed to reach completion when the Soviet army overran Eastern Europe. SPLEE historians had thought that the retreating Nazis had destroyed the Bell and the much smaller and older Trubka to prevent them from falling into enemy hands. However, as Mathers now could see, when the Soviet forces overran the Nazi positions, they must have recovered the Trubka from deep inside the Wenceslas Mine in Poland. This location was where the Meri-Isfet "wheel" development took place under the code name "Der Laternenträger" (Lantern Bearer), a lightly veiled reference to the Satanic

---

[297] The Thule Society (Studiengruppe ür germanisches altertum).

goal of releasing darkness and chaos associated with the infernal device.

Of course, the complete history of the Trubka was much older than this, being an item of technology that had survived from the massive cataclysms that marked the end of the Pleistocene and the beginning of the Holocene geological epochs[298], triggered by a worldwide series of air burst explosions from cometary fragment impacts[299].

In order to preserve an example of their technology for later generations, the Trubka had been transported by those few Meri-Isfet adepts who survived the cataclysms to a retreat on the highest plateaus of Tibet amongst the Himalayan peaks. They hoped this location would escape the global tsunamis and rising sea levels[300] caused by the release of massive glacial meltwaters from the two-mile-thick ice sheets covering much of the Northern Hemisphere.

After it had been moved, the Trubka remained hidden from the world for the ensuing millennia, awaiting a time when civilization recovered to the point where its technology could generate the substantial amounts of electrical energy needed for the Qliphothic wheels to operate. During the thousands of years of waiting for civilization to recover, a dark magickal sect was formed to guard the Trubka. Eventually, this sect would become a well-known branch of

---

[298] A series of cometary high air burst "impacts" starting 13,000 years ago and finally ending 11,564 years ago.

[299] Geologists report a layer in the soil between 13,000 and 11,500 years ago called the Younger Dryas boundary. This layer contains signs of cometary impacts suggesting temperatures in excess of 2200 °C and the burning of more than 10% of the planet's vegetation (biomass); explaining the mass extinction of the large mammals (megaflora) thriving at the time.

[300] A 400-foot rise in global sea levels.

LHP esoteric Buddhism, the infamous "Brothers of the Shadow".

Then, after nearly twelve thousand years of waiting, the first large-scale electrical power generation was pioneered in the 1880s in the United States[301] and then slowly, the technology spread around the globe. By 1883 the first street lighting occurred in the Russian Capital, St Petersburg[302]. Still, it was not until the late 1890s that there was a genuinely stable electrical power generating infrastructure[303] in the Russian capital.

Coinciding with the advent of a reliable electrical supply, in the spring of 1899, the Russian Geographical Society launched The Russian Tibet Expedition, led by Captain P.K Kozloff and assisted by a Dr R.T. Semenov. In addition to being a renowned scientist, Dr Semenov was also a fifth-degree adept within the Meri-Isfet lodge in the Russian capital of St Petersburg. Although it was unsuspected by the Russian Geographical Society or Captain Kozloff, Dr Semenov was, in fact, undertaking the expedition to make contact with the Brothers of the Shadow and transport the Trubka back to Russia. The Meri-Isfet planned to begin utilising the relatively new electrical power grid within the Russian capital to power the infernal device and resume opening gateways to the chaos and darkness from previous creations.

After reaching Tibet, Dr Semenov unexpectedly resigned from the expedition and, assisted by the Tibetan guardians of the Trubka, used oxen and primitive wooden carts to

---

[301] In 1882 Edison helped form the Edison Electric Illuminating Company of New York, which brought electric light to parts of Manhattan.

[302] Where Nevskii Prospect was illuminated.

[303] Over 100 electrical power plants.

undertake a 3,500mile-long trek through mountains, dense forests and the vast open grasslands of the Eurasian Steppes before finally reaching the comparative luxury of the newly built railway. The entire journey took over ten months and cost the lives of dozens of the Brothers of the Shadow who accompanied the Trubka on its epic trip. At the end of the journey, in June 1904, when they finally unloaded the device in St Petersburg, Dr Semenov had fallen gravely ill from the mysterious illness that seemed to afflict everyone who came into close contact with the Trubka. The full scientific explanation for these ailments would not come until 1915, for although the young University of Zurich PhD student, Albert Einstein, would publish his theory of special relativity in 1905, it was not until ten years later that his work would be further developed into an understanding of how space/time was related to gravity[304].

Once you understand the full implications of Einstein's work, the illnesses associated with proximity to the Trubka were not mysterious at all because each time the device was moved, the two intersecting cylinders that formed the Trubka rotated slightly, causing minor disruptions to space/time that projected Gravitational Waves (GWs) around the immediate proximity of the device. Although small, these GWs tore at the atomic structures of everything in their vicinity, causing accelerated wear to the wooden carts and catastrophic damage to the internal organs of any living organism unfortunate enough to be close to the device when it moved. One further side effect that is only evident to those not in frequent proximity to the device is neurological damage. The operators become increasingly fixated on the device and on increasing the forces being

---

[304] Special relativity with its famous equation, $E=MC^2$

generated, leading to a form of mania and madness where they cannot comprehend the dangers they are unleashing.

When one understands that the purpose of Qliphothic Wheels is to tear apart our universe's structure and allow the influx of influences from beings from previous creations, one can begin to appreciate the dangers of operating these wheels at anything approaching their full intended speed. If the emission of gravity waves from minor accidental motion causes slow death, the full operational forces unleashed by the wheels, even a tiny version, such as the Trubka, produce catastrophic consequences. This was discovered by the St Petersburg Meri-Isfet Lodge members when they finally began to experiment with the device. It took them nearly four years before they finally succeeded in running the small Trubka wheel at anywhere near its intended power. By that time, Dr Semenov had passed away, and the St Petersburg Lodge was led by a charismatic mystic called Grigori Yefimovich Rasputin from Siberia. In an infamous ceremony, during the Summer Solstice of 1908, the St Petersburg lodge succeeded in a momentary opening of the Qliphothic gates with the specific intent of granting Lodge Master Rasputin sufficient esoteric power that he could influence political leaders into creating global instability that would indirectly lead to the world's first truly global conflict for over 12,000 years. As history shows, within three years of this ceremony, social instability and rivalry within Europe had deteriorated to the extent that it instigated one of the worst wars in modern history[305] , and Rasputin's influence over the Russian Royal family directly led to their

---

[305] World War One – 1911 to 1918 was one of the deadliest conflicts in history, with over 8 million combatant deaths and over 13 million civilian deaths. It also led to numerous genocides and the Spanish flu pandemic that caused over 100 million deaths.

unpopularity and indirectly to the October Socialist Revolution of 1917.

Aside from its dark humanitarian impact, the Solstice Ceremony of 21st June 1908 also generated significant disruptions to space/time and the momentary exertion of massive gravitational forces originating from the Earth. These GWs diverted a relatively small, near-earth object from its stable solar orbit into the path of our planet. This 150-foot diameter block of rock and ice reached Earth at 07:17 HRS on 30 June 1908, flying into our planet at over 30,000 miles per hour and exploding some five miles above the earth's surface over the Podkamennaya Tunguska River in Siberia. The resulting air burst yielded a thirty megaton[306] explosion with a shock wave that measured 5.0 on the Richter scale. It flattened over eighty million trees in eight hundred and thirty square miles of forest. History would remember this impact as "The Tunguska Event".

Sadly, this was not the last time the Trubka would be activated during the twentieth century. The Soviet Union (Russia) and the successors to The Weimar Republic (Germany) would eventually end up embroiled in some of the bloodiest conflicts of the Second World War. However, immediately after the end of the First World War[307], both nations were outcasts[308] from the rest of the developed nations. Naturally, under such isolation, they were forced to increasingly cooperate. The Treaty of Rapallo[309] formalised some aspects of this warming of relations and permitted

---

[306] 13 petajoules, roughly 3614 gigawatt hours.

[307] The armistice was signed 11 November 1918.

[308] The communist nature of the Soviet regime and the memories of the German actions during the war made many countries reluctant to trade with either nation.

[309] Signed April 16, 1922 in Rapallo, Italy.

extensive military and cultural exchanges that continued as late as 1933. It was during such an exchange visit in early August 1930 that four members of the Berlin Meri-Isfet lodge visited Leningrad (formerly called St Petersburg before the revolution) and, while posing as cultural historians from Humboldt University, gained access to the basement of the Hermitage Museum located in The Winter Palace. This was where Meri-Isfet records indicated that the Trubka had been stored, mistakenly attributed as a Tibetan prayer wheel, after the fall of the Romanoff dynasty in 1917.

At 23:45 HRS, on the first of August 1930, the four German adepts conducted a Celtic-themed Lughnasadh ceremony. Although, it should be noted that the Meri-Isfet's interpretation of a harvest festivity is more focused on celebrating the ending of life rather than thanks for a bountiful crop. At the stroke of midnight, they succeeded in briefly opening the Qliphothic gates to empower the then struggling and embryonic Nazi Party (NSDAP) to gain more influence over the German people. Although due to the enormous power demands required to operate the small wheel, it overwhelmed the weakened electrical grid of the Russian city and the Qliphothic gates were only opened for less than one minute. Even so, this brief period produced effects that were nearly as dramatic as those of the previous ceremony that used the Trubka, conducted in 1908.

During the German federal election on 14 September 1930, just over a month after the infamous "Leningrad Lughnasadh Ceremony", the Nazi Party (NSDAP) dramatically increased its number of seats in the Reichstag from 12 to 107. This event marked the start of the Nazi party's mysterious and meteoric rise to power. Not surprisingly, since the Lughnasadh ceremony that initiated the rise of the Nazis was dedicated to the "harvest of death", the results of this opening of the infernal Qliphothic gates produced the highest death toll[310] in modern warfare and some of history's most terrible humanitarian atrocities.

As before, in addition to the social and humanitarian results of opening the Qliphothic gates, another near-earth object became attracted by the gravity waves emitted by the Trubka wheel, causing it to head towards our planet. On this occasion, the forces pulled the object so powerfully that it fractured along its weakest points and broke into three smaller objects, forming an "iridescent string of pearls" so familiar to astronomers from the Shoemaker-Levy 9 comet impact into Jupiter in July 1994. However, on this occasion, the streaming ice tails from the three objects went unappreciated as astronomical observations were considerably less advanced in 1930. So, it was not until the 13th of August 1930, some two weeks after the Meri-Isfet's Lughnasadh ceremony in the basement of the Winter Palace, that the three blocks of ice and rock, each weighing over 1,000 tons, slammed into the earth at 25,000 miles per hour over the area of Curuçá River in Brazil. Fortunately, like the area of Tunguska in Siberia that was struck by the earlier icy meteor, this area of the Amazon Forest was largely uninhabited. At the height of four miles, the three objects caused a series of massive airburst explosions, each yielding nine kilotons of blast that levelled over two hundred square miles of rainforest and initiated an enormous fire storm. History records this meteor airburst as the "Curuçá River Event", and, due to the remote location, it would probably have gone unrecorded by astronomers but for the dedication of a Franciscan Friar, Fedele d'Alviano. He visited the site five days after the series of explosions and

---

[310] 85 million people.

interviewed eyewitnesses[311]. Friar d'Alviano's account was recorded in L'Osservatore Romano[312] in 1931.

As Mathers recalled the dark history associated with the small, dark green metallic cylinder that protruded from the broken wooden crate, a chill of foreboding ran through her as she realised that she was utterly alone, potentially facing the entire Meri-Isfet.

---

[311] He conducted a hundred interviews with witnesses that describe how at 08:30HRS, three bodies fell from the sky into the forest, changing the colour of the sky, making a rain of dust and a massive tremor that could be felt sixty miles away, in the city of Tabatinga.

[312] 'The Roman Observer' is the daily newspaper of Vatican City State.

17 HARD TO KILL

"In training, our constant goal is to make our operatives not just good, but superlative." – Lubyanka Square, Operations Manual, Komitet Gosudarstvennoy Bezopasnosti (KGB).

Third-floor washroom,
Улзварт hostel (Crossroads hostel),
On the great Gobi plateau,
Outer Mongolia,

01:49HRS (GMT+8), 10th Sept, Present day

The mix of scalding water and pressurised steam continued to torrent from the end of the broken titanium pipe. It filled the atmosphere with choking vapour and streamed, like a fire hose, over the impaled remains of Huan Su-Fin, that hung suspended on the tiled rear wall of the third-floor communal washroom. The force of the water pressure, combined with the extreme heat, caused the exposed top layers of skin[313] on the former commander of the Falcon force to blister and peel away from the deeper tissue[314] of the head and hands. The shredded skin and hair formed a thick plug of organic matter that blocked the washroom drain, causing a growing pool of warm, red liquid to form around Abdul Issuin's ankles. The sensation of the hot fluid soaking through his old leather boots was not wholly unpleasant. Still, the hawk-faced assassin did not delay using the thick white towel to grasp the large, red, circular shut-off valve and turn it anticlockwise, gradually stopping

---

[313] Epidermis (The outermost layer of skin) and dermis (The tougher connective tissue under the epidermis).

[314] Hypodermis

the stream of boiling water from cascading over the body of Su-Fin.

So far, the hawk-faced man's improvised plan had simultaneously terminated his opponent and removed the body's primary means of rapid identification. The next priority was to stage Su-Fin's physical remains so they would pass as his own. Abdul Issuin was acutely aware of the need to complete the switch in identities quickly. The remaining SF team members were currently undertaking their search and destroy mission elsewhere in the building. By his estimate, there was a seventy-six per cent likelihood that they would reach the communal washroom within the next four minutes and twelve seconds.

He waded through the red liquid that had formed into a putrid-smelling mix of blood, post-mortem bowel discharge, skin and water. After locating the drain covers, he removed the combination of materials that had accumulated there as a result of the stewing of the Chinese commando's flesh and threw it into the second cubical from the end of the row of toilet stalls. He knew that, statistically, people were most likely to select the first, middle or last booths.

Once the stinking fluids had flowed away, his next action was to remove the eight-foot-long titanium pipe from the dead commando's chest and unpin the body from the tiled wall to undress the corpse. Most people do not realise the difficulty of undressing and redressing a corpse to look "normal". But the hawk-faced man had received extensive training on the most effective methods at the SVR[315] Academy's facility, North of Moscow.

---

[315] Academy of Foreign Intelligence – Russia's premier espionage academy. Known internally, within the KGB (now renamed the FSI) as the 101st School, K1 or Gridnevka.

Since the two men were of a similar height, it was a simple act for Abdul Issuin to switch clothing. Although the Chinese commando was of a heavier build, the extensive flesh burns on his face and hands would mean that, when dressed in Abdul Issuin's second world war expedition clothes, the body would pass short-term scrutiny as "The most dangerous man in the world". That short-term deception would give the hawk-faced assassin the freedom to assume the commando's identity and move within the building with impunity. Once the body was dressed, the hawk-faced man used the SS dagger to cut a suitably sized hole in the chest of the expedition jacket, reinsert the length of titanium piping through the chest, and re-attach the body with its titanium piping back into the hole in the tiled wall.

Abdul Issuin then commenced working his way through the personal effects that he had systematically laid out on the floor from his own belongings and those of Su-Fin. He recalled the grizzled old instructor at the KGB espionage school, deep in the woods North of Moscow, showing him how to lay out the sets of personal effects, so they formed the shape of a human body. Each item was then set on the floor at its position on both the source and target bodies, so there would be a seamless swap.

In his exchange of belongings with the Falcon operative, the only items that the hawk-faced man retained were the linen-bound log book from the cave, a collection of what looked like boiled sweets, the SS dagger and the Skull-headed ring. All the other items he had acquired in the cave were placed in the appropriate locations on the commando's body. The ancient Laco watch that he had acquired in the cave was swapped for a tritium-filled Chinese clone of the Luminox watches that he was familiar with from his time with Maelstrom. Not surprisingly, since they were made from identical components[316], the "HNLGNOX" watch had the same carbon fibre construction and even sported the US NAVY's Special Warfare insignia[317] on its case back. The only difference was the wolf's head logo on the dial.

Before donning the Chinese operative's black military uniform, the hawk-faced man ran it under the hot shower to remove the biological waste that soaked the chest and groin areas. Then, after wringing out the material as best he could, he stepped into the one-piece uniform. The Chinese commando's suit fitted very loosely on Abdul Issuin's thinner frame, but given the darkness inside the hostel, that difference would probably go unnoticed. The Falcon operative's boots[318] were slightly too large for the hawk-faced assassin, so he wrapped some of the stiff paper toilet tissue[319] around his feet, so the boots did not move around too much during activity.

He then pulled on the heavy body armour[320] that was a clone of the US-designed Interceptor[321] and a classic, open-

---

[316] Outsourcing saves manufacturing costs for Western companies but often means that "fakes" come off the same production lines as the "real" luxury product.

[317] Called "the Trident" or "The Bird" by Serving US Navy SEALS.

[318] Copies of Solomon Quest 4 GTX boots, constructed on the Solomon production line after "official" hours.

[319] Similar to the Izal Medicated Toilet Tissue so popular in the post second world war period.

[320] The front and rear ceramic plates are excellent at preventing bullet penetration but add extra bulk and weight to what is already cumbersome clothing.

[321] Interceptor Multi-Threat Body Armor System.

faced[322] balaclava mask[323] that protected against flash-bang injuries and would conceal the operative's identity[324]. This feature would be especially useful to Abdul Issuin in the current situation. A full-face gas mask[325] that was designed to fit over and around the balaclava completed the task of obscuring his identity.

The hawk-faced assassin examined the name and rank badges on his black, flame-resistant military fatigues. He was not fluent in Chinese, but he knew enough to understand that he had assumed the identity of the unit commander, Huan Su-Fin. Having served in special forces units, he understood the numerous advantages that being the commander could afford and the risks of being identified due to the greater scrutiny to which he would be subjected.

He then went through his weapons. The silent firing, twenty-round, armour piercing QSW-06 handgun was technically superior to the eighty-year-old Walther he had been carrying. But the 9mm rounds on the older weapon were much more readily available than the very specialised 5.8mm Chinese ammunition. The matt black combat knife that Su-Fin had worn was a beautifully balanced piece of carbon steel that Abdul Issuin recognised as being similar[326] to the blades issued to the US special forces.

---

[322] Providing maximum field of vision.

[323] Clone of the Israeli designed Agilite SF Balaclava.

[324] With the increasing presence of phone photography special forces operatives do not want to be exposed to recrimination for their actions.

[325] Cloned copy of the M-40 gas mask issued to the US military.

[326] It is not just similar. It is *identical* to NATO stock item 1095-00-391-1056 from the Ontario Knife Company. With a six-inch double edge blade made from 440A steel.

Finally, after a complete check of the scene, the hawk-faced assassin picked up the QCW-05 submachine gun and turned on the Chinese commando's body cam, ensuring that whoever was viewing the staged scene got to see the remains pinned to the wall.

Seven hundred miles to the East, back in the underground Falcon command, the tension of the past seven minutes had been excruciating for the command-and-control team. Each member of the control room team knew that their future and the futures of their entire families depended on the outcome of a primal contest of unarmed martial prowess taking place in a washroom nearly a thousand miles away. The smoke-filled air inside the silo acquired that taint of stale stress-laden perspiration familiar to anyone who frequents casinos at the end of a night of hectic business. The stress had been worse for Jip Keing. As a supervisor, he would have borne the full brunt of the wrath of his superiors for such a high-profile failure. Not just the usual demotion and being posted to some remote shit hole. As the scapegoat for the party leaders, he would disappear. His apartment would suddenly become vacant, and one of his staff would be unexpectedly promoted, just as had happened to him some three years earlier. Unsurprisingly, the delight on Jip Keing's sweat-soak-faced face was palpable when the body cam images came online. He insisted that screen shots of the impaled figure shown on the grainy body cam be sent immediately to the Shao Jiang (major general) Ying, who was overseeing the entirety of PLA activities that night.

Closing the door to the third-floor washroom behind him, Abdul Issuin assumed the arrogant swagger so typical in SF commanders worldwide, striding confidently along the corridor. He noted the regularly placed, red[327] coloured glow sticks that had been set to provide illumination after the EMP weapon attack had destroyed the building's electrical systems. The hawk-faced assassin assumed that the glow rods had been placed by Su-Fin, the Falcon commander, as he made a preliminary search of the third floor after finding the first roof entry team incinerated in Abdul Issuin's room.

Just as the hawk-faced man reached and opened the double doors to the stairs, he encountered the second Falcon SF team of five men coming up. As cool as a cucumber, Abdul Issuin gestured, using standard Visual Signals[328], common amongst military units worldwide.

"Stop"

"Silence"

"Target Acquired"

"Go"

and he then signalled towards the communal washroom doors, some ten yards further down the corridor.

Keeping in strict formation, the five men hurried down the hall and stormed the washroom, thinking they were following instructions from their commander. Inside the sparsely lit, tiled room, they found a mutilated body pinned to the end wall and dressed in their target's clothing. Although the target's face was missing and burnt off during

---

[327] The rhodopsin in the rod cells of the eye is insensitive to longer wavelengths of light, so red light preserves night vision.

[328] Visual Signals were originally developed after the second world war. The current standard is laid out in US Field Manual 21-60 and Training Circular 3-21.60. They are standardised so that troops can rapidly integrate into multi-national operations and can communicate during an operation when silence is essential.

the fight with their unit's commander, they confirmed that the body's clothing exactly matched those worn in the grainy web cam images they had been provided at the mission briefing. The size and height of the body also roughly corresponded to the descriptions they had been provided for 世界上最危险的人 (the most dangerous man in the world).

At the other end of the third-floor corridor, the hawk-faced assassin waited until he heard the loud shouts of delight before descending the stairs down to the ground floor to prepare for the next stage of his plan.

Back in the third-floor wash room, the five members of the second Falcon assault team took the formal identification pictures that were required to confirm "the kill". They sent these pictures to the Falcon command and control centre, who, moments later, congratulated the team on their successful completion of the assignment. They were to stand down and await further instructions from their unit commander, who was now to be recognised as the new holder of the title 世界上最危险的人 (the most dangerous man in the world). The team members were permitted to temporarily disable their body cams to give them some well-deserved privacy.

The five men visibly relaxed, removing their face masks and balaclavas before posing for selfies with their phones besides the body. The most senior of the group took the old-fashioned watch and Luger pistol as souvenirs of the kill. Similar scenes of celebration were taking place throughout the Chengdu Special Forces Units in Beijing. Men were roused from their garrison beds and gathered in the refectories for toasts to Operations Commander Su-Fin, who had brought long-sought international recognition for their unit's prowess.

In the ground floor kitchen area of the hostel, everything was laid out from the previous evening, when the kitchen staff had prepared the room for the mine worker's breakfast the next day. The kitchen was set out with the utensils ready for cooking the various mutton-based delights for which the hostel was renowned.

Although, the actual guests were waiting outside in the early morning chill and pre-dawn gloom for the all-clear so they could return to their beds for a few precious moments before starting another hard day's graft.

The five members of the second Falcon unit returned downstairs to discover that their beloved unit commander had set up some candles and raided the hostel's drinks cabinet. He had opened three large CHANDON[329] champagne bottles and poured generous drinks for the five men in tumbler-sized plastic beakers. As the five men toasted their success at eliminating the world's most famous assassin, they were not in the least bit surprised that Commander Su-Fin declined the opportunity to join them, instead opting to take a tray of the fine champagne to the helicopter crews and remaining five Falcon troops who had been standing by at the operational perimeter.

The news of the kill had reached the men waiting at the helicopters, so they eagerly took the offered champagne glasses from their unit commander and toasted their unit's success. Many of the men insisted on taking selfies with the hero of the hour, commander Su-Fin. Showing his authentic leadership, he was so focused on ensuring all his men got their celebratory champagne that he had not taken the time to remove his gas mask or balaclava.

---

[329] From vineyards in the Ningxia Hui Autonomous Region in the eastern foothills of Helan Mountain, China.

Ten minutes later, the command-and-control centre in Beijing recorded that one of the three Harbin Z-20 helicopters had taken off and was headed in an Easterly direction. Strangely, the aircraft had not engaged the onboard BeiDou navigation system and was, instead, flying entirely on manual control. The single remaining control operator in Beijing put this down to the operatives consuming too much of the expensive drinks they had seen handed around to the helicopter crews before their body cams were disabled.

As the helicopter continued on its unauthorised trajectory East, it ignored all attempts at communication. It assumed an extremely low altitude, even lower than the thirty feet minimum achieved with the advanced automated flight systems.   After a further six minutes, the operator became so concerned that he risked interrupting supervisor Jip Keing from his sixth glass of Wuliangye[330]. The corpulent manager resented the interruption but eventually staggered over to the console and demanded that all the operational web cams be remotely enabled.

The grainy cockpit camera in the Harbin Z-20 eventually began transmitting its picture of the aircraft's interior, showing a pilot who was in the process of removing his mask and balaclava. The interior lighting inside the helicopter had been turned off, so the images were too indistinct for identification. All that they showed was the outline of the person flying the aircraft. The man was searching in his top pocket, where he retrieved a large Montecristo No.4[331] and lit it with a single stroke of a match, drawn from a cardboard matchbook promoting somewhere

---

[330] A brand of Baijiu: a type of rice and barley liquor.   Often compared to vodka.

[331] A Montecristo No.4 Cuban cigar.

called "Vics Club"[332]. As the flame ignited the cigar, it illuminated a distinctive hawk-faced profile, smiling directly at the camera and blowing a stream of smoke towards the lens.

As if that was not shocking enough, the web cams from the Falcon operatives started to show their feeds as well. They were revealing images that made even the heavily inebriated blood of Jip Keing run ice cold. Scenes of death were everywhere. The bodies of the Falcon teams were lying on the ground, both inside the hostel and at the operational perimeter, their faces contorted hideously, a white foam visible on their lips. The other two Harbin Z-20 helicopters were blazing infernos on the Gobi sands.

On the hostel's kitchen floor were some small squares of eighty-year-old greaseproof paper embossed with an IG Farben logo, lying next to small, smashed, rubber-coated glass vials.

---

[332] Vics is one of China's most famous nightclubs. Located in Beijing's Chaoyang District it is well frequented by PLA officers.

18 FORTRESS OF EVIL

*"Put on the full armour of God, so that you can make your
stand against the devil's schemes. For our struggle is not
against flesh and blood, but against the rulers, against the
authorities, against the powers of this world's darkness, and
against the spiritual forces of evil in the heavenly realms! -
Ephesians 6:12*

*Godinje (Годиње) village,
Municipality of Bar,
Montenegro, near the Albanian border.*

14:35HRS (GMT+2), 10th Sept, Present day

Within twenty minutes of the Trubka's wooden crate having
fallen from the rig, the local farmers had been coerced by
the three Russian truck operators to wrap the remains of the
broken wooden crate, and the partially exposed Qliphothic
Wheel, in a large, triple-layer, grey canvas tarpaulin taken
from the back of the Ural-4320. They then bound the canvas
with seven thick black nylon straps connected to a massive
galvanised steel carabiner. As Mathers occupied herself
browsing the local market stalls spread around the cobbled
square, the air became filled with the distinctive "chuf-chuf"
sound of whirling helicopter rotors. The sound grew in
intensity until finally, over the hill top, an old-fashioned-
looking transport helicopter, adorned in dirty blue and
white "AFGZ" livery, came into view and hovered above the
square. Although Mathers was not an expert on such
matters, she vaguely recognised the shape of the aircraft[333]

---

[333] A French SA 321 Super Frelon helicopter. The model ceased
being used by the French Airforce in 1981 and this particular
example subsequently passed into the hands of "AFGZ AD", a local
Moldavian construction company.

from her childhood as something that occasionally flew over the Paris sky in the 1970s.

The hovering helicopter lowered a long steel line while the French Adept haggled with one of the market stall holders over some locally produced yoghurt. The three Russian men efficiently attached the steel connection from the nylon straps wrapped around the Trubka crate. The old helicopter then tried to lift the object. Based on the copious amounts of black smoke belching from the three turboshafts[334] that powered the aircraft and the ominous sounds issuing from the helicopter, the weight of the wrapped crate vastly exceeded the expectations of whoever had planned this pickup. After two further attempts, the container rose some four to six feet above the ground. It began a slow journey in a Southerly direction, through the green vegetation of one of the nearby vineyards, down to the blue waters of Lake Skadar. Unfortunately, the object's weight meant that it remained only a few feet from the ground, catching and then pulling over the entire North-South orientation of several rows of trelliswork that formed an essential component of a local farmer's viticulture. As the destruction of the vineyard continued, the weighty object was straining the thirty-year-old engines of the helicopter as the Trubka crate began ploughing into the soil, creating deep gouges in the well-tilled, rich dark earth of the vineyard.

One of the market stallholders ran from his old, white Lada Niva van, with its rear double doors open, displaying numerous deep red Vranac wine bottles. Based on the angry man's reaction to the ongoing damage to the vineyard, Mathers assumed that he was the owner. Since she had only recently purchased a bottle of wine from him, the French Adept attempted to strike up a conversation in

---

[334] Turboméca Turmo IIIC engines.

English. She had already discovered that he was one of the few people in the market who admitted to having any multilinguistic abilities.

The wine seller was a large, heavily tanned man with a shock of short brown hair. His broad shoulders were contained in a red and black plaid shirt, a brown leather waistcoat, well-worn cargo pants and long rubber boots, partially covered by a full-length, blue canvas apron. The man put his hands on his hips and, as he watched the heavy object finally leave his fields and fly erratically out over the blue waters of the lake, he exclaimed.

"Гребаные ублюдки!" (Fucking bastards!)

Mathers came alongside him and gestured towards the three Russian men, who were now getting back into the six-wheeled lorry and preparing to leave.

"Maybe you can get compensation from them?"

The man turned to the French Adept with a look of disbelief before remarking,

"I would have a better chance of growing wings myself. These people are a rule unto themselves."

He gestured to the assembled townspeople, who seemed noticeably less stressed now the outsiders were leaving.

"We have learnt to our cost that it is best to go along with whatever *they* want. Less trouble that way."

Mathers looked carefully at the man and could see in his aura a life filled with hard physical work and numerous troubles, many not of his own making. She remarked,

"You are the only person I have interacted with who is prepared to acknowledge they exist. My name is Mathers, by the way." She offered her hand.

The man looked at the auburn-haired woman with her scholarly round glasses and stylish dress sense and, after some reflection, offered his own large and roughly calloused right hand.

"Ivanović. Pavel Ivanović."

As they shook hands, the two turned to watch as the Ural-4320 military truck drove away down the narrow lane that led out of the village, its six wheels raising copious dust clouds high into the air.   Mathers then enquired,

"Are they all Russian, like those three?"

Ivanović looked at Mathers more carefully, "You ask many questions, Miss Mathers. What are you, a reporter trying to stir up trouble?"

"Not exactly, but I am here to find out all I can about the people in that old Ottoman castle out there in the lake." Replied Mathers as she followed Ivanović past her classic VW, over to the edge of the market square, where the vineyard started, to survey the damage.

"If you want my advice, you will get back in that old camper of yours and head to some sunny beach and find something less dangerous, like shark hunting!" The big man smiled, clearly pleased with his attempt at humour as he walked over the rich dark earth of the vineyard.

Mathers followed close beside him, "Sadly, that's not an option, Pavel. You are the only one around here who is not afraid of these people; surely you want something done about them, so no one needs to live in fear?"

Ivanović paused and pulled up the first line of the wire trelliswork that had been toppled over by the passing helicopter. After Mathers began to help in the work, he looked at her from the corner of his eye and decided to support this strange woman.

"It all started about ten years back, just after the latest round of regional troubles ended. Some wealthy Scandinavian charity decided they wanted to buy Grmožur. We all welcomed it, lots of money coming to the area and well-paid work for us all. Then these rich foreigners came and began rebuilding the old ruin. But there was something odd right from the start."

"Odd. In what way?" Queried Mathers.

The winemaker continued, "Well, for a start, they dug foundations like they were expecting earthquakes, tidal waves and tornados all simultaneously! We all thought they were mad, but we were so glad of the money that we went along with their crazy construction ideas. By the time they had completed the building works, the entire structure had levels of reinforcement that could probably survive an atomic bomb!"

Mathers nodded, "and?"

Ivanović continued to talk as he and the French adept worked together, pulling up the rows of the fallen trellis as they progressively moved down the hillside, gradually bringing the vines upright.

"Then they started making demands. Small ones at first, suggesting what crops we should grow, and then it was the church. I am not what you would call a believer, but Godinje has always had a small chapel. They promised regular annual payments, big payments if we had the church moved. They even offered to have a new church built for worship, provided it was on the other side of the hill." Ivanović nodded towards the landscape that rose above the village behind them.

"Did they say why?" queried the French Adept.

"Not really. It was not until much later that we discovered that the *residents* disliked any kind of religious symbolism!

Christian, Jewish, or Muslim makes no difference. All of the symbols were banned. They even forced those of us doing work for them to remove crucifixes and never to mention God's name, not even in swearing." Explained the winegrower.

Mathers nodded, "I have heard this about these people in other places they have set up a centre."

Ivanović seemed interested that the French adept had encountered these people elsewhere, he commented.

"Seems they follow some pagan system. A few of the *residents* from the castle have tried to convert some of the villagers to their beliefs. And strange beliefs they sound as well, like something straight out of fantasy movies. A few of us pretend to have converted, just to help business, but we still all pray to God in our homes when these strangers have left us."

The French Adept smiled and wondered how Mr Ivanović would react if he knew the truth about Mathers herself. She decided to find out if there were any Meri-Isfet adepts that she would recognise, so she would be better prepared for the confrontation that now seemed inevitable.

"Is there any one of them who seems to be in charge?" Asked Mathers as they both struggled to pull up one of the longer sections of trellis that had been cleaved clean in two by the airborne crate as it ploughed into the ground.

"As far as I can tell, there are three seniors in the cult; all are men. The three of them always come by helicopter for the more important events on the island. Two of the three senior men are older. One is in his thirties with long dark hair, a deep tan and a keen dress sense, always wearing very expensive-looking clothes. The other older man is smaller, with glasses, and dresses like a bank manager. He is probably in his fifties." Stated the winegrower as he struggled with the effort of righting the long trellis.

Mathers had to prompt him to continue, "You said there were three who seemed to be senior?"

Ivanović nodded, "When these two are absent, the cult is run by the third man, who appears less senior than the other two. He is a young man in his twenties with a shaved head and many strange tattoos. Rather arrogant. He treats his fellow cultists with scorn, and I have even heard him sneering at the other two older leaders, saying how they are past it."

As she recognised the description, the French Adept could not help exclaiming, "Ironheart".

The farmer looked thoughtfully at Mathers, "Yes, that's his name. IronHeart. You know him?"

Mathers shook her head, "Only by reputation."

"Nasty bugger from what I have heard. Enjoys suffering, watching it anyway." Stated Ivanović before continuing, "Listen, there has been a lot of activity recently, helicopters and a large food order placed for a few days. So, I think they are planning some big event."

The big man looked at Mathers. They had reached the end of the field and brought all the vines back up into their neat rows.

"Thanks for your help with these repairs. If you insist on staying, then you can camp overnight near my house and use my electricity and water, if you want."

"Thanks." Mathers shook hands with Ivanović and headed back up the hill to the market square, where she completed purchasing food for her lunch and dinner. She planned to have a special meal that evening with some local red wine as she gazed at the stars in the night sky, as the lack of light pollution promised a rare opportunity for appreciating the constellations as the ancients would have seen them.

After finishing her shopping, she drove the VW down the rough track leading to Ivanović's stone farmhouse. After a quick wash using the farmhouse water, she unloaded her Triumph from the back of the van and, using the superior manoeuvrability of the bike and its thick, new tires, continued along the coastal track to the East. She found the ideal spot further along the winding, unmade lakeside path. It was near the top of an eighty-six-foot-high cliff that overlooked a stone-walled building constructed on a small island, about a mile away from the clifftop, on the blue waters of Lake Skadar. From reading the guide books that she had purchased the day before, she already knew that the original Ottoman fortress Grmožur had been built in 1843. Still, she was more interested in the details of the additional works mentioned by Ivanović, as she hoped they would begin to reveal the intentions of the Meri-Isfet.

The auburn-haired French Adept unpacked some items from her red Hermes leather backpack and sat crossed-legged on a bright and colourful Trek Light Gear midweight woven blanket[335] that had accompanied her on numerous travels. She had deliberately fasted since her pre-dawn breakfast, and although she was hungry, she delayed starting her lunch a bit longer. There was a particular esoteric technique that she intended to utilize that was most effective when the bloodstream was untainted by terrestrial influences.

But, before she commenced the precise consciousness projection technique that she had been taught by a senior Rosicrucian adept, she opened a small battered leather case. She pulled out a pair of 1970s, East German binoculars[336] and surveyed the island and the stone buildings covering most of its surface. Mathers could see that the fortress had

---

[335] A "Halley's Comet" Adventure Blanket from Trek Light Gear.

[336] Carl Zeiss Jena Dekarem, 10x50

not simply been restored. It had been completely rebuilt, with massive stone walls that must have been at least twenty feet thick and showed evidence of containing numerous steel and concrete reinforcements. The winemaker's observation that the structure had been designed to withstand earthquakes and hurricanes was not an exaggeration. However, Mathers speculated that these structural reinforcements were indications that the Meri-Isfet planned to begin again with their reckless attempts to open the Qliphothic gateways between this existence and those of prior creations. This fortress was explicitly designed to conduct such infernal experiments.

The fortress, its associated helicopter landing pads and jetty were deserted. There was considerable damage to the pathway to the fortress gates, which must have been from the delivery of the small Qliphothic Wheel or Trubka, by helicopter earlier that afternoon. Clearly, the modern custodians of the Meri-Isfet tradition underestimated the extreme mass associated with the small object. The other visible feature from high on the cliff top was the two large underwater cables connecting the small island to Montenegro and Albania. Mathers guessed these would be dedicated electrical supplies fed by the national grids from the two nations as the energy required to operate the wheels was considerable.

Putting the field glasses down, Mathers considered what she should do, she needed to investigate further, but she was aware that doing so would put her at considerable personal risk. If she was found, as was entirely possible, then it was sure that she would be killed, and any knowledge that she had accumulated so far about the Meri-Isfet's acquisition of the Trubka wheel would be lost. Picking up her large unbranded Android phone, she tried calling her mentor, Frater Gabriel, in Geneva, but the call to his landline at home went unanswered. Knowing that the elderly Gabriel often had to attend medical appointments related to his heart condition, she instead sent a short email to Frater Aron. Although he did not own a mobile, he embraced modern technology enough to regularly use electronic communication.

Having completed a summary of her situation, she placed her phone beside her, returned the binoculars to their case and commenced her projection meditation. Since, during the coming moments, certain aspects of her non-physical essence would be separating from her physical body, she first took precautions to protect her physical form from the possibility of a psychic attack. Such attacks could include invasion by another human consciousness or even one of the many inhuman non-physical entities that are unseen by our physical senses but inhabit the super-physical realms and surround us every day.

As the French Adept sealed the seven sacred gateways of her body, just over a mile away deep in the stone fortress that she had been observing, the shaven-headed Meri-Isfet adept known as Magister Ironheart stopped his work. He had been supervising the installation of the newly arrived Qliphothic Wheel that now stood upright as the centrepiece in a large, underground vault. He felt the presence of another advanced magical practitioner exercising their True Will. He could not determine who had performed the act, where the Magical Will had been exercised, or even what Magical act had been performed- he could only appreciate the technical excellence and purity of the Magic.

His piercing blue eyes narrowed as he dismissively waived away the group of twelve less advanced adepts. This group had been assisting him in connecting a set of eight massive Northrop Grumman HTS[337] ship propulsion motors that had been installed into the floor of the underground chamber

---

[337] High temperature superconductor (HTS)

before the walls and ceilings had been constructed. These eight 36.5-megawatt[338] motors dwarfed the much smaller, green, Trubka cylinder that had recently been delivered to the fortress, as did the six-foot-thick, riveted steel electrical conduits connected to each of the HTS engines. These conduits drew their electrical supply from dedicated offshoots from the national grids of Montenegro to the northwest, Kosovo to the northeast, North Macedonia to the east and Greece to the south, through a series of underground and underwater cables.

While remaining standing, Ironheart began his own preparation to project his consciousness, to determine if he could identify the source of the recent Magical disturbance. He knew from the quality of the technique and its purity that it did not originate from within the Meri-Isfet fortress. Unlike Mathers's cautious and detailed precautions on her hilltop, a mile away, Ironheart had no concerns about other entities possessing his body. It was not that such possession could not happen to him or that he was ignorant of the protection mechanisms and techniques that he could apply. It was that he possessed a supreme arrogance and was convinced that he had been chosen by the very darkest elements of this creation and by similar forces from previous creations to rule and lead.

Within moments, Ironheart's breathing slowed, his massive chest hardly moving, and his shaved head bowed forward, not through submission but rather a relaxation of his physical form. For those gifted with what the ancients called "second sight", a dark, scintillating mist could be seen forming from behind the large man's thick neck, emerging from a region close to the base of his skull. The strange fog flowed like gently exhaled cigar smoke and formed into an anticlockwise rotating ball, around four inches in diameter,

---

[338] 49,000 horsepower

that glowed with a series of dark colours, ranging from red through to pitch black. This ball of astral energy flew from its stationary, rotating position above the Magister's head through the thick stone walls with a sudden upwards and sideways motion. It was instantaneously visible again, half a mile above the fortress ramparts.

A mile away, to the North, Madeleine Mathers had completed her protective measures and was focusing her consciousness in a manner that the Ancient Taoist Alchemists termed "creating the pearl of Chi". This was a singularity of consciousness that could be moved to any location within the body by an act of will. This technique enabled Taoist Masters to perform what appeared impossible feats- or, as the French Adept was about to demonstrate, that same singularity of consciousness can be projected outside of the body to any location in space-time. Unlike the vaporous form of projection completed by the Meri-Isfet adept, Mathers' projection was not visible, even to those gifted with second sight.

The ways that the two senior adepts approached their preparations for the projection of consciousness highlighted the fundamental differences between Mathers and Ironheart. Whereas Ironheart left his physical body unprotected and manifested his projected consciousness in a rather crude, semi-physical form, the French Adept had taken much greater care. Not only had she sealed the seven sacred entrances to her physical body, she had also formed what the ancient Rosicrucian Masters called the "Nubes Lucet", or the Luminous Cloud. This cloud is the basis of the Rose-Croix's claims to have mastered the secret of invisibility. Through an effort of will and a form of material projection, Mathers had manifested a condensed cloud of astral matter from her fingertips- in a series of hand motions that were not unlike pulling yarn from the core of a skein. Except these motions were in mid-air in front of where Mathers was sitting. This technique gradually formed a glowing white cloud that the French Adept eventually manipulated- so it hung over and around her seated form. The glow of the astral material rapidly subsided, becoming the greyish hue of the projected materials that were so frequently photographed in early 20th century mediumistic seances and were termed ectoplasm.

Unlike the bold claim of the seventeenth-century Rosicrucian Brotherhood, this cloud of astral matter did not make Mathers' body invisible but rather obscured it. If anyone from the twenty-first century had taken a digital photograph directly where the French Adept was seated, then when they reviewed the picture, they would have presumed some digital editing had censored elements of the composition. Although it might be supposed that any passing observer would instantly notice such a mass of nebulous grey, that is not the case. Human and animal visual perception (even astral perception) has evolved to detect motion or objects in stark contrast to the other sections of the field of view. An obscured element within such a field of view is almost impossible to detect, which is a blessing for most people who have numerous "floaters[339]" in their eyeballs.

Once these precautions were completed, Mathers focused her True Will on the battlements of the fortress she had been observing through the old binoculars. In the time it took for her memory to recall the minute details of the stonework and the narrow walkway that lined the interior of the battlements, she found herself at the location. Decades of daily, dedicated practice had refined the French Adept's magic technique to that sublime level where there was no longer any need for conscious awareness of the complex processes required to achieve her magical intent. Although

---

[339] Small specs of material within the vitreous of the eye.

her mentors in the Geneva Lodge would never tell her, she had surpassed the abilities of any other adept in the modern history of the Meri-Maat.

The non-material body she was using for her reconnaissance of the fortress was formed of such refined forms of ethereal material that it had hardly any detectable interaction with the physical world[340]. It was unlikely that anyone would detect her unless they, too, were operating in a similar refined projection. Raising the vibratory rate of consciousness to such a level was a feat that very few human beings could achieve for less than a few seconds. The fact that Mathers was comfortable operating at this extraordinary level of vibration was a signature of her prowess in the Great Art- although her constant striving for self-improvement meant that she would have denied such recognition.

In stark contrast, Ironheart's gently spinning, red and brown ball- which now hovered approximately half a mile above the fortress, was composed directly of his ethereal or astral body. This astral form is called the *Liṅga Śaṅra* in Vedic esoteric teachings or the Ikiryō (生霊) in Japanese occult schools. Not only was Ironheart's projection semi-physical in nature, but it was also intimately linked to his vital life force and his multi-fold constitution[341]. This connection

---

[340] Just the odd stream of Quarks, Hadrons and positively charged, Muons, interacting here and there with the surrounding space-time field. We could debate, at some length, if Mathers' consciousness was in fact causing these particles to manifest and *form* space-time, but that would be a significant diversion from the story.

[341] Occult lore teaches that the incarnated, living human being has a number of bodies, ranging from the gross physical to the absolute, immortal, non-physical essence. The exact number and nature of these bodies varies from occult school to occult school. Some say three, some seven and others, like the Western Esoteric

meant that any damage to Ironheart's coarse ethereal body while projecting would cause a corresponding injury to his physical body. Most LHP adepts feel that such a risk is outweighed by the advantages offered by such semi-physical ethereal projections. Since such kinds of astral bodies are composed of physical matter, they can be formed by the Magickal will into visible appearance in any image desired by the projecting adept's imagination. This makes this technique ideal for manifesting terrifying encounters on unsuspecting victims. With such coarse astral forms, it is also possible to interact with objects in the physical world, knocking over things, causing air drafts, or even physical injuries. These near physical (coarse) astral projections are the foundations for the numerous shapeshifting creatures[342] so common throughout the folklore and legends of the world[343].

Back on the fortress ramparts, half a mile beneath the floating, red and brown, ethereal body of Ironheart, who was unsuccessfully using his projected senses to detect her; the French Adept willed her consciousness down through the thick stonework. She found herself in a large entrance space, twenty feet wide, forty feet long and fifteen feet high. The massive surrounding masonry made the area pleasantly cooler than the warmth from the sun outside.

---

path followed by both Mathers and Ironheart teach there are ten bodies, linked to the symbolised structure of the Tree of Life.

[342] Such as the "Fetch" in Celtic Lore, Vampires and Werewolves in Eastern Europe and the Wendigo in North America.

[343] It is this phenomenon of corresponding damage that explains many of the accounts from folklore where injury to a witch or shaman when she or he occupied the form of an animal, such as a crow, wolf, fox or hare, was later found on the body of the magical practitioner.

The hall floor was tiled in a pattern of interlocking, red and black marble squares. In the centre of the tiled area was a five-foot-tall bronze statue of a striking cobra, with two prominent fangs made of highly polished steel. The snake's eyes were formed by two large red rubies that caught the light cascading from four large stained-glass windows on the left side of the hallway. In contrast, the right-hand side of the entrance hall had no windows. Instead, hanging from the white plaster wall, there were a series of five full-colour photographic montages, six feet high and four feet wide-each devoted to one of the prime magical elements; Earth, Water, Air, Fire and Spirit. Directly in front and beneath the bronze cobra was a dried human skull that had been cracked open to serve as an incense burner, filling the space with a musky aroma laced with cannabis.

The images portrayed in the fifteen-foot-high stained-glass windows were related to War, Famine, Pestilence and Death in a panorama showing events and individuals from the past four hundred years. The window associated with War focused on images of the carnage of humans and animals during the two world wars in sickening detail. Famine showed skeletal humans and animals with bulging eyes alongside empty crop fields in Africa, North Korea and Asia. Pestilence started at the top of its glass area with a detailed portrayal of the so-called American Plagues that brought a cluster of Eurasian diseases to the Americas by Europeans, that caused the deaths of 90% of the indigenous population in the Western Hemisphere and the collapse of the Inca and Aztec civilizations. Tableaus beneath these images of white Europeans standing over thousands of dead and dying natives included more recent plagues and infections that culminated in Ebola, The Spanish Flu, Covid-19 and the Red Death. The final of the four windows focused on Death. It showed the numerous genocides that have taken place within the last few centuries; the Tutsi in Rwanda; the Khmer Rouge in Cambodia, and culminating in an extensive series of images showing graphic detail of the Nazi genocide of the Jews, Gypsies and other minorities.

On the right-hand wall was a series of photographic compositions, each under the banner of the prime magic elements; Earth, Water, Air, Fire and Spirit.

Earth showed enormous landfills in Africa and Asia, crammed with the developed nations' discarded consumer goods: cars, fridges, TVs, computers, and phones. Beneath these images were Alberta's oil sands, the deforestation of the Amazon, and finally, open cast mining operations. Inset within each image were the resulting congenital disabilities in humans and animals unlucky enough to live near such destruction.

Water showed the oceans and rivers choked with plastics, chemicals, and effluent with dead and dying marine creatures.

Air showed the thick smog and smoke from factories, power stations, chemical works and vehicles, alongside dying victims who had inhaled the toxic output related to human greed.

Fire showed the burning of city garbage, alongside other images of deliberate burning of tropical rain forests and finally, from developing nations, the burning of plastic and chemical waste next to shanty towns.

The final esoteric element, *Spirit,* was depicted in a series of images under the banner "*Do what thou wilt be the whole of the law*". These compositions showed peoples of all ages and all nations obsessively focused on themselves and their own pleasure while displaying gratuitous consumption, regardless of the impact on the planet, their fellow-creatures, or fellow human beings.

Reaching the end of these sickening celebrations of suffering, pain, disease, destruction and narcissism, the

French Adept moved further into the fortress complex. After passing through some additional walls, she found herself in a clinically clean long room, laid out as a hospital ward with eleven beds. The furthest bed in the ward was empty. Each of the other ten beds was occupied by a person, lying, sedated from drips hanging above their beds. On the wall above each sleeping form was a whiteboard listing the name of the bed's occupant, their latest medical assessment and a flag from one of the ten kingdoms and principalities of Europe[344].

From the rarefied state of her high vibratory projection, Mathers could see, floating about four feet above each of the sedated individuals, was their etheric double. These astral forms were connected to their physical sleeping body by a scintillating, thin silver cord that originated from the heads of the sleeping forms. The ripples of colours flowing through the floating etheric bodies suspended above each bed showed them in a deep dream state. Beside each bed was a tall wooden cabinet made of camphor wood that, based on the swirling astral energies that flowed from and around the storage units, contained something that emitted considerable esoteric force.

The French Adept could not open these wooden containers, as her projected form lacked sufficient physical force and mass. But she was able to move close enough to the first three cabinets labelled SPAIN, DENMARK and NORWAY, respectively, to read the descriptions neatly handwritten on the fronts of the storage units. Although Mathers was not a historian, her knowledge of European Esoterica was considerable, so she immediately recognised the things listed as items the Nazis had seized during their occupation of Europe. These items were thought to have been lost at

---

[344] Denmark, Norway, Sweden, Netherlands, Belgium, Spain, Andorra, Liechtenstein, Monaco and Luxembourg.

the war's end. They were: *The Lobera* (Wolf Slayer), the legendary sword of the king Saint Ferdinand III of Castile, Spain; *The Sauvagine*, one of the two magical swords of Ogier the Dane, a knight of Charlamagne; and finally, *The Gambanteinn*, a wooden staff mentioned in the Poetic Edda of the Norse sagas.

Whether these cabinets contained these genuine items, Mathers did not know. Still, she could tell that whatever was inside the chests had been imbued with significant energy and belief by numerous people over a considerable period.

Looking at the powerful relic-powered vortexes swirling beside the unconscious bodies of the European royal heirs, Mathers remembered her briefing in Geneva- opening the Qliphothic gates required significant occult relics, royal blood and a Qliphothic wheel. With a cold dread, the French Adept realised that the Meri-Isfet were far closer to their terrifying goal than anyone in SPLEE had dared to contemplate.

19 INTERCEPTOR

"A fighter pilot must maintain constant aggressiveness for success. All else is rubbish." - Manfred Albrecht Freiherr von Richthofen (The Red Baron).

Three hundred feet altitude AGL[345],
Two miles West of Yoliin Am Valley[346] (Valley of the Vultures)
Gurvan Saikhen Mountains,
Gobi Desert,
Southern Mongolia.

05:09HRS (GMT+8), 10th Sept, Present day

The darkness inside the front of the Z-20 helicopter was broken only by the cockpit instruments, the glowing end of Abdul Issuin's Montecristo No 4 and the tritium vials on the dial of his "HNLGNOX" watch. Glancing at the information displayed on his heads-up display (HUD), he could see the aircraft's altitude and attitude[347] of the aircraft and based on

---

[345] Aeronautical term for the height above ground level (AGL or HAGL).

[346] Yol (Vulture) in Mongolian, gives its name to the Yoliin Am Valley.

[347] Attitude is the angular differences between an aircraft's axis and the Earth's horizon.

his BeiDou[348] GPS reading, that sunrise was just over an hour away[349].

Although the hawk-faced assassin could not understand all of the Chinese symbols on the controls, he did not need to as he was thoroughly familiar with the instruments on the Sikorsky UH-60[350]. He had completed the US military's advanced training[351] at Fort Rucker in 2010 while serving as a "military advisor[352]" for the oil-rich Gulf state of Bahrain[353].

On entering the aircraft back at the hostel, Abdul Issuin had removed his heavy body armour before strapping himself into the left-hand pilot's seat. Once airborne, he guided the fast-moving aircraft at just over one hundred knots over the undulating, rock-strewn floor of the desert plateau with a series of delicate, coordinated movements on the Central

---

[348] Chinese military had to develop its own GPS as, if there was a conflict with Western forces, they would be denied access to Western GPS or worse it would be deliberately altered to provide misleading data.

[349] At this location and altitude (8202 feet) on the 9th of September, dawn occurs at 06.09HRS.

[350] Otherwise known as the Blackhawk.

[351] United States Army Aviation Center of Excellence in Alabama.

[352] A term which can mean almost anything but in this case was pretty certain to have been related to personal protection to the Al Khalifa family (the royal house of Bahrain).

[353] Based on Abdul Issuin's assessment of the aircraft after his training Bahrain ordered several Blackhawks.

Cyclic[354] and Pitch levers[355] along with the floor pedals[356]. In front of him, an integrated augmented reality display projected his immediate terrain onto the cockpit windows, labelling all free-standing objects larger than four square inches in volume with a suggested target identification[357].

Of course, not being fluent in technical Mandarin, the hawk-faced assassin could not understand all the possible suggestions that could be displayed by the CTIS (complex target identification system) if they had been flying over more varied terrain. However, since pretty much everything around him was either 岩石 (Rock) or 悬崖 (Cliff), Abdul Issuin did not pay much attention to this miracle of artificial intelligence.

Except that is when he noticed a row of small objects rising above the cliff top and then disappearing back down behind the cliff edge as the helicopter passed below them, causing him some concern. These were labelled 秃 (vulture) on his display. Although Abdul Issuin did not recognise the mandarin symbol, he did recognise the distinctive shape of the heads and necks that poked above the ridge and could identify these as the same kind of birds[358] he had encountered at the watering hole when he had regained consciousness. He ignored the fancy augmented display.

---

[354] The "stick" enables the pilot to tilt the craft to either side or forward and backward.

[355] The Pitch controls change the height of the aircraft.

[356] The foot pedals control the rear tail rotor to change the direction of the aircraft.

[357] The 你是做什么的 or Nǐ shì zuò shénme de (literally "what are you") system was derived from a particularly successful cyber hacking initiative against the US DARPA "third wave AI" systems.

[358] Eurasian Black Vulture: Aegypius monachus, who specialise in eating bones, a fact that tells you much about the Gobi Desert.

Instead, he steered the Z20 along the wide valley floor, looking for the distinctive rock fall that indicated the cave's location, where the linen-bound log book said there were ten kilos of gold.

Suddenly, the augmented display showed a small flying object, travelling to the left of his aircraft, labelled as 小猫头鹰 (small owl[359]). Noticing the slow, arcing wings and rapid descent of the target until it merged with a second target, labelled 啮齿动物 (Rodent), Abdul Issuin quickly dismissed the episode as one of the desert's many nocturnal birds of prey hunting. However, moments after his encounter with the owl, there was a sudden loud buzzing that made the black plastic cockpit fascia inside the Z20 vibrate and produced a bright, red symbol 直升机 (helicopter) with a red flashing 贝尔525 (Bell 525) to appear beneath it on the screens. Although the hawk-faced man could not understand the detail, he instantly recognised the potential threat. This new target was not biological, as it was sixty feet long, eight feet wide, with a set of five, fifty-five feet long rotors on the top of its structure. The rapidly cooling engine mountings[360] showed that this medium-sized helicopter had been stationary for over thirty minutes. This new aircraft was on a small plateau, some four hundred yards ahead on the left side of the broad valley, six hundred feet higher than Abdul Issuin was currently flying.

Bringing his stolen Z20 to a stationary hovering position, three hundred feet above the valley floor and next to the large fallen boulders that had formerly drawn him to the concealed cave, the assassin recalled seeing a similarly sized helicopter to the one highlighted on his night-vision

---

[359] More accurately: Little owl, Athene noctua.

[360] The mountings housed a pair of General Electric CT7-2F1 turboshaft engines.

systems some days earlier when he had encountered the adventure tourists[361] posing for photographs at the top of a steep cliff face.

Based on what the Z20s augmented night vision systems were showing, the same group of people were now assembled to pose for a series of pictures on a large, off-road motorbike[362] just as dawn rose over the Eastern tail of the Gurvan Saikhen Mountain range. Based on the copious amounts of fake mud and dirt the adventure tourists were applying to their faces and clothing, the staged photographs implied that these modern-era explorers had just completed an arduous, all-night, off-road adventure. However, the Z20s thermal imaging showed that the bike's engine had not been run for a considerable time.

Although Abdul Issuin was not overtly aware of it, his presence in the hovering Z20 went utterly unnoticed by this group of seventeen people. His engines were practically silent, and the sophisticated camera and projection systems mounted on the helicopter's frame made it blend almost perfectly into the rocky surroundings of the valley floor, especially in the pre-dawn light. The hawk-faced assassin gently manoeuvred his aircraft down and landed in a gap between two of the larger boulders that had fallen from the cave. The stone blocks were of such a size that the entire length of the Z20's fuselage was hidden between the massive rocks, and when the Z20 had touched down, the rotor blades were well beneath the tops of the boulders.

Six hundred feet above where the Z20 stealth helicopter was hidden, the two Australian tour guides, Oliver and Jake, were taking a well-deserved break. It had been a very early

---

[361] "Xtreme Tours – creating the definitive selfie record of the world's ultimate adventures".

[362] BMW R 1250 GS Adventure - Edition 40 Years GS.

start, and getting the fifteen "extreme explorers" dressed and ready for the predawn photo opportunity was very trying. Based on the numerous complaints during breakfast, if any of this group had experienced four AM before, it was because of the extended hours at some exclusive private nightclub.

Both of the guides had classic, sun-bleached hair that looked like it had never seen any attention but was, in reality, the result of hours of careful, daily grooming and preparation. The two men, who were trying much too hard to look like they were still in their early thirties, were sitting in North Face canvas directors' chairs and sipping their third, chilled, Carlton Draught[363] of the morning. Their clothing reflected the rugged images they were trying to project, a mix between Crocodile Dundee and Indiana Jones.

A golden Buddha, suspended by a leather strap, hung around Oliver's neck, nestled amongst a mass of thick, black chest hair, revealed under a denim shirt with too many buttons undone, especially for the chilly, pre-dawn conditions in the Gobi. The open denim shirt was partially covered by a blue Patagonia windcheater and faded blue jeans.

Jake, meanwhile, was cultivating the "ageing surfer dude" look with a red, signed "Italo Ferreira[364]", Rip Curl[365] hoodie and some shredded, tan RVCA chinos. Both men wore large, steel Japanese pilot watches equipped with circular

---

[363] An Australian lager – unlike many of the lagers advertised as being Australia's favourite, this one is the real deal.

[364] Ítalo Ferreira is a Brazilian professional surfer who won the world title in 2019.

[365] The young explorers would probably have informed Jake that Rip Curl is "so last season".

slide rules and complex dials[366]. Their choice of footwear was identical; tan-coloured Timberland boots that are so common with adventurers, real or imagined.

Some twenty feet in front of the blue Yeti cooler box, filled with chilled beer, that lay immediately between where the two guides were sitting, a group of fifteen men and women were busy making themselves ready for their moment to pose on the motorcycle. The four females in the group had strategically applied a specialised spray[367], either to their legs, if they were wearing shorts, or to their cleavage, if they had low-cut tops. Each hoped that they could accentuate their natural curves before post-production editing, and filters were applied to their pictures prior to being posted to numerous social media feeds.

In contrast, the male "adventurers" were busy applying copious amounts of fake mud and sand dust over themselves. Once the phoney dirt was applied, they pushed in front of each other to take unofficial selfies on their thousand-dollar mobiles while posing beside the large, red and yellow, liveried off-road motorbike that had been set up on the hillside, ready for the imminent dawn photoshoot.

All fifteen of the tourists shared the same dream, familiar to most young people of the modern era; to be noticed enough to gain hundreds of thousands of followers on the numerous social media streams that flooded the world's mobile devices on an hourly basis. Previous generations had fantasized about becoming rock or sports superstars, but such exalted fame demanded extensive practice, innate ability, and luck. Today's path to wealth is different. It involves projecting an image on social media that is so startling that it attracts followers who try to wear the same

---

[366] Citizen Skyhawk.

[367] Mar Tan's Contest Sheen & posing oil.

clothes, adopt the same postures and consume the same foods or drinks. Such is the world of the social media influencer, the modern generation's definition of success. This vision had motivated this group of fifteen to pay thousands of dollars to gain the chance to pose in some of the world's most dramatic scenery and pretend that they had single-handedly explored its dangers and delights.

Six hundred and eighty miles to the East, back in Beijing, the news that *the most dangerous man in the world*- terrorist mastermind, Issac bin Abdul Issuin, had single-handedly evaded and destroyed three elite falcon teams spread like wildfire through the PLA high command. The depth of the crisis, from such a loss of face[368], meant that, reluctantly, senior aides had roused the deputy party chairman[369] from his bed in his luxury villa surrounded by Jasmine trees, located in the Xicheng District of the Chinese capital.

Within moments of Major General Ying (in charge of military operations) hearing the news of the Falcon mission failure, he replaced supervisor Jip Keing. Six, armed PLA officers dressed in their dark olive green uniforms had stormed into the Falcon command and control centre and, after passing a plain manila envelope to Keing's assistant, promoting him, they frog-marched the terrified Keing from the room.

Less than an hour later, Jip Keing had been sedated and transported to a dilapidated but highly secure medical facility- where he awoke to find himself chained to a bed in

[368] Loss of face is, in oriental tradition, one of the worst things that can occur to a person, an organisation or a nation. Such pride in performance and integrity is incomprehensible to many in modern Western societies.

[369] Deputy Chairman of the Central Committee of the Chinese Communist Party (CCP).

a large ward containing numerous others in a similar state to himself. All of the men and women who were strapped to the beds had committed some offence against the State[370].

The loss of vision in Jip Keing's left eye after it had been removed, along with the searing pain in his chest and abdomen, confirmed that he had already undergone extensive surgery to remove several of his body parts. Having risen to a supervisory role in the PLA, he knew that his organs would already be on sale for donor transplants into the illegal black market. His fate would be as rapid or as slow as the demand for his remaining organs.

Back in a sparsely furnished fourth-floor office located in the tall white stone-fronted August 1st Building in Beijing, Major general Ying, the officer responsible for overseeing PLA activities that evening, was acutely aware that unless he took some immediate action to regain control over the Abdul Issuin fiasco, he would be likely to be joining Jip Keing in the organ donor ward.

Since, like most of us, Ying preferred to keep his internal organs internal, he picked up one of six phones on his desk and called the senior duty officer of the People's Liberation Army Air Force (PLAAF). Ying instructed that two of China's fifth-generation fighter jets be diverted from their current duties, patrolling in the disputed Air Defence Zone (ADIZ) "East China Sea[371]". The new mission brief for the two

---

[370] See the China Tribunal's report of Nov 2020, delivered by Sir Geoffrey Nice QC, to the British Parliament that provided evidence of an illicit trade of forced organ harvesting from ideological prisoners, contrary to Article 3 of the Universal Declaration of Human Rights.

[371] This contentious air exclusion zone exists in the intersection between CADIZ (China), KADIZ (Korea) and ADIZ Taiwan, respectively.

fighters was simple. Having been provided with the current location and the BeiDou (GPS) transponder details of the helicopter currently flown by Abdul Issuin, they were to seek and destroy the Falcon unit's remaining Z20 helicopter with utmost urgency by any means necessary.

Two hundred nautical miles[372] South East, from the August 1st Building in Beijing, where Major general Ying had issued his command, a Chengdu J-20[373] "Mighty Dragon" and a J-31[374] "Gyrfalcon" diverted from their scheduled patrol. Due to the nature of their revised commands, they took the shortest route towards a Xian H-6[375] airborne refuelling tanker that was located just off the Sino-North Korean border. The revised flight path took the two fighters directly over South Korea's air exclusion zone (KADIZ). It attracted the attention of the advanced radar surveillance systems[376] of the USS Carl Vinson (CVN-70)[377], the United States Navy's

---

[372] Equal to 230 statutory miles.

[373] The J-20 is a 50 million US dollar, single-seat, twinjet, all-weather, stealth fifth-generation fighter aircraft developed by China's Chengdu Aerospace Corporation.

[374] The J-31 is a twin-engine, mid-size fifth-generation fighter developed by Shenyang Aircraft Corporation. It's designs are based on a massive data hack from the US DOD Joint Strike Fighter program. The J-31 aircraft is intended for the export market as a much cheaper alternative to Western 5th generation fighters, such as the F22.

[375] The Xian H-6 refuelling tanker is a modified version of the Soviet Tupolev Tu-16 twin-engine jet bomber.

[376] Using the E-2 Hawkeye Airborne Early Warning Aircraft produced by Northrop Grumman.

[377] The USS Carl Vinson (CVN-70) carries 5,000 crew and 65 aircraft. It is the flagship of Carrier Strike Group One, based out of San Diego.

third Nimitz-class supercarrier, that was patrolling just off the South Korean coast.

The officer of the deck (OOD[378]) on the US nuclear-powered vessel assigned four F35s[379] to intercept the two Chinese fighters and escort them out of South Korean restricted airspace. Unfortunately, one F35 failed its preliminary launch tests. Shortly after take-off, a second F35 developed a software error in its navigation and avionics systems and returned to the Carl Vinson[380]. That left only two F35s available to scramble to intercept the two Chinese fighters. The US fighter jets flew in close trail formation (one behind the other) and accelerated to over five hundred and twenty knots[381]. Although the Navy F35 has a maximum speed of nearly eight hundred and sixty knots[382], it can only maintain that top speed for less than one minute. Consequently, the two F35s held to a lower cruising speed on a trajectory that would bring them within visual confirmation range with the two Chinese aircraft, some twenty nautical miles South of the North Korean border.

The assigned mission for the USS Carl Vinson was to provide South Korea, Japan and Taiwan with a demonstration that the United States would ensure that the KADIZ restricted airspace was monitored and defended. However, the F35's mission goal was most definitely not to

---

[378] The officer of the deck (OOD) represents the ship's commanding officer.

[379] The Lockheed Martin F-35 Lightning II. A 180-million-dollar, fifth generation fighter.

[380] The failure rate of the F35 is very well documented by the US DOD. The mission capable rate is so low that only 36% of F-35s are available for any required mission.

[381] 600 mph.

[382] 1000 mph (Mach 1.3).

engage in combat with the Chinese fighters. In the modern geopolitical landscape, where China was one of America's biggest trading partners and held over a trillion dollars of US treasury bonds[383], any rhetoric made against China by US politicians is almost entirely for the benefit of the US vassal states in the Pacific region. The reality was that regional tensions in the South China Sea provided excellent motivation for increased weapons purchases by nervous nations who looked to the US to protect them from actual and imagined threats. The visible presence of the US war machine provided not only reassurance but also acted as an excellent sales showroom for the expensive weapons technology that could be acquired from the US[384].

Although twenty-first-century combat pilots spend months training for classic aerial dogfights, as depicted in films like Top Gun, the modern reality is that massive investment and research over the past thirty years has transformed modern aerial combat into a sophisticated electronic game of cat and mouse. The future of warfare will focus on remotely controlled, un-crewed[385] weapons platforms, not on large and expensive aircraft that require a human operator inside to steer and control them. Modern combat aircraft and massive aircraft carriers still exist for the same reasons that mounted fusiliers (horse-riding cavalry) were deployed at the start of the Second World War by many nations-

---

[383] Dumping of the US Federal bonds would cause worse devastation to the United States than sinking one of their massive aircraft carriers.

[384] A strategy of stoking regional tensions to promote massive weapons sales is a common policy worldwide, not just for the US but also for other nations with a weapons industry.

[385] Unmanned is so gender specific I have opted for this alternative.

tradition and machismo. These motivations are often highly irrational and wasteful of lives and money.

The modern goal of air combat is to achieve *air supremacy from a distance*, where the distance between the hunter and target can be as far as two hundred miles from each other. In such a setting, complex, remote monitoring systems compete to be the first to achieve a target acquisition. Weapons systems designers compete with aircraft designers, each aiming to overcome the capabilities of the other. Aircraft designers aim to build aircraft that are invisible to tracking technology[386]. In contrast, weapons designers create weapons systems that can defeat the aircraft designer's attempts at invisibility. This ongoing contest means ever-increasing complexity in the aircraft and associated weapon systems. Such complexity is incredibly expensive and produces aircraft and weapons that become obsolete before they are finished[387] and are, by implication, unreliable.

For their part, the two Chinese fighter pilots were utterly focused on their assigned task of finding and eliminating the rogue Falcon Z20 helicopter in the wastelands of Outer Mongolia. Their airborne warning system[388], which was currently in North Korean airspace, had made them aware of two incoming targets from the South West. The extraordinarily low radar profiles and radar blocking

---

[386] So called stealth technology.

[387] Needing endlessly upgrades and changes to the requirements specifications that quickly render even the best designs into a chaotic set of improvised fixes.

[388] A KJ-500 ("Air Warning 500") is a third-generation airborne early warning and control (AEW&C) aircraft built by Shaanxi Aircraft Corporation.

countermeasures indicated these targets were fifth-generation stealth fighters with a size and speed profile that conformed with the United States F35 Lightning.

The Chinese KJ-500 airborne early warning and control (AEW&C) system predicted that the two F35s would come within close visual range with their current speed and course setting, literally seconds before the J-20 and J-31 would cross over into North Korean airspace. The two Chinese pilots briefly discussed the pending interception, and both agreed that the "baakgwai", or white ghosts[389], were merely making a show of force for their South Korean puppet regime. This non-confrontational solution to their incursion into the South Korean air space suited them perfectly. The reality of the situation was that neither side desired to engage in an unnecessary dog fight that could risk damage to their aircraft. Although both sides were flying the very latest fifth-generation air supremacy fighter aircraft, both planes were plagued with technical issues that would make actual air combat an extremely high-risk activity.

Although the F35 costs the US taxpayer nearly two hundred million dollars each, its design and development have involved numerous compromises and changes. For example, a congressional committee refused funding for an improved infrared search and track (IRST) system on the F35. Consequently, the fighter is not fast enough at acquiring a missile-firing solution[390] at distances over 79 miles to be utterly reliable- instead, having to wait until targets are within twenty miles to be sure of a kill. Further, the F35's 25mm cannon only carries 220 rounds, a total that would be quickly spent when firing at 3,000 rounds a

---

[389] A term for Caucasian Westerners.

[390] Called a weapons "lock".

minute[391]. If that was not bad enough, firing the F35's cannon is known to cause the aircraft's fuselage to crack.

Things are not much better for the Chinese J-20 and J-31 aircraft. Both planes result from extensive cloning and reverse engineering of designs taken from Western weapons development programs. The quality of the base components used in the construction of the Chinese aircraft can be quite variable. The engines and weapons systems are prone to catastrophic failure when subjected to extreme stress, such as in real-time, close range, aerial combat. Of course, these severe weaknesses are closely guarded state secrets. In public, both the Americans and the Chinese loudly proclaim that their aircraft are superior and would prevail in any head-to-head confrontation. The reality is that if the F35, J-20 and J-31 were to engage in combat[392], neither side would be clear winners, and such a contest would boil down to a battle between the US AIM-120[393] and the Chinese PL-15[394] missiles.

As it was, the four fighters briefly came within twenty miles of each other before the two Chinese jets passed into North

---

[391] Less than five seconds, in case you were too lazy to do the math.

[392] In considering such a confrontation it must be kept in mind that the Chinese strategy for using the J-31 is not to directly fight US F35s or F22s during a confrontation in the South China Sea. Instead, they intend to destroy the airborne fuel tankers and airborne radar aircraft required by the F35 and F22 in order to operate.

[393] The AIM-120 Advanced Medium-Range Air-to-Air Missile (AMRAAM) has a range of 86 Nautical Miles.

[394] The Chinese PL-15 (Thunderbolt-15) is an active radar-guided air to air missile designed to destroy Airborne Warning And Control Systems (AWACS) and Airborne Fuel Tankers, with a range of 160 Nautical Miles.

Korean airspace and the two F35s turned back on a course to re-join the USS Carl Vinson.

Later that morning, the American Secretary of Defense, Jane L. Maskins, held a press conference to announce that F35 fighters, deployed from the USS Carl Vinson patrolling in the South China Sea, escorted two hostile Chinese jets from Korean airspace.

Almost simultaneously, the North Korean Defence Minister, General Ho Ye-jun, announced a successful collaborative mission with their glorious allies to the North, overflying the rogue state to their South with complete impunity from Imperialist American forces.

20 HIDDEN BENEATH YGGDRASIL

"Fenrir, the great Wolf, will be fettered by Gleipnir[395] under the roots of Yggdrasil until the time of Ragnarok." – Chapter 34, Gylfaginning, Prose Edda. (Early 13th century Icelandic Saga)

880 Yards above Fortress Grmožur,
Lake Skadar,
Montenegro (near the Albanian border)

17:02HRS (GMT+2), 10th Sept, Present day

The swirling mass of red and black etheric matter that contained the projected consciousness of Magister Ironheart passed some seven hundred and eighty feet above where the physical body of the French adept was seated, near the top of the cliffs overlooking Fortress Grmožur.

Mathers' magical sealing of the seven sacred gateways to her body had temporarily halted the powerful signature of theurgic forces. These forces usually made the area around the French Adept's body appear as a swirling vortex of bright white and blue light to anyone gifted with clairvoyant vision. In addition, the thick grey mass of projected essence that surrounded her physical body, from her utilization of the Rosicrucian "Cloud of Invisibility", effectively obscured her physical form from all but the most curious of observers, including, in this case, the passing astral projection of Magister Ironheart.

---

[395] Gleipnir is as thin as a silk but stronger than any iron chain. It was forged by dwarves in their underground realm of Niðavellir to bind the great wolf of destruction.

Having failed to find the source of the focused Magical intent that he had detected while attending to the installation of the Qliphothic wheel, Ironheart had decided to expand his search and approach the nearby village of Godinje. He knew that there was another adept of advanced rank somewhere nearby, with an exceptionally pure technique. Such skills were rare and even rarer in the ranks of the Meri-Isfet, where most practitioners took the attitude that once they had acquired a technique to the minimum required level necessary to move to the following degree, they ceased to practice it. The magical operation that he had detected was of such purity that it spoke to decades of repeated practice. Only one magical order cultivated such an obsessive trait for perfection, the Meri-Maat. Typically, the two orders did not interact. Rather, it would be more accurate to say that adepts of the Meri-Maat avoided any form of magical confrontation with their rivals. For their part, the Meri-Isfet regarded the Paris council decision of 1682, where the Meri-Maat had sworn to only adopt defensive techniques, as just an excuse for the weakness that is always associated with cowards. In contrast, the Meri-Isfet promoted the aggressive use of Magick, believing that an attack was always the best response in any situation.

If an advanced adept of the Meri-Maat *had* dared to come looking for the Meri-Isfet in their headquarters, that was a disturbing development that needed to be handled with the utmost ruthlessness. Since he believed he was the rightful and future leader of the beloved of Isfet, Ironheart felt it was his responsibility to handle this situation without any need to confer with his fellow high adepts. He had already started planning the ruthless methods that he would use to deal with this upstart, to make such an example that the fate of this intruder would be remembered for generations. The fact that this intruder had hidden himself, yes, the Magister instinctively assumed his rival would be a male, indicated he was looking for the usual timid type who followed the way of harmony. Such idiots were best suited to reading and meekly practising whatever useless elements of the Great Art remained in their order after three hundred years without any actual tests of their powers.

Progressing slowly inland, at last, Ironheart noticed a very fine vortex of force projecting some twenty feet into the air above a point within the toad green leaves of one of the vineyards that faced the edge of Lake Skadar. Moving his astral body down, closer to the ground, he discovered that the source of these rotating spirals of fine etheric force was a classic, green and white Volkswagen camper van parked near one of the local farm houses. A water hose and a long blue power cable led from one of the outhouses of the farm to the camper van. One of the locals had decided to help this unwelcome guest. Approaching even closer, the Magister could sense, from the direction of the clockwise rotation of the spinning vortex of energies, the essence of a Right-Hand Path (RHP) adept of significant ability.

Although he still could not detect where the adept had concealed himself, Magister Ironheart rapidly recalled his projection to where his physical body remained, back in the fortress. After a few moments of deep breathing, he opened his piercing blue eyes. He then systematically moved his hands along his arms, legs, head, and torso, following the direction his hair grew, up the outer side of each limb and down on the inner side in the direction of the flow of the subtle energies that animate the physical form.

When performed with intent, such movements manipulate the ethereal body and reintegrate it with the chakras of the physical body. This procedure is necessary after any substantial or prolonged withdrawal of the ethereal body from the material. Having completed this astral reintegration, Ironheart rose and walked across the large stone chamber, past the newly installed Qliphothic Wheel, up a narrow stone stairway and into the command-and-control room for the fortress. Once in the control room, he barked orders for two boats to head immediately to the village. The first boat would contain four Wolfsangel operatives. The second boat would take a contingent of six, Meri-Isfet adepts, leaving the ten newly advanced seventh-degree adepts, who had arrived at the fortress the previous night, to continue with their preparations for the coming ceremony.

Meanwhile, some forty yards away from where the Magister coordinated the operatives under his control. The essence of the French Adept was in the medical facility of the fortress. Her projected consciousness glided past each of the sedated bodies lying on their beds within the long, white-tiled room. Mathers regarded the bodies of the European royal lines and the mysterious objects associated with each nation's history. Each of the camphor chests was surrounded by swirling esoteric force vortices. Depending on the nature and use of the items, these vortices rotated in either clockwise or anticlockwise directions. The colours of the associated fields varied between the dark reds and browns of violence and the purer whites and blues associated with more positive and constructive actions and intentions.

The French Adept reflected on the decades of preparation work represented here. Still, the question remained, why had the Meri-Isfet waited until now to gather these relics in one place, abduct the representatives of the European blood lines and obtain the St Petersburg Qliphothic Wheel? Mathers hoped that she could find a clue elsewhere in the vast island fortress.

Mathers' projection moved out from the medical area. It drifted along a narrow stone corridor, some twenty feet long, four feet wide and seven feet high, illuminated by electrical lights embedded into the ceiling. This walkway terminated with a grey metal-framed door that could have been taken from the bulkheads within a sizeable ocean-going vessel or a submarine. Fortunately, even though the door was sealed shut from the other side, the French Adept's projected form could pass through the reenforced steel without any hindrance. She found herself in another large, tiled room that looked like a freshly cleaned changing room at a sports centre. The area was furnished with long benches for seating, each in front of a row of grey metal cabinets. There was a flurry of activity taking place within the changing area. A group of four very athletic-looking men and women were outfitting themselves with a range of tactical gear, including night vision equipment and, ominously, knives and loaded pistols.

Beyond the section of the changing area that contained these four operatives, another entirely separate group of six men and women were becoming sky clad (completely naked) before dressing in far less threatening clothing, namely, dark red linen robes. The French Adept was not surprised when she saw the classic striking cobra motif embroidered on the backs of each red linen robe. If there had been any doubts in the French Adept's mind about the fortress being used and occupied by the Meri-Isfet, these robes dispelled them. Based on the initiation sigils that Mathers could detect in the auras of these individuals, five of this group were second-order adepts, holding the fifth degree of Adeptus Minor. The other, sixth individual, who was donning a purple vestment, carried the initiation sigils of all the second-order degrees, fifth through to seventh, and, in addition, two other distinctive features.

The first was an initiation sigil that the French Adept had never seen anywhere other than in ancient texts on the theoretical degrees beyond the mortal realm. If the sigil was genuine, this adept had successfully crossed the abyss that marks the limits of the second-order and had achieved the eighth degree, earning the magical rank of Magister Templi[396]. Although, on paper, this was only one degree higher than Mathers' seventh degree[397], the French Adept remembered the warning by her three mentors during their briefing in Geneva that they had no idea what powers or capabilities such an exalted adept might possess. Since Mathers already knew the names of the senior Meri-Isfet adepts, she could only conclude that she had encountered the Swede, Oscar Pedersen or, as he preferred to be addressed, "Magister Ironheart".

The second distinctive feature in Magister Ironheart's aura was more disturbing, for there was another entity, a non-human entity, integrated tightly into his entire incarnating essence. This other being was not just attached to his etheric body, as one frequently sees with a parasitic "dweller on the threshold" encountered in the aura of those who dabble with the occult communications, such as Ouija. Nor was it one of the non-physical entities (often artificially created) that delight in attaching to the lower three principles of living humans to manifest phenomena that encourage negative behaviours to induce strong passions in the victim's emotional bodies, on which they "feed".

In contrast to these kinds of astral parasites, this entity was fully sharing in all of Ironheart's vehicles of consciousness and manifestation, apart from the eternal tenth principle, which is impossible to share or integrate with another[398]. Clearly, at some point, Magister Ironheart had voluntarily permitted this nonphysical entity to bind and integrate into

---

[396] Denoted as 8=3.

[397] Denoted as 7=4.

[398] This tenth principle is immortal and is a part of the mystery of the manifestation of the universe, consciousness and the unknowable God.

all his mortal principles. Theoretically, such a connection would continue for as long as Ironheart remained in the cycle of incarnation[399]. Mathers knew that such a complete binding, called an "indwelling" in esoteric lore, would give the human partner significant advantages in terms of physical and occult powers. But this kind of conjoining came at a terrible price- the indwelling entity had complete control over all the incarnating principles of the adept. Such an indwelling meant that when the entity decided to terminate its indwelling, as they invariably did, the human host died horribly, their non-physical bodies fragmenting as the integrating entity violently separated away. If that wasn't a bad enough fate, the other outcome was worse. The surviving, eternal tenth principle of the human host would be unable to incarnate ever again within this current cycle of the universe[400].

Mathers reflected on the dangerous lengths to which some magical students would go to gain power and then returned her attention to observing Magister Ironheart. He was a physically huge man, in his late twenties, with piercing light blue eyes. He stood over six feet four inches tall, and Mathers estimated he must have weighed nearly two hundred and sixty pounds- with the size and build of an American football player. His large, muscular head was utterly devoid of hair except for a long, blond goatee beard on his chin that had been braided and adorned with Scandinavian bead decorations, including the Mjölnir[401] and other protective rune symbols. Ironheart's powerful, muscular body sported numerous tattoos and ritual

---

[399] Occult students are taught that we repeatedly incarnate with the same souls.

[400] Esoteric lore says that we are in one of an endless cycle of universes.

[401] Thor's Hammer.

scarification marks over it, most devoted to Nordic mythology. The one exception to the Nordic theme was shown on his right forearm and portrayed the classic Meri-Isfet striking snake's head.

The rarefied nature of Mathers' consciousness existed at such a high vibratory rate that the molecules that triggered the sensations of taste and smell were no longer perceived. However, the auric colours surrounding the body of the senior adept indicated that Ironheart had adopted the relaxed attitude towards personal hygiene so frequent in the Viking Age and, in more modern times, within the Aghori sects of India, where filth is regarded as a holy state of existence.

Looking around her, the French Adept felt compassion for the more junior adepts who attended on Ironheart[402]. Based on the customs of the Meri-Isfet, the personal disciples of a senior adept were expected to be available for any Magickal practices. Both male and female disciples were used in Ironheart's sex magick rites and were mandated to consume Ironheart's bodily fluids as a holy sacrament, in much the same way that Catholics consume the wine and bread at the Sacrament of Holy Communion.

Forcing individuals to submit to the sexual desires of senior adepts was regarded as a perverse abuse of power by SPLEE. In contrast, SPLEE viewed each individual as having the right to decide if they wished to participate in any form of ritual, let alone sexual magic and if they did want to participate, they could choose with whom they partnered in

---

[402] In reality Mathers should not have expended too much concern, as the junior adepts viewed Ironheart in much the same way as Ironheart viewed his fellow secret chiefs of the third order; namely as inconveniences that needed to be removed so he could assume their power and knowledge.

such rites. The consumption of excrement or its worship did not constitute any part of the SPLEE's magical practice.

While Mathers was reflecting on the fate of the junior adepts, the two groups of men and women in the changing area responded to a command from Ironheart. They abruptly filed out of the changing rooms, through a double swing door, down a descending stone staircase, and out onto a small internal jetty constructed in the lowest levels of the fortress. This jetty led into a concealed cave entrance set into the island's bedrock on its Eastern side. Moored to the jetty were several small vessels, primarily devoted to cargo transport, but there were also two twenty-two-foot-long, rubber Pro 7, Zodiac dinghies. The assortment of ten people, six dressed in robes and four in black tactical clothing, entered these two Zodiacs and, after starting the 250 horsepower Yamaha outboard motors, proceeded out of the concealed cave and headed in a Northerly direction towards the mainland.

Resuming her search through the fortress, the French adept returned from the jetty to the changing area. Then, after passing through another locked and sealed grey metal bulkhead door, proceeded down an unlit stone-walled corridor that led to a pair of large, oak doors with ornate carvings inset into the wooden surfaces. These ornate wood carvings included sigils from classic Goetia[403] that would have been familiar to anyone with a copy of the *Lemegeton*

---

[403] Goetia is the ritual evocation of evil. The term is derived from the Ancient Greek "γοητεία" meaning "sorcery or witchcraft". As Heinrich Cornelius Agrippa stated, "Now the parts of ceremonial magic are goetia and theurgia. Goetia is unfortunate, by the commerces of unclean spirits made up of the rites of wicked curiosities, unlawful charms, and deprecations, and is abandoned and execrated by all laws."

Clavicula Salomonis[404]. Passing through the thick wooden door, Mathers found herself in a large space, one hundred feet long, sixty feet wide, with a high classically vaulted stone ceiling some twenty-five feet high. The area had been designed from its initial construction as a ritual space, as the floor and walls had the requisite markings carved into them in preparation for one particular ritual. Such specificity is unusual in ceremonial magic, as normally, such spaces are used for a wide variety of ceremonies. The banners and floor designs are laid out for each ritual. Then, after the ritual is completed, the items are packed away in storage.

Mathers recognised the arrangement of the temple, from her research in some of the oldest of the SPLEE's archives, as the layout for the "Decem et Aperire Portas" or Opening of the Ten Gates (OTTG). The OTTG is one of the most ambitious ceremonies in ritual magic and can be performed in both its positive (creative or Life) or negative (destructive or Death) aspects. The OTTG ceremony had not been performed for many centuries within the SPLEE due to the need for seventh-degree adepts to be posted at each of the ten spiritual gates to be opened.

Many modern esoteric scholars believe that the concept of the ten emanations[405] of the "Tree of Life" or, for LHP adepts, the "Tree of Death" within the Hermetic Western Esoteric Tradition (WET) are derived from some fifteenth and sixteenth-century Jewish Kabbalistic texts[406]. The truth is that the concept of the "Tree" with spheres that show the aspects of the manifested creation is, in fact, much older,

---

[404] Lesser Key of Solomon. A classic grimoire of Goetia.

[405] Sefirot, ספירות, meaning emanations from the unknowable godhead.

[406] Such as the Bahir, Zohar and Gikatilla's "Gates of Light".

appearing in ninth-century BCE Assyrian texts[407] and the most archaic, hand-carved ceramic tablets within the SPLEE library.

As the French Adept contemplated the enormous resources needed to construct such a dedicated temple structure, she focused her astral perception on ten red-robed figures who were busy practising their respective roles within the LHP version of the OTTG ceremony. At first glance, they looked like any other group of ceremonial magicians preparing for a significant ritual. However, a closer examination showed some unusual features. The auras of all these ten individuals showed very recent additions of all three of the second-order initiation sigils, indicating that they had made extremely rapid progress through the fifth, sixth and seventh degrees. The Meri-Isfet was famous for enabling the rapid progress of students who could aid the order's goals, but these initiations were so recent that the auras had not yet healed around the grade sigils. Such fresh sigil "burns" within the aura of a recently initiated candidate were not unusual. Such burns were always only for the most recent initiation, not for all three initiations and not for a group of ten individuals. Normally, even within the Meri-Isfet, there was a gap of years between each degree as the candidate studied the curriculum and completed the requirements to advance to the following degree. In Mathers' order, progress between each of the three, second-order degrees usually took decades to complete, not the mere days indicated in the sigil burns evident on these ten individuals. In addition, these ten adepts were exhibiting techniques so rough and imprecise that they would pose a danger to themselves and everyone else inside the ritual space if they performed many of the

---

[407] See Parpola, Simo (1993). "The Assyrian Tree of Life: Tracing the Origins of Jewish Monotheism and Greek Philosophy". Journal of Near Eastern Studies. 52 (3): 161–208.

techniques they were trying to complete. Finally, as the French Adept concluded her assessment, it was clear that these ten individuals did not understand the meaning of the ceremony they were rehearsing. There was something seriously wrong with the entire situation. Why had the Meri-Isfet expended such enormous effort to construct a specialised temple dedicated to a specific advanced ceremony and then deploy such completely unprepared magical practitioners, wondered Mathers?

The strange rehearsal was being coordinated by an eleventh individual, who was also dressed in what Mathers recognised was the red, working ritual robes for the second-order within the Meri-Isfet. This Director of Ceremonies had more normal initiatory sigils, showing he had advanced to the sixth degree of Adeptus Major at a more normal pace. The director of ceremonies was guiding the practice from a large red leather-bound book propped open in the centre of a podium. This lectern was located outside of the central ceremonial space, marked by a pair of silver circles inlaid into the stone floor, with a diameter of thirty feet.

Since the French Adept was not that familiar with the LHP OTTG ceremony, she approached the lectern. She began to read over the shoulder of the director of ceremonies from the pages of the book that were currently open. She immediately noticed that the OTTG ceremony they were practising was significantly different from the standard versions she had seen described within the SPLEE Geneva library. This LHP interpretation of the ceremony had a distinctive Scandinavian flavour, which was not entirely surprising, given Magister Ironheart's involvement, but what was shocking to Mathers was the source book guiding this ritual practice. Standing on the lectern was one of the most infamous texts of Scandinavian magical lore, *The Rauðskinna*- the grimoire of grimoires for the Nordic dark art of Galdr! The text had been thought by occult scholars to have been lost when it was buried with Bishop Gottskálk "grimmi" (the cruel) Nikulásson of Hólar on the eighth of December 1520. However, annotations in the margins of the text indicated that legendary Galdr master Loftur Þorsteinsson (better known in the history of the Nordic dark arts as *Galdra-Loftur*) had acquired the book and tried to understand and master its numerous secrets.

The *Rauðskinna*[408], also known as "The Book of Power", was alleged to provide its reader with the procedure to summon and control the manifestation of ultimate evil, the giant wolf of destruction described in the Viking Sagas, Fenrir. As Mathers gazed at the ink sketches of the enormous baying canine depicted on the bound human parchment, the French adept noted, with considerable disquiet, that the images in *The Rauðskinna* were identical to the pictures Thomas O'Neill had sent to her phone yesterday- drawn by the possessed patient, Mrs Susan Widee.

There was also a handwritten astrological chart beside the opened, flesh-coloured pages of the Rauðskinna that Mathers recognized had similarities to the charts for the current period shown to her by her mentors in Geneva. But, if it was to be believed, the chart lying beside the Rauðskinna had been drafted in Paris, as a paid commission[409] by one Michel de Nostredame[410], to portray the ideal times for opening the Qliphothic Gates for a six

---

[408] Literally "Red Skin" – This unusual name is derived from the colour of the binding and pages, that were made from the skin of Saint Veiðimaður; one of the Christian settlers found on the Icelandic islands when the pagan Vikings first took possession of the Icelandic islands around 873 CE.

[409] In return for immunity to the plague that had been unleased in Europe at the time.

[410] You probably know him better as "Nostradamus".

hundred year period from when the chart was cast, in August 1550.

These charts showed peak astrological alignments for performing OTTG ceremonies on June 21st 1908, August 1st 1930 and several dates during the early 1940s. Then there was a gap before another suggested optimum period around the current year, which explained the timing of Nissa Ad-Dajjal's recent attempts to acquire the Emerald Tablets. The optimum alignments subsided for the weeks immediately following Ad-Dajjal's death[411] but returned to a maximum in the middle of the current month of September and then continued for two further months before subsiding for the next fifty years. Having read the chart, the French Adept finally understood why the Meri-Isfet had decided to move the St Petersburg Wheel to their base here in Montenegro at the current time.

A hand-scrawled footnote, written in English[412] at the bottom of the old astrological chart, noted that September also aligned with the annual appearance of the Perseids meteor showers[413]. Mathers realised that any Qliphothic Wheel activity would trigger substantial cometary fragment impacts on the earth, possibly onto centres of population,

---

[411] On August 14th

[412] Presumably by Magister Ironheart.

[413] The rock and ice fragments that impact our planet each fall to create the annual Perseids meteor shower originally formed part of a 16-mile-wide comet called "109P/Swift-Tuttle" that still orbits around the sun, passing our earth every 133 years. Swift-Tuttle is at least twice the size of the meteor that caused the Cretaceous–Tertiary (KT) extinction event 66 million years ago. This massive comet was discovered in 1862, independently by both Lewis Swift and Horace Tuttle, hence its name. Three years after its discovery, Giovanni Schiaparelli identified that Swift-Tuttle was the source of the Perseids.

increasing the sum of suffering on the planet- one of the dark goals of the Meri-Isfet.

Now that the French Adept had solved one riddle related to the timing of the current activity of the Meri-Isfet, she turned her astral perceptions back to the Temple that her refined consciousness was currently inhabiting. The one thing that remained a puzzle to her was that the St Petersburg Wheel did not feature as the centre piece of the sacred ritual space where the group of ten red-robed adepts were practising. Instead, where she would have expected The Wheel, there was a very detailed silver inlaid floor decoration in the centre of the magick circle, depicting a circular pattern of Icelandic characters spelling the single word, "Urðarbrunnr"[414]. Mathers recognised the name as the Sacred Well that the Viking Sagas described as existing beneath the sacred Ash tree called Yggdrasil[415]. The French Adept quickly concluded that this indicated something significant under the ground, so she willed her consciousness through an immensely thick series of reinforced concrete, stone and steel layers beneath her feet to find herself in an underground chamber, roughly twenty feet square.

In stark contrast to the recreation of an ancient Ritual Temple in the chamber above, this space was a sleek modern installation. It featured massive concrete, titanium and steel fixings supporting the small but incredibly heavy, opaline-coloured St Petersburg Wheel that Mathers had seen delivered on her arrival at Godinje. There were thick titanium tram rails set into the floor, leading from the wide double doorway to the centre of the small square room, obviously used to bring The Wheel through the fortress. These rails passed beside several six-foot-wide, rivetted

[414] Known as the Well of Wyrd that formed and controlled destiny.

[415] The World Tree.

steel electrical conduits connected to eight massive turbine engines that dwarfed the small, green, Trubka cylinder.

Everything that the French Adept had seen during her prolonged astral observation of Fortress Grmožur confirmed that the Meri-Isfet planned to resume the accursed, Qliphothic obsessed practices of their ante-diluvian predecessors and recklessly endanger all of creation in the process. As Mathers considered what actions she could initiate to prevent the operation of the St Petersburg Wheel, she suddenly became aware that a non-human consciousness had begun to observe her physical body back on the cliff top, a mile away.

21 THE ART OF WAR

"Appear weak when you are strong, and strong when you are weak." - Sun Tzu

Two miles West of Yoliin Am Valley (Valley of the Vultures)
Gurvan Saikhen Mountains,
Gobi Desert,
Southern Mongolia.

05:49HRS (GMT+8), 10th Sept, Present day

The most dangerous man in the world sat on the torn and stained, black rubber flooring in the open, left-hand, rear-side sliding door of the black Z-20 helicopter, his legs dangling over the edge of the door ledge. His black, synthetic, tactical boots rested on the thick gravel, dirty sand and small rocks scattered over the uneven ground between the massive boulders that currently concealed the Harbin Z-20. The pre-dawn air of the Gobi Desert provided a refreshing change from the stuffy atmosphere inside the helicopter, filled as it was with a potent mix of sweat, rubber, cigar smoke and oil. In the stillness of the morning, the only noises were from the WZ-10 turboshaft engines, creaking and groaning as they cooled down above the black, armoured airframe of the helicopter.

As the hawk-faced assassin sat in the door frame, he pondered if he had physically recovered enough from his injuries and malnutrition to successfully storm the tourist group who were posing for photographs on the motorcycle, some two hundred yards above him on the steep sandy slope. Abdul Issuin estimated the incline to be twenty-six degrees[416] , and he knew, instinctively, that, when fit, he

---

416 Roughly a forty eight percent angle.

would cover such an inclined, six hundred feet in well under thirty seconds. Given that there were only two men, both armed with 9mm pistols, watching over the group and neither would be expecting an attack, if he was in perfect health, there was a 98% probability of killing both armed guides before either had drawn their weapons. However, when the assassin measured the pulse at his carotid artery, he found it elevated at fifty-six beats per minute, not the forty-eight that he would typically expect when at rest at 8000 feet above sea level.

Having discovered mention of ten kilograms of gold in the linen expedition journal, he knew that, if it existed, it would make his escape considerably easier- so it was worth waiting to see if the tourist group would move off soon. He was acutely aware that the Chinese PLA would be reacting soon to the termination of their three elite commando units, so he would need to leave this location within the next forty-five minutes. For now, he was content to sit and wait. He decided to enjoy another of the five inches long, Montecristo No 4s, from the crumpled paper pack that he had acquired from the body of Su-Fin, the Falcon unit commander. The unit commander had a taste for the finer things in life, and Abdul Issuin decided that if he acquired the gold, he would treat himself to a supply of these Habanos[417], among other things. His recent close brush with death and the cruel way his leader, Ad-Dajjal, had treated him at the end convinced him that life was much too short not to indulge in its many luxuries. From now on, he would serve only himself and his interests- after dealing with the Scotsman.

---

[417] The Cuban company that controls export of premium cigars for Cuba worldwide. The company name is often used to refer to a high-end Cuban cigar, such as the Montecristo No 4.

As the hawk-faced assassin drew deeply and exhaled the cigar smoke, he continued to skim read through the linen-bound log book that described a long expedition from Berlin on the pioneering commercial passenger flights that operated, even during wartime. The four German explorers had used fake Swedish Passports[418] to fly from Lisbon in Portugal to Shannon International in Ireland and to the United States. Once having crossed the American continent, these four fake Swedish explorers embarked on a sixty-hour, multi-stop journey via Pan Am[419], from San Francisco to Manila in a 'China Clipper[420]. They then went on to a series of smaller planes through Japanese-occupied Shanghai and finally to Peking[421].

If the log book was to be believed, along the way, the four men visited numerous sacred sites located in or near the places they stopped. They looted several priceless religious icons and artefacts before moving on. When the four explorers finally arrived in the Chinese capital, they acquired two local guides and equipment before heading out on the final length of their journey to Mongolia.

Interestingly, Abdul Issuin noticed that on the back pages of the journal, it stated that the expedition had decided to leave most of its gold with the local Union Bank of

---

[418] Sweden was famously neutral during the second world war.

[419] The once famous airline company, Pan American Airlines.

[420] A Martin M-130 seaplane. This massive propeller driven aircraft could carry over thirty passengers for ranges over 3,500 miles.

[421] Peking (so named during the 1937 Japanese invasion of China) was renamed to Beiping in 1945 (after the surrender of Japan) and then renamed to Beijing in 1949.

Switzerland[422] (UBS) representative at an address in Peking. The handwritten addendum described how the team leader opted to bring only thirty gold, twenty-mark[423] coins. The remaining bullion would be retrieved when the expedition returned to Peking. According to the journal, the presentation of the expedition leader's silver ring, with its unique inscription, was the only identification required by UBS to recover the deposited gold.

As the most dangerous man in the world looked thoughtfully at the distinctive skull-shaped ring on his finger, his thoughts were interrupted by some excited chatter on the cockpit radio and the sudden sound of an insistent low buzzing from the interior of the Z-20. Rising from where he was seated, Abdul Issuin resumed his position in the pilot's seat and examined the complex onboard combat surveillance systems. The heads-up display showed two distinct incoming targets, both flying low and at supersonic speeds. From their behaviour, they were fighters, and from their different profiles, they were two different types of aircraft. Surprisingly, the sophisticated A.I. classification system that had effortlessly identified vultures, owls, rats and the Bell 525 Relentless helicopter could not get sufficient information to identify the aircraft. The hawk-faced assassin concluded these incoming targets were sophisticated fifth or even sixth-generation[424] stealth fighter jets. Clearly, the Chinese had

---

[422] UBS was the favoured international banker for certain individuals during the second world war.

[423] Minted until 1915 these 20-mark coins provided 0.25 ounces of .900 fineness gold.

[424] The Chinese claim their latest fighter jets are sixth generation while all other fighters, including the F22 and F35 are merely fourth generation.

decided to send their most cutting-edge weapon systems to make sure of eradicating the hawk-faced assassin.

Abdul Issuin needed to estimate the ETA[425] for the two jets. He checked his watch and noticed, for the first time, that the icy air from the pre-dawn Gobi had chilled his HNLGNOX watch, causing the glass to steam up. The scalding water from the hostel washroom had defeated the watch's rubber gaskets. He checked the UTC[426] time shown on the instrument panel, the speed of the incoming targets in knots[427] and their distance from him in nautical miles. There were roughly twelve minutes before the two aircraft would arrive and unleash their wrath on him.

Stepping out of the Z-20, he calmly walked out onto the rocky floor of the broad valley, encountering the chill of the desert morning that reminded him of his native Egypt. As he walked into the valley's centre, planning how he would deal with this latest threat, the hawk-faced assasin pondered if he would ever return to his beloved Egypt. Maybe, he decided, after settling the score with that devil, Tavish Stewart.

He dismissed his thoughts of revenge and focused instead on the task at hand; how to best use his terrain. He was in a vast, steep-sided valley, some fifty yards across and several miles long, heading roughly West to East. The wind was blowing gently from the East at around three knots. Although his watch was water logged and no longer trustworthy, he could sense, from the colour of the sky, that dawn was now less than ten minutes away. He knew instinctively that in early September, at this altitude, latitude

---

[425] Estimated Time of Arrival.

[426] Coordinated Universal Time or UTC is the primary time standard.

[427] A Knot is a nautical mile per hour.

and longitude, the sun would rise almost precisely along the alignment of the broad valley.

Walking calmly back towards the parked Z-20, he gazed up at the sight of the adventure tourists, who were now busy posing for their set motorcycle photographs. The two Australian guides took numerous pictures on a large Canon EOS-1D digital camera. The loud giggles and chattering showed that the group were utterly unaware of Abdul Issuin, his helicopter and the potential for violent chaos that was about to unfold in their immediate vicinity. In anticipation of what was to come shortly, a wicked smile began to form on the hawk-like face of the most dangerous man in the world. Once back inside the Z-20, he removed a large aluminium suitcase and an orange distress flare gun. Stepping outside the main sliding door, he carefully placed both objects between some of the larger rocks so they would be shielded from the debris scattered from the rotor downdraft when he restarted the helicopter.

He resumed his cockpit seat, strapped himself in and then restarted the WZ-10 turboshaft engines. While he waited for the rotors to reach full speed, he enabled the aircraft's BeiDou encrypted military satellite navigation system, announcing his precise position to the incoming Chinese jets. He then decloaked the Z-20 and flew the aircraft slowly and deliberately out into the centre of the gorge, rising high enough to be clearly seen above the high-sided valley's rims. Two adventure tourists noticed the sleek, black helicopter and broke away from the group. Using their mobiles, they began to take numerous selfies with the sleek, black military helicopter hovering behind them. Soon the entire group followed suit, apart from the two Australian guides, who were the only members of the seventeen viewing the strange aircraft with any concern.

Meanwhile, back in the cockpit of the Z-20, the hawk-faced assassin was assessing the position of the incoming jets, waiting for them to adjust course and altitude now that they had a clear position for their target. Once the two fighters had moved into what would be the start of their first approach run from the East, heading through the narrow valley towards him, Abdul Issuin activated his helicopter's weapons guidance systems. After taking a deliberate aim at the side of the valley, some three miles ahead of him, he launched one of the eight LJ-21[428] missiles located in the pair of stub wings mounted on either side of the Z-20.

The seventy-three-inch-long missile sped away from the helicopter's left side with a bright yellow flame trailing from its rocket engine. It accelerated to just under six hundred miles an hour before the high-explosive anti-tank (HEAT[429]) warhead detonated into the high-sided valley wall. The explosion raised dust and rubble into the air and sent a cloud of fine sand high into the atmosphere- completely obscuring the valley to the East of where the Z-20 was hovering.

The chatter on the encrypted inter-aircraft communication channel that was fed to the throat microphone and earpiece worn by the hawk-faced assassin indicated a reaction of hilarity from the two Chinese fighter pilots. Abdul Issuin's grasp of Mandarin was sufficient for him to understand the two pilots laughing at the complete incompetence of their target; to aim and miss with a computer-guided, fire and forget weapon. So much for the most dangerous man in

---

[428] The LJ-21 ("Blue Arrow-21") has a range of eleven miles, carries twenty pounds of high explosives and, by a strange coincidence or excellent espionage, is remarkably similar to the United States, AGM-114 Hellfire missile.

[429] A HEAT warhead utilizes a shaped charge explosive that employs the Munroe effect (ejecting super-heated material into the target rather than explosive force) to penetrate heavy armour, such as a tank, an armoured aircraft or a cliff side.

the world! An arrogant complacency grew in the two pilots at how easy this kill would turn out. While the two fighter pilots were busy congratulating themselves over their anticipated success, the thick smoke and dust from the explosion into the valley wall began drifting slowly, carried in the three-knot prevailing wind, down the valley towards the West.

Up on the valley slope, where the adventure tourists were busy posing for selfies with the Z-20 in the background, excitement turned rapidly from wonder to terror at the missile's launch, followed by a massive explosion so relatively near to them. The two Australian guides began urging the group to get back into the Bell helicopter. Once all seventeen people were aboard, they started the Bell's General Electric T700 engines in preparation to leave, abandoning the items laid out for the photoshoot in preference for imminent escape.

Back on the Z-20 helicopter, the hawk-faced assassin waited until the cloud of debris that he had deliberately created obscured the Z-20, at which point he returned the helicopter to its place between the two massive boulders on the valley floor, turned off the location transponder and enabled the visual shielding. By the time the cloud of dust had passed on further down the valley to the West, the Z-20 had vanished from sight and from all the sophisticated weapons guidance systems fitted to the Chinese fighter jets.

The two Australian tour guides, Oliver and Jake, had now taken off and headed down the valley to the West at nearly one hundred and sixty knots. The Bell relentless quickly passed into the thick clouds of dust and debris floating down the valley and became so obscured that only its outline was visible.

Seconds later, a blur passed through the valley, followed by the roar of twin jet engines, as a Shenyang J-31 stealth fighter[430], the first of the two Chinese jets, arrived. The mass of airborne debris and dust floating down the valley obscured and deflected the sophisticated target identification systems of the fighter sufficiently to prevent a positive target identification. However, the fighter pilot could make out the distinctive shape of the spinning rotor from a medium-sized helicopter, making its way at over one hundred and fifty knots away from the scene of the recent missile discharge.

The People's Liberation Army Air Force (PLAAF) command-and-control centre back in Beijing, supervising the fighter operation, authorised the aircraft to engage. At the same time, the pilot of the second jet, currently waiting its turn to make its attacking pass down the valley, added his support by yelling through the encrypted communication channel.

"Kāi qiāng" (take the shot!).

Inside the concealed, hovering, Z-20 helicopter, a smile spread over the lips of the most dangerous man in the world. He continued enjoying the smouldering Montecristo and watching his plan unfold.

Due to the floating debris cloud, the weapons systems of the J-31 fighter jet were unable to gain a definitive lock on the fleeing target, so the pilot resorted to the aircraft's 30mm cannon, firing directly into the obscured shape that was inside the thick dust cloud. The armour-piercing rounds systematically shredded the fuselage of the unarmoured Bell helicopter until the fuel tanks were penetrated with one of the fighter jet's tracer rounds[431]. The

---

[430] The Shenyang J-31 (F-60) is a fifth-generation, multi-role, twin-engine stealth fighter aircraft capable of 1200 knots which is just under 1,400 miles per hour.

[431] Tracer ammunition (tracers) are bullets with a small pyrotechnic charge in their base that burns brightly and makes the trajectory

entire helicopter exploded in a gigantic fireball, killing all seventeen occupants instantaneously. The smouldering metal remnants of the Bell Relentless cascaded over the valley floor as the Chinese J-31 fighter sped through the remaining dust cloud and soared back up into the morning sky.

The J-31 fighter celebrated completing its mission by soaring into the air, completing a turn, half loop and waggling its wings in an exaggerated victory roll[432]. The pilot then brought his aircraft to a higher altitude, above the long valley, heading back in the opposite direction (to the East), to where the jet had started its attacking run some moments earlier[433]. While the J-31 returned to the origin of its attacking run, the second fighter, the larger Chengdu J-20[434] "Mighty Dragon", commenced its passing run down the narrow valley to check that there were no survivors. The pilot held the powerful fighter at close to its stalling speed of just two hundred knots to carefully scan the area.

As the slow-moving J-20 Mighty Dragon passed by the two large boulders, where the hawk-faced man's concealed Z-20 helicopter hovered, Abdul Issuin reacted with cat-like speed. Aware that this second pass down the valley would quickly reveal that the first jet had taken down the wrong target, he manoeuvred his aircraft up and round ninety degrees, in a single smooth motion, so the nose of his Z-20 pointed

---

visible, allowing the shooter to see the flight path of the projectile and correct their aim, if needed.

[432] A manoeuvre used by fighters since the second world war to mark a successful operation.

[433] This is a variant of a Chandelle, one of the Basic fighter manoeuvres (BFM) used by fighter jets in classic dogfights to gain positional advantage over their opponent's aircraft.

[434] The Chengdu J-20 is a stealth air superiority fighter.

towards the flaming, rear jet engine of the J-20 fighter. Abdul Issuin then accelerated his helicopter to its top speed, chasing close behind the powerful jet fighter.

The hawk-faced assassin locked his weapons systems onto the J-20's Turbofan, Xian WS-15 engine, that was not stealth shielded and prepared to fire his 50mm cannon. Inside the cockpit of the J-20, a loud warning siren screamed, alerting the pilot to the weapons lock from his rear and causing the pilot to begin performing violent evasive side to side movements and engage the full thrust of his Xian WS-15 engine. Once the engine had reached full power, the J-20 Mighty Dragon began to perform a steep, vertical climb to try and escape its pursuer. However, the warning siren commenced again as the Z-20 helicopter exhibited its incredible manoeuvrability[435] by coming to a stop and raising its nose to follow the path of the powerful J-20 fighter.

Moments later, the J-20 Mighty Dragon exploded in a massive fireball in the blue desert sky as one of the Z20's LJ-21 air-to-air missiles detonated its HEAT warhead into the fighter jet's engine. The hawk-faced assassin then scanned the air above the massive explosion until he could see the plume of a grey-coloured parachute deployed from the fighter's ejector seat. Once he had located the slowly drifting parachute canopy, he pitched the helicopter around in the air towards the descending target. He fired his 50mm cannon, tearing the small object into multiple pieces that fell rapidly to the rocky desert ground.

---

[435] Tests by the US Airforce (J-CATCH, short for Joint Countering Attack Helicopter tests) have shown the helicopter to be five times more manoeuvrable than fighter jets under actual combat conditions. Helicopters achieve a five to one kill ratio against fighter jets. Prompting the US TOP GUN instructors to inform their pilots to "Leave the f**king helicopters alone."

The most dangerous man in the world relished this confrontation as he smiled and savoured an extra-long draw on his Montecristo No 4. Although he had enjoyed the contest, he had paid the price, for the g-forces and violent manoeuvres of the last few minutes had reopened the wound in his side, causing a growing blood stain to form on his flight suit. His enjoyment of the kill was momentary, as the heads-up display showed the J-31 'Gyrfalcon' had turned and was moving back towards where the Z-20 helicopter had just shot down its companion jet and the ejecting pilot.

The pilot inside the J-31 'Gyrfalcon' had seen the consummate skill with which the helicopter pilot had dealt with the J-20 Mighty Dragon. It was clear that the two pilots had vastly underestimated their opponent and had been unwittingly drawn into a masterfully planned ambush. The remaining pilot resolved not to make the same mistake twice, so he remained flying well above the confined space of the valley and outside of the range of the Z-20's LJ-21 air-to-air missiles. Using the sophisticated weapons target tracking systems of the Gyrfalcon, the pilot locked on to the hovering Z-20 and prepared to engage his PL-10 'Thunderbolt-10[436]' short-range air-to-air missiles.

Meanwhile, in the Z-20 helicopter's cockpit, multiple alarms were sounding to alert Abdul Issuin of the full weapons lock against his aircraft and the imminent launch of air-to-air missiles. For his part, the hawk-faced assassin attempted to get his own weapons guidance systems to lock on to his

---

[436] The PL-10 'Thunderbolt-10 is a 9 foot long, "look and shoot" missile with 15-mile range and a conventional explosive "blast frag" (like a giant hand grenade) warhead.

rival's aircraft, but the J-31's stealth design[437] made it impossible.

Accepting that the destruction of the Z-20 helicopter was imminent, Abdul Issuin enabled his 50mm cannon. He fired while deliberately tilting his aircraft nose down, so the aim of the machine gun was low. Instead of firing toward the J-31, the machine gun razed the ground fifty yards in front of the helicopter with fully automatic 50mm shells. Desert sand and rocks were blasted fifty yards into the air, creating another dust cloud that was quickly caught in the three-knot wind and carried East to West down the valley towards the doomed Z-20 helicopter.

Back in the J-31 'Gyrfalcon' fighter, the pilot was non-plussed. He began to wonder if he had overestimated his opponent and that his success so far had been down to pure luck. No matter, he thought, it was time to end this idiot's life once and for all.

As the small dust cloud reached the Z-20 helicopter, Abdul Issuin leapt from the hovering aircraft through the open side door. Before the dust cloud he created had time to disperse, he ran over to the cover provided by the two massive boulders he had used earlier to conceal his aircraft.

Seconds later, a streak of steel and fire lashed down from the sky. The magnificent Harbin Z-20 rocked violently before exploding in a loud and violent detonation reverberating around the valley's high walls. Finally, scorched, red hot metal fragments began cascading down from the sky as what remained of the transport helicopter rained down to the valley floor.

---

[437] Acquired by a particularly attractive intern who was "mentored" (at least that was how the executive described the relationship to the CIA) by a senior executive at Lockheed Martin Aeronautics Company "Skunk Works".

High above the valley, the J-31 fighter pilot took a long, slow turn to pass by again to double-check that no one was left alive. As the fighter commenced its turn, a lone figure sauntered into the middle of the broad valley, carrying an aluminium suitcase and an orange flare gun.

After aiming high into the air, the solitary figure fired once, straight up with the pistol, sending a distress flare high into the sky and highlighting his exact position to the approaching fighter.

The pilot of the J-31 'Gyrfalcon' looked on in disbelief at the solitary figure standing beneath the slowly descending flare. The man was wearing a black outfit that could not have stood out more prominently against the lighter coloured desert floor of the broad valley. It was almost like this man was taunting the fighter to come and finish him.

"愚蠢的混蛋" (Stupid Bastard!)

Exclaimed the pilot as he brought his fighter jet back down into the narrow valley and commenced a low strafing run. As the J-31 jet came within two miles of the lone figure, it began unleashing its 30mm cannon into the ground, anticipating the massive bullets tearing the solitary figure into small pieces.   But, rather than trying to run away, as any sensible person would, the lone figure instead bent over and opened an aluminium suitcase. He unfurled a large, thirteen-foot diameter antenna dish from inside the case before standing behind the unfurled electromagnetic projector that now pointed towards the incoming jet.

As the hawk-faced assassin looked up into the oncoming J-31 jet that was unleashing the full wrath of its 30mm cannon towards him, he watched a large arc of lightning issue from the suitcase. The static charge caused the hair on the hawk-faced man's body to rise as a massive sizzling sound of intense static electricity began to fill the air.

The most dangerous man in the world looked directly at the J-31 and smiled as he drew deeply on his Montichristo No 4.

By the time the pilot of the J-31 'Gyrfalcon' recognized the NNEMP weapon, known as Wú yān long or "Smokeless Dragon, it was too late. His aircraft had utterly lost control. The fifth-generation fighter had been deliberately designed to be aerodynamically unstable to increase manoeuvrability. This instability required sophisticated artificial intelligence and fly-by-wire technology to remain airborne. The jamming of all its electrical systems meant the J-31 became nothing more than a lump of garbage, even its ejector seat failing to operate. Seconds after the Smokeless Dragon had started working, the J-31 flew straight into one of the cliff sides, creating the biggest explosion of the entire confrontation.

A jet black, unmanned space craft called Yaogan 31A[438], flying some seven hundred miles above the Gobi, had recorded these dogfights. The images were streamed live to the party deputy chairman as he consumed his breakfast of soybean milk and deep-fried golden dough sticks on the veranda overlooking the Jasmine trees in a spacious garden in the Xicheng District of Beijing. Twenty minutes later, just after Yaogan 31A moved out of observation range and before Yaogan 31B took its place, a large BMW off-road motorcycle sped down the long valley towards Beijing in an Easterly direction.

---

[438] YAOGAN-31 A is part of a trio of Chinese military reconnaissance satellites.

22 AT HER MAJESTY'S DISPLEASURE

"No one truly knows a nation until one has been inside its jails. A nation should not be judged by how it treats its highest citizens but its lowest ones." – Nelson Mandela

Holding Cell 2, Exceptional Risk Wing
Her Majesty's Prison Belmarsh (HMPB)
Thamesmead,
Western Way, London, SE28 0EB

10:30HRS (GMT+1), 10th Sept, Present day

During her arrest, after the demonstrations the previous evening in New Bond Street, Dame Cynthia Sinclair had been immediately hooded. This unprecedented violation of Sinclair's rights was based on direct instruction from the new Prime Minister, overruling The Cabinet Office Consolidated Guidance (COCG) that prohibits the use of blindfolds on Captured Persons (CPERS).

Sinclair had been assessed as an "Exceptional Risk[439]" detainee and was transported, by two, armed SO15 officers, in a distinctive red liveried Diplomatic Protection Group (DPG) BMW 5 Series estate car to Thamesmead, in the East End of London. Where, still wearing her hood, Sinclair allowed herself to be frogmarched across a large gravel courtyard that was one hundred and fourteen paces long[440]

---

[439] The highest category of risk for a detainee within the British Criminal Justice system. The risk assessment can be in terms of the danger the prisoner poses to staff or other prisoners and the probability that the prisoner might escape.

[440] It is standard operating procedure for an agent to count the number of paces when escorted over any space so they have an accurate estimate of distances for any attempted escape.

, leading to a North facing[441] building. The air was filled with the distinctive, pungent aroma that is only associated with the proximity of sewage plants. The strength of the odour was such that even the material of the black hood she was wearing did little to detract from its pungent, penetrating stench. Given the gusting, variable wind, and the consistency of the odour, Sinclair estimated that such treatment plants surrounded her. Although she had not been informed of where she had been brought, only one location in the capital matched the current olfactory evidence, Belmarsh.

Her Majesty's Prison Belmarsh (HMPB) is between Crossness Sewage Treatment Works and the Beckton Sewage Treatment Works. Opened in 1991, this category "A" prison usually only deals with the most dangerous convicted male criminals. However, after the closure of Paddington Green Police station, Belmarsh is also used to detain those arrested under the provisions of Part 4 of the Anti-terrorism, Crime and Security Act 2001. Such prisoners can be detained indefinitely without charge or trial and effectively made to "disappear" from the British Criminal Justice System and public scrutiny until their long-term fate is decided.

Most prisoners at Belmarsh enjoy the extensive recreational facilities of two gyms, a sports hall and a fitness room, run in partnership with Charlton Athletic FC, which offers these dangerous individuals coaching courses. However, those prisoners like Sinclair, arrested under the Anti-Terrorism Act, enjoy far fewer facilities and are kept separately from the other 910 inmates.

On Sinclair's arrival, her fingerprints were taken, and she was subjected to the standard front, and side mug shot photographs. She was then escorted under heavy guard to

---

[441] Determined by Sinclair from the direction of the warm sunlight on her back as she was led from the diplomatic protection vehicle.

"Exceptional Risk" Holding Cell 2A. This was a regular, one-person cell, twelve feet long and six feet wide. The small room had heavily scuffed, black vinyl flooring, wipe clean, painted, light blue walls, fluorescent strip lighting, a matching steel WC & sink combination and a metal-framed bed without a mattress. Later, Sinclair was provided with a thin plastic-covered mattress and a single grey woollen blanket as prisoner-specific issued items. On the wall opposite the bed was a black 20-inch unbranded wall-mounted TV with fifty stations devoted to sports or 24-hour news coverage.

Once seated on the bed in her cell (there was nowhere else to sit), a male warder provided Sinclair with basic white polycotton underwear and a standard grey marl polycotton sweat suit that is issued to all new British prison inmates. She was also given a single bar of unperfumed soap, one towel and a standard HMP toothbrush. Before leaving the cell, to permit the former SIS director to wash and change, the warder asked Sinclair to put the clothes she had been wearing during her arrest into a clear plastic evidence bag. It was noticeable that when the warder returned, forty-five minutes later, to take away the evidence bag, he also collected the soap, towel and toothbrush, presumably to avoid giving Sinclair any possible weapons or means of suicide.

Unlike the substantial three-course meals offered to ordinary inmates, at the five-thirty pm dinner time, a warder brought Sinclair a sad-looking sandwich made from two slices of dried stale white bread containing a single piece of processed cheese, presented on a white paper plate. After consuming this meal, a short series of interrogations commenced. These interviews were just formalities that had to be completed to document that due process had been followed.

Sinclair was questioned in rapid succession by two different groups of rather non-descript, middle-aged men. The first pair were dressed in the dark polyester off-the-peg suits that, based on Sinclair's experience over the past two days, seemed to be standard issue for MI5 operatives. As these two agents left Sinclair's cell, they were immediately replaced by another two more elegantly dressed officers from her own Foreign and Commonwealth Office (FCO). Both pairs of interviewers brought their own sets of near-identical government quartermaster-issued equipment, a JVC camcorder, Mnemosyne brand ring-bound notebooks and disposable, clear plastic BIC pens. Neither interview lasted more than ten minutes.

During the first interview, the two domestic security officers produced the Raffica gun that had, they alleged, been used in the indiscriminate New Bond Street shooting. The weapon had the same serial number as the weapon confiscated by MI5 from Sinclair the previous day, which she witnessed being taken by Wolfsangel operatives, along with the dead bodies of the two MI5 agents. The fact that Sinclair's lookalike had then used this same weapon at New Bond Street before reappearing now in the hands of MI5 after her arrest confirmed Sinclair's existing suspicion of significant collaboration between the domestic security service and Cortez's Wolfsangel forces.

She was more disappointed by the attitude of her own FCO colleagues towards the preposterous accusations that she was a terrorist who was stupid enough to open fire on unarmed civilians in front of live TV cameras. She had, after all, been successfully leading SIS for several years, and she thought she would have earnt some respect from her agency. The change of government had realigned people's loyalties. After the abrupt removal of Sir Richards from the FCO Principal Private Secretary role that morning, the new leadership of the FCO were happy to throw the former SIS

Director "under the bus[442]" to save their department's reputation with the new Prime Minister.

After these two perfunctory interrogations were over, Sinclair was visited by a Mr Brown, a smartly dressed young man with short brown hair and glasses, who was Belmarsh's Prison Service Welfare Officer (PSWO). Brown asked numerous questions to determine if Belmarsh's latest inmate needed to be placed on suicide watch. After Brown finished his gentle, very obviously targeted chat and was satisfied that the new inmate was not a risk, he left the small cell shortly before 23:00HRS, just as the prison lights were turned out for the night.

After almost forty-eight hours of minimal sleep, Sinclair was so exhausted she would fall asleep almost anywhere- so the thin mattress was not an obstacle to her getting nearly nine hours of deep and dreamless sleep.

She woke when a shrill bell and the cell's fluorescent lighting returned at eight AM. Shortly afterwards, the cell door opened. She was presented with a paper bowl containing two Weetabix, a white plastic spoon, a paper cup of instant coffee, and sachets of whitener and sugar, all presented on an old, green plastic tray. As Sinclair sat on her bed and started to consume this welcome breakfast, the TV on the wall opposite her came to life and started showing the news summary from one of the morning breakfast shows that are a staple of daytime TV.

The smartly dressed female announcer, who was wearing a dark trouser suit, stood beside a wall-sized screen showing the mass protests that had taken place yesterday in every major capital city around the world. The images switched from city to city, showing angry people of all ages and nations demanding action against Stewart and Curren for

---

[442] A slag term meaning to callously discard.

their misdeeds.   The news presenter then introduced the next segment filmed yesterday in Hyde Park, London. Over a million people had assembled to demand Stewart receive punishment for "the murder of billions of people and the largest criminal extortion in human history".

The new British Prime Minister, Sir Reginald Twiffers, and the former opposition leader, Sir Johnathan Premble stood on the podium in the centre of Hyde Park. However, through their repeatedly shouted demands, the crowd insisted that the new coalition party Chairman, Senor Cortez, address them. Cortez made a big show of not feeling that he should be the one to "represent the wishes of the people".

For their parts, Twiffers and Premble looked at first surprised and then frightened as they realised that, in the blink of an eye, they had lost control over the situation. They had grown accustomed to being treated with deference due to their democratically elected leadership positions. However, the power of an angry mob transcended those of democracy and the rule of law.   Thanks to some masterful social manipulation, Twiffers and Premble were now just irrelevant older men, facing an angry mass of over a million people, all shouting and demanding,

"Cortez!"

"Cortez!"

"Cortez!" over and over.

The Argentinian smiled slyly as Twiffers and Premble reluctantly stood to one side and gestured for Cortez to approach the podium, which he did, after making another big show of modesty.   The elegant Argentinian was wearing a long grey cover coat, which he removed and passed to one of his numerous assistants. This disrobing revealed a T-Shirt that showed an image of Stewart grinning as he held his blood-soaked hands facing whoever was taking the picture. Behind this photoshopped image of the Scotsman were many bodies of older men, women and children. All covered in a series of gruesome wounds and cuts. Under the picture, written in dripping blood from the two gore-soaked hands of Stewart, was the slogan, "Return the Trillions! Justice for the Billions!".

The cameras focused on the image and text printed on Cortez's shirt in a mastery of timing. The image played perfectly to the emotions running through the psyche of the crowds since it was an image and pair of slogans that had been filling social media streams from social influencers for the past hours. The sight of Cortez's T-Shirt made the crowds explode into screams of delight, as clearly, they felt there was one person who understood the intentions and passion of the people.

Cortez acknowledged the adulation and gestured for silence then; as that silence spread not just through the crowd in Hyde Park but also through the similar mass gatherings around the world- who were watching the live streaming of this event, he addressed his spellbound global audience,

"Friends, this is not a time for words. This is a time for action. While weak democracies,"

Cortez subtly gestured towards Twiffers and Premble beside him, who looked startled and increasingly out of their depth.

"...struggle to respond, with their pathetically slow bureaucracies, that are institutionally biased in favour of those with backgrounds of wealth and privilege, like *SIR*, Tavish Stewart...."

Cortez made an artificial exaggeration of the pronunciation of Stewart's title, prompting boos, jeers and hisses from the crowd. A smile formed on Cortez's face as he raised his hands for silence again before continuing,

"I want what you want. No, I demand what you demand! Immediate action! Since I am a simple man, I will offer a simple solution. I offer one billion euros to anyone who brings this monster, Tavish Stewart, to justice!"

At this announcement, the worldwide crowds went wild with screams and cheers of joy. Clearly, the millions of people all felt they had a leader, a real leader, who could take action, not mislead and obfuscate through weasel words and corrupt deeds, like their elected representatives.   The news coverage showed similar responses of delight and rapture from the gathered millions in every other world capital as the Hyde Park meeting was being televised live.

Suddenly the crowd began to pump their right fists into the air in unison together, in what looked like a spontaneous act but was, in reality, being led by specific influencers in the crowd. The mass of over a million people in Hyde Park chanted,

"Cortez!"

"Cortez!"

The news broadcast showed this mass salute and chant spreading across the crowds gathered in all of the world's capital cities until it reached a loud, repeated salute. This phenomenon struck fear into the elected world leaders standing on their respective podiums similar to those set up in Hyde Park in each nation around the world. The enthusiasm of the angry crowds caused the normally calm politicians to look genuinely terrified as they realised their authority had been usurped. After brief consultations with their advisors, each made the same decision- rapidly leaving every event and scurrying away to waiting black luxury limousines, surrounded by their security details.

Sinclair shook her head at the images of the mesmerised crowds in London, Paris, Berlin, Moscow, Washington, Tokyo and every major nation, all shouting and saluting in unison for one single man. The pictures looked like they had come straight from 1930s Nazi Germany for anyone with even the weakest grasp of European history.

Sinclair sighed in despair, "The Nuremberg rallies all over again."

The news presenter then moved to the next segment.

"In separate news, during the London protests yesterday, there was a tragic event – viewers are advised that some of the following scenes may cause emotional triggers."

The following clip showed Sinclair coming out of Stewart's showroom and shooting down numerous police, protesters and TV crews. Noticeably, the footage had been edited and enhanced to include more blood and death than had actually taken place.   The footage then switched to pictures of Sinclair being forced into a blue Ford Transit police van, even though, in reality, it had been a red, DPG, BMW estate car. A short clip of Sinclair followed this footage in an interview room, where she acknowledged she had been working for decades at the deepest levels of the government to undermine the British people and their corrupt values while secretly working for Stewart and his Maelstrom group.   Again, at no time had Sinclair made such an admission, and the surroundings shown in the deep fake interview were far more luxurious than the small cell that she occupied in Belmarsh.

After cutting from these deep-faked images, the news switched to a live press conference held at 10 Downing Street by Prime Minister Twiffers and Chairman Cortez. It was noticeable that Twiffers looked considerably more tired and stressed than usual and was distracted by a short, strange-looking, older woman with large rose-coloured glasses who stood nearby.

Twiffers cleared his throat and began,

"People of Britain, I have been shocked and horrified by the unprovoked carnage that took place yesterday in New Bond Street and the recorded statements given by the former Director of the Secret Intelligence Service, Cynthia Sinclair. It is clear that Dame Sinclair is not and has never acted for or on behalf of the interests of the United Kingdom. Therefore, she is to be stripped of her title, and her assets are to be seized both in the UK and in her home in Jamaica, with immediate effect.

The press conference showed police in Jamaica arresting Sinclair's parents and seizing the Sinclair family property. While in the UK, Sinclair's Horseferry house apartment was shown as being emptied of its contents.

Twiffers continued,

"In consultation with The Palace, we have also decided to strip Tavish Stewart of his titles and military decorations and seize his ancestral estate in Scotland."

The TV coverage switched from Downing Street back to the news presenter.

Sinclair sighed. Her title loss did not bother her; it was just a vanity after all. She was more distressed by the arrest of her family and their loss of income from the rum distillery that had been in her family for generations. Similarly, she was sure that Stewart cared little for his titles or decorations, but he would be distressed by the loss of his family estate. Cortez was clearly determined to destroy their reputations before he had them both killed. For, by this time, there could be no doubt that death could be the only outcome of this grim pantomime.

Back on the TV, the news presenter then smiled as she announced,

"In some rare good news from this breaking story, Helen Curren, Stewart's lawyer, who we now know, played the role of Nissa Ad-Dajjal in the recent UNITY scandal, was found wandering around Rome Airport by Italian authorities late last night. Italian police are understood to be interrogating Ms Curren. However, she appears to be under the effect of powerful sedatives assumed to have been administered by Tavish Stewart, the evil mastermind behind the recent global massacre of over four billion innocent people and the extortion of trillions of dollars from members of the public and the world governments."

Sinclair was shocked, at least Helen was alive, but her drugged state immediately caused the former SIS head to wonder at the fate of the Scotsman who had, after all, set out the previous day to rescue Curren.

The newscaster drew her news summary segment to a close,

"Finally, a review of the video evidence by a panel of judges at the Hague has resulted in a global Interpol warrant for Stewart's arrest. Sources at the Hague confirmed that once Stewart is found, he will be escorted by the United Nations Police (UNPOL) to be detained at the International Tribune for Crimes against Humanity in the Hague. Because of Stewart's crimes, the judges will almost certainly make an extraordinary revocation of Article 114 of the Dutch Constitution and implement the death penalty. This execution will be the first since March 21, 1952, when SS Officer Andries Jan Pieters was shot by firing squad for the torture and execution of Dutch resistance members.

As of this news release, Tavish Stewart remains at large. Thanks to the generosity of Chairman Cortez, an unprecedented reward of 1 billion Euros has been issued for information leading to the capture of the Scotsman."

The news summary ended, and the broadcast returned to the breakfast studio.

Sinclair rose, turned off the TV, and emptied her coffee cup before crushing the paper container and dropping the crushed cardboard remains onto her breakfast tray, remarking coldly.

"What a fucking mess. Even Tavish may not be able to escape from Cortez's tangled web."

23 THE DARK FORTUNA

*"And now we must pass mention of those relics of antiquity
that came to reside in Italia (Italy). The strangest and most
powerful being a small female figure known as Fortuna
Tenebris (The Dark Fortuna). This effigy was claimed by its
worshippers to be that of Aset (the Goddess ISIS) and was
brought from the Temple of Philae in Kemet (Egypt). For
many centuries this effigy resided in the Temple of Fortuna
Primigena." - Publius Cornelius Tacitus, Annales (Annals),
116 CE.*

*Presidential Suite,
The St. Regis Rome,
Via Vittorio E. Orlando, 3,
00185 Roma RM, Italy*

11:30HRS (GMT+2), 10th Sept, Present day

Mr Tavish Stewart woke from a deep, dreamless sleep,
blissfully unaware of the infamy that had descended on his
reputation during the past twenty-four hours. A fall that was
courtesy of numerous social influencers, their countless
followers and the expertise of the digital media editors at
Beyond Facts Inc. As the Scotsman slowly returned to
consciousness, he was at first uncertain of where he had
been sleeping for the past ten hours. Before his eyes
focused, his nostrils had already detected the aroma of fresh
linen. As he slowly raised his head from the crisp white
pillow to take in his surroundings, he noted he was lying
alone in a king-sized bed, his naked body covered only by
the cool white sheets of a hotel bed. But this was not just
any bed. Pulling back the mattress cover, Stewart noted the

"Vi-Spring Monarch" label that denoted one of the world's finest mattresses[443].

Sitting up on the edge of the bed, the Scotsman took in his luxurious surroundings. He was in a large bedroom, twenty-five feet square, with a twelve-foot high, ornate plaster ceiling and wide, partly opened sash windows letting in streams of sunlight and the sound of nearby traffic. In addition to the traffic noise, there was also the sound of an antique clock ticking; its 19th-century ivory dial showed 11.30 am, a late start for the Scotsman, but he had been without rest for over 48 hours.

Resting on a black marble bedside table to his left was a traditional hotel room key, with a large brass keyring decorated with a long red tassel that would presumably make it difficult to lose the key. Seeing the long red tassel acted as a trigger that prompted the Scotsman to remember the events of the previous evening.

After the violent clashes in the Meri-Isfet Temple buried deep under the Coliseum, Stewart and O'Neill took a few moments to reflect on the conflicting emotions running through their minds. There was, of course, immense relief at having dispatched the demonic monster known as Sister Christina. Still, that joy was tinged with the frustration of failing to save Helen Curren, combined with the shock and grief at the violent death of their friend, Conrad De Ven, whose warning phone call had brought Stewart to Rome in the first place. O'Neill's injuries made him look like he had been in a horrendous car accident, and, as a result, he was unable to articulate even the most straightforward phrases

---

[443] The Vi-Spring, Monarch is a blended mattress filled with cashmere, lambswool, and mohair. A hollow bamboo frame absorbs moisture and helps with ventilation around the body, making it one of the most comfortable mattresses in the world but also one of the most expensive.

from his bloody and misshaped mouth. Consequently, Stewart made a simple prayer over the body of De Ven as O'Neill administered the last rites, as best he could, without any of the usual oils or vestments. O'Neill's beloved iPhone and Nite Mx10 were smashed into numerous fragments, but he recovered his sim card by scrabbling on the stone floor and feeling around the smashed phone casing. The last thing he wanted was for the Meri-Isfet to get hold of his contacts list or call history and place the French Adept Mathers in danger. Sadly, his treasured watch was beyond any recovery.

Stewart and O'Neill then walked very slowly and carefully, avoiding falling over any of the numerous bodies in the smoky darkness that permeated the vast hall. They were guided by the sole remaining candle flame that flickered in the hallway entrance that had survived the recent ceremony. On reaching the stone doorway, the lighting improved considerably as the pairs of torches that lined this end of the corridor remained burning.

Stewart was keen to move through the hallway back to the exit but was stopped by O'Neill, who gestured that he wanted them to examine the contents of some of the numerous, large plastic crates that had been stacked outside the temple entrance. The injured priest had specific boxes in mind for examination. He rapidly separated two containers with paper labels, written in a fine script, one for "Magus Regio" and the other for "Magus Salvador".

Regio's storage box contained a two-piece Gammarelli suit in worsted wool, a matching black clerical shirt, a white dog collar, oxford lace-up shoes, a leather wallet with a Vatican ID card, a VISA credit card and 2,000 euros in cash. Stewart made a point to soak these items in the blood of the dead samurai, Kenzo-San and then left the ID card, Visa charge card and cash in a prominent position so they would be found by the police and link Regio with the decapitated body.

Inside the other crate, labelled for Salvador, was a three-piece suit in dark grey worsted wool. According to the label inside the jacket, it had been hand-tailored by Luigi De Carlo, who Stewart recognised as one of the leading bespoke tailors in Buenos Aires.

"Expensive."

Remarked Stewart as he went through the other items left in the dead Magus' storage chest. There were a pair of polished Loake Foley leather brogues, a fine white Egyptian cotton Oxford shirt, and a blood-red Thai silk cravat. Embedded into the fine red silk was a highly distinctive, 18kt gold tie pin, carved in the shape of an aggressive, hooded snake that was posed and about to strike. Alongside the clothing was a dark leather Montblanc wallet, an 18kt gold IWC watch on a dark leather strap, and a red tasselled old-fashioned hotel room key with the words "St. Regis – Presidential Suite" and finally, a set of car keys with a remote-control key fob.

A business card inside the wallet described the recently deceased Magus as "Señor Edwardo Salvador" and gave his address as Villa Salvador, Petrona Eyle 450, Buenos Aires, Argentina, on the Puerto Madero Waterfront; one of the most exclusive regions not only of Buenos Aires but the whole of Latin America. Salvador's wallet had over 22,000 Euros in high denomination notes that Stewart pocketed before throwing the credit cards and the rather flamboyant gold watch back into the plastic crate.

The Scotsman could see the disappointment on O'Neill's face, so he explained,

"These bastards caused all your injuries, so it's only fair that they cover your medical bills."

Stewart then continued, as O'Neill had pulled out his Vatican health insurance card from his wallet,

"Put it away. If I know Regio, he has already phoned all the local health providers to be on the lookout for that health insurance card. You will have to go private and claim you had a car accident. You certainly look like it. I would become....." Stewart peeled off the sticky label from the plastic chest, "Mr Salvador."

O'Neill nodded his agreement as he took the name sticker from the Scotsman and put it in his wallet.

Having reassured the priest, Stewart took the white cotton shirt from the plastic crate they were examining and wiped down the Fabarm Martial Pistol he had used to blast the demonic form. He did the same with Kenzo-San's 9mm pistol, the Teales leather ammunition belt, the holster and finally, the Gladius sword; until he had removed all traces of his fingerprints. After everything had been cleaned, Stewart placed the items in the plastic crate, along with his blood-soaked Canali coat.

Stewart then gestured to O'Neill to continue making their way to the stairway exit at the far end of the long corridor, highlighted by the shafts of bright sunlight that streamed down from the level above. On the way along the dimly lit corridor, the Scotsman paused twice. Once to wipe the fingerprints from the hilt of the Roman gladiator's dagger protruding from the face of one of the dead operatives, and again, to pick up Kenzo-San's sword and wrap it in the discarded grey robe that the samurai had worn before his deadly charge at Stewart.

As they progressed, O'Neill became increasingly shocked by the carnage around them and began to fully appreciate the odds that the Scotsman had faced to save him. Reaching the top of the stairway, they could hear the sounds of pitiful animal cries, interspersed with an angry growling that matched the violent shaking of one of the trapdoor flaps within the raised wooden platform. O'Neill looked quizzically at Stewart, who explained,

"Attack dog."

And then halted the well-meaning, animal-loving priest from lifting the wooden trap door and freeing the dog inside, adding,

"Trust me; it is best to leave Fido inside. Let animal welfare deal with him."

When the two men finally descended the Coliseum's main entrance ramp, they found the outer wire gates had been unlocked and left open. Around twelve of the sleek black executive limousines that had been parked when Stewart arrived were now missing, including Regio's massive BMW seven series.

"Must have driven it himself."

Remarked Stewart as he pressed the car key remote they had taken from the Argentinian Magus' storage crate. An old-fashioned low sprung red sports car that was partially hidden behind a large black Mercedes S Class with EU flags responded with a loud bleep, prompting Stewart to exclaim,

"Bloody Hell, Salvador certainly had expensive taste."

O'Neill, who knew very little about sports cars, looked towards the Scotsman for a further explanation.

Stewart clarified, "It's a Ferrari[444]. If it's genuine, then it's worth a small fortune[445]. Only a few hundred were made between 1962 and 1964."

---

[444] It is a 1964 Ferrari 250 GT Berlinetta Lusso.

[445] Millions of USD.

O'Neill looked less than impressed, so Stewart explained, as he walked around the car admiring its sculpted form,

"Its sleek lines, balance, and performance make it one of the finest sports cars ever made by Enzo Ferrari."

The priest shrugged; he preferred the thrill of being the first to explore an ancient site; as far as he was concerned, cars were just a means to get from one place to another. The priest pulled open the passenger door to the big Merc and went to get inside but was stopped by the Scotsman, who preferred the bright red Ferrari. O'Neill looked surprised and mimed, with gestures of shielding his eyes as if the Ferrari was brightly illuminated, that he felt the car was too conspicuous.

The Scotsman nodded but then explained his preference for taking the sports car,

"The great thing about such a car is that it is so famous that no one will pay attention to us. Especially in Rome, it would be like walking beside Monica Bellucci along Via del Corso[446]."

O'Neill grimaced in pain from an involuntary chuckle as the Scotsman guided the priest over to the Ferrari and opened the side passenger door. O'Neill's chest injuries meant that Stewart had to help lower the priest into the red leather bucket seat. Once Stewart was in the driver's seat, he turned the ignition and listened to the beautiful burbling noise from the three-litre V12 engine.

The Scotsman's theory proved correct, as the heavy traffic stopped dramatically along the entire length of Piazza del Colosseo and cleared a way for the red Ferrari to pass. The air became filled with the sounds of numerous car horns and repeated shouts of,

---

[446] Via del Corso is the busiest shopping street in Rome.

"Viva Enzo! Viva Ferrari!"

Stewart and O'Neill waved thanks to the repeated gestures of goodwill, and O'Neill grinned through his badly bruised face for the first time that afternoon. The triumphant beeps and shouts followed the progress of the red sports car as it headed around the Coliseum, South along the Via Celio Vibenna and then North on the Via Corso di Francia toll road. It took just over twenty minutes before they arrived at their destination- an exclusive private clinic known for the quality of its health provision and its highly discrete treatment of the rich and famous. With the funds they had recently acquired from the Argentinian playboy, Salvador, the Scotsman was optimistic that they could get the treatment that O'Neill urgently needed and maybe even some for himself after all his recent close-quarter combat.

The Clinica Sola in Villa Flaminia is a five-storey white modern building set off the Via Luigi Bodio. O'Neill was becoming increasingly stiff from his injuries when the Ferrari drew into the car park. Stewart had to get assistance from one of the clinic orderlies to extract the badly injured priest from the low bucket seat and into one of the centre's wheelchairs.

As O'Neill went into the clinic, Stewart placed the red Ferrari under the watchful eye of the car park attendant, thanks to a one-hundred-euro tip and the promise of a similar sum on Stewart's return. By the time the Scotsman re-joined O'Neill in the clinic's reception area, the topic of payment had already begun to be discussed.

The receptionist clearly anticipated problems with this new arrival based on her experience with non-Italian walk-in patients- especially those who claimed to have been involved in an automobile accident but had injuries obviously related to physical violence. Thankfully, these reservations evaporated when Stewart withdrew a thick wad of 200 Euro notes and made a substantial deposit for the immediate start of O'Neill's treatment.

As if by magic, suddenly "Mr Salvador" became one of the clinic's most important clients. He was assigned one of the two overnight emergency beds and put into the care of a senior visiting physician who specialised in head and upper torso trauma. The man's name was Dr Georg Henriks, a tall thin Swede with a shock of dark blond hair, square glasses and a kind face, who appeared beside O'Neill's bed. After a preliminary examination, Henriks announced that Thomas had lost all his teeth, had four fractures to his jaw and cheek bones, and multiple fractures to his ribs. He queried if the clinic needed to notify the police about the brutal beating that "Mr Salvador" had suffered and looked dubious when Stewart said "No," and O'Neill shook his head. But the Dr accepted their assurance and continued,

"Very well. This evening, we will schedule surgery to insert pins and wires into the jaw and then fit tooth implants. The procedure will take around eight to ten hours, and Mr Salvador will need to wear full-face bandages and protection for some days afterwards. He may be able to be discharged late tomorrow afternoon if all goes well. He must return to us or his local medical facility every seven days to see if there is no infection and the healing is progressing well. We will provide a course of painkillers to alleviate the pain during recovery when he has left the clinic."

Henrik then looked at the extensive bruises and cuts that were in evidence over Stewart's hands, arms, neck and face and remarked,

"Did you need me to examine your injuries as well?"

The Scotsman thanked the Dr but declined the examination, preferring instead to let Henriks begin prepping O'Neill for his surgery, promising to return to check on progress in the afternoon of the following day. Stewart then went into the hospital wash room and cleaned himself as much as possible before heading back to the Ferrari and settling his debt with the car park warden.

Stewart picked up the distinctive hotel key they had recovered from the plastic crate and reflected on his situation once inside the classic sports car. It was inevitable that Regio would have started searching for O'Neill and for Stewart, involving more of those private security goons he had encountered at the Coliseum and the resources of the Vatican, which were considerable. However, if Salvador had already checked into the Regis Hotel, then there was a possibility that Stewart could use his room, avoiding a hotel registration process and potentially evading any ongoing searches. They would probably be looking for two men, not one. Given the promiscuous nature he assumed for the deceased Argentinian playboy; it was perhaps not unusual for "additional guests", both male and female, to stay with Salvador when he was in Rome.

The St. Regis Rome is one of the Italian Capital's finest hotels, if not the finest. As the classic red Ferrari drove along the Via Vittorio E. Orlando, the hotel's doorman, dressed in an old-fashioned top hat and matching long brown coat, clearly recognised the car. Thankfully for Stewart, the Scotsman's theory about the highly flexible attitude to guest occupancy demanded by the high paying, dead Argentinian playboy proved correct. Opening the driver's side door, the hotel's porter invited the Scotsman into the hotel,

"Buonasera signore, farò parcheggiare la macchina, per favore andate nella suite."

(Good evening, Sir, I will have the car parked, please head up to the suite.)

If the elegant doorman or the waiting baggage attendant thought anything about their new arrival's stained and torn clothing or his bloodied face and hands, they said nothing. Clearly, the wealthy Argentinian invited a wide variety of individuals to come and share his room while staying at the Regis. Stewart thanked the doorman while discretely folding a twenty Euro note into his gloved hand and then followed the baggage attendant through the foyer and towards one of the old-fashioned cage door elevators. Stewart nodded to the two women in reception and held up the presidential suite key as they passed by the check-in desk. They smiled warmly back, clearly accepting Stewart's use of the room. As he passed through the lobby, the Scotsman thought to himself that the interior of the Regis had been decorated and furnished in the style of a 19th-century palace, with marble tiled mosaic floors, crystal chandeliers and plinths decorated with the heads of Roman politicians. The seats in the hotel lobby were filled with a mix of the wealthy and those who aspired to meet the wealthy.

The old-fashioned concertina-style doors on the elevator concealed that the elevator walls were made of glass, permitting a panoramic view over the interior of the palatial hotel foyer. The luggage attendant pressed the first button, and they went up a single floor, and then exited the grand elevator and made their way to a dark wooden door labelled "Presidential". This door proved to be merely an external soundproofing barrier, and the suite's entrance proper was at the end of a short hallway. The attendant took Stewart's key and then opened the door, making a grand gesture for the Scotsman to enter.

Inside the Presidential Suite was a long, narrow hallway with a black and white marble floor that led to the main bedroom on the right and a living room and bathroom to the left. A tall sash window was at the far end of the hallway, looking out over Via Vittorio E. Orlando. The master bedroom had a king-sized bed with a mirrored headboard and an ensuite bathroom with black marble walls and fixtures. The large living room was furnished with two sofas positioned in front of a vast high-definition LG television. Beside this seating area were a dark wooden business desk with a high-backed leather office chair, a brushed aluminium 27inch iMac computer and an HP colour laser printer. Beyond the computer desk was a double glass door that led out onto a small balcony that looked out over the Via Vittorio E. Orlando directly beneath and, to its right, the Fontana del Mosè and the busy Piazza di San Bernardo.

After the Scotsman had finished his brief tour of the suite, he tipped the attendant with a twenty Euro note, and with the loud click of the entrance door closing, he was finally alone. Stewart's first act was to sit at the Apple computer and, after opening a safari browser, he typed in a search for "Edwardo Salvador".

The search results showed numerous iconic pictures from leading fashion and business magazines, where Salvador had featured on the covers of Time, Fortune, Vogue and even Hello. Fortune magazine described how the flamboyant playboy was descended from Spanish nobility and was one of South America's wealthiest businessmen. His business interests included cattle, agriculture, real estate, oil, precious metals and gemstones.

Leaving the living room, Stewart headed to the main bedroom and entered the walk-in wardrobe, where the Argentinian had deposited his Louis Vuitton luggage set. The butlers, who serviced the presidential suite, had been busy, as all of Salvador's clothes had been put out neatly on the racks, shelves and drawers that filled the entire right side of the twelve-foot-long closet space. The air smelt of a strange mixture of fine leather and mothballs.

Stewart assessed that the dark magician's dress sense was entirely focused on the cost of an item rather than its intrinsic quality or classic design. The clothing, belts, and shoes were all from a range of top-tier labels; Burberry, Dolce & Gabbana, Gucci, and Brioni. Salvador was slightly taller than Stewart and had a smaller frame so that nothing would have fitted. Besides, although the clothing was expensive, it was too flashy for the Scotsman's more subdued taste. Moving back to the row of expensive monogrammed luggage lined against the left side of the walk-in closet, Stewart picked up a dark leather holdall with subdued Louis Vuitton logos embossed into the fine hide. Stewart recognised the bag as a Keepall Bandouliere, a re-creation of the classic 1930s original soft travel bag.

"At least there is something classy."

Reflected the Scotsman to himself as he sat crossed-legged on the floor, unzipped the bag and began to unload its contents onto the cold tiles that someone could have used as a chess board. Inside was a black Dunhill leather folder bag with a monogrammed set of silver dice on the clasp that Stewart recognised as one of the accoutrements frequently associated with professional gamblers.

Looking through the folder's contents revealed a somewhat different picture of the income sources for the international playboy than had been listed in the flattering article in Fortune magazine. There were itemised travel itineraries and plans going back over the last four months and forward for the next two months for all the major casinos in the world, including a list of those who had barred the man due to "irregularities". This phrase was often a polite way of saying the man cheated or, as Stewart now believed was the case for the Dark Magician, had exhibited such extraordinary luck that he risked breaking the casino or, as it was termed, "the house".

Going further through the folder's contents, the Scotsman found a thick pre-printed booklet of IOUs made out to Salvador, complete with a perforated tear-off strip as a receipt for the unlucky individual who had played a game of chance and lost to the Argentinian. Clearly, the Dark Magician won frequently enough to require such pre-printed paperwork. Stewart flicked through the stack of over fifty IOUs from other gamblers who, when unable to pay a debt in cash, had opted to give the Argentinian some item that they possessed and which Salvador had signed as being accepted as part or full payment of "gambling debt."

Interestingly, although Stewart was unaware of its significance, there was an IOU slip from a Russian General Zarkov from a poker game in St Petersburg only six days earlier, agreeing to supply a specific relic "as demanded". The object that the Argentinian had expressly specified was described as a "khor lo" (Prayer Wheel) from the reign of the Tibetan king, Trisong Detsen, in the 8th century CE. The prayer wheel was listed as item number 234c (which is 234s in English) in the exhibition "Abode of Charity: Tibetan Buddhist Art" in the Winter Palace in the Hermitage Museum. It was odd, reflected Stewart that a professional gambler would know the Hermitage's catalogue number for an eighth-century Tibetan prayer wheel. The Scotsman began to consider that all of these apparently "random" gambling debts might have been deliberately planned to target key individuals who had access to something that would be of value to the Meri-Isfet.

At the end of the I.O.U. booklet was an open (uncrossed) cheque from the "Kaiser Casino" in Nuremberg, Germany, for 100,000 Euros with a handwritten note from the principal manager asking Herr Salvador to refrain from revisiting their casino. Stewart had no idea of the final costs for O'Neill's treatment, and given the threat from both Cortez and Regio, it was almost sure that Stewart would need funds for the coming confrontations, so he folded the cheque and placed it in his wallet, remarking,

"That will do nicely."

Resting at the bottom of the Keepall, was a chocolate-coloured leather, Scatola Del Tempo, watch roll that contained a series of expensive watches. Opening the seven-watch container revealed one unoccupied space, presumably, thought Stewart, for the gold IWC watch that the Scotsman had left in the Coliseum. Each watch in the roll had a gambling IOU attached to it (proving legal ownership). They were all top-of-the-range models from Audemars Piguet, Patek Philippe, Vacheron Constantin Jaeger-LeCoultre, and Rolex. Having traded his plastic Casio for the loan of a motorcycle while in London, Stewart was currently without a timepiece- but all of these watches were too pretentious to fit with the Scotsman's rather utilitarian preferences. It was true that Stewart had an old Omega chronograph[447]. But he had purchased that watch as a tool to time military operations back in the days when people had just one watch and used it to tell the time rather than to make some public statement about their financial success.

Oddly, one additional I.O.U. was included in the watch roll; the transfer of ownership for a red 1964 Ferrari 250 GT Berlinetta Lusso and one set of car keys from an Arab Sheik in Monte Carlo.

In amongst all this gambling paperwork was a sheet of A5-sized paper from The Ritz-Carlton in New Orleans that smelt strongly of Chanel No 5 and had a prominent lipstick kiss embedded on the paper along with the contact details of

---

[447] A 1969 Omega Speedmaster Professional, currently being assessed after sea water ingress. Stewart is awaiting an estimate for the repair work but was already certain that he would be unable to afford it.

one Jane Maskins, a name Stewart recognised as being the current Secretary of Defence for the United States. In handwritten blue ink, Maskins had written her personal mobile number just below the red lipstick kiss mark along with the text,

"Thank you, my *wonderous* teacher, for guiding me. I promise to devote my life to your teachings and our beloved order, *your Jane.*"

The Scotsman's suspicions about the exact nature of this "beloved order" were confirmed when he tore open a large, plain brown envelope marked "Private and Confidential for J. Maskins' eyes only". Inside the envelope was a folded parchment certificate for the initiation of one "Soror Tenebrosis Cupiditatibus Turbulentam" (which Stewart roughly translated as "she who desires or loves destruction"). The certificate confirmed that Maskins had been admitted to the sublime degree of Adeptus Minor at the Meri-Isfet Temple in New Orleans ten days earlier. Stewart sighed. So, the Meri-Isfet had the US Secretary of Defence in their pocket.

"Cortez does not intend for the good old US of A to come and free Europe from the master race, this time around." Concluded Stewart to himself.

Looking at the evidence in this one bag, Stewart could see that the Argentinian playboy was a professional gambler who spent six months of the year on a circuit of the world's high stakes gambling venues. He had terrific luck, as the combined value of all the items would have funded a small nation. Then, at the bottom of the folder, the Scotsman found what he could only conclude must have been one of the sources of the Argentinian's amazing success. In a small, dark wooden case, there was what looked to be an ancient carved bone figurine of a seated woman, who was moving a set of scales, so they favoured one side rather than the other. The figure was around four inches high, with a square of letters[448] engraved into a small space under the seated woman.

S E Q O R

E Q A M O

Q A S A Q

O M A Q E

R O Q E S

Under this square was the text; "Fortunae deae direxisti tenebris" (an evocation to the dark goddess of fortune)

Intrigued, Stewart walked from the master bedroom into the lounge and, accessing the iMac, used its web cam to photograph the statue and conduct a reverse image search that came back as having identified the statue as the historical artefact known as "The Dark Fortuna". One of the statue images was taken in August 2021 during an inventory stocktake at the Smithsonian Institute shortly before the item was reported missing, presumed to have been mislaid or incorrectly catalogued. Under this image was a brief history of the relic taken from the Smithsonian website.

"The recorded history of "The Dark Fortuna" begins in 71 BCE when, during the Third Servile War[449], the city of

---

[448] This square of letters looks very similar to a magical square listed within the Sacred Magic of Abramelin for manifesting material gain. This Abramelin system of magic is said to be derived from a Hebrew manuscript from 1438 but many components of this magical system can be found in much older sources from antiquity.

[449] Plutarch called this the Gladiator War, history remembers it as the War of Spartacus.

> *Praeneste[450] was sacked during the slave*
> *uprisings inspired by Spartacus. When*
> *General Marcus Licinius Crassus restored*
> *order to the area with his army, legend*
> *tells that the grateful townspeople*
> *presented the general with the small*
> *statue of "The Dark Fortuna" that had*
> *been one of the treasured relics of the*
> *Temple of Fortuna Primigena. After*
> *Crassus' death in 53 BCE, the*
> *whereabouts of the statue became*
> *uncertain. As is frequently the case with*
> *historical relics, there was then a long*
> *gap in the recorded history of "The Dark*
> *Fortuna" before it reappeared again, this*
> *time in the United States, where it was*
> *recorded as a personal possession of*
> *one, John D. Rockefeller, having been*
> *acquired by him through his Standard*
> *Oil Company agents when prospecting*
> *for oil in North Africa in the late 1880s.*
> *Rockefeller donated the statue, along*
> *with numerous other personal effects, to*
> *the Smithsonian Museum on his death*
> *in 1937."*

After reading the article, the Scotsman looked critically at the small statue he held in his left hand. It looked harmless enough. Like so many other antiquities that had passed through his showrooms over the past years. Except, this item had some very serious providence that suggested that it did affect the fortunes of whoever used it, especially when

---

[450] Now called Palestrina, a city in Lazio, 22 miles East of Rome.

considered in conjunction with the gambling receipts and IOUs in Salvador's luggage.

Stewart's personal and professional financial situation was dire, so it was only natural that, just for a moment, he contemplated if he should keep the statue for himself, just for a while, until he had recovered some of his finances. Unknown to the Scotsman, similar thoughts had passed through the minds of every single previous owner of the Dark Fortuna. Each thought they would use the statue for a short period until they gained just enough money and influence to satisfy their needs.

But this temptation was part of the seduction of the idol, for there is never enough to satisfy human greed and the Dark Fortuna had another "gift"- one that prompted the ancient priests to name it the Dark Fortuna. In addition to changing the fortunes of those who owned it, it also corrupted them, exaggerating every negative trait. The ancients placed the idol in their temple not to venerate it but to keep it away from the hands of human beings because they knew too well that the average human was unable to resist the seductive temptation of power and wealth promised by the Dark Fortuna.

Fortunately, Mr Tavish Stewart was far from ordinary. After briefly experiencing the seductive temptation of using the idol to solve his current financial situation, his rational mind countered that impulse with the realisation that for the Meri-Isfet to have acquired the statue, it must have some significant negative aspect associated with its possession and use. The previous owners listed in the Smithsonian article did, it is true, all become extremely powerful and immensely rich after coming into the possession of the statue, but they also became renowned for their cruelty. Many of these people lived at a time when brutality was commonplace, so for contemporary accounts to have labelled these individuals in such a way meant that they must have been barbarically savage.

With that realisation, the Scotsman took the statue and put it in the metal wastepaper basket that sat on the floor next to the desk. Stewart then set about searching through the Presidential Suite's well-stocked bar; having dismissed the use of Glenfiddich as an accelerant with a short,

"Unthinkable..."

He finally picked up a bottle of "Hine Antique XO" brandy and a box of Tres Estrellas matches. After walking out onto the balcony, he soaked the carved bone statue with the liquor and repeatedly burnt and resoaked the Dark Fortuna until the carved bone was reduced to nothing more than a pile of fine powder. The whole process took nearly forty minutes, and most of the bottle of Hine brandy. Stewart then unceremoniously poured the remaining dust over the edge of the hotel balcony. It scattered over the street below before being blown away.

The Scotsman then had a shower, put on one of the complimentary white towelling robes and called the Suite's duty butler, Sebastiánto, to have his clothes sent for an overnight clean and order a meal to be delivered to his room. After quickly reading the menu, Stewart selected a medium, grilled fillet steak, new potatoes, asparagus and stuffed tomatoes in a mint leaf sauce. He declined, what had been the Argentinian Magician's default wine, Château Lafite Rothschild, instead opting for a half bottle of Fontodi 2017 Chianti Classico.

Sebastiánto nodded his approval at the selection of Italian wine before dressing the table in the Suite's lounge for the meal with a table cloth and cutlery from storage cupboards in the hall. Stewart was impressed. The St. Regis certainly knew how to treat its guests to old-style luxury. Some forty minutes later, Sebastiánto returned with two waiters, one for

the food and the other for the wine. All three men entered
the lounge and served the meal with great flourish. The
aromas made the Scotsman's mouth water even before the
silver cutlery touched the food. Stewart relished the
perfectly cooked dinner, as he had not had a substantial
meal since his breakfast in New Bond Street that morning,
although he limited himself to just half a glass of the wine
as he did not want to spoil the coming night's rest. He
thought that he would need to be sharp the following day.
After using the complimentary toiletries, he retired to the
large master bedroom and fell into that wondrous deep,
dreamless slumber that often follows a night or two without
sleep.

Ten hours later, he awoke, and after calling room service
and ordering a late breakfast, he used the room phone to
call the Royal London Hospital to check on Jeffery Sonnet's
status. The Major Trauma Centre nurse who came on the
line confirmed that Sonnet's emergency surgery was over,
but he remained in ICU as he was in a critical condition.
Stewart's call to Sinclair went unanswered, making the
Scotsman worry that something untoward may have
happened. He resolved to follow up once he had got
O'Neill out of the clinic. The sooner the two men could get
away from Rome and into hiding, the better, as Stewart did
not doubt that Cardinal Regio's search for them would only
be intensifying.

Another trio of men brought the Scotsman's brunch of
scrambled eggs on toast with strong Caffè Vergnano Gran
Aroma coffee, this time with a different Suite Butler as
Sebastiánto had gone off duty at midnight. The new butler,
Antonio, also returned the clothes that Stewart had sent the
previous evening, all pressed. The Scotsman noticed where
the material on his Chinos and shirt had been cut or torn;
they were neatly repaired. Again, the St. Regis was proving
that it had earned its reputation.

Once he was washed and dressed, Stewart called Antonio and asked for the car to be brought round. The Scotsman was never one to watch TV, so he remained blissfully unaware of the global man hunt underway for "The Wickedest Man in the World", as he was described in the British morning newspapers.

Twenty minutes after driving away from the St. Regis, Stewart parked the red Ferrari in the car park beside the Clinica Ars Biomedica. After making the usual arrangement with the parking attendant, the Scotsman made his way to the reception and asked about the status of Mr Salvador.

The receptionist explained that Salvador had been moved to a private room when Dr Georg Henriks, who had been supervising the treatment, appeared beside the Scotsman. The Swede seemed unusually happy to see Stewart and led the way to a private room on the left side of a long corridor of treatment rooms.

"The operations went well, but Mr Salvador will need to wear face wrappings for the next few days." The doctor explained.

As Stewart and Henriks entered the private room, they found O'Neill sitting on the side of the bed, looking like the invisible man with bandages covering his entire head, except for two small holes for his eyes. O'Neill was watching the international English language news that had just started playing on the wall-mounted TV. The news coverage showed the deep-fake images of Stewart and Curren, followed by footage of Sinclair firing her Raffica machine pistol into the crowds outside the burnt-out remains of Stewart's showroom.

Stewart looked at the news coverage in sheer disbelief. Still, his shock became even greater as the coverage switched to the images of Cortez standing on a podium in Hyde Park, in front of tens of thousands of protestors, making an offer of one billion Euros for information leading to the capture of Tavish Stewart.

Dr Henriks looked directly at Stewart and, shrugging, apologised,

"A billion is a lot of money, Stewart,"

He opened the door to the private room and let in a dozen UN Military Police (MP) with HK MP5[451] submachine guns that all pointed toward Stewart. Entering immediately after the UN officers was a tall, blond man in a fine suit, who Stewart recognised as having been seated next to Cortez on the stage at Wigmore Hall and introduced as Cortez's grandson.

"Come to make sure the frame fits?" Asked the Scotsman.

"Oh, it fits perfectly, Mr Stewart." Responded the blond man in an Argentinian accent.

O'Neill interrupted the conversation by holding up his hands before passing the Scotsman a scribbled note. Stewart read it and then turned to Dr Henriks and Cortez's grandson, asking.

"Can I at least say goodbye to my friend?"

The blond Argentinian laughed,

"Weak and sentimental. That is why people like you will always lose. Very well, you have five minutes, no more. The Military Police have surrounded the building, so there is no escape."

Cortez's grandson and the doctor walked from the room, closing the door behind them. Before it shut, the Argentinian issued a command to the UN MPs.

---

[451] Heckler & Koch GmbH (H&K) MP5 (Maschinenpistole 5).

"Wait outside for a few minutes, then cuff and hood that bastard for transportation to the Hague, where he will face a summary trial before his execution."

Three minutes later, four of the heavily armed military police officers pushed their way into the room and grabbed "The Wickedest Man in the World", dressed in his blue, short-sleeved, sea cotton shirt, pair of light khaki chinos and a pair of worn, tan leather, deck shoes. Standing behind Stewart, the senior UN MP pulled a dark hood over their victim's head, brutally interrupting whatever conversation was taking place between the Scotsman and the injured Irish American priest. Having captured their target, the UN MP exclaimed,

"Come on, you Scottish bastard! Time to face justice for your crimes!"

The hooded figure was then roughly bound with PlastiCuffs and frogmarched from the examination room down the corridor. The elegantly dressed, blond-haired grandson of Cortez began to follow when Dr Henriks ran behind him, demanding,

"Excuse me, what about my reward?"

The blond Argentinian turned and looked at the bespectacled Swedish doctor and smiled,

"But of course...."

He led the doctor into an empty side room further along the corridor, pulled out a long black, suppressed 9mm Glock 17 polymer pistol and shot Henriks point-blank in the head. The blond Argentinean returned his weapon to its concealed holster inside his suit jacket and walked into the corridor. He left the greedy Dr Henriks with a surprised look on his face, lying prone on his back in a growing pool of his blood that expanded slowly from a gaping head wound over the polished linoleum floor.

Cortez's grandson strode confidently down the clinic corridor towards a long-bodied, former Russian military Mi-8 copter in its distinctive white and blue U.N. livery that had landed in the clinic's car park. He smiled at the sight of the hooded figure of the Scotsman sitting, helplessly restrained inside the aircraft cabin. Turning behind him, he looked back and could see a pathetic bandaged figure sitting on the bed, alone in the treatment room. Cortez would be a delighted man tonight, as would Cardinal Regio, who had already been told where to find the errant priest.

24 ACROSS THE ABYSS

"Within the Magickal system of the Meri-Isfet, "Crossing the Abyss" is the culmination of the first two orders and marks the adept's confrontation with those contradictions that manifest between the conscious and unconscious mind. For those who successfully transcend the challenge of CHRNZN[452], they gain a sublime unity and graduate to the degree of Magister Templi, or "Master of the Temple". For those who fail, they are cursed to find their mind fragmented into the unending chaos of madness." - Notes for candidates to the Third Order. Soror Lupus et Exitium, Imperatrix of the Meri-Isfet.

Ten Miles from Godinje (Годиње) village,
Municipality of Bar,
Montenegro, near the Albanian border.

18:35HRS (GMT+2), 10th Sept, Present day

Knowing that some unknown inhuman consciousness was scrutinizing her physical body, the French Adept drew her projected awareness back towards the clifftop, a mile from the Meri-Isfet Temple, where she had been observing the St Petersburg Qliphothic Wheel.

Before returning to her physical form, she hung, some fifteen feet in the air, above the grey cloud of "invisibility" that obscured her seated form to all but the most careful scrutiny. Looking down from her vantage point, she could see that there was an indistinct, shimmering astral form, around eight feet tall, that was floating inches above the

---

[452] Vowels are frequently omitted from the names of powerful entities to prevent accidental acts of empowering the entity or causing aspects of the entity to manifest within the magician's psyche.

ground level of the clifftop. It swayed slowly like some kind of giant, long-stemmed grass, ten feet away from where Mathers' body was seated.

In her decades of study of the hidden forces of nature and the numerous non-physical beings that inhabit the invisible realms, the French Adept had never seen anything like the entity that was focusing on her physical body. The creature had a highly developed aura but was free of any sigils that might help identify its allegiances. The colours of the aura, which are usually an accurate indicator of the inherent nature, were oddly devoid of any colourings. There was, therefore, no way to judge the intentions of the swaying entity or if it posed any kind of imminent threat. Mathers had no alternative but to return to her physical form and assess what response to make to this strange intruder.

The French Adept gathered her consciousness slowly and gradually back into her physical body, which had remained seated, cross-legged near the cliff top, shrouded with the mysterious cloud of grey ectoplasmic material for nearly seventy minutes. Returning consciousness to her body automatically reactivated and opened the seven sacred gateways she sealed before beginning her projection. She then ceased to will the cold, grey cloud of projected matter into manifestation, after which it slowly started to dissipate in the gusty cliff-top breeze. She then commenced a series of deep kundalini[453] breaths, typical of the Kapalabhati Pranayama technique[454], to induce heat[455] and re-energise

---

[453] An ancient Vedic system of energy manipulation based on the interplay between the breath and the vital energies of life within the body.

[454] Often informally known as the "Breath of Fire" since it warms and reenergises the physical body.

[455] It is also often called the "skull-shining" breath since, in addition to raising heat it cleanses the air ducts inside the skull

her body. After an hour of projection from within the cloud, this technique was essential since prolonged exposure to the material composing the "Rosicrucian Cloud of Invisibility[456]" significantly drained the physical body of its warmth and vitality.

It was only after these essential steps of corporeal reanimation that the French Adept finally opened her physical eyes to look at whatever had taken such a profound interest in her during her meditation. As her eyes focused and her gaze rose, the first thing that she noticed was that the consciousness that was observing her, whatever it was, cast a definite shadow on the brightly coloured, woven blanket where she was seated. For an astral form to cast a shadow was highly unusual, as they are generally composed of very fine matter that would not block light. For an astral form to cast a shadow implied that it was capable of interaction with the physical world and could, as a consequence, be extraordinarily dangerous.

As Mathers' gaze took in the shape of the shadow, she noted, with some alarm, that it was an outline that looked remarkably similar to one cast by a giant snake when roused into a classic striking pose. There was also that highly distinctive, musky smell that the French Adept recalled experiencing near the giant diamondback rattlesnakes at the Vincennes Zoo[457] in Paris. The French Adept had an instinctual dislike of snakes[458], so with growing dismay, she

---

[456] Sometimes also referred to as "The Alchemical Cloud" in more modern Rosicrucian literature. Since it utilizes aspects of transmutation.

[457] The Paris Zoological Park, formerly known as the Bois de Vincennes Zoological Park.

[458] Ophidiophobia (fear of snakes) is believed to be a genetic predisposition based on the real-life threat often posed by many species of snake.

braced herself to find out exactly what had been focusing its attention so closely on her while her consciousness had been out of her physical body.

It was, therefore, a complete surprise when, as she looked up, she saw an attractive man in his mid-thirties, with long flowing shoulder-length dark brown hair. This man had a highly stylised plaited beard with four segments extending down almost to his waist, in a style worn by men of status in many ancient Mesopotamian civilizations[459]. This strange figure wore a brightly coloured, full-length robe adorned with a golden border. On his feet were a pair of sandals, again formed from a golden thread. This man had the most striking blue eyes that were in complete contrast to the rest of his appearance. He exuded an indefinable sense of serenity and authority. The strange man strongly reminded Mathers of the images of Helena Blavatsky[460]'s Mahatma[461], Kuthumi, and how Aleister Crowley described the appearance of his guiding discarnate entity, Aiwass[462].

However, the astral figure that appeared in front of the French Adept shimmered in and out of focus. Mathers realised that the image was an illusion caused by an act of Magical Will directed towards her perception. With an effort, the French Adept swept the hallucination aside and

---

[459] Chaldean, Babylonian, Assyrian, Median, Aramean, and ancient Persian.

[460] Founder of the Theosophical Society.

[461] Blavatsky claimed that these enlightened beings dictated her esoteric teaching, The Secret Doctrine.

[462] Crowley claimed that this being dictated his esoteric teaching, The Book of The Law. In The Equinox of the Gods, Crowley described Aiwass: "He seemed to be a tall, dark man in his thirties, well-knit, active and strong, with the face of a savage king, and eyes veiled lest their gaze should destroy what they saw. The dress was not Arab; it suggested Assyria or Persia."

saw a composite creature that appeared to be a type of chimaera, with a body formed from several different species. Such hybrid entities are frequently encountered on the astral planes, as evidenced by the numerous images of composite bodied "Gods" portrayed by most ancient cultures and the strange entities encountered during many hallucinations.

The astral being confronting Mathers had a thick, segmented body, like an enormous serpent but was much larger, around three feet in diameter, with similar dimensions to a medium-sized tree. A blur of rapid motion halfway down this strange creature's body emitted a distinctive fluttering sound, like a gigantic dragonfly's wings. There was no indication that this creature had, or ever would, fly in the physical sense since it was semi-astral in its manifestation. As the French Adept would soon discover, these fluttering appendages had evolved for this astral being to manifest sound on the material plane.

The base of the entity's thick, segmented body transitioned into long, root-like tendrils, most of which trailed away from where it stood. The "head-end" was made up of seven gently swaying elongated necks, around the diameter of a human arm, which terminated in round gaping, sucker-like mouths filled with numerous small, sharp teeth arranged in consecutive circular rows. These teeth seeped a green viscous fluid that slowly dripped down to the ground, causing an instantaneous reaction similar to that of powerful acid on whatever was unfortunate enough to become impregnated with the green slime. Consequently, the immediate atmosphere around the creature stank from the unusual combination of chemicals and burning.

As Mathers took in the chemical evaporation, rising from numerous small holes appearing in both the rocks and ground-hugging vegetation that littered the cliff top, she quickly pulled herself back and stood up to face the thing.

She had no doubt now that it, whatever it was, had been sent by the Meri-Isfet to deal with her after they had detected her inside Fortress Grmožur. The only question was, why hadn't it attacked her while her consciousness was away from her body. While the French Adept considered these questions, she stood facing directly whatever the Meri-Isfet had conjured against her. Although the entity was only partially manifested onto the material plane and would appear as a shimmering apparition to normal sight, it looked as solid as any other material object to Mathers' highly developed senses.

The strange creature's body rose to match her height, and the seven "heads" swayed menacingly before her. Although no eyes were visible, the beast could accurately detect her proximity, like some multi-headed, blood-sucking leech or lamprey.

Mathers had never seen any manifestation like this entity in her many decades of esoteric practice. The only thing that even vaguely matched was a creature described on an ancient ceramic cylinder at the Bibliothèque Nationale de France in Paris. This 22nd-century BCE cuneiform inscription was associated with the Sumerian King Gudea from Lagash in Southern Mesopotamia. The description talked about a creature called the MUŠ.ŠÀ.TÙR[463] that terrorised the lands of ancient Sumer; destroying buildings, crops, animals and humans with a venom that was deadly to every living thing. The terror felt by the people was vividly described in the cuneiform text, which talked of a vaporous multi-headed, worm-like creature with fluttering wings that

---

[463] An ancient Mesopotamian monster, sometimes described as a horned snake with two forelegs and wings and at other times as being a venomous serpent many miles long that devoured all creatures. It was also the Akkadian name of the Babylonian constellation (MUL.DINGIR.MUŠ) or Hydra.

delighted in disease and suffering[464]. Several notable warriors attempted to slay the monster, but all perished. The beast had an extraordinary ability to regenerate from any injury. When spilt, its blood was even more toxic than the venom that poured from every one of its seven fang-filled orifices. Mathers tried to recall more about the Sumerian legend from her time as a student researching in the Paris Library many years before. She hoped for information that might provide her with a clue about the best way to escape, as she had no illusions about trying to defeat the creature by physical means.

According to the ancient tale, King Gudea had ended the monster's reign of terror when a little-known order of Gal.Lu[465] devotees came forward with an offer to engage the MUŠ.ŠÀ.TÙR in some kind of alliance that, the priests promised King Gudea, would provide a way to contain and control the destruction that had been ravaging the land. In return, the strange priests wanted only to be gifted a temple for their worship of the MUŠ.ŠÀ.TÙR. To the desperate King, this proposal sounded like an ideal solution. It was not until some time afterwards that reports came to the monarch of unspeakable acts of cruelty at the temple. The complaints from the nearby townspeople eventually became so numerous that King Gudea had to renege on his agreement with the mysterious order and dispatch his army to sack the temple and put the cult members to the sword. This grisly mission succeeded, except for the cult leader, who escaped despite having numerous mortal wounds inflicted on him with swords, arrows and clubs. From inscriptions found inside the temple, it emerged that the

---

[464] This semi physical creature was the basis for the Greek and Roman mythical tales of the Lernaean Hydra.

[465] The Assyrian term for the great demons or devils that ruled the ancient Mesopotamian underworld.

order had made a deal with the MUŠ.ŠÀ.TÙR, whereby it would inhabit the physical body of the high priest of the sect, giving the hierophant all the supernatural powers of the demon but at a price of becoming it's permanent physical incarnation.

At that moment, the French Adept recalled seeing the thick astral tendrils of an "indwelling" entity embedded throughout the Meri-Isfet adept, Magister Ironheart, when she had projected to Fortress Grmožur. With a sense of horror, Mathers realised Ironheart had made a pact with this ancient horror of evil and had sent it to deal with her.

Involuntarily, the French Adept gasped,

"MUŠ.ŠÀ.TÙR..."

The creature's body rose six inches from the ground in response to the utterance. Its swaying heads now towered above the French Adept, and it hissed with delight. This hissing indicated one thing, realised Mathers. The creature recognised human speech. The French Adept decided that if she were to stand any chance of surviving, then she would need to start interacting with the entity immediately,

"You are what inhabits Ironheart?"

She queried, in English, hoping that the thing would be able to differentiate between itself and the human being it inhabited.

The creature responded by making a vibration in the delicate membranes on its midsection. It was hard to understand at first, but it was just possible with an effort. It droned in French,

"HOST"

Mathers swallowed. So, the creature understood that it was a kind of parasite, but, more surprisingly, it could tell the native language of the person addressing it, even when that person was addressing the entity in a non-native tongue. The French Adept was not sure that either of these facts was good news. Still, Mathers knew she had to keep the dialogue going; while the thing was talking, it was not killing her. There was no point in trying to avoid the most crucial question, so she went straight ahead with it,

"Why did Ironheart send you?"

"KILL"

It buzzed. With such a direct response, the French Adept wondered if she should try and make a run for it. Unfortunately, her trusty Triumph Bonneville was almost thirty feet away over rough ground. If this thing had destroyed entire Sumerian cities and dispatched their leading warriors with ease, it was sure it could move with extraordinary speed. The creature understood her instinctive reaction because it added,

"WASTE"

Mathers was unsure if she should be flattered or even more frightened; if an apex parasite did not want to kill you, it could only have one other motive. This deduction was confirmed when the thing buzzed excitedly,

"HOST"

A chill ran through the French Adept; this thing had concluded that she would make a better target to inhabit than Magister Ironheart. However, its subsequent response made the situation more intriguing.

"CROSS ABYSS"

Now Mathers was confused. To the best of her knowledge, the Meri-Isfet had three living adepts[466] who had passed the legendary Abyss that marked the transition from the seventh degree to the higher initiation grades of the eighth, ninth and tenth degrees. She and all other members of the Meri-Maat assumed that such an advancement involved some trial of ability followed by ceremonial conferment of the following degree. Now this strange creature was intimating that the promotion, if it could be called that, was, in fact, simply the result of an indwelling by an ancient non-physical entity.

The more that Mathers considered this idea, the more sense it made. The lore of her order, the Meri-Maat, maintained that no living human being could attain the higher degrees but becoming a host removed your humanity, transforming it in unknown ways. The ancient Sumerian texts recounted the powers these creatures possessed and their propensity for causing suffering. These intentions matched closely with those of the Meri-Isfet so that an alliance would be mutually beneficial. The entity would be able to incarnate on the physical plane, and the human adept would gain many of the attributes and abilities of the most ancient evils of creation.

However, Mathers had devoted her current incarnation to the pursuit of harmony and the reduction of suffering. If she died now on this cliff top, her work on the path of light would become limited to the nonphysical planes until her next physical incarnation, which could take seventy to one hundred years. Based on the preparations she had just witnessed in Fortress Grmožur, the world did not have more than a few days before it would be irrevocably plunged into

---

[466] Mathers is currently unaware that one of the three senior masters had recent perished under the Colosseum in Rome, during a failed attempt to resurrect Nissa Ad-Dajjal.

chaos unless she took some immediate action. Since she had not had the chance to inform anyone of what she had discovered at the fortress, no one else would know the plans of the Meri-Isfet. But she had to wonder, if she were to become the "host" for this ancient evil, would she retain her current morals or free will? Or would she become corrupted to fulfil the desires of this monster on the material plane?

While the French Adept pondered the terrifying possibilities inherent in her imminent future, North from the cliff top where Mathers was standing, Magister Ironheart had his own crisis. He felt uncharacteristically anxious as he stood proudly near the bottom of Pavel Ivanović's vineyard, close to the French Adept's classic Volkswagen camper. His highly developed intuitive senses told him of great mortal danger. So solid and compelling was this growing feeling of dread that he had opted to stay beside the intruding adept's base rather than seeking to confront them directly, himself. Instead, he had decided to send his Holy Guardian Angel[467], as he referred to the in-dweller[468], to seek out and destroy the intruder adept. The Holy Angel was practically indestructible; at least Ironheart was unaware of anything that could harm it. So, he asked himself, why did he still feel this deep and growing sense of dread? He should feel supremely safe and confident. His Meri-Isfet disciples surrounded him, and if their combined magical defences proved insufficient, he always had the guns of the highly

---

[467] This is a similar attribution made by English occultist Aleister Crowley about the discarnate entity Aiwass: "My name is called Aiwass," and "in The Book of the Law did I write the secrets of truth that are like unto a star and a snake and a sword."

[468] Ironheart is clearly unaware of the true appearance of the indwelling entity.

trained Wolfsangel operatives to protect him. Besides, it was incomprehensible even to consider that a mincing seventh-degree Meri-Maat adept could defeat the god-like abilities of the Holy Guardian Angel.

Ironheart was contemplating the possible reasons why he felt so strangely insecure when he suddenly noticed an unfamiliar weakness in his body. It started with nausea in his stomach as if he was going down with the flu. Then his legs began to feel progressively weaker as though he had just risen from a bed where he had been lying ill for weeks. He began to shiver as he felt a growing chill starting in his fingers and toes and gradually spreading through his limbs. Just as he was about to consider asking for one of his acolytes to help him, his astral vision noticed movement by his feet. A series of long, grey, rootlike non-physical tendrils were dragging over the ground, away from his body and withdrawing down the gravel path leading towards the cliffs.

The Magister went to scream his protest but found his breathing becoming increasingly difficult, as if his lungs had suddenly become smaller, so much smaller that he could not get enough air. He clutched his chest and fell to his knees, gasping for each new breath that was shorter than the last. Finally, his consciousness faded, and his dead body slumped to the ground to lie beside the green-leafed vines of the vineyard. The entire process was over within a few short minutes, and although his acolytes saw their master was in distress, not one of them moved to help him. Instead, they behaved as they had been taught- to be without pity or compassion for any living thing.

South from the scene of Magister Ironheart's rapid demise, Mathers's astral vision could see numerous long, grey tendrils moving alongside the track beside where she was standing. These plant-like roots pulled back into the base of the segmented body of the swaying multi-headed snake creature that stood close before her.

"What should I call yo...."

The French Adept went to ask, but her sentence was never completed. Instead, she gasped in pain as the first astral tendrils began to wrap themselves around the toes of her right foot. Instinctively she tried to pull her leg away, but dozens more of the grey, root-like shoots had wrapped themselves around her foot with a powerful grip that held the French Adept firmly to the spot. The first physical contact with the creature stung like a powerful jellyfish sting, but that pain became a numbness that paralysed those parts of the body enveloped by the binding roots. This numbness was replaced by a growing sense of calm. Then a series of powerful waves of pleasure began to pulse through her. Each time the French Adept surrendered another level of her resistance to the infestation, she received more powerful waves of pleasure. The constant bliss disrupted any hope of focusing her Magical Will in her defence. As the French Adept's consciousness fell deeper into a form of rapture, the creature's non-physical tendrils began to wrap themselves over Mathers' physical and non-physical bodies. First around her calves, then her thighs, midsection, chest and finally, her neck. Just as the long, delicate tendrils began to entwine themselves around Mathers' head, her pupils dilated, her lips parted, and her breathing increased as her now entirely inhabited body fell backwards to the ground. All the time this infestation proceeded, the multi-headed creature's vibrating wings hummed at an ever-increasing pitch.

Moments later, Mathers' entire physical and non-physical essences became encased in a semi-transparent shimmering, immaterial shroud of tightly binding tendrils. Rather than fighting the transformation, she now embraced it, thinking she was like a caterpillar when it became a chrysalis. Whether these thoughts were her own or were being placed in her consciousness by the creature no longer mattered to Mathers- her consciousness was now the same as the inhabiting entity.

As the French Adept lay prone on the floor, in an almost invisible cocoon of grey tendrils that were growing not only through her physical body but also each of her non-material ones, she became aware of another mind, infinitely superior to her own, accessing her memories, re-living each moment of her life. It was not an unpleasant experience; she had lived a good life, and she felt some pride that her experiences were of interest to her new teacher. There was even a moment of sadness when the review concluded. But that disappointment was quickly overcome by awe and wonder as the entity began to share some of its own life experiences with its new host.

It referred to itself as one of the Jawān[469], which Mathers' human memory recognised as coming from some of the most ancient Middle Eastern traditions as the serpentine or dragon-like beings who inhabited the earth before humans or animals. The Jawān were described in ancient sources as being formed out of a primordial fire, as contrasted to Angels, who were said to be composed of primordial light and mortal humans and animals, who were created from primordial matter. According to the Holy Quran[470], the Jawān were the ancient precursors of the supernatural

---

[469] Known in Arabic as the جَوَان – it is the plural for a proto-supernatural entity known as the جَانّ (jānn).

[470] Surah 15:27 and Surah 27:10 of the Quran refers to the Jawān as a supernatural creature or a serpent.

entities known as Djinn, and before the time of Adam, they were ruled by a king or father entity called Jann ibn Jann[471].

As the entity began to recall its life, Mathers became aware of the vastness of the primordial, lifeless oceans and the eternal loneliness of the desolate water planet that was the early earth. Then there was the emotion of delight as life emerged; simple forms at first and then, rapidly, ever more complex ones. The entity enthusiastically inhabited these primitive creatures, gathering energy from the perceptions experienced by the organisms it came into contact with while incarnated on the physical plane. Early in these series of inhabitations, the entity discovered that pain and suffering produced the most extreme reactions in consciousness. So it began to actively seek to increase the sum of suffering on the material plane.

Many hours later, the transformed body of Madeleine Mathers rose from where she was lying. The thick layers of semi-transparent grey fibrous astral roots that had encased her physical and non-physical bodies were no longer visible, and all evidence of the strange creature was gone. In its place was what superficially looked like the female form of the Meri-Maat adept who had encountered the MUŠ.ŠÀ.TÙR several hours before. However, this woman's skin tone, musculature and body shape exceeded those impossibly perfect features seen on professional fashion models after extensive photo manipulation.

The French Adept slowly got to her feet and strode, fearlessly, to the cliff edge, where she stood for a few minutes looking out over the moonlit, shimmering waters of Lake Skadar towards Fortress Grmožur. Her senses buzzed with an awareness of literally every living consciousness in

---

[471] Some Islamic scholars assert that the father of the Jawān, called, Jann ibn Jann, is synonymous with Iblīs, the leader of the devils (Shayāṭīn).

her vicinity. She took a deep breath and reached up to untie her red hair, delighting in how it flowed behind her in the lakeside night breeze. Before walking to the Triumph Bonneville parked nearby, she removed her golden initiate's ring, reversed it- so the pentagram was inverted, and returned it to her right ring finger with a sensual smile.

25 ESCAPE AND EVASION

"Our goal is to teach our operatives indomitable spirit combined with supreme adaptability. They must be able to manipulate negative circumstances in such a way that insurmountable obstacles become our weapons and those who hunt us become our helpless prey." - Lubyanka Square, Operations Manual, Komitet Gosudarstvennoy Bezopasnosti (KGB).

Two miles West of Yoliin Am Valley (Valley of the Vultures)
Gurvan Saikhen Mountains,
Gobi Desert,
Southern Mongolia.

07:09HRS (GMT+8), 10th Sept, Present day

After destroying the J-31 'Gyrfalcon' fighter by the NNEMP[472] weapon, known as Smokeless Dragon[473], the air in the long rift valley became heavy with the thick acrid fumes from burnt aviation fuel and the mix of exotic materials used in the construction of the fifth-generation jet.

The most dangerous man in the world seemed oblivious to the choking smoke as it obscured the light from the rising sun that streamed down the narrow gorge. After the thick smoke began to be carried away by the morning breeze, the shafts of sunlight cast long shadows from the protruding rocks on the valley floor and the growing warmth tempted numerous desert reptiles[474] to emerge from their night-time shelters.   The lizards blended almost perfectly with the

---

[472] NNEMP = Non-Nuclear Electro Magnetic Pulse weapon.

[473] Also known as "Wú yān long".

474 Mostly the Mongolian Agama (Paralaudakia stoliczkana) which is an 11-inch-long, brown reptile with a very long tail.

browns and khakis of the sand and rocks that made up the valley floor. As relative silence and peace returned to the area, some of the larger reptiles, which were almost a foot long, took up what must have been their established positions on the highest points. They bobbed up and down and displayed bright blueish green colouring on their long tails in an attempt to attract a mate.

Adbul Issuin watched these lizards for a moment, appreciating their magnificence, as he continued to savour his Montecristo Number 4. The hawk-faced man reflected on the danger that the bigger male lizards placed themselves in from the ever-watchful eyes of the predatory hawks that frequented the Gobi. Gazing into the clear blue sky, he reminded himself that he was hunted by unseen eyes high in the sky, just as ruthless in their pursuit.

He resolved that he would need to move quickly to determine a way to evade the hunters that would come after him and identify a route out of the region. He deactivated the electromagnetic jamming weapon, folded it into its aluminium case, carried it back to the valley edge, and proceeded up the steep slope towards the concealed cave that he had discovered a few days earlier.

The hawk-faced man did not increase his breathing or exhibit any other signs of physical exertion while carrying the forty-two-pound case up the two hundred yards of thick sand on the twenty-six-degree slope in the growing heat and altitude[475]. Whereas most individuals would have been gasping and sweating as they exerted such physical effort, Adbul Issuin hardly noticed it. He continued to reflect on his hunters. Gazing up into the clear blue sky, he was aware that there were four separate trails of smoke from crashed

---

[475] 78F and 8,000 feet above sea level.

aircraft[476] drifting on the morning's desert thermals high into the sky above him. These marked his position to the Chinese Government's Yaogan surveillance satellites that constantly circled the globe. Given such clear evidence of his location, he did not doubt that the authorities would observe his subsequent actions with enormous care and respond with road blocks and border checks. His description would already be with the People's Police and the more fearsome paramilitary People's Armed Police (PAP).

Six hundred and eighty miles to the East, in Beijing, the destruction of the J-31 had been streamed live to the Deputy Party Chairman, Zhu Zhing. Zhing was an octogenarian career politician whose shrewd intelligence had allowed him to survive the numerous regime and ideological changes that had dogged the Chinese government for the past fifty years. The elderly figure wore a classic grey polyester Sun Yat-sen suit (more commonly known as "a Mao suit").

Although the classic ideology[477] characterised by the garment had ceased to be fashionable for the neo-capitalists within the Politburo[478], Zhu Zhing was aware that China's economic dependence on the West's endless debt-fuelled consumption was an unsustainable model that was bound to end badly. Experience had taught him that such

---

[476] The two fighter jets, the J-31 and J-20 and the two helicopters, the Z-20 and Bell Relentless.

[477] The five big buttons symbolize the separation of five powers (administration, legislation, jurisdiction, examination and supervision) whereas, the three smaller cuff-buttons, represent "the Three People's Principles" (Nationalism, Democracy and the People's Livelihood).

[478] Politburo of the Communist Party of China. This supreme governing body has 25 members.

"bad endings" resulted in a dramatic return to classical values; it was, therefore, prudent to appear old-fashioned.

The inner calm exhibited by Zhu Zhing, as he sat watching the streaming video feed from the satellites on a brushed aluminium ten-inch Lenovo tablet that was held in front of him by one of six smartly dressed attendants, was exemplary. Apart from a momentary pause, as the final of the two, multi-million-US-dollar fighters crashed into the valley wall in a massive fireball, the elderly politician had not stopped his enjoyment of the freshly made golden dough sticks wrapped in noodles.

As the final Zhaliang roll left the chopsticks and passed into the Deputy Chairman's mouth, he delicately wiped his lips with a white linen napkin. He then sat back into his oversized white wooden high-backed chair, drew a deep breath and then barked a series of harsh commands that had the six attendants around him scurrying fearfully away. After they had gone, the elderly statesman drew a deep contented breath. He settled back into enjoying the bird songs that filled the air on the wide veranda, overlooking the fragrant Jasmine trees in the most exclusive section of the Forbidden City.

Six hundred and eighty miles to the West of the Forbidden City, Adbul Issuin had reached the concealed cave and placed the Smokeless Dragon near the rear wall in case he would ever need it again. He then returned to a more detailed examination of the cave contents

Within a few minutes, he had effected a change of clothing. He had taken off the Falcon commando suit, folding it into a cotton laundry bag. He put on a khaki-coloured Hugo Boss cotton shirt, cargo trousers and safari jacket, all of which had been in the bottom of one of the large rucksacks. The clothes were slightly too small but were undoubtedly less conspicuous than the black paramilitary fatigues he had been wearing. He opted to keep the Falcon combat boots as the dead men's footwear inside the cave was too damaged by decomposition to be viable. Once dressed, the hawk-faced man resumed his systematic search through the dead bodies and the large rucksacks. He only found eight, twenty-mark gold coins, worth a few thousand dollars, that might be useful for a bribe but not nearly enough to pay for the kind of escape that Adbul Issuin needed right now if he was to complete his goal of killing that Scotsman, Stewart.

A detailed accounting inventory stored near the clean laundry showed how the other gold coins had been spent covering the expedition costs. There was no sign of the ten kilograms of gold that had initially prompted Adbul Issuin's return to the cave. The hawk-faced assassin had to assume that the gold had been left with the Union Bank of Switzerland (UBS) representative in Peking (now Beijing). At the back of the expenses inventory book, Adbul Issuin found a note storage sleeve with a receipt from the UBS branch in Peking, dated Sept 28th 1944. The paper was the documentation related to the deposit for a single item, listed as

"Deutsche Reichsbank 999/1000[479] Goldbarren, 10 kg."

It stated in German that the gold would be transported to UBS, Geneva, should it not be collected within two years from when it was deposited. The small print on the rear of the deposit slip stated that the gold could be collected from UBS Geneva on presentation of the number engraved inside Obergruppenführer[480], Henrik von-Gustoff's totenkopfring

---

[479] 24 Kt gold.

[480] Senior group leader – the second highest rank in the SS, equivalent to a three-star general in NATO.

der SS. Adbul Issuin touched the skull-headed SS ring, which was currently on his right hand's ring finger. So, his final destination was determined, Geneva. The only decision that remained was how to reach Switzerland without being captured by the Chinese authorities. He considered his options. He had checked the large off-road bike as he came up the valley slope and confirmed that it had a full gas tank, meaning it had a range of just under four hundred miles on good made-up roads; however, that range would be less over rough terrain.

To the North of his position were the high mountain ranges of the Gobi, and beyond that, a vast, harsh, empty region of Russia filled with lakes and forests over a thousand miles from Moscow. The terrain to the West was not much better, filled with desert and then the Himalayan Mountain range. The South would take him into mainland China, where he would stand out like a sore thumb in the rural countryside, especially since he was, by now, on the nation's internal security agency "most wanted" list. That left one other option: to head directly towards Beijing, to do what the people searching for him would regard as the least likely response.

With his itinerary determined, Adbul Issuin let his subconscious mind begin to work on how he would achieve his goals of travelling to the Chinese capital and from there on to Geneva. He focused his conscious mind on continuing his search through the objects in the cave. At the bottom of the last rucksack were two boxed items that Adbul Issuin reflected must have been the relics mentioned in the travel journal as being "acquired" from temples by the SS explorers as they made their way through the Philippines and mainland China. The first was a tiny finger bone[481] wrapped in ornate silver filigree, and the other was a small tortoise carapace[482] with some ancient Hanzi[483] engravings on its surface. There was also a hand-drawn map[484] on goatskin vellum. This map included a highly stylised portrayal of the Gobi Desert, with a camel train en route to Metropolis Diablo. This ancient map was inside an acrylic folder with a 1940s aerial survey map of the local terrain printed on silk, as many combat maps were during the second world war. The relics and ancient map were of no value to the hawk-faced man's current mission, so he left them in the cave. However, he did retain the 1940s silk survey map; even though much had changed over the past eighty years, the basic geography of the region remained so that the map could help plan routes.

The only items that he took from the cave and placed in the paniers of the large motorcycle were the eight gold coins, silk map, goggles, a compass and the laundry bag containing the black Falcon paramilitary suit.

Having completed his search of the cave, he sat on the sandy hillside beside the BMW 1250 and lit another Montecristo No 4 as he consulted the silk survey map and a steel and brass Breithaupt compass. The bright red and white colouring of the large bike was not what he would

---

[481] A relic from the revered Taoist Master, Lü Tung-pin. He was an alchemist and one of the Eight Immortals. Although having part of his skeleton casts some doubt over his immortality.

[482] The hard shell of a tortoise.

[483] Characters used during the Shang Dynasty (1600 – 1046 B.C.). Probably an example of a carapace-bone-script – used for divination.

[484] The map constructed by Albertinus de Virga around 1411 that was alleged to have been stolen by the Nazis before the second world war.

have selected, not because he was especially aesthetically critical, but because the global surveillance satellites would have taken an incredibly detailed image of the motorcycle[485]. Unlike other fictional assassins[486], Adbul Issuin's KGB training had instilled in him that any possession that made him more distinctive and more easily identified was a liability. So, although the bike, with its eight-inch wheel travel, was one of the finest vehicles he could have selected for traversing rough and varied terrain, he knew he would have to ditch it as quickly as was reasonably possible.

Having started to formulate a plan, he put on a pair of Neophan desert glasses, mounted the bike and started the 1.2-litre engine. With a smile and deep draw on the Montecristo, he kicked away the bike stand and drove down the hillside with a trail of dust rising behind him.

Back in Beijing, the Police and Paramilitary Police had been alerted to watch for a suspect matching the hawk-faced man's appearance, travelling alone on a red and white BMW R 1250 GS Adventure motorcycle and heading towards the coastal ports of Southern China.

Simultaneously, the internal security apparatus had started to deal with all those personally involved in the successive failures in dealing with *the most dangerous man in the world*. Five miles away from the tall white stone-fronted August 1st Building in Beijing, where Major General Ying had presided over the PLA responses to the initial sightings

---

[485] Regardless of the urban myths and CIA propaganda, the cameras of the global surveillance satellites that orbit the globe are not capable of reading newsprint. They can make out objects around five inches in size at reasonable resolution. So, identifying a six hundred pound, off road bike would be easy.

[486] You know his name.

of Adbul Issuin, the unfortunate former Major General woke to the sound of screaming. He found himself strapped to a wire-framed bed in the same donor organ hospital as had "treated" the former Falcon command and control supervisor, Jip Keing.

Five thousand miles to the West of Beijing, in an exquisitely furnished bedroom within the upper floors of The Apostolic Palace, Cardinal Regio was seated in a reclining red leather, Xten Chair that exuded the design style that only Pininfarina can achieve. Two attractive dark-haired women, gifted with the same sultry looks that once drove Sophia Loren to worldwide cinematic fame, attended on the Cardinal. Both wore tightly fitting Gucci and Prada couture that accentuated their voluptuous bodies. One of the women was gently mopping Regio's creased brow with a Chanel-branded white flannel cloth soaked in Le Labo Santal 33 cologne that filled the air with the distinctive aromatic tones of cardamom, iris, violet and cedarwood. The other woman poured the troubled Cardinal a generous measure of a rich, golden-coloured Vecchia Romagna XO cognac into a fine Murano[487] cut crystal balloon glass.

It had been a disastrous day, reflected Regio. For reasons that his preternaturally enhanced intellect[488] was unable to understand, the resurrection ceremony had failed. A team of elite special forces and a demonic incarnation had been unable to prevent a single, middle-aged Scottish antique dealer from storming the heavily fortified temple and rescuing an incompetent priest. So complete was the disaster that he and his acolytes only just managed to escape the Coliseum with their lives. Given what she may

---

[487] Venetian glass.

[488] Courtesy of his inhabiting MUŠ.ŠÀ.TÙR entity.

have overheard of his plans, the English lawyer Helen Curren had been too risky to leave behind. After dosing her with the "WB[489]" formulae, that he had previously used to erase the minds of Venchencho and Kwon[490], he had his men deposit her at the main airport, where she was rapidly identified and had joined the Scotsman for trial and execution at the Hague.

As the Cardinal sipped the fiery liquor and savoured its distinctive smoky flavour on his tongue, he reflected that at least the meddling Scotsman had been apprehended to face execution. He reassured himself by wondering how far could a heavily bandaged priest, driving a classic red Ferrari, get when the world's finest special forces operatives were now hunting him?

---

[489] Wahrnehmungsblock (patent pending) – Regio's suggested alternative for spiritual deliverance.

[490] According to the late Conrad De Ven both men were currently inmates at the dreaded Sanatorium of St Michael.

26 GAMES PEOPLE PLAY

"Certain souls may seem harsh to others, but it is just a way, beknownst only to them, of caring and feeling more deeply." – The Marquis de Sade.

Hohhot (呼和浩特市) Service Station,
G7 Beijing–Ürümqi Expressway,
Inner Mongolia (China).

11:09HRS (GMT+8), 10th Sept, Present day

Nine hundred miles to the West of Beijing, a red and white BMW off-road bike was cruising at sixty miles per hour in an Easterly direction along the G7 Beijing–Ürümqi Expressway[491]. Although China keeps strict control over its citizens, it has not, as yet, implemented the same extent of camera surveillance as many Western nations, except for strategic zones within cities and near military sites. So, after four hours of travel, Abdul Issuin reached a service station at Hohhot (呼和浩特市) in Inner Mongolia without being detected. Still wearing the dark Neophan glasses, he had wrapped the silk 1940s survey map around his face like a mask to protect against the airborne sand and dust and prevent recognition.

He positioned the big, red and white BMW so it was partly obscured within a long row of other, similar, large off-road bikes. Walking away from the motorcycles and towards the service station shop, the hawk-faced assassin passed a friendly compliment to each fellow biker. It was noticeable that each exchange was deliberately made out of the

---

[491] This 1,500-mile-long toll highway runs from Beijing to Ürümqi, the capital of the Xinjiang Uygur Autonomous Region.

earshot of the previous one and in a different language to minimise any consistencies in witness statements.

The hawk-faced assassin still had some of the Mongolian money he had taken from the group of twelve nomadic traders, who had perished at the oasis some days earlier. He intended to use these limited funds to gain supplies essential for the next stage of his plan to reach Geneva.

The service station supermarket was a single-storey prefabricated building- constructed from sheets of white corrugated plastic. On entering, the senses were assaulted by a mix of scents: body odour, garlic and plastic. Once you had overcome the shock of this strange mix of smells, the next revelation was how much merchandise was crammed into such a relatively small space. There was row after row of eight-foot-high display stands containing an extraordinary variety of low-quality, mass-produced items unified by one factor- their low price.

Abdul Issuin took one of the blue plastic shopping baskets stacked by the entrance and wandered around the indoor market. He filled his basket with what looked like a completely random selection of goods but were, in fact, a precise list of items: a children's stationery kit, paper glue, scissors and a length of laundry rope. Finally, having completed his purchases, the hawk-faced assassin placed his new belongings in one of the store's free, blue plastic bags and then used the service station "photo me" booth to take a set of passport pictures.

The hawk-faced assassin spent the rest of the afternoon sitting alone at a white plastic table near the front window in the service station restaurant. Although he had repositioned the silk map to appear as a neck scarf, he retained his dark glasses, which, along with two days' growth of beard, kept his features reasonably well disguised. After eating a bowl of watery and tasteless chicken noodle soup, he nursed a pot of jasmine tea so that it lasted for over two hours. At that point, a series of six tourist coaches travelling in a mutually supportive convoy along the lonely highway pulled into the service station.

This arrival was something that the hawk-faced assassin had been waiting for, as he quickly abandoned his cold tea, left his table and pulled his dust mask up. Having left the café, he slowly walked past each large coach as the passengers disembarked. The drivers began to unload the luggage for an overnight stop at the small motel, located towards the rear of the service station.

Abdul Issuin paused at each windscreen to read the itinerary until he reached a large, red and gold coloured "Xiamen King[492]" coach that had a paper sticker on the windshield proclaiming, in Chinese, Russian and English:

通往紫禁城的丝绸之路

来自俄罗斯、莫斯科的金熊猫之旅

俄罗斯联邦公务员

Шелковый путь в Запретный город.

Golden Panda Tours из России, Москва.

Государственная гражданская служба Российской Федерации.

Silk road to Forbidden City.

Golden Panda Tours from Russia, Moscow.

Civil Service of the Russian Federation.

---

[492] One of China's leading tourist coach manufacturers.

Abdul Issuin permitted a slight smile to cross his hawk-like features as he seamlessly inserted himself into the line of twenty-three passengers who had exited the Golden Panda tour bus. Each traveller picked up their luggage and slowly walked across the parking lot towards the row of sixty prefabricated, single-storey flat-roofed motel rooms.

As they walked, the hawk-faced assassin watched each of the passengers with extraordinary care, taking in every detail of each individual. He noted their appearance, their gait, and, most importantly, which of them were travelling alone and were not interacting with the other tour members. After this detailed analysis, that only took his experienced eyes a matter of moments; he began to focus on two of the tour members: a larger, short set, older woman dressed in a rather shapeless, grey, full-length polyester skirt with thick glasses, who was rapidly consuming a packet of potato chips and a middle-aged male, with greasy, dark collar-length hair, who was dressed in a black, leather jacket and matching leather trousers. Hanging from the man's belt was a long, thin, steel chain holding a key ring, decorated with a pair of tiny handcuffs. Such a clear signal of the man's propensity towards bondage and discipline sealed his fate.

The moment the coach group approached their motel rooms, this man started to raise his voice threateningly to one of the female motel workers who was just exiting his room, presumably having just completed cleaning. Abdul Issuin directly followed this rather aggressive lone male, arriving just as the man began to snarl and raise his arm towards the more petite cleaning woman, who cowered in evident terror, anticipating a violent, back hand blow across her face. Just as the strike was about to be executed, the hawk-faced man intervened, grasping the man's striking arm and saying quietly, in flawless Russian,

"Сэр, я ученица Донатьена Альфонса Франсуа"

(Sir, I am a student of Donatien Alphonse François[493].)

The man looked startled and then smiled with genuine warmth as he gestured into his motel room,

"Тогда заходи, я обещаю научить тебя"

(Come in then, I promise to teach you.)

Abdul Issuin nodded his appreciation, took over carrying the sadist's luggage and entered the motel room, saying,

"Спасибо, сэр. Я не сомневаюсь, что вечер будет познавательным."

(Thank you, Sir. I have no doubt the evening will be *educational*.)

Moments after the motel room door had closed behind the two men, a sudden cry of pain filled the air, followed by a thud that shook the entire motel complex and then silence.

Inside the room, the leather-clad sadist was lying prone on the floor, hog tied with the clothes line from the hawk-faced man's blue plastic shopping bag. A red silk map was stuffed into his mouth, and his eyes bulged in evident terror at the brutal and effective way he had been rendered utterly helpless. His gaze followed the hawk-faced stranger, who had opened the sadist's luggage onto the motel bed and systematically worked his way through the contents.

For his part, Abdul Issuin had no interest in the numerous sex toys, gags and restraints that came out of the bag. He was only interested in one thing, the man's identification documents. The hawk-faced assassin had focused on this coach because it contained Russian Federation government

---

[493] Perhaps better known as the Marquis de Sade. This 18th century French aristocrat is renowned for his works of fiction related to acts of sexual cruelty that are the basis for the modern terms of Sadism and Sadist.

employees engaged in a knowledge-gathering cultural exchange with the People's Republic of China. Russian Civil Servants were given special privileges during such "cultural exchanges", most notably being able to travel using Russian Federation internal travel documents rather than the more formal laminated biometric passports required for most tourists. Russian internal identity documents were easy to alter for a skilled covert operative, and cultural exchange guests also had special dispensations that included reduced scrutiny at customs and immigration checkpoints. A perfect match for the assassin's plans.

Abdul Issuin opened the old-fashioned red cardboard Russian Federation Internal Identity Passport (RFIDP). He checked the handwritten visa stapled to one of the blue watermarked pages. He noted that the cultural exchange tour visited Beijing and then some highlights of the ancient Silk Route that once linked Cathay[494] to the rest of the world. The assassin checked the dates for each stop on the itinerary and saw the coach had already visited the Forbidden City[495], Ulaanbaatar[496], Karakorum[497], the Huiteng Xile Grasslands and was on its way back to Beijing. A PJSC Aeroflot[498] return ticket for flight SU1287, folded into the rear cover, indicated that the tour was scheduled to fly from Beijing Capital International Airport the following evening at 23:45HRS (GMT+8), arriving back in Moscow at 07:00HRS (GMT+3) on September the 12th.

---

[494] The ancient name for China.

[495] The Forbidden City was the imperial palace of the Ming and Qing dynasties (1368–1912).

[496] Capital of Mongolia.

[497] Capital of the Mongol Empire in the 13th century.

[498] The Russian Federation's National Airline.

This information confirmed his original assumption that the sadist was of potential use in his escape plan. The hawk-faced assassin took the RFIDP[499], walked over to the room's small desktop table and, using the student stationary kit, scissors, glue and passport photographs he had taken earlier, changed the picture to one that confirmed his new identity as:

"Василий Васильевич" (Vasiliy Vasil'yevich)

After burning the actual photograph he had extracted from the RFIDP, the hawk-faced assassin held the freshly glued picture close to the single, hundred-watt bulb table lamp that illuminated the room, so the glue was firmly set. He then lit one of his last Montecristo Number 4s and repeatedly blew thick cigar smoke over the new picture, so it more closely resembled the ageing of the original.

The hawk-faced assassin then practised pronouncing his new name a few times. This repetition caused the hog-tied sadist on the concrete floor to struggle momentarily against his bonds.

Ironically, Abdul Issuin noticed that the identity papers revealed that Vasil'yevich was a permit renewal officer working in the Russian White House[500]- where he managed identity permits within the Presnya[501] district of Moscow. After being satisfied that the new name flowed smoothly and readily from his tongue, the assassin then spent the next hour practising signing his new signature to match the sample on the identity document until it was second nature when writing.

---

[499] Russian Federation Internal Identity Passport.

[500] The central government offices, that includes the office of the President.

[501] Moscow's Presnensky District.

It was improbable that anyone would test these skills. Abdul Issuin vividly recalled the wrinkled former Sicherheitsdienst[502] officer. This old instructor taught the intricate details of cover identities at the KGB's SVR Academy[503], providing accounts about the remarkable number of agents whose covert identities had been compromised by some relatively trivial error.

Once he was satisfied that he was fluent with all aspects of his new identity, the hawk-faced assassin checked the bonds on the hog-tied sadist before leaving the room. He returned moments later with the linen bag from the panniers on the BMW bike and an innocent-looking paper bag from the shop.

The hawk-faced assassin pulled the Sadist up into a sitting position before removing a litre bottle of "безудержный як" (Rampant Yak) from the crumpled brown paper bag, announcing,

"Давай, Василий, злорадство только начинается."

(Come on, Vasiliy, the schadenfreude[504] is about to begin...)

Five thousand miles to the West of the small motel room, Cynthia Sinclair was seated on her cot bed in holding cell 2, eating a meal of cold baked beans on a single slice of burnt toast from a paper plate, using a set of white, plastic cutlery. A lengthy documentary was being shown on her TV and all other media outlets across Europe, describing the social injustices and discrimination that numerous world

---

[502] Sicherheitsdienst des Reichsführers- was the intelligence agency of the Nazi SS.

[503] The Russian Academy of Foreign Intelligence.

[504] The enjoyment of another person's suffering or discomfort.

410

governments had perpetrated against the Fourth Republic over the past eighty years.

Sinclair pulled a face,

"Surely no one can believe this bullshit?"

The broadcast was interrupted by a news flash. An announcer with the striking Nordic looks that now seemed to be the only ethnic group represented on global media came on and stated:

"We bring you some breaking news. Interpol and the United Nations have just informed us that the terror mastermind behind the red death and the UNITY organisation, Tavish Stewart, has been arrested in Rome,"

Some grainy video footage showed a hooded figure being led to a UN helicopter parked in a city-centre car park. The TV announcer continued, in her stern Germanic accent,

"Stewart is currently being transported to the Hague, where he will face trial for his crimes against humanity. A guilty verdict is expected within hours, and the Netherlands government has confirmed that the death penalty will be implemented."

"Kris la, yo te resevwa ou tou, Tavish!" (Christ, they got you too, Tavish!)

Exclaimed Sinclair, just as Brown, Belmarsh's PSWO[505] entered her cramped cell, looking sincerely dejected. He looked down on Sinclair with pity,

"Ms Sinclair, the Home Secretary has just informed us that you are to be transferred to the Hague to face trial alongside Ms Curren and Mr Stewart."

---

[505] Belmarsh's Prison Service Welfare Officer (PSWO).

"Did they indicate when?" queried Sinclair, thinking she might have some time to begin to formulate a plan.

Brown shook his head, "No, they just said we should stand by for the arrival of a UN helicopter. The exercise yard is being cleared as we speak."

Four thousand eight hundred miles to the East of Scheveningen[506], where Sinclair would soon reside, the following morning found the hawk-faced Vasiliy Vasil'yevich, comforting the potato chip-eating female tourist. The two sat together on one of the right-hand front seats of the coach. The sobbing woman had her head buried in the hawk-faced man's shoulder and was holding on to him for comfort due to a horrific accident the coach had just passed. Some unfortunate motorcyclist had been riding a large, red and white off-road bike when it collided with a massive pig transportation truck. The violence of the impact had utterly destroyed the much smaller vehicle and left minimal physical remains of the rider. The police had cordoned off a large section of the highway, reducing traffic down to a single lane. The PLA had also become involved in dealing with the incident, as three Changhe Z-8[507] helicopters had landed beside the highway, and armed troops were carefully examining the accident debris.

The large, sobbing woman pulled herself back from Abdul Issuin's shoulder momentarily and looked into his face, asking,

"Зачем кому-то ехать на встречную полосу ?"

---

[506] The United Nations Detention Unit for people awaiting trial by the International Criminal Court (ICC).

[507] The Changhe Z-8 (Zhishengji-8) is a medium lift transport helicopter used by the PLA.

(Why would anyone ride into the oncoming traffic?)

"Вероятно, они искали острых ощущений."

(They were probably seeking the ultimate thrill.)

Stated the assassin in a calming voice intended to soothe his companion's distress. The woman nodded and hugged her new friend. Strange how these things happen, she thought. She had not noticed him over the past few days until they had met by accident at breakfast that morning. Now it felt like she had known him all her life. It was a fortunate coincidence, as they had so much in common. He was such a lovely, kind man. He had even brought her some more potato chips and guessed her favourite flavour correctly! She put her fat stubby fingers back into the large bag of "Lay's", "pickled cucumbers" flavour chips on her lap, thinking to herself, yes, finally, this man could be "*the one*".

Eight hours later, the couple disembarked from the coach at Beijing Capital International. They passed together through Chinese customs and immigration (the security staff were looking for a Western male travelling alone) and boarded a sleek, two-year-old, eighty-seven-seat SSJ100[508] aircraft for the 23:45HRS Aeroflot flight SU1287 to Moscow.

The potato chip-loving woman relished every moment with her new companion during the flight. He continued to show his appreciation towards her, even letting her eat his dessert from the in-flight meal. She felt so comfortable that she shared details of her hobby of Russian cursive calligraphy. To her delight, she found her companion remarkably well informed on the complex demands of replicating many of the distinctive characters of the script, especially if, like the woman, one could not afford an expensive fountain pen.

---

[508] Sukhoi Superjet 100

After the twelve-hour flight, the Sukhoi Superjet 100 finally landed, just twenty-three minutes late, at Terminal F of Sheremetyevo International Airport and disembarked its fifty-two passengers. At baggage reclaim, the hawk-faced man carried his companion's luggage, and the couple were waved through immigration and customs as "favoured status" state employees.

Inside the busy main lounge of the airport, the couple finally had to separate. The woman had a connecting flight to Rybinsk[509], where she worked as a junior controller for the local port authority. The pair exchanged phone numbers and promised to keep in contact. The crisp-eating woman looked back before stepping onto one of the express moving walkways to Terminal B, where her internal flight was due to board.

Once his crisp eating travel companion had vanished from view, the hawk-faced assassin walked with a slight stoop, still exactly replicating the gait and mannerisms of Vasiliy Vasil'yevich. He soon reached the left luggage unit within the airport. He cited a memorised ticket number[510] at the desk and showed his forged Russian Federation Internal Identity Passport (RFIDP). After a short delay, he was given a small black plastic suitcase. This bag was one of five that he kept in different international locations for when he needed to change "skins"- as identities are known in the espionage profession. The hawk-faced assassin remained in the character of the leather-clad sadist and carried the innocent-looking suitcase into one of the Gent's washrooms. Like the other five suitcases that the assassin had prepared, this case provided everything needed to change appearance and identity, including credit cards,

---

[509] A city that is 166 miles from Moscow.

[510] Left luggage can be stored for a maximum of six months at Moscow's Sheremetyevo International Airport.

onward travel options, and an address kept running by a discreet management service as an occupied dwelling. Noticeably, the case did not contain any weapons or a mobile phone- from the perspective of a covert intelligence operative, weapons attract attention, and phones are simply a way to be tracked

A supremely elegant-looking figure emerged from the same washrooms twenty minutes later. This man's gait, posture and bearing were radically different from the rather shabby, leather-clad man that had entered earlier. Abdul Issuin had shaved, washed his hair, and wore an elegant, dark blue Lufthansa pilot's uniform with a captain's coveted four gold arm bands. His distinctive hawk-like features were hidden behind tinted Ray-Ban aviator glasses and the shadow cast by his peaked cap. Hanging from his jacket's right lapel was a red "Crew Member Certificate" (CMC) photo identification that acted as a visa exemption for flight crew passing through airports[511]. The CMC could also conveniently explain the absence of visa stamps within identity papers.

Poking out from the top of his breast pocket was a burgundy coloured, Bundesrepublik Deutschland (German/EU) biometric passport for Herr Otto Hynsek, from Altstadt[512] in Munich. Herr Hynsek had a distinctive hawklike face and was of the same height and description as Abdul Issuin- except that the assassin had a noticeable loss of weight and face colour that a recent illness or stress could explain. Approaching one of the departure gates, the

---

[511] ICAO Convention on International Civil Aviation states: Contracting States shall accept CMCs, issued according to the requirements of Standard 3.63, for visa-free entrance of crew members when arriving in a duty status on an international flight and seeking temporary entry for the period allowed by the receiving State.

[512] The exclusive and very expensive area of the "old town".

pilot checked his gleaming, steel-cased Breitling Navitimer and presented a valid crew travel authority pass to Geneva.

The tall, blonde stewardess smiled at the newly arrived, handsome, off-duty pilot, who smelt delightfully of a masculine woody scent that spoke of very expensive cologne[513]. After some quite overt flirting, the stewardess booked the newcomer onto the next flight, into first-class, where she informed him she would,

"Personally, see that you get *everything* you need, Sir..."

Issac bin Abdul Issuin beamed his most delightful smile and responded,

"Liebling, please, just call me Otto,"

The stewardess giggled and led the captain down the gangway to the plane, well before the other waiting passengers.

Back in the departure lounge for Terminal B, the former travelling companion of Abdul Issuin was called to her gate to commence boarding. As her ticket was scanned, the attendant checked a typed list and, reaching under the counter, withdrew a small parcel wrapped in Mont Blanc logo themed paper and, handing it over, said,

"Ваша мадам по магазинам."

(Your shopping, Madam.)

As the potato chip-loving woman took the small package in her short, thick fingers, she saw there was a note, written in perfect Russian cursive script, attached.

---

[513] Xeryus Rouge Givenchy: Annick Menardo designed this classic men's fragrance in the mid-1990s, with top notes of Cactus, Chinese Orange and Tarragon.

"Хорошая каракули !"

(Good scribbling!)

Fifteen miles to the West and 15,000 feet above the Russian countryside, Lufthansa flight LH207[514] from Moscow to Geneva was still in a long climb to its cruising altitude, eight miles above the ground for its five-hour flight. The hawk-faced assassin was relaxing, seated in his luxurious grey fabric reclining seat, cocooned in a private first-class cubicle. His tie was loosened and his top button undone as he sipped Moet Imperial champagne from a fluted glass and listened to Mozart[515] on a pair of complimentary Apple earphones.

However, his relaxation was short-lived as he watched the inflight news bulletin in growing disbelief on the high-definition display within his cubicle. His curiosity at the radical changes that had taken place within the short time he had been out of circulation caused him to switch audio streams to listen to the news summary with his full attention.

The first news item was coverage of worldwide mass rallies, all demanding what was being called a *universal political revolution*. This revolution aimed to replace the weak democratic governments with an alternative that promised to restore society's lost values and make humanity strong again.

"That could mean almost anything,"

Muttered Abdul Issuin to himself as he watched and listened to the newscast.

---

[514] An Airbus A380-800

[515] Serenade No. 13 "Eine kleine Nachtmusik"

According to the blonde, blue-eyed news anchor, who spoke English with a slight German inflexion, this new movement had first risen to prominence in South America but had, in recent weeks, rapidly gained popularity within Europe and then in the rest of the world.

Video clips showed mass rallies in all of the world's major nations, except Russia, China and North Korea, where governments had forbidden mass gatherings and had suspended social media.

A second newscaster, who was also striking in his Nordic looks, took over to explain that this universal political movement was led by a charismatic figure called Cortez, who had achieved such universal respect from the general population that the top global social media hashtags were now,

#ChangeforBetter

#ChangetoCortez.

Video clips of Cortez were highly favourable; either this man was fortunate with the footage that had been selected, or he had considerable control over the global media. Closeup images showed a distinguished older man with white hair swept back from his face into a long ponytail that emphasized a classic profile and deep, penetrating blue eyes. Perhaps in his late fifties, Cortez was extremely fit and exuded that rare authority seen in hereditary leaders or dictators who know they have absolute power. Having encountered such authoritarian leaders in many Middle Eastern and Asian dictatorships where he had worked, the hawk-faced assassin suspected this reluctant leader was highly manipulative. The adoring swarms of people would find a very different experience if Cortez were allowed to replace the world's democratic governments.

Abdul Issuin was speculating on what could be responsible for Cortez's meteoric rise in popularity when the first female newscaster returned. This time with a short segment providing an update on the detention by the United Nations of the three key figures responsible for the recent extortion of trillions of dollars and the deaths of billions: Helen Curren, Cynthia Sinclair and the evil mastermind, Tavish Stewart.

The deep-faked videos of Tavish Stewart performing many of Abdul Issuin's most notable recent activities caused an uncharacteristic loss of emotional control in the usually icy cold assassin. The news summary concluded with the statement that Cortez's growing widespread recognition was due entirely to his capturing Tavish Stewart and making him face the death penalty for his crimes.

Abdul Issuin's hand crushed the plastic champagne flute into a pulp as he realised that this man Cortez had framed Stewart for Ad-Dajjal's world domination by digital deceit! Cortez had also transformed the hawk-faced assassin's reputation as *the most dangerous man in the world* into nothing more than a children's fable.

Five hours later, at the automated glass and steel exit doors to the Geneva headquarters of the Union Bank of Switzerland (UBS), a smartly dressed Lufthansa pilot momentarily halted his progress towards the nearby taxi rank. Putting down the moderately heavy[516] black, plastic attaché case, the hawk-faced man removed his pilot's cap and the aviator sunglasses that had been obscuring his features. The hawk-faced man then slowly and very deliberately looked up into the super high definition Siemens CCTV camera that recorded all exits from the bank and smiled directly into the lens.

---

[516] After exiting the bank the bag is probably twenty two pounds (ten kilos) heavier than when it went in.

The megabytes of streaming image data from the Siemens CCTV were intercepted within milliseconds of their arrival into the nearby Cisco router located within the UBS branch.

Abdul Issuin's image was then stored, analysed and catalogued by the complex artificial intelligence systems of the US National Security Agency (NSA) program SIGAD US-984XN (code name PRISM)- in the same way as all other worldwide data are processed by the covert systems buried within US-designed hardware and US-designed software[517],

Buried, some thirty feet beneath the pavements of New York's Fifth Avenue, a spotty-faced junior NSA analyst repeatedly looked back and fore between an image that had just appeared on his screen and a picture that had been framed for posterity on the nearby wall, alongside other notables such as Osama Bin Laden. After several double-takes, he called his group supervisor,

"Clive! Clive! You are going to want to see this...."

---

[517] Under Section 702 of the FISA Amendments Act of 2008.

27 PLOTS AND SUBTERFUGES

"Pride is an admission of weakness; it secretly fears all competition and dreads all rivals." - Fulton J. Sheen.

Borgia Apartments,
Apostolic Palace, Vatican City,
Rome, Italy.

17:23HRS (GMT+1), 13th Sept, Present day

The golden, late afternoon sunlight streamed through the high set windows. The 14th-century inset window casings cast growing pools of shadow over the seven-hundred-year-old oak flooring. The auburn beams of light from the descending September sun began to highlight the exquisitely painted walls of the Room of Mysteries[518]. Above these elegant wall decorations were a series of world-famous Renaissance ceiling frescos by di Betto that perfectly complimented the refined sound of Bach's Goldberg Variations[519] being broadcast through a set of Naim, Mu-so[520] speakers. The rich aroma from the blend of Arabica[521] and Robusta[522] beans wafted from a fine, white

---

[518] The Room of Mysteries was the final room built by Nicholas V (1447-1455) and reserved for the private use of the Pope. Famous for the flawlessly painted faux niches depicting liturgical devices, grotesques and papal symbols on its walls and the ceiling frescos.

[519] BWV 988 by Johann Sebastian Bach, performed by Lang Lang.

[520] A 24-bit/192kHz digital stream from a dedicated 100BASE-TX (100 Mbps) ethernet connection.

[521] From Brazil.

[522] From Africa.

porcelain cup that Pope Alexander VI had once used[523].
This delightfully decadent odour was mixed with the exotic
fragrances of incense and Indian spices from Regio's Bleu
Lazuli[524] cologne.

Soaking in this sophisticated ambience, the bespectacled,
sixty-two-year-old Vatican Secretary-General, Cardinal
Regio, was dressed in his customary, black Gammarelli suit,
matching black clerical shirt and a white dog collar. He held
a primitive single-handed, wooden-handled implement with
a narrow, stylised, gleaming metallic adze[525] in his soft,
white hands. He had just removed it from a bespoke,
velvet-lined, cedar wood storage box that lay open on the
elegant, leather-topped, fifteenth-century desk.

His Eminence was seated under Pintoricchio's[526] classic
fresco depicting the "Adoration of the Magi". The theme of
this Renaissance work appealed to Regio's sense of the
ironic since he would soon be the most powerful entity on
Earth and would become the target of such adoration.

His Wolfsangel counterpart, Cortez, had his dream of
restoring his beloved Fourth Republic to Europe, but the
Argentinian would soon discover that Regio wielded the real
power. That is, the Cardinal reflected after he had dealt with

---

[523] Born as Rodrigo de Borja, better known to history as "Borgia",
he was Pope from the 11th of August 1492 to the 18th of August
1503.

[524] By Giorgio Armani.

[525] The Adze is an ancient cutting tool (usually for wood) that is
similar to an axe but the cutting edge is set perpendicular to the
handle rather than parallel.

[526] The artist's real name was Bernardino di Betto, (1454-1513), he
was an Italian Renaissance painter of small stature, hence his
nickname.

the other MUŠ.ŠÀ.TÙR[527] soul parasite entity that was now his rival for the ultimate power granted to those beings that could survive the completion of the ceremonial opening of The Ten Gates. The death of his fellow Magus and MUŠ.ŠÀ.TÙR sibling[528], who indwelt within Señor Edwardo Salvador, at the Colosseum had initially felt like a significant loss but, after reflecting on the situation, Regio had realised that the fact that only one other MUŠ.ŠÀ.TÙR remained in existence was, in fact, a great opportunity.

As every practitioner of the Great Art knows, there is no such thing as a coincidence. While gathering every possible esoteric relic for the Meri-Isfet, destiny brought Regio the key to removing the single remaining rival preternatural parasite that inhabited Magister Ironheart's body. While cataloguing the Vatican Secret Archive, the Cardinal had acquired a famous Assyrian adze, known to scholars of the most ancient cuneiform tablets as the "UG-ZI-ZU[529]". This ancient Mesopotamian artefact was the only known weapon that, if struck directly into the Sahasrara[530] chakra of an inhabited human host, could kill the indwelling MUŠ.ŠÀ.TÙR entity. The cultural recognition of the item's significance

---

[527] An ancient Mesopotamian mythological creature described as looking like "a horned snake with two forelegs and wings." This semi-immortal soul parasite was the basis for the Greek tale of the Hydra.

[528] The MUŠ.ŠÀ.TÙR entity that had indwelt within the Magus was genderless and the question of its blood relationship to the other, similar, entities was long lost in the mists of time. Besides it is unlikely anyone would be willing to administer the DNA testing required to determine the answer.

[529] Translated literally from primitive cuneiform as the Death-Soul-Blade.

[530] The Sahasrara or Crown Chakra provides the spiritual connection to the higher self and the universe.

was demonstrated by the numerous civilizations that adopted representations of the UG-ZI-ZU as a symbol of supernatural authority, including the "Was Sceptre[531]" carried by Egyptian Gods, Pharaohs and, of course, the British monarchs Sovereign's Sceptre.

As Cardinal Regio reflected on how this ancient object had survived countless millennia to serve its final purpose of enabling his destiny, a seventeenth-century wall clock gently chimed. The noise prompted Regio to check his white-dialled Lange & Söhne gold dress watch.

The cardinal sighed,

"Yes, it's time."

After packing the legendary weapon into its carrying case and walking across the room, he opened a concealed door painted to resemble a tableau of the Crucifixion. Walking through the doorway, he encountered the two smartly dressed female companions who had been tending to him the previous evening. The pair of bodyguards had been seated, patiently waiting, outside *The Room of Mysteries*. Unlike the formal gowns they had been wearing last night, they were now all business, wearing white cotton shirts[532] under black Prada, business suits with calf-length skirts complimented by flat, black leather security[533] shoes. On each woman's left jacket lapel was the Wolfsangel motif. Unnoticed by all but the most experienced eye, who would notice the distinctive distortion in the lines of the jacket,

---

[531] Also called the Heqa sceptre. A symbol associated with the divine rule of the Pharaohs.

[532] The cotton shirts concealed Level IIIA Kevlar Stealth armour by Safeguard.

[533] By Ambler with reenforced toe caps, enhanced grip and shock protection.

both women carried the latest variants of the full-framed M9 Beretta[534] in Galco[535] quick draw holsters.

As Regio started down a long, windowless corridor, decorated on both sides with priceless artwork, the two women fell into step, six paces behind the Cardinal. Moments later, they descended a long, white, marble stairway that led to one of the six side exits from the extensive buildings of the Papal Palace.

Outside the palace, Regio's black BMW limousine was waiting to transport him to the Vatican Heliport, located at the westernmost bastion of the Leonine Wall[536]. Decorated with the gold and silver livery of Simon Peter[537], this Airbus H155 helicopter was scheduled to make the short flight to Fortress Grmožur on Lake Skadar.

Before entering the BMW, Regio turned to his two beautiful bodyguards,

"Have Sichern increase the surveillance around O'Neill's apartment. That idiot will undoubtedly head there, and when he does, I want that to be the end of that meddling priest."

---

[534] The M9A3A is a revised version of the classic, 9mm, Beretta 92F with a 17-round magazine, improved reliability, threaded barrel for suppressors and self-lubricating internal mechanisms.

[535] Galco Miami Classic II

[536] The wall is named after Pope Leo IV, who constructed the massive walls after the Old St. Peter's Basilica had been sacked by Muslim raiders in 846 CE.

[537] The two keys of St. Peter symbolise spiritual authority and temporal authority, respectively which hints that heaven has a spiritual *and* temporal (physical) existence. They are the *keys of the kingdom of heaven* and not *the keys to the gates of heaven* as many believe.

He looked into the heavily made-up faces of the two women before demanding,

"Check it yourselves, understood?"

The two female operatives nodded before watching the large black, stretch limousine draw away into the growing twilight.

Eight hundred and ninety miles North West from the Papal Palace, heavy clouds had flowed over the London skyline all afternoon, dropping temperatures and reminding commuters that they should begin to prepare for autumn. In the garden[538] at the rear of 10 Downing Street, the leaves on the silver birch trees standing beside the large lawn had begun to turn a wonderful golden hue and drop the odd leaf over the carefully tended turf. The few staff who were blessed with office windows overlooking the green space, enclosed within the wire-topped high walls at the rear of the Prime Minister's official residence, felt blessed.

Inside the British Prime Minister's three-hundred-year-old residence, which was originally three separate dwellings until Walpole[539] merged them, the lights gradually came on in most of the one hundred rooms. Inside the White State Drawing Room[540], the subdued interior lighting cast Terry's ornate Baroque style central ceiling[541] and corner mouldings

---

[538] Half an acre.

[539] Robert Walpole, 1st Earl of Orford, KG PC, was the first Prime Minister of Great Britain (1720-1742). He commissioned William Kent, leading architect of the 18th century, to merge the three houses.

[540] Known within Downing Street staffers as "The White State".

[541] Leading British Architect, Quinlan Terry, completed the redesign of the interior in the 1980s.

of the national flowers of the Four Kingdoms[542] into stark relief. On the walls, as is the custom for each new Prime Minister, Sir Reginald Twiffers had his personal choice from the artwork on display at the National and Tate, including, for this room, one of van Gogh's "Sunflowers" and Picasso's "Nude, Green Leaves and Bust". Twiffers had opted to hold the urgent briefing requested by GCHQ in this room to show off these acquisitions.

Usually, the "White State" is furnished with uncomfortable eighteenth-century Adam-style furniture, with exposed wooden frames and woven fabric structures. Especially for this meeting, they had been replaced by three large, brown leather Queen Anne, Chesterfields, with buttoned detail, and one single, captain's style chair, placed directly in front of the three principal chairs. The three larger, more comfortable chairs had matching small mahogany side tables, where copies of the GCHQ briefing notes were placed along with Waterford crystal glasses. Unlike the briefing notes, these glasses were in constant use, receiving top-ups from the latest of three opened bottles of the finest, Emilio Lustau Amontillado VORS[543], sherry brought over from the extensive multi-million-pound Whitehall wine cellars.

Seated in the centremost of the three Queen Ann chairs was the newly appointed Prime Minister, Sir Reginald Twiffers. To his left was the former opposition leader and new Foreign Secretary, Sir Johnathan Premble and, to the Prime

---

[542] Rose for England, Thistle for Scotland, Daffodil for Wales and Shamrock for Northern Ireland.

[543] V.O.R.S. stands for "Vinum Optimum Rare Signatum" (Wine Selected as Optimal and Exceptional). Many native English speakers define VORS as "Very Old Rare Sherry". Such extraordinary sherry is of the supreme quality and is at least thirty years old.

Minister's right, was the new Home Secretary, Lord Jeremy Kenner.

The only slightly inebriated[544] Twiffers turned to Kenner on his right and asked,

"No Clive today, Jezza?"

Jeremey "Jezza" Kenner, who as Home Secretary had direct responsibility for the Security Service, MI5, momentarily stopped the consumption of his sherry and responded, with only the slightest slur in his speech,

"No, Reggie, old chap, I decided Basildon[545] did not need to come. He has a *dinner engagement,*"

Lord Kenner paused, made eye contact with his two colleagues, and gave a wink, producing knowing smiles from both men. Kenner continued,

"With that pretty little *señorita*, you know, the one who Cortez introduced us to at his last soirée. Flirty little thing with legs to die for. What was her name? Angelica?"

"I know what I called her, totally fuckable!" Interrupted Premble.

All three men laughed at the Foreign Secretary's coarse remark, and then Kenner continued,

"Anyone know what this bloody briefing is all about? The notes are like a sodding maths test!"

"Everything from The Doughnut[546] always is," retorted Premble.

---

[544] It was still early afternoon.

[545] The director of MI5, Clive Basildon.

[546] The insiders name for GCHQ – named after the shape of its headquarters building in Cheltenham.

"Isn't that the bloody truth." Confessed Twiffers.

"Comes from hiring the wrong kind of people. They are all geeks, with thick glasses, acne and no sex lives." Asserted Kenner.

At that moment, there was a knock on the oak double doors that led from the Terracotta Room next door and the Prime Minister's personal private secretary, Sir Michael Peters, announced the arrival of the representative from GCHQ,

"Ms Twop, for your 5.30, Sir."

Twiffers consulted the bejewelled face on his 18kt gold Rolex day date and, gesturing to the secretary who had opened the door, said,

"Send her in."

In her thirties, a slim, tall woman with short, bobbed, dark hair and large round, red-framed glasses that made her look like an owl walked into the room carrying an old, black plastic-cased Acer laptop that was covered in various sci-fi-themed stickers[547]. Twop wore a dark blue polyester trouser suit with black leather Puma trainers. Her top jacket pocket had three clear plastic biro pens of various colours, and her jacket lapels were covered in more sci-fi-themed metal badges. Understandably, Twop looked uncomfortable. She had been summoned to give this presentation with such short notice that she had not had time to dress more appropriately.

She walked towards the three men and extended her hand. But, instead of a handshake, she was greeted by a cursory nod towards the captain's chair from the older man seated in the middle of the three chairs, who Twop recognised as the recently appointed Prime Minister, Twiffers. Now she had moved closer to the three senior Ministers; she noticed

---

[547] Thunderbirds, Dr Who and Lost in Space.

a powerful smell of fortified wine, cigar smoke, stale sweat and ammonia[548].   As she took her seat in front of the three men, she could not help but notice residual smears of white powder around and beneath their nostrils.

It was Twiffers who started,

"Where is the director of GCHQ?" he demanded.

"Playing golf," responded Twop.

"Good for Timmy..." responded the Prime Minster.

"Timmy, who?" Asked the Foreign Secretary, Premble.

"I think the Prime Minster is referring to my Director, Lord Timothy Uwefult, Sir," added Twop, helpfully.

"He works for you, old man," added Kenner, less helpfully.

"Ah yes, of course, he does," Premble said, trying to save face.

"Now what can we do for you, Miss... urr.. sorry, Ms Twop?" asked Twiffers, trying to regain control of the meeting so they could conclude as quickly as possible and resume their enjoyment of the world's finest sherry.

"If you read my report, you will see that we have detected a pattern in social media activity over Europe for the past few days." Stated the GCHQ officer.

"Very good, my dear," commented Twiffers as he took another long sip from his sherry glass.   Then, realising he was expected to have a further reaction, he added,

"And this, umm, pattern, concerns you?"

"Yes, this pattern does concern me. It should concern you as well." Twop retorted.

---

[548] The Prime Minister had enjoyed a lengthy *meditation* session with the High Lama.

"Why my dear, you can see we are not concerned." Interjected the Home Secretary in a very fatherly tone.

"But the data suggests a systematic attempt to overthrow the democratic government!" Said the GCHQ analyst indignantly.

Twiffers chuckled, "Now that is rather fanciful, don't you think, my dear?"

The GCHQ analyst looked stunned. After a few moments, she recovered her composure enough to ask,

"Have you actually read my report?"

Twiffers coughed loudly and reached for his briefing papers buried under two empty bottles of Sherry that had made dark red, circular stains on the paperwork. The other two senior Ministers were also busy pretending to refamiliarize themselves with the report. In fact, they were ignoring the detailed five-page summary of social media activity over the past few days. Instead, they were entirely focused on the single-page summary of Twop's civil service record.

The Home Secretary made some quick, handwritten notes on the paper with his gold Cross fountain pen, reached over and showed The Prime Minster and Foreign Secretary a highlighted section of the woman's personnel record. Reading the paper, the Prime Minister raised his eyebrows in shocked horror. The highlighted section on the page was devoted to the woman's education. Next to the area related to school, Lord Kenner had scribbled, "*State Secondary School*," and next to the University were the two words "*Former Polytechnic!*".

Seeing the horror in the men's faces at what they were reading, the GCHQ officer thought that, at last, the men had seen the dangerous trends in the data, so she enquired,

"You see the problem?"

Twiffers looked again at the Home Secretary's handwritten comments related to the non-elite nature of the analyst's education before responding, gravely,

"Yes, my dear, we see the problem now. Thank you for bringing this to our attention."

"What will you do? If this is not addressed, there is a real risk the British Government will be overthrown."

The Prime Minister tried to calm the increasingly irate intelligence analyst.

"Now we all know that will never happen, don't we, my dear? Men of experience, with the right background[549], know that social change is unthinkable in the United Kingdom."

The GCHQ officer looked unconvinced and resumed her plea for immediate action,

"You must do something, Prime Minister! You could authorise GCHQ and MI5 to launch a joint investigation into all key individuals within Government to see who could be involved, as there must be major financial transactions that could be traced."

The colour visibly drained from the faces of the three senior Ministers. The last thing any senior politician wants is a detailed audit of their finances. Fortunately, years of experience evading the detection of countless illegal "donations" made Twiffers quickly react,

"Don't worry, my dear, we will take immediate steps to deal with this. I will write to your director and have some action taken."

Twop looked relieved,

---

[549] Eton and Oxbridge.

"Thank you, Sirs."

Twiffers smiled, looking like a benevolent leader,

"Not a problem, my dear. Leave it to us, "

He gestured towards the door she came in through.

After the analyst had left, the Home Secretary scribbled a note on the woman's civil service record to be passed to the central administration. The other two men chuckled as they read what he had written in his fountain pen,

"Unsuitable for current position, transfer to Welsh Assembly[550] at soonest. Kenner."

The Foreign Secretary took Lord Kenner's pen and changed the proposed destination from "Welsh Assembly" to the "Falkland Islands",

Twiffers nodded his approval and co-signed the instruction before asking,

"Now then, gentlemen, having concluded today's business, who fancies some Niepoort in Lalique 1863 Port and Fortnum's[551] stilton cheese biscuits?"

One thousand, one hundred miles to the South East of London and two hours later, the silence over the toad green vineyards of Godinje was disturbed by the sound of the two Safran Arriel 2C2 turbine engines from a low flying, long-range helicopter with distinctive Papal livery. The H155 Eurocopter flew at over 160 knots, swooping low over Lake Skadar's waters as they glistened in the dying rays of the

---

[550] The "Metro-Elites" have a misguided view of Scotland and Wales, and the rest of the UK, for that matter.

[551] Fortnum and Mason are an exclusive department store in Piccadilly, London.

setting sun, before circling once around Grmozur Island and coming into a perfect landing on one of the four floating helipads located at the Southern end.

The bespectacled Cardinal Regio had spent the short flight listening to one of the many debates systematically broadcast from every media outlet in Europe. The languages and experts were different in each nation, but the discussion's focus and conclusions were identical. This was not a surprise, as social influencers at *Beyond Facts* had carefully choreographed each debate.

Regio reflected that one of the benefits of the modern, internet-fed, post-fact-world was that there was always "an expert" prepared, for a fee, to speak with solemn certainty in support of any idea, no matter how inaccurate, absurd or dangerous.

In this case, "authorities" from leading universities systematically informed populations throughout Europe that democracy was a harmful waste of humanity's ever-dwindling resources. The experts argued that each successive government spent countless billions of taxpayers' money reversing the policy decisions of the previous government. To add to this wasteful situation, the experts argued that over the past fifty years, the political parties in Western nations had moved closer and closer to a single core ideology of social democracy that only differed in the mechanisms of implementing that core ideology. The experts concluded in a masterfully choreographed end to the debate that sounded spontaneous that a single, strong leader would bring a stable, coordinated path of progress without the chronic waste characterised by the bloated bureaucracies needed to support the constant changes of government. The debates concluded with the presenter summarising hundreds of thousands of supporting posts from numerous global social media streams, all with the

hashtags #endwastefuldemocracy
#freeeuropefromdemocracy.

The Italian Cardinal chuckled at how well the Wolfsangel plan was progressing; the social media-obsessed, post-fact-world made the ideological takeover of Europe much easier and quicker than the last attempt with its crude panzers[552] and blitzkrieg[553]. This time, the population believed whatever their beloved social media devices told them to believe. They had decided to implement change and would shortly be guided to start demanding it.

Regio paused before exiting the Papal aircraft. After opening the cedar wood carrying case, he took out the "UG-ZI-ZU" adze and placed it, striking head first, into a specially designed inner pocket that he had instructed his tailor to make inside his jacket. The inside pocket concealed the adze but permitted its rapid drawing to strike Ironheart's Sahasrara Chakra when the opportunity arose. The Cardinal held such a low opinion of Magister Ironheart that he thought it inconceivable that the Swede would expect the much smaller, older Regio to initiate an attack. Ironheart's obsessive fixation on Viking magick and his complete disinterest in the more profound history of the occult would mean he would probably not even be aware of the existence of the ancient Assyrian weapon. Let alone its unique ability to kill the semi-immortal MUŠ.ŠÀ.TÙR soul parasites.

Exiting the side door of the Eurocopter, Regio approached the senior of the six attendants who had come to escort the Magus to the fortress where, in under five hours, the ceremony for which the building had been created would commence.

---

[552] Nazi tanks

[553] Literally, rapid war. Imploying aircraft and rapidly moving tanks and troops to overwhelm an opponent.

Regio turned his attention back to the present and asked the lead assistant, a tall man with dark hair and a Meri-Isfet striking cobra symbol embroidered on his dark linen jacket,

"Updates?"

The man looked genuinely apprehensive as he stated hesitantly,

"Some setbacks I fear, your Eminence."

Regio had anticipated that things would go wrong. Just so long as nothing prevented the opening of the Ten Gates, he would deal with whatever had happened *after* the evening's ritual.

"Nothing that will prevent *The Ceremony*, I trust?" Regio calmly enquired.

The tall attendant gulped,

"I do not think so, your Eminence."

Regio looked relieved,

"Good, then they are of minor importance. What are they?"

"When our two sisters visited O'Neill's apartment in Rome to check on security, as you instructed on your departure, they found the four Sichern guards had already been subdued. The operatives were tied up. Their uniforms and equipment were gone along with Venchencho's black Mercedes."

Stated the attendant nervously. He had seen first-hand how Magister Ironheart handled bad news, and he thought the Cardinal was likely to react just as violently.

Thankfully, Regio took the news calmly,

"O'Neill has more balls than I anticipated. No matter. Increase the guards at the Sanatorium of Saint Michael....."

The Cardinal could see the nervous reaction of the assistant to this last instruction, so he asked,

"What?"

The attendant was terrified of the Cardinal's reaction to this next item of news, as he paused before finally answering,

"It's too late, Sir. The Sanatorium was stormed some six hours after the incident at O'Neill's apartment."

"Stormed? How many men were involved?" demanded Regio.

"The six guards claim it was an overwhelming force, but when our two sisters from Rome reviewed the CCTV footage of the attack, they could only see one person."

"One man?"

"Yes, sir, he arrived in what looked like Venchencho's old car. He was dressed in Sichern body armour and using one of the MP7 rifles. He quickly stormed the building and freed two of the patients."

"Venchencho and Kwon." The cardinal stated calmly,

"Yes, your Eminence."

The attendant still looked apprehensive, so Regio asked,

"Is that it?"

The attendant shook his head,

"No, Sir. The Magister is dead."

This time Regio looked shocked. He had not felt any discontinuation within the power of the Meri-Isfet. But the Cardinal did not mourn the passing of his colleague. Indeed, he had been planning to terminate him but only *after* he had assisted in opening the Ten Gates. It was impossible for a single high-grade adept, even one as accomplished as Regio, to complete the ceremony alone. Centuries of preparation would have been wasted if they could not complete the planned operation that night.

Regio looked at the attendant as one would look at an imbecile,

"Brother, how is it that you think that Ironheart's death will not affect The Ceremony?"

The attendant smiled for the first time in the entire interaction,

"Because, your Eminence, he has been replaced by another Master of the Great Art."

"What?!" Regio's face suddenly matched the crimson colour generally associated with members of his ecclesiastical rank. He brushed the attendant aside and hurried towards the open gates of Fortress Grmožur.

28 FRIENDS IN LOW PLACES

"Several early magical texts, including the Eighth Book of Moses[554], Testament of Solomon[555] and the Ghâyat al-Hakîm fi'l-sihr[556], make mention of a most ancient ritual called, the Claudendo Infernum[557] or 'iighlaq aljahim. If these accounts are to be believed, this ceremony was regarded by the ancients as the ritual of last magical resort. Although no copies of the Infernum remain extant, we can guess at the nature and intent of the ceremony, since the grimoires that mention it have the common theme of conjuring a more powerful evil to cast out lesser evils that have been summoned into the physical realm. The ceremony was certainly not to be undertaken lightly, since the cost of summoning such an ultimate evil was the death of the magician(s) performing the ritual." - Hand written addendum to History and Principles of Theurgy by Elias Ashmole, 1667. MS 3444, Ashmolean Museum of Art and Archaeology, Oxford.

*Place du Bourg-de-Four
1204 Genève, Switzerland*

23:30HRS (GMT+1), 13th Sept, Present day

The distinctive bells of the twelfth-century St. Pierre Cathedral marked the half-hour, echoing across the damp

---

[554] A fourth-century CE Greek papyrus part of the Papyri Graecae Magicae.

[555] A first century CE Greek papyrus that was later used and adapted by magicians of subsequent centuries.

[556] A tenth century Arabic magical text. Ghāyat al-Ḥakīm (غاية الحكيم) means Goal of the Wise.

[557] Literally, "closing hell".

cobblestones of the Place du Bourg-de-Four, temporarily masking the cascading sound of water from the ornate fountains. The few remaining street lamps illuminated the deserted central square as the staff at the cafes finally headed home after a long day. Most of the shops had brought in their tables and withdrawn their awnings in preparation for the first mountain storm of the season. Given the city's altitude, it was even possible that the morning would find the ancient cobblestones gifted with their first light scattering of snow.

This tranquil evening scene was disturbed by the arrival, from up a side street, of a small, curved, green and white, autonomous electric minibus marked with the distinctive TPG[558] livery. The only sound that the twelve-seater minibus made as it pulled up close to the concealed entrance to SPLEE[559] was a chime that marked that the small vehicle was about to halt to allow passengers to disembark. As the bus side double doors opened, three figures, two men and one woman, stood and slowly exited the cabin. A male and the female stepped out first, and they then assisted the other man, who was quite unsteady on his feet, down from the raised interior of the minibus.

All three individuals required walking sticks to help them negotiate the uneven cobblestones made more slippery by the recent passing of the city road cleaners. During the three figures' slow progress towards the SPLEE doorway, they could be heard complaining. Their complaints included how their arthritis was always worse before a storm, that their balance was terrible tonight, and that they would be

---

[558] TPG: Transports publics genevois also known as Geneva Public Transport.

[559] SPLEE: Société pour la préservation des lignages ésotériques européens.

unlikely to sleep that night as it was so late after their accustomed bedtime.

Frater Gabriel led the group, dressed in his usual tweed jacket and matching trousers. By his right side was Soror Emmilia, wearing a long black velvet dress, her thick, white hair braided into a long pony tail that went down the entire length of her back. Frater Aron walked to Gabriel's left and was having balance problems. His thick-set body struggled over the slick wet cobble stones, one hand on his three-pronged stability cane while the other clasped his beloved brushed aluminium Dell laptop close to his side.

The group were met at the SPLEE building doorway by Frater Léon, his shock of white hair highlighted in the red light[560] cascading out from the lodge's interior. Léon's heavily wrinkled face looked grim after receiving the news that had prompted this late-night meeting of the chiefs. Léon's right hand held the trusty Sphinx 2000 pistol covering the square behind the three senior adepts. The overt presence of the weapon showed that the time for the pretence of antiquated weapons had passed. With Mathers compromised, the Meri-Isfet could launch an attack on the Geneva lodge.

Once all four adepts were inside the building, Soror Emmilia was the first to speak.

"Gods, it's cold in here!" She exclaimed, rubbing her hands together.

"The heating goes off at five when no meetings are scheduled." Explained Frater Léon with a note of sympathy.

"It will be even colder in the Temple," added Frater Aron, before looking expectantly towards Frater Gabriel and adding, "Could we not meet here in the foyer, Gabriel?"

---

[560] A colour selected to minimise the loss of night vision.

Gabriel smiled at the constant complaints from his two colleagues,

"No, for a matter this serious, it is best we position ourselves within the Brocken-Rennes[561], for we need every advantage we can muster."

While Frater Léon pulled across a massive medieval wooden draw bar to seal the innermost door to the building, the three senior adepts made their way slowly to the temple, Aron complaining as they did,

"Why so many bloody steps?"

Emmilia laughed, "You know damn well why."

By the time all three of them had completed their unsteady descent of the ten steps and entered the dark hall, Frater Léon had passed beside them and had begun lighting the tall, beeswax candles that were the sole illumination to the sacred space.

Gabriel called to him,

"No need for all of them, Léon. We will sit here on the nearest bench,"

as he gestured towards the oak pews on the left-hand side of the long room with its high vaulted ceilings and stone floor. A distinct chill had started to permeate throughout the temple, matching the more significant chill that was soon to spread through the world, reflected Gabriel. The few candles at the end of the first pew flickered as they cast long, dark shadows that vanished into the impenetrable darkness at the far end of the long room. The four adepts stood in front of the pew in a roughly semi-circular formation as Frater Léon ignited a small tree of rose incense

---

[561] The major European ley line running through the Meri-Maat Geneva temple.

on a silver tray located on a specially designed incense shelf carved into the end of the bench's hand rail. The glowing essence began to fill the air with a subtle scent of roses.

The four adepts then joined hands in their small semi-circle. They began to chant a series of deeply resonating intonations similar to Egyptian God names but were actually vowel-rich resonances known to enhance psychic energy flows and preternatural receptiveness.

"RAAaaaaaa... RAAaaaaaa... RAAaaaaaa... RAAaaaaaa... RAAaaaaaa[562]"

"MAaaaaaa... MAaaaaaa... MAaaaaaa... MAaaaaaa[563]"

The mantras complete, Gabriel hobbled towards the centre of the hall and performed the Lesser Banishing Ritual of the Pentagram[564], followed immediately by the Lesser Banishing Ritual of the Hexagram[565]. Notably, both rituals were completed without notes or prompting. Although the three senior adepts were not intending to perform a ceremony, at that moment, they needed to avoid being overwatched by some unseen astral form.

As the nonagenarian turned to face the direction of the other two adepts, the magical force from his banishing guttered the flickering candles. This event temporarily cast the temple into total darkness until Frater Léon, who was expecting the occurrence, relit them using a long wax taper and a box of Swan safety matches.

---

[562] Five intonations – an odd number, associated with a positive polarity.

[563] Four intonations – an even number, associated with a negative polarity.

[564] Banishing the magical prime elements of Air, Fire, Water, and Earth respectively.

[565] Banishing magical influences or entities from the higher planes.

As the temple's atmosphere became charged with powerful, invisible, astral forces, Frater Léon returned to the Temple door, where he stood on guard, his steady hand holding the 9mm Swiss Army automatic ready, should it be needed.

The precautions completed, the three elderly adepts gathered themselves onto the nearest oak pew and began to discuss the recent developments in the situation related to their prodigy, the French adept, Mathers.

"The last we heard from her was Aron's email." Stated Emmilia in a tone that intimated that the blame for the current situation lay with the two men.

"She would have done an astral projection before physically entering that fortress," said Aron trying to reassure.

"Yes. But something has happened to her," Affirmed Emmilia before continuing, "I have tried to.."

Gabriel interrupted, "Yes, Emmilia, we all have tried to reach her numerous times."

"My readings indicate that she is still alive, in a form, but we must face the reality that whatever the Meri-Isfet did to her has transformed her nature." Said Aron.

"Yes, I tried to reach her, but all I got was a profound sense of evil looking back." Gabriel acknowledged.

Emmilia looked pointedly at the two men sitting beside her, "It is our karmic responsibility for sending her."

"She made her own decision." Replied Aron, but it was clear from his tone that he also felt tremendous guilt for what had happened.

"Don't just feel sorry for yourself. It is down to us to do something!" Emmilia exclaimed, adding, "In her email, she said they had The St Petersburg Wheel."

"Impossible." Responded Aron, not wanting to accept the terrifying possibility.

"If she says she saw it, then they have it." Responded Emmilia coldly, then continuing, she added,

"If they open the ten gates with the wheel running, unimaginable evil will be released."

"The rise of the Nephilim all over again." Agreed Aron.

"That would require many wheel operations, but I agree even one use will threaten the world," admitted Gabriel.

"And raise the senior Meri-Isfet adepts to unimaginable power." Added Aron.

Emmilia sighed, "Even in our prime, we three would not have been powerful enough to stop them. But now we are so weak and old; we are next to useless."

"We must try!" said Gabriel forcefully, fearful that his two colleagues were losing heart to continue the battle against evil.

"What about that person Madeleine said was an ally?" Asked Aron.

"He is not an initiate; just a man Wolfsangel has targeted." Responded Emmilia gloomily.

"He must be a threat to their plans if they are targeting him." Argued Gabriel.

"You have a point," conceded Emmilia reluctantly, "Let us at least inform him of her disappearance and her change in loyalty."

"We owe him that in case she comes for him and misuses his trust." Agreed Aron.

"After we have told him, we three have no option but to perform the Claudendo Infernum," Stated Gabriel solemnly.

There was a long moment of silence as the other two adepts took in the full implications of their leader's demands. Completing the Claudendo Infernum was not just a death sentence for all three adepts- it would release an evil capable of destroying whatever nightmare was being summoned by the Meri-Isfet. The karmic consequences of releasing such a supreme evil were far more frightening to the three adepts than the end of their current mortal incarnation.

"But it is forbidden unless under extreme threat!" Said Emmilia forcefully.

"Can you think of a more extreme threat than opening the ten gates with the wheel?" Asked Aron.

"We are too infirm to perform it," Countered Emmilia.

"Can you think of anyone else who could?" Gabriel asked both of his oldest friends, looking sadly into their eyes. The two other adepts shook their heads.

"That's settled then," said Gabriel, "Let us go back to the foyer and use the hall phone. Then we come back in here and do what we must."

A few long minutes later, Gabriel's arthritic fingers struggled with the grey, 1960s wall-mounted rotary dial phone set up in the foyer, dialling each number as Aron read it from Mathers' email. When the line finally connected, it rang for over a minute before it was finally answered.

Gabriel asked in English,

"Hello? Please forgive me for calling at this late hour. I believe that you know a Ms Madeleine Mathers?"

There was a response, but only Gabriel could hear it.

"Yes, yes, we are associated with Ms Mathers."

Another muffled response.

"Sir, we need to talk with you most urgently. Yes, right now."

The speaker on the other end of the line made some query.

"How important? The entire fate of the world depends on it."

Another muffled response.

"No, sir, I assure you I am not exaggerating."

Four hundred and twenty miles to the North of the SPLEE Lodge in Geneva, at the United Nations Detention Unit at Scheveningen, Chairman Cortez was making an impromptu visit from the UK. He intended to visit the three UNITY/Maelstrom prisoners facing trial for Crimes Against Humanity[566] the following morning at the ICC[567].

The UN ICC commandant, Kapitein De Jong, was dressed in the smart grey-green trousers, jacket, dress shirt, tie and beret of the Royal Netherlands Army[568] service dress uniform[569]. De Jong had met Cortez's distinctive maroon-coloured Royal helicopter[570] at the Scheveningen Heliport, located some thirty yards outside the prison's twenty-foot-

---

[566] Under international law, crimes against humanity refer to specific crimes committed in the context of a large-scale attack targeting civilians, regardless of their nationality.

[567] International Criminal Court.

[568] Koninklijke Landmacht.

[569] Dagelijks tenue or DT.

[570] An AgustaWestland AW109, modified for fewer passengers and greater comfort. This aircraft is from The Monarch's Helicopter Flight. The aircraft is available for senior UK Government use.

high perimeter, electrified razor wire fence, search lights and armed K9[571] patrols.

"Good evening, Chairman," said De Jong, in flawless English that is so often spoken by Dutch nationals. He escorted the visiting UK Government representative through the checkpoints at the main gates and into the prison complex. The armed guards came to smart attention as the men passed by them. Cortez, dressed in a black, worsted wool, Hugo Boss, three-piece suit, and matching Barker, black leather Burford shoes, took the VIP treatment by the prison authorities in his stride, as if he had always been accustomed to such exceptional treatment all his life[572].

Once inside the modern brick building, the pair made their way through long, grey and white corridors that smelt of pine disinfectant. Their progress towards the specialised UN Detention Unit was halted now and again as they completed numerous security checkpoints at each of the "Sallyway" sets of paired locked gateways.

De Jong informed his guest, "Your three detainees are quite the celebrities. Since their arrival, we have had nonstop media interview requests."

"All denied, of course." Replied Cortez forcefully.

"Yes, yes, of course, as specified by their arrest documentation." Said De Jong, realising that his guest was fixated on these prisoners. The Dutch officer continued,

"I just meant that these detainees make a change from the normal guests we have from around the world's war zones."

Cortez made no response. He did not care about the other prisoners or the mundane duties of this boring glorified

---

[571] Belgian Shepherd Dog (Groenendael).

[572] He had.

policeman. All the Argentinian wanted was to see that bastard Stewart suffering on the night before he faced a trial that Cortez had exquisitely manipulated to ensure the final destruction of this Scotsman's reputation. In addition to the shocking deep fake materials related to the UNITY multi-trillion USD extortion and the mega deaths[573] associated with the Red Death bioweapon, he had prepared something extra. This addition took the form of faked evidence from Stewart's military service, showing that even before the UNITY atrocities, the Scotsman had been routinely violating the Geneva Convention.

They finally arrived at the UN detention unit. It contrasted with the main prison's stark grey and white colour scheme by the UN's signature blue and white on the walls. As De Jong signed his guest into the visitor log, the Dutchman asked,

"Did you want to see Curren and Sinclair?"

"No, just the main prisoner." Answered Cortez abruptly.

"Yes, of course." De Jong responded, "Stewart is in our special high-risk facility. It is a large cell with a clear glass front, so the suspect always remains visible. A guard has been posted around the clock to monitor the suspect."

Cortez smiled, "Excellent." The Argentinian thought to himself how such continuous observation would weaken the morale of even the strongest man.

"What has he been doing?" Asked Cortez.

"He seems to have found God and spends most of his time praying. Often in Latin," answered De Jong.

---

[573] A unit used in quantifying the casualties of weapons of mass destruction. The unit is equal to the deaths of one million people.

The Dutchman noticed how his VIP visitor looked puzzled, so he added, "It sometimes happens when people face the consequences of their actions."

At that moment, they arrived outside an extensive glass frontage some twelve feet tall and twenty-five feet wide. The window looked into a single, large room, around twenty feet square. The cell was equipped with a bed, steel toilet, wash basin, table and chair, all fixed to the floor. The entire room was in darkness, making it hard to see what the occupant was doing.

"Can we raise the lights?" enquired Cortez.

De Jong nodded to the uniformed guard seated in front of the large window. Moments later, the room was illuminated by fluorescent bulbs in the ceiling.

At the far end of the room was a dark-haired man dressed in a one-piece, orange jumpsuit. He was facing away from the window and kneeling in prayer.

"Mr Stewart, you have a visitor." Called De Jong into a steel, Philips branded microphone and speaker system embedded into the blue coloured wall beside the massive area of armoured glass. The dark-haired man rose from his prayers and turned, walking towards them. His face was severely bruised, and his grin showed extensive metal braces around his teeth.

Cortez exploded at the Dutch Kapitein, "Is this a fucking joke? This man isn't Stewart!"

One hundred and ninety miles to the West of the Hague, one of the private Park Lane facing balconies of the Dorchester Hotel was partly illuminated. Beyond the high sash windows of the Eisenhower Suite, a distinguished man, wearing a gleaming white dishdasha with a long-embroidered cape embellished with golden threads[574], sat on the edge of the same grand, four-poster bed used by Eisenhower when planning the D-Day landings. This man had booked into the Dorchester a few hours earlier as HRH Prince Ahmed bin Khalifa and had paid in advance for a week-long stay in cash.

Placed on the bed beside him was a suite of highly specialised apparatus that the Prince had purchased, again in cash, at Lorraine Electronics Surveillance[575], shortly after his arrival at the London St-Pancras Eurostar terminal, before his check-in at the Dorchester. The equipment consisted of a grey DVD-player box, with a matt, black laptop resting on its top. Numerous connecting cables linked the grey, Gossamer GSM Interceptor base unit to the black Stealth ColorWare, MacBook Pro running a Mil-Spec variant of Fishhawk, Over-The-Air special signal software[576] attached to a specialised Harpoon range-extending amplifier.

The speakers on the Mac were playing a phone conversation between a forceful sounding man with an Argentinian accent who was, based on the background noise, a passenger in an executive helicopter. The second person in the overheard conversation spoke with a British accent. Based on the tracking information displayed on the laptop screen, the aircraft was currently on a route from the Netherlands to bring it into London City Airport within the next half an hour. The other speaker in the monitored phone conversation was located in St James's Square

---

[574] Called a "Bisht".

[575] Located near Leyton Midland Road Rail Station in London's East End.

[576] Monitors GSM (Global System for Mobile communications) phone calls and breaks the encryption.

London[577], less than a mile from where the white dishdasha-wearing Prince Ahmed bin Khalifa was seated on the four-poster bed.

"Resume the search for the Scotsman immediately! Use all our resources and find him. It should not be difficult. No one on earth will assist a man with his reputation." commanded Cortez.

"Understood, Sir." Said the British voice.

"I should be landing in around....." there was a pause while Cortez spoke to the pilot, "forty minutes. Have the Maybach ready to meet me on the tarmac."

"Yes, Sir," the obsequious voice agreed.

The line disconnected. Prince Ahmed bin Khalifa rose from the bed and walked purposefully over to the balcony doors and, after stepping out into the night air, he struck a match and lit a Montecristo No. 4. The glowing end of the Petit Corona cigar briefly illuminated a distinctive, hawk-faced profile.

One thousand six hundred miles to the South East, from where Prince Khalifa was enjoying his Montecristo, a classic red 1960s Ferrari 250 GT and a jet black 1970s Mercedes 450 SEL 6.9 stood alongside a white Toyota Land Cruiser and a Fiat Ducato Ambulance[578]. The ambulance and Land Cruiser were covered in numerous biohazard symbols

---

[577] The location of "The Silver Club".

[578] Emergency Ambulance Fiat Ducato Box Body Type B / Light A+E 4.25 T.

demanding HAZMAT[579] level A[580] precautions and "WHO Ebola Response Team" livery. These four vehicles were all parked on an area of hard standing that surrounded an eighteenth-century, classic, single-storey Mediterranean-style villa with whitewashed walls and terracotta roof tiles. The engines on the vehicles were emitting those tell tail clicking noises made by automobiles that have been driven hard over long distances. Copious layers of dead insects and dust added to the evidence of a seven-hour journey undertaken by the four vehicles on the E45[581]. They had travelled from San Pietro della Ienca[582], in the mountains of Abruzzo, down through the countryside to the tip of the "boot of Italy", at the Villa San Giovanni ferry port.

Although the off-white-coloured gravel provided a classic elegance to the trained eye, it also gave a twenty-yard clear space between the villa and any surrounding vegetation or rocky outcrops that could have acted as cover for unwelcome visitors. The noise caused by walking on the shingle combined with the light colouring of the small stones meant that visitors made considerable noise and were greeted by the highly territorial flock of seven Tufted Roman geese[583] who called the hard standing their home.

---

[579] Hazardous Materials.

[580] The highest level of protective equipment and protocols against direct and airborne chemical contact.

[581] European Route E45 is a 3100 mile long north-south highway between Gela in southern Italy to Alta in northern Norway.

[582] The location of the infamous *Sanatorium of St Michael*, devoted to the care of Exorcists who have fallen under the "extraordinary influence" of Evil.

[583] Traditional and highly effective guard animals – said to have saved the city of Rome from a clandestine attack by Gauls in the fourth century BCE.

The villa's location at the summit of one of the highest hills near the small Sicilian town of Riesi required anyone intending to visit to travel two miles up an exposed, winding single-lane track. The track had been paved with the same gravel as the hard standing but deliberately combined with a mix of fine sand that raised a significant dust cloud. These passive security measures did not look significant to the untrained eye but, in reality, guaranteed that anyone intending to visit Villa Donne would give away their intentions almost immediately.

As one approached the dwelling, one noticed the chirping of numerous male cicadas singing as they gathered in the oak trees, brambles and poison ivy that covered the hillside. Closer to the villa, a deep exotic, tropical scent wafted from the numerous Pomelia[584] trees planted in large clay urns on the veranda.

Inside the house's kitchen and living area, a group of ten tough-looking men and women with dark hair and short stature had gathered around a long oak kitchen table. Each wore similar medical-themed white cotton shirts and dark trousers. Almost all of them smoked Marlborough brand cigarettes, making the air thick with grey smoke and an intense aroma. Due to the humidity, many had removed their white medical coveralls and hung them on the backs of their chairs, revealing numerous empty leather pistol holsters. Their weapons, a mix of Italian and American sidearms with small calibres[585], were stacked neatly on a table, near the living room door, beside an assortment of secondary weapons that included throwing knives, stilettos and, of course, razor wire.

---

[584] Frangipani

[585] These men were not interested in showing off – only with effectiveness and ease of use.

Seated at one end of the table, with his back towards the unlit hearth, was a man who bore a strong familial resemblance to the figure shown smiling in an old black and white photograph of Stewart's late friend, Mario Donne. Mario ran the Stewarts showroom in Rome before being brutally tortured and killed by Maelstrom. Capomandamento[586] Donne was a short, clean-shaven, well-built man in his sixties with greying hair. As Mario's oldest son, he had taken over the "Cosche" (family business) when his father had opted to retire to work with Stewart in Rome.

On his old Nokia phone, at the other end of the long table, Tavish Stewart had just finished the speakerphone call with Frater Gabriel from the Geneva SPLEE lodge. Before the unexpected call, the assembled Capos[587] discussed how to help Venchencho and Kwon. After being rescued, both men sat on a nearby sofa, looking vacantly into the distance, while being fed some minestrone by two women, one of whom Stewart recognised was Mario's widow.

Unlike the stark medical attire of the people gathered around the table, Stewart wore an unbranded light blue oxford cotton shirt, lightweight grey chinos and a pair of leather deck shoes, which he had picked up in one of the many tourist shops that fill Messina.

The assembled group had listened to the interruption from the mobile phone conversation in silence. They now waited for their leader to make some assessment.

Capomandamento Donne looked at Stewart and cut straight to the point,

---

[586] A Capomandamento is the head of a "mandamento" territory of three geographically contiguous cosche (Mafia families), that control specific areas of Sicily. Such a high-ranking "boss" is entitled to be part of the Mafia Commission or "Dome Quarry".

[587] A Capo is the head of a Mafia unit.

"You believe what this Gabriel said?"

"I do," said Stewart, "I know it sounds farfetched, but I have seen first-hand some of the abilities of the people planning this ceremony at Fortress Grmožur tonight. I have no problem believing that they intend to try and perform a ritual to bring untold evil into the world."

The Capomandamento grunted and then continued,

"And what of this wheel contraption? You believe that as well?"

Stewart was more cautious, "I have not had first-hand experience of it, but yes, I believe these devices could magnify the effects of any ceremony."

The Mafia Boss looked at Stewart, clearly assessing how seriously he should take this threat before he continued,

"And you say these are the same bastards who did this..." he gestured towards the blank-faced Venchencho, "... *outrage* to the Holy Father? And," he added with even greater disgust, "they kidnapped the royal heirs, including mere children, in order just to kill them for *pleasure*?"

A look of anger crossed the faces of all those assembled at the table. Whatever the nature of their own "family businesses", abducting and drugging The Pope and kidnapping and then murdering children for what was essentially sick entertainment was a step too far, even for them.

Stewart nodded. "Yes. These are the same people."

The Capomandamento assumed a calm but menacing tone.

"These *bastardos* begin their ritual in," he consulted a white gold Vacheron Constantin Patrimony[588] watch, "twenty

---

[588] Reference: 81180/000G-9117. White dial, 18k white gold. Who says crime does not pay?

minutes. Stewart, do you have any suggestions on what we, humble," the Boss looked around his Capos, "*Men and Women of Respect* [589] can do to help you throw a spanner into these Pazzo[590]'s plans?"

Stewart smiled at the understatement of the capabilities of the assembled men and women who, he knew, formed a significant proportion of the infamous "dome quarry"- the legendary governing body of La Cosa Nostra, and nodded his gratitude for their offer of assistance.

"Lake Skadar is too far for us to launch any kind of physical assault with such short notice,"

The Capomandamento nodded his agreement at the Scotsman's assessment. Stewart continued, "But Gabriel said these people need massive amounts of electrical energy to run this infernal wheel. If we can identify the most significant power stations in the surrounding regions, then...."

Before Stewart finished his sentence, the Capomandamento clicked his fingers, causing four Capos to hurry from the kitchen table and retrieve their phones from where they had been left in a metal cabinet near the door[591]. As the four men with smartphones called out the names of the major regional power stations, two other men began writing with chalk on an old blackboard. They listed, Pljevlja and Mratinje Dam for Montenegro; Koman, Fierzë and Vau i Dejës for Kosovo; Tikveš and Vrutok for Macedonia and finally, Agios Dimitrios & Kardia for Greece.

---

[589] A term exclusively used by the Sicilian Mafia to refer to themselves.

[590] Mafia term for "crazy/insane".

[591] To minimise the risk of electronic eavesdropping.

As the list was written, the Capomandamento looked again at Stewart and asked a single-word question. "Explosives?"

Stewart smiled, "I was thinking of a less messy alternative; you and your colleagues are famous for being highly persuasive. Maybe you could find a way to *convince* the power station staff that they should take a break."

The Capomandamento smiled for the first time as he nodded and gestured for one of his Capos to hand him his phone. "I will talk to my regional *representatives* and see if they can *persuade* the shift workers at these power stations," he gestured towards the list on the blackboard, "to take a well-deserved *vacation* tonight."

29 OLD DREAMS NEW NIGHTMARES

"The victor will never be asked if he told the truth." - Adolf Hitler

Fortress Grmožur,
Lake Skadar,
Montenegro.

23:47HRS (GMT+1), 13th Sept, Present day

The stark white of the tiled walls and floor were highlighted in a light blue hue from the far-UVC[592] fluorescent lighting that automatically kept the air and exposed surfaces sterile in the medical section of the Meri-Isfet fortress. The strong, sweet aroma of Sevoflurane anaesthetic filled the air of the long room, which was like a hospital ward, with eleven beds, only one of which was empty at the end.

Over the past hours, the entity that inhabited the French adept had utilised her exalted status as the most senior adept at the Fortress. The parasite had accessed the almost unimaginable financial resources of the Meri-Isfet, to transform Mathers' formerly restrained appearance into something more striking. To say that she now looked like a million dollars would be to grossly underestimate the costs involved in her meticulous preparations for the coming Ten Gates ritual.

Standing in the medical room, supervising the preparation of the ten representatives of the European bloodlines, Mathers wore a bespoke, purple ritual robe created by a team of designers and seamstresses who had been flown in

---

[592] 222 nm wavelength far-UVC light from krypton-chlorine excimer lamps. Kills all bacteria and viruses without causing tissue damage to humans or animals.

from Maison Valentino in Rome. The dress was cut to emphasize her flawless figure and included an intriguing décolletage pattern of fabric strips cut into an inverted pentagram over her breasts. The tightly cinched waist had high slits that exposed her bare legs and naturally led the eye down to her black Manolo Blahnik wrap-around ankle strap, six-inch stiletto high heels. Her exposed arms were adorned with bespoke Cartier snake pattern, wrap-around bracelets in gold, inlaid with dark enamel, that mimicked the scales of a cobra- the heads of which were embedding their exposed fangs into the French adept's wrists.

Her entire body had been meticulously prepared for the coming ritual by a spa team flown in from Clinique La Prairie, in Clarens-Montreux, Switzerland. In addition to the usual massage, wraps, exfoliation, waxing, pedicures and manicures, Mathers' auburn hair had been styled into a golden topknot, adorned with real gold thread, by one of Wella's top stylists, to resemble a Greek Goddess. The rarefied air around the French adept was filled with an intoxicating aroma of black coffee, white florals and vanilla that characterised Yves Saint Laurent Black Opium. Her face had been enhanced by a team of professional makeup artists from Loreal, Paris. These artists had emphasized the look of a Goddess from the ancient world through heavy kohl around her eyes and the addition of blood-red gloss on her lips.

Under Mathers' supervision, once all the ten royal bloodline heirs had been sedated, four Meri-Isfet acolytes had moved the ten unconscious bodies onto specially designed gurney trolleys with a receptacle tray underneath which contained the charged relic associated with the kingdom. Blood grooves on the upper level of the steel trolley fed down to the relic tray beneath to ensure that the victim's life blood would soak the artefact at the appropriate moment in the ritual.

When the French adept started administering a semi-transparent, off-yellow solution of Heparin[593] via an injection gun, a breathless Cardinal Regio, dressed in his purple ritual robes, stormed into the medical area. He initially looked startled at the provocatively dressed French adept who, thanks to her raised Grecian hairstyle and wicked-looking high heels, towered over the much shorter, balding, sixty-two-year-old Regio. Trying to recover his composure, the Cardinal looked over the top of his glasses, so he could better use his astral sight and proclaimed, in English,

"So, you changed host form?"

"Mmm... Yes," Replied Mathers in the sensuous tone that only the French can truly master. She passed the blood-thinning injection gun to one of the assistants and then walked, like a predatory cat, towards the increasingly disturbed Regio.

"It's an improvement, n'est-ce pas ?" queried the French adept seductively as she moved her hands along the tapered lines of the tightly fitted robe. She was relishing her exploration of how easily she could disturb the magical focus of her rival senior adept as she noticed Regio's aura taking on the tell-tale crimson hue of lust. Moving even closer, she saw that Regio's breathing had increased and that his pupils had dilated significantly behind the Cardinal's round glasses. So, she thought, her rival's weakness was exposed, and now she knew she could use this knowledge to her advantage. She moved even closer, slipping her hands inside his robes, close enough to smell the garlic and wine from the older man's lunch, and she pursed her blood-

---

[593] With the label: "10,000 IU Heparin Sodium. Final medical resort acute arterial embolism or thrombosis." Helps avoid annoying blood clotting during ritual blood sacrifices, allegedly.

red lips seductively, as if to kiss Regio, but pulled away at the last moment saying, breathlessly,

"I must control myself! We will explore such delights *after* the ceremony. For now, we should preserve our energies for the ritual. We will both need to be at full performance...."

With that, she turned away from her aroused rival, back towards the four attendants who were prepping the ten ritual sacrifices, proclaiming, as she gestured theatrically to the sedated bodies,

"Bring the Royals to the temple. We must begin immediately!"

And then, turning to the bemused Regio, she took the Cardinal's hand like a child and led him from the medical ward down the corridor towards the temple. The ten loaded gurney trolleys followed behind in a linked train of bodies dragged and pushed by four adepts, two at the front and two at the rear.

The temple was ready for the two ceremonies that would take place that night. The first, a blood sacrifice, would pave the way for political supremacy for Wolfsangel within the European continent. Once that ritual was complete, they would naturally transition into the more complex and demanding "Decem et Aperire Portas[594]".

Mathers strode assertively, like an amazon, through the open double doors, adorned with their carved goetic sigils, and into the vast temple space, with the still flustered Regio struggling to keep up. He was looking increasingly like the French Adept's junior. Electric lights lit the one-hundred-foot-long hall in the high vaulted stone ceiling. Additional light came from a series of tall, red candles set on six-foot-high pillars. The ceremonial space was enclosed within the

---

[594] Opening of the Ten Gates (OTTG).

pair of silver circles inlaid into the stone floor, with a diameter of thirty feet. The assembled group of ten adepts, all dressed in their red, silk, Meri-Isfet robes, bowed towards the two seniors when they arrived and then lined up into two rows of five in front of where Mathers and Regio stood in their purple robes at the Northern end of the sacred space. Both senior adepts stood within their own smaller silver inlaid, protective circles beside the wooden plinth that held the large red, leather-bound book of power.

With their sedated Royal heirs and associated national relics, the gurneys were carefully laid out into a series of ten prepared positions denoted by specific runic inscriptions meticulously copied from the Rauðskinna onto the floor, inside the inner circumference of the larger protective circle.

A series of four banners were displayed in the cardinal directions on the temple walls, showing the goals of their first ceremony. The banner in the East showed a Teutonic knight, in older middle age, with long white hair, dressed in shining steel armour, riding a powerful black Criollo[595] Stallion. The knight was carrying the Spear of Destiny[596] held aloft in triumph. Although the facial bone structure of the knight was that of Chairman Cortez, there was also a striking similarity to an infamous Austrian painter turned politician from the 1930s.

---

[595] The famous horse of the Argentinian gauchos (cowboys).

[596] The spear, also known as The Holy Lance, and the Lance of Longinus, is believed to have pierced the side of Jesus Christ. It is also believed that whoever carries the spear will control the destiny of the world.

The banner in the North showed the symbol of the Black Sun[597]. In contrast, a third banner in the West showed an assortment of oddities: a strange bell-shaped object with lightning surrounding it[598], a saucer-shaped aircraft[599], and finally, a rocket with stars behind it[600].

The final banner, in the South, showed the sideways "Z" with a bar through it (the Wolfsangel symbol) with an embroidered picture beneath showing the inner circle of the Third Reich, all proudly wearing the symbol long before the Swastika was adopted. Superimposed over these faces were the images of Cortez's inner circle.

A large pillar of specially prepared incense, shaped into the form of a hooded, striking cobra, the symbol of the Meri-Isfet, glowed menacingly under the Black Sun banner in the North. The burning concoction slowly released an intense mixture of musk, human blood and hallucinogenic chemicals to enhance the passive and active psychic facilities of those performing the coming rituals.

The assembled group of ten adepts and the two seniors turned towards the North and made obeyance to the

---

[597] Called the "Schwarze Sonne" by the SS, the symbol shows the SS rune (Sowilo) in a repeating sequence around a black central point.

[598] Die Glocke (The Bell) is, we know after reading this story, a much larger version of the St Petersburg Qliphothic wheel installed under Fortress Grmožur.

[599] The legendary "Haunebu" saucer shaped aircraft that, allegedly, in protype form in 1943 reached speeds up to 6000 km/h and was the source of the "Foo Fighter" sightings by allied pilots during the second world war.

[600] The V-2 A4 rocket that was the first known man-made object to reach outer space on October 3, 1942.

glowing cobra. All then performed their obscene variant of the Pater Noster:

"Magna Bestia" (Great beast);

"Noster Accipere Tributa" (Accept our tributes);

"Deorum De Tenebris" (Gods of darkness);

"Ligatis Pedibus Nostris" (Bind our wills);

"Ad Communem Vobis Fore" (To your desires)!

Mathers, who still dominated the smaller figure of Regio, then led the assembled adepts through the Meri-Isfet "Ritual of the Inverted Man" (RIM).

Having completed these preliminaries, Mathers strode to the temple's Western side, where a control wheel was set on the stone floor that looked like a ship's Engine Order Telegraph (E.O.T.)[601]. Grinning mischievously, she pulled the control through all four denoted speeds, SLOW, MEDIUM, and FAST, until it clicked into the final setting marked as "FULL".

A measured engine whine began deep beneath the temple floor. Powerful vibrations started spreading throughout the fortress structure. Regio looked concerned as he approached beside the French Adept, who, in contrast, appeared to be exhilarated by the powerful shaking that was coming through the floor. She exclaimed,

"Feels like a washing machine's spin cycle!"

 Regio looked increasingly uncomfortable. He remarked cautiously,

"We should start the wheel slowly," as the electric lights above them began to flicker and dim.

---

[601] Also referred to as a Chadburn.

"Nonsense. After all, this is a *tiny* wheel; it has been over 12,000 years since it was put through its paces. It wants to *play*."

Mathers laughed seductively at the increasingly frightened reaction of Regio, "Mmmm... you can really feel that vibration in the body, though, can't you?"

The MUŠ.ŠÀ.TÙR infestations of their human forms granted both Mathers and Regio exceptionally robust physiology that could withstand extreme environmental conditions. The human adepts were, unfortunately, less fortunate. They all started to feel physical pain, nausea, and blurred vision. Some began bleeding from their nose, eyes and ears.

The plasterwork on the walls and floor of the temple began to show hairline cracks that rapidly spread over the entire interior surfaces, causing the adepts, including Regio, to become increasingly alarmed. Seeing a growing panic, Mathers shouted,

"Be calm! This is to be expected," and then, ignoring Regio, she abruptly strode to the centre of the temple and commenced the ceremony before the Cardinal had a chance to halt the proceedings.

"Etiam tenebrarum dominis exaudi me!" (Lords of Darkness, hear me!)

There was a violent gust of wind as Mathers continued,

"Vnum verum rectorem sanguis ab his vetusta progenies proferat." (Let the blood split from these ancient lineages bring forth the one true ruler!)

"Fortitudo et puritas consilii fabricata est, et adorabunt eum gentes" (One built of strength and purity of purpose, and the nations will bow down before him)

"Domini tenebrarum sacrificium nostrum suscipe!" (Lords of darkness accept our sacrifice)

Mathers then took a long silver dagger with Sowilo (SS) runes on the hilt from the plinth and processed in an anticlockwise direction to each gurney in turn, savagely cutting the unconscious figures at the throat and in the groin at the top of the thigh. Copious amounts of blood spurted violently. By the time the French Adept had completed her grisly task with all ten bodies, her face and robes had become soaked in blood. The atmosphere inside the temple was heavy with the stench of iron. Mathers then walked back to the plinth and opened two boxes of black obsidian, carved with ornate symbols of a Black Sun and the Wolfsangel rune.

Inside the first box was a human skull, notably without the two bullet holes (entry and exit) associated with committing suicide with a .32 calibre Walther PPK/E handgun. Instead, the head showed signs of reaching extreme old age, with bone resorption, pitting and shrinkage. Forensic examination would have estimated the age at death as being in the late 80s.

The other object that the French Adept extracted from the second box was a red canvas flag with a central white circle containing the hated, anti-clockwise rotating (LHP widdershins) Swastika. If the flag had been subjected to accurate dating techniques, it would have been found to be from the early 1920s and to be of German manufacture[602].

Mathers processed again anticlockwise around the gurneys and soaked both objects in the copious ritual blood that continued to pulse from the bodies. By now, the massive

---

[602] The Blutfahne or Blood Flag, is a Nazi Party flag carried during the attempted Beer Hall Putsch in Munich, on November the ninth 1923, during which it became soaked with the blood of one of the SA men who died.

turbine engines beneath the temple floor had accelerated the St Petersburg wheel to such an extent that sections of the walls and ceiling began to fall to the temple floor. One could also hear that a massive storm had started to form outside the building.

The spurting blood overflowed from the gurneys down over the runic symbols painted onto the floor. The gathering blood formed into a puddle shaped like the outline of Europe. As the painted runes dissolved in the blood, they created a sound that grew in volume. It was a ranting male voice, making a speech in a harsh tongue, accompanied by the frenzied chants of thousands upon thousands of adoring voices. After some minutes, the distinctive voice faded to silence as the puddle of blood drained away through conduits on the temple floor.

As this marked the end of the first of their two intended ceremonies, Mathers wiped the blood from her face with a towel from the plinth. At the same time, Regio supervised the replacement of the red candles with black ones and changed the wall hangings from their Germanic themes to black inverted pentagrams inscribed with Enochian and Hebrew curses. The blood-soaked gurneys were moved on mechanisms to re-position the sacrificed Royal victims into an upright position.

Mathers and Regio exchanged a knowing look before the French Adept commenced, in English (for the benefit of the newly initiated seventh-degree adepts),

"Brethren, it is one week before the equinox and a dark lunar phase, on the Jewish Sabbath day, in the hour of Saturn, in an aspect of Capricorn. The perfect alignment if we are to summon and open the ten Qliphothic gates successfully[603].

On hearing this announcement, the ten adepts dutifully took their places, as they had rehearsed over the past days, each standing in defined spots inscribed on the floor precisely in front of each exsanguinated upright body.

Mathers and Regio now stood side by side in their own smaller, protective circle and jointly proclaimed,

"עשרה קרבנות, אחד לכל אחד מהספירות ההפוכות בהגינותם לתופת!"

(Ten sacrifices, one for each inverted Sephiroth in their descent to the infernal!)

The ten adepts then proclaimed,

"לעלות לעלות לעלות!" (Rise Rise Rise!)

Regio and Mathers then continued,

"הו העתיקים ביותר" (Oh, most ancient ones)

"פתחנו את השערים כדי שתוכלו להיכנס" (We have opened the gates so you may enter)

"לעלות לעולם החומר" (Come up to the material world)

"להורות לנו את הראויים!" (Instruct us who are worthy!)

There was nothing except the vibration and noise of the spinning wheel beneath them. Then, slowly a gradual transparency appeared in the walls, ceilings and even the bodies of the gathered adepts, including Mathers and Regio. The Cardinal and the French Adept looked disconcerted as they had thought they would be spared this effect of the dark magick by their protective magic circle.

---

[603] "The Tree of Death" related to the realm of Evil termed "Sitra Achra" (The Other Side).

Behind the translucent surfaces were tantalizing glimpses of the forms of the surviving entities from previous creations. These manifested to human senses in our limited three dimensions as; pulses of blinding light, sound waves, vibrations, heat, cold, touch, taste, pain, pleasure and, more abstractly, the conscious awareness of mathematical and geometrical concepts[604].

The temple's floor, where the newly initiated magicians were standing, issued forth sparks of lightning that leapt up into the bodies of the ten adepts as they stood in their respective allocated locations within the sacred space. Similar sparks flew up from the floor into the bodies of Mathers and Regio- but the inhabiting MUŠ.ŠÀ.TÙR entities protected their human host forms from the mortal damage inflicted on the less fortunate humans. As Regio and Mathers watched, the life force drained from the bodies of the ten magicians.

This circle of lifeless figures stood with their arms hanging loosely by their sides. One by one, each of the carcasses opened their mouths unnaturally wide and emitted a piercing scream that changed tone gradually into rasping speech, each voice speaking in a different ancient language proclaiming blasphemies against God. This evil choir glorified hate, pain, lust, betrayal, destruction, hunger and disease. The sheer ferocity of their rasping delight in all that was evil gradually disintegrated their bodies and those of the young royal heirs suspended in front of them.

The dust and debris from these remains blew across the temple floor and gradually accumulated to build the outline of a body composed of human ash, forming the ceremony's

---

[604] I know, you were expecting tenticles and "unspeakable horrors".

thirteenth participant, Dumah[605], the Kabbalistic and Islamic Angel of Death. This terrifying figure read from the red book of power in a language so ancient that the two high adepts couldn't recognise it. As the Angel of the Dead continued his exaltation, the earth shook more violently. Regio started in shock as his gold Cardinal's Ring shattered into fragments onto the floor at his feet. Mathers' initiates ring turned from gold to jet black.

The moment the French Adept had pushed the Wheel's engine control towards its maximum setting, the overhead lights in the temple had flickered momentarily as massive amounts[606] of electricity were diverted from the surrounding national grids- causing blackouts in large areas of neighbouring countries. The mechanism inside the small green St Petersburg wheel gradually began to turn. Its sheer mass caused the entire fortress structure and surrounding bedrock to vibrate, with a low buzzing that caused a dull ache in the ear and made vision blur, even for those not inside the temple. Although modern occult scholars focus almost exclusively on the gravitational effects generated by the Qliphothic wheels, the wheels produce what is more accurately described by the most ancient Vedic sources as distortions of Brahman (space, time and consciousness).

These reality distortions were gradual; the melting wax flowing from the candles increased and reversed. Mathers and Regio momentarily saw images of themselves processing into the temple moments before. In addition, the pair noticed that objects, including their bodies, felt heavier and then lighter. As the wheels continued

---

[605] Dumah (דּוּמָה), the angel with authority over the "wicked dead", in both Rabbinical and Islamic lore.

[606] In the region of 300000000 Joules per second.

accelerating, they began projecting a Coriolis field[607] within the temple that spread out into the surrounding space-time-consciousness field, using massive graviton waves[608] that propagated in all directions at the speed of light. These gravitational effects were variable, related to the slight irregularities within the construction of the Trubka cylinder (wheel), which meant that, as they rotated, the generated reality disruption forces varied. If one were to try and describe such disparities, the nearest approximation would be those between a rotating black hole and light particles[609].

These effects spread out around the globe and well beyond. The location of the centre mass of the earth became slightly distorted by the wheel's gravity projection, causing movements within the soft iron and hard iron sections of the earth's core, generating electromagnetic disturbances,

---

[607] One of the apparent gravitational fields felt by a rotating or forcibly-accelerated body, together with the centrifugal field.

[608] In accordance with Einstein's theoretical projections from his 1916 general theory of relativity.

[609] Using Newton's universal laws of gravitation ($F = Gm_1m_2/r^2$), Einstein's mass-energy equivalence relation ($E = mc^2$), the quantum theory of radiation ($E = hv$) and the Schwarzschild radius for spinning black holes as given by the following equation.

$$F' = \frac{hc^3}{GM\lambda}$$

where λ is the radiation wavelength.

plate tectonic activity, and increased movement of magma in the asthenosphere[610].

Compasses became erratic. Bright auroras filled the skies during the day, and animals began to move away from coasts, volcanoes, and tectonic plate edges. Our nearest celestial body, the moon, began to have its orbit imperceptibly altered, triggering rougher seas and violent storms around the globe.

The motion of the moon, combined with the activity in the Earth's mantle, triggered earth tremors from New Zealand, around the East coast of Asia, Canada, the USA and down to the southern tip of South America. As these tremors grew in strength, increased amounts of steam began to rise ominously from the volcanos of Vesuvius, Rainier, Novarupta, Pinatubo, St. Helens, Agung, Fuji and Merapi. Far out in space, massive lumps of rock and ice that had frozen together for countless billions of years began to be pulled apart and diverted from their long-established orbital paths around the sun.

Exactly eight minutes and twenty seconds after Mathers' started the wheel's motion, the Sun emitted a massive coronal ejection that would, in turn, eight minutes and twenty seconds later, disable all the world's navigation and communication satellites.

---

[610] The super-heated, fluid rock beneath the crust that powers the movement of the tectonic plates of the Earth.

30 THE QLIPHOTHIC GATES

"Know that in those days before the Manvantara-Sandhya[611](great calamity), the children of the path of Mara[612](Evil) did indulge in abuses of the divine wisdom that had been bequeathed by the Manu[613] (Lords of Light) to humanity to bring harmony throughout creation. Instead of balance, the followers of Evil sought to concentrate all knowledge, pleasure and possessions on themselves. Soon they discovered there was a forbidden knowledge and power possible to be drawn from before the first breath of Brahma[614] (existence) by the construction of Vinaash Ke Pahiye[615] (wheels of destruction) that accessed the depths of chaos before Brahman (space, time and consciousness)." - Only remaining transcript from the lost scrolls of Pavitr Shuruaat (Sacred Beginnings).

Lake Tashmoo Town Beach,

---

[611] Manvantara-sandhya (मन्वन्तर सन्ध्या) – one of the periodic ends of an age of existence by fire or water. The Ancient Greeks called these "*Kataklysmos*" and "*Ekpyrosis*", cleansing by fire and water respectively. The most recent was, allegedly, by water – known in Western myth as the great deluge or the flood.

[612] Mara – Esoteric Buddhism's personification of evil.

[613] Manu - Higher beings, who were, allegedly, the progenitors of life.

[614] The first breath of Brahma would mark the start of our creation. A creation that, according to the ancient Vedic Sciences, lasts 311,040,000,000,000 human years.

[615] Vedic Science knows these as Vinaash ke pahiye (विनाश के पहिये) – "wheels of destruction". Tibetan Esoteric Buddhists know them as Niṣēdhita mēśinaharu (निषेधित मेशिनहरु) - "forbidden machines". Western Occultists are more familiar with the term, Qliphothic Wheels (גלגלים קליפתיים).

Martha's Vineyard, South of Cape Cod, Massachusetts, United States.

19:47HRS (GMT-4), 13th Sept, Present day

The President of the United States and his senior staff were enjoying a delicious barbeque of New York Strips of A5-Certified Kobe Beef and ice-cold Samuel Adams Whitewater IPA beer, near President Wilson's holiday residence at Lake Tashmoo Town Beach in The Vineyard[616]. The relaxed atmosphere of the evening, sitting at a long wooden bench watching the unprecedented aurora displays, was interrupted by a series of earth tremors, followed by distant flashes of lightning, out over Vineyard Sound. The wind began to pick up, and twelve-foot-high waves formed in rows and drove into the sheltered coastline.

"What the hell?" exclaimed President Wilson.

As the earth tremors increased in violence and huge hailstones began to rain down on the group, the six dark-suited Secret Service agents gathered around the President. They ushered him to cover under the long trestle table along with the Joint Chiefs of Staff (JCS).

"Status?" Demanded the President towards his senior aide, a young man with a stubble designer beard and an iPad pro in his hand. The aide tapped ineffectively at the device, "Sir, all the satellites have ceased working. Before they were lost, the last information I had was from NASA reporting a massive solar flare. It seems to have fried all our surveillance."

---

[616] Martha's Vineyard, often called "The Vineyard" is an island located South of Cape Cod in Massachusetts. It is frequently used for recreation by *the elites*.

"Then we are blind," declared the President, "Go to DEFCOM 1!"

The four aides tried their sat phones, mobiles and other devices before shaking their heads, "Mr President, Sir, we have lost all communications."

As the men struggled to accept the failure of their beloved technology, the Secretary of Defense, Jane Maskins, the only Meri-Isfet initiate in the group, smiled to herself, saying quietly, "It's beginning."

Three thousand three hundred miles to the North East of Martha's Vineyard, in the White State Drawing Room of Downing Street, Prime Minister Sir Reginald Twiffers, Foreign Secretary Sir Johnathan Premble and the Home Secretary Lord Jeremy Kenner were in the final stages of what is often termed by hardened drinkers "a bender[617]." Twiffers and Premble were in a stupefied state, lying on their backs on a silk Isfahan Persian rug, under a swaying, Waterford crystal chandelier, looking dumbly at the fine cracks that were spreading across the ornate plaster ceiling above them. Lord Kenner was occupied throwing up a mixture of Emilio Lustau Amontillado sherry, Niepoort Port and stilton cheese biscuits into an antique, lacquered, wastepaper basket with a portrait of King Edward VII[618] on its side.

On one of the eighteenth-century Chesterfield walnut tables nearby were four empty Lalique decanters of 1863 vintage port and three empty cardboard boxes of Fortnum's cheese biscuits. Beside these discarded empties were a stack of

---

[617] A wild drinking spree, often called in Government circles "a work event."

[618] King of the United Kingdom, British Dominions, and Emperor of India from 1901 until his death in 1910.

"URGENT ACTION" memos that had been brought into the room by Downing Street aides over the past hours. Some were from the Treasury, while others were from the Governor of the Bank of England. These "Urgents" were related to an ongoing systemic hedge fund attack shorting Sterling that had lowered the pound's value to unforeseen depths and placed the British currency on parity with the Venezuelan Bolivar. Unprecedented sell-offs against British Companies on the stock market mirrored this loss of confidence in the country. The FTSE had instigated circuit breaker halts in trading that afternoon at 7%, 13%, and 20% losses, respectively, wiping trillions of value within hours.

Blissfully unaware of these developments, Twiffers and Premble were remarking on the faces they could see in the spreading cracks in the ceiling plaster when a shrill alarm sounded throughout the building, and four dark-suited RaSP[619] police operatives burst into the room. The lead officer looked at the three men, rapidly decided to ignore the obvious inebriation, and proclaimed,

"Prime Minister, due to the earth tremors and extreme weather damaging the structures of government buildings, the threat level has been raised to critical[620]. We have to evacuate you to a safe location."

"What?!" slurred Twiffers.

The detective gestured to the shaking chandeliers, the falling plaster from the ceiling and the rattling empty crystal decanters, "Sir, the building *is* falling apart."

---

[619] The Royalty and Specialist Protection (RaSP) branch of the Metropolitan Police.

[620] Critical is the highest of the national threat levels in the UK.

"Oh, it is actually moving..." remarked Premble, "thought it was the DTs[621], again."

Twiffers giggled.

Initially, the RaSP operatives tried to get the three senior Ministers on their feet, but ended up having to throw the empty port, sherry and wine bottles from the three drinks trolleys and pull the three drunken men onto them. They then wheeled them out into the corridor and through a concealed doorway behind some wood panelling that revealed a lift with a thick, airtight, blue metal sliding door.

"Bloody hell. Been in Whitehall for thirty years and didn't know this was here!" proclaimed Kenner indignantly. After his recent emesis, he was the soberest of the three senior ministers, although still, appropriately, given his aristocratic title, as "drunk as a Lord.[622]"

"Installed in the 1990s as part of Pindar[623]." Explained one of the detectives as they wheeled the three incapacitated Ministers on their trolleys into the lift and descended over one hundred feet. The lift opened into a narrow blue walled tunnel that led North East, deep under Whitehall. It sloped downwards for nearly a quarter of a mile towards a series of massive, blue-coloured, metal blast doors, one hundred and sixty-five feet under the Ministry of Defence buildings at Horse Guards Avenue.

---

[621] Delirium tremens (DTs).

[622] Proverbial in British society even as far back as the 1600s. Some traditions continue unabated.

[623] Pindar was an ancient Greek poet, whose home was the only one left standing after Thebes was sacked in 335 BCE. More than 165 feet under London, it is the prime military control bunker to be used to govern the UK after a cataclysm. It is so classified that even the Prime Minister and Defence Minister do not know all its secrets.

"Welcome to the Defence Crisis Management Centre."
Stated the lead detective as he handed control of the three
trollies over to a group of four soldiers, who wheeled the
three senior Ministers along bustling corridors with a vibrant
cocktail party atmosphere. The area was filled
predominately with older, corpulent men, who looked
vaguely similar to King Edward VII[624], dressed in smoking
jackets and holding glasses of their chosen beverage and
paper plates filled with hors d'oeuvres[625]. These men were
accompanied by a mix of women, dressed either in evening
clothes or tweed country wear, depending on where they
had been when the emergency was declared. Some women
were young and blessed with extraordinary good looks,
while others had a striking resemblance to a horse, which in
British society often means upper class and wealthy.

The top-secret underground shelter had initially been
intended to house one hundred essential military staff and a
handful of political leaders to maintain essential services.
However, over the decades, the list of those selected to
escape the apocalypse changed to reflect those who
contributed the most to whatever political party happened
to be in power or whichever senior civil servant was in
charge of *emergency preparedness*. Consequently, "*The
Pindar List*" had become the ultimate mark of social status
in the United Kingdom. With this change in the anticipated
occupants, the dried military rations had been replaced by
the very finest food from Fortnum and Mason and, of
course, unlimited access to the multi-million-pound,
taxpayer-funded Whitehall Wine cellars.

---

[624] In British Society looking like this former King is, typically, a sign
of high social status and probably advanced liver disease along
with gout.

[625] Party food and snacks.

The three senior Ministers, still lying prone on their trollies, eventually worked their way through the busy corridors and arrived in The Situation Room, where the bunker complex's blue colour theme continued. Thick metallic air conduits and cables covered the ceilings. The walls were covered with old-fashioned computer screens[626], chalkboards, world maps and a row of six clocks showing the main cities around the world. The air inside the long narrow room was cool and had a distinct metallic odour caused by the air filtering systems.

Seated at the head of the long dark wood table was a short, fat man with thick gold-rimmed glasses and a badly miscoloured wig. He was wearing a British Army Major General's mess dress uniform, with a vulgar display of medals and decorations that would have made a South American dictator uncomfortable. Below these rows of decorative brass, silver and gold was a black plastic name badge that declared the wearer to be "M.G. H. Smegett". The recently promoted General Smegett had been transferred from the former Maelstrom base in Grindelwald to oversee the smooth transition of power that Cortez anticipated. General Smegett consulted his white dialled Bremont, Martin Baker MBII[627] watch[628], looked at the sliding plastic wall sign that proclaimed "Current Threat Level is: CRITICAL", the incapacitated Ministers, then at the senior officers from the three armed services and the one

---

[626] Budget priorities focus on essentials, such as fine wines, brand new executive limousines, private executive jets and all the trappings of the elite lifestyle demanded by modern career politicians and senior civil servants.

[627] The Martin Baker ejection seat manufacturer who, under license, permits their name on some Bremont watches.

[628] A new acquisition that he had purchased to celebrate his promotion.

white-coated scientist, all of whom were looking expectantly to the General for leadership. Smegett decided he should at least act the part of a *Modern Major General*[629] and, looking at the tall, thin, bespectacled man in the lab coat first, asked,

"So, umm," Smegett struggled for how he should correctly address the boffin, "Professor, what does science have to say about these strange phenomena we are experiencing?"

The tall man smiled benignly, "You have made a perfectly understandable mistake General. Since Government introduced the commercially funded research reforms to British Universities, we scientists now focus exclusively on providing service-driven knowledge generation."

Smegett looked confused, so the professor continued,

"Put bluntly, General, you tell us what you would like us to find, and we will provide the data and supporting theories to back your desired findings. For a small additional fee, we will stand beside you at press briefings and provide convincing evidence to support whatever action you are planning to take."

Smegett nodded, thinking how he longed for the days when real scientists knew enough to provide useful answers. Giving up on modern science, Smegett turned to the Royal Navy Commander and asked,

"Commander, since we are at the critical threat level, alert our nuclear deterrent to be on full preparedness in case of a first strike by an enemy."

The Naval officer looked embarrassed,

---

[629] Don't worry we will not be bursting into song.

"Sir, all four boats are at HMS Neptune[630], awaiting the release of additional budget funding to enable essential repairs."

Smegett tried to reassure himself of the deadly capabilities of Great Britain,

"But the warheads are still operational?"

The Naval Commander looked even more uncomfortable,

"The Trident 2 D5 nuclear missiles are leased from the United States, Sir, and, well, due to budget constraints, we have not kept up the payments."

Major General Smegett looked at the RAF Wing Commander instead for reassurance, who coughed and said,

"Not much better for us, Sir. The maintenance facilities for our F35s are also leased from the United States. We await the next spending review to get our fighters operational again."

Smegett sighed as he looked towards the Army Major,

"But Major, you can reassure us that our troops are ready for action?"

The Major coughed,

"Well, Sir, after so many complaints of British troops being aggressive to enemy combatants, the most recent defence review decided we would sell our tanks, weapons and heavy support to Saudi Arabia. We are awaiting additional funding to purchase more ecologically sustainable transportation."

"Tanks?" Asked Smegett, hopefully.

"We are focusing on less *hostile* options, Sir."

---

[630] HM Naval Base Clyde, twenty-five miles West of Glasgow, Scotland.

Smegett looked confused,

"Less hostile?"

"Indeed, Sir. Under advisement from the Crown Prosecution Service (CPS), we have decommissioned our weapons. All Army personnel are undertaking extensive re-education programmes for anger management and conflict resolution, followed by surrender negotiation masterclasses."

While Major General Smegett struggled to understand the challenges facing the modern British Military, nearly two hundred feet above him, on Horse Guards Avenue, outside the Ministry of Defence building, Chairman Cortez was addressing the national and international media. Behind him, the assembled cameras showed politicians, corporate leaders and senior civil servants looking terrified as they were hurriedly escorted up the steps and through the two tall, stone, Tuscan pillars[631] to the Ministry building, where they were led to the underground shelter. Meanwhile, seismic tremors continued to cause widespread damage to much of the City of London. While the elites were panicking, Cortez appeared supremely calm and confident as he addressed the traumatised citizens of Britain.

"Friends, the other leaders are unable to address you tonight. However, as a man of the people, I feel that I should share these hazards alongside my fellow citizens. I realise that many of you are now homeless, hungry and helpless. For this reason, I have mobilised my own personal resources to create a Freedom Force (FF) that, as we speak, is creating relief centres in each major city to provide free housing, food and medical care that will commence operations within an hour."

---

[631] Plain pillars without the ornate decorations typically found on Doric or Ionic styles.

Behind Cortez, a group of six smartly dressed young men and women wearing a distinctive white Hugo Boss manufactured uniform with a white cap, and a red armband emblazed with the two letters "*FF*" in a black slanting text marched up and came to attention beside the Argentinian. Cortez gestured to them before continuing,

"Sadly, I am also aware that some people are taking advantage of the situation and have started looting homes and businesses. Therefore, I have asked the weapon-carrying FF members (weaponed FF) to intervene and detain these undesirables to protect the ordinary citizens who are suffering. I ask that you cooperate with the weaponed FF whenever you encounter them performing their duties. Thank you."

With that, Cortez walked from the camera and, in a scene that would be relayed around the world on social media with the hashtag #CaringCortez, he put bandages on an injured senior citizen sitting on the Ministry of Defence steps. Behind the crying senior citizen, a stream of escaping elites passed by on their way to the underground shelter.

Six hundred and twenty miles to the South East from the Ministry of Defence building in London, at the SPLEE lodge, in Geneva, the etheric atmosphere along the Brocken-Rennes ley line had started to glow in bursts of white light, each burst brighter than the last. The three elderly Meri-Maat adepts stood proudly and fearlessly as they performed the ancient *Claudendo Infernum* ritual of final magical resort. Chunks of masonry fell around the three figures, filling the air with a fine covering of dust that was beginning to gather over the adept's clothing and faces. The sound of their powerful invocations was occasionally overwhelmed by loud crashes as benches, candles and other ritual items fell to the temple floor about them in the growing earth tremors. The ancient building shook again, more violently than before, and the hypocaust flooring began to split open. Still, the three continued.

Seven hundred miles to the South East of Geneva, in the Meri-Isfet Temple within Fortress Grmožur, Mathers delighted at the sight of the Angel of the Dead evoking the opening of the Ten Qliphothic Gates, while Cardinal Regio's sweat-soaked face exhibited blissful contentment as he looked at his own aura and could see a new, additional sigil that prompted him to remark excitedly,

"Mathers, look! We are granted the superlative degree of ten circles and one square[632]!"

The dark figure of the Angel gestured with both of his skeletal hands towards the temple in front of them, proclaiming,

"The seven divisions of darkness demand entry to this realm."

Now that Regio and Mathers had achieved the ultimate magical degree, they had an understanding of the tongue of angels, the ancient language from before creation that the Angel of Death was uttering. As the Angel made this pronouncement, seven indistinct, black silhouettes manifested high in the air along the length of the temple.

The Angel's rasping voice then intoned,

"First, Tzoah Rotachat, the abode of the archangel of the abyss, Abaddon!"

The floating dark shape nearest to them became noticeably darker, creating the illusion of an abyss opening before

---

[632] Ipsissimus (10°=1□): The highest degree of Magical perfection.

them. From the bottomless darkness emerged a terrifying roar of some caged beast that demanded release.

The Angel of the Dead continued his evocation,

"Second, Be'er Shachat (בְּאֵר שַׁחַת) the pit of corruption!"

The next dark vortex opened, but it emitted a foul miasma instead of a feral cry.

"Third, Mashchit; Bor Shaon (בּוֹר שָׁאוֹן) the cistern of sound!"

The air in the temple was split by a deafening scream and various discordant sounds.

"Fourth, Tit ha-Yaven (טִיט הַיָּוֵן) the clinging mud!"

The next dark emanation commenced sucking the immediate surroundings into its gaping void.

"Fifth, Sha'are Mavet (שַׁעֲרֵי מָוֶת) the gates of death!"

The next black abyss filled the temple with an icy chill that caused a mist to form in the air, and even Regio and Mathers began to shiver.

"Sixth, Neshiyyah (נְשִׁיָּה) oblivion!"

An empty nothingness opened in the air.

"Seventh, Eretz Tachtit (אֶרֶץ תַּחְתִּית) the lowest earth!"

A tremendous weight was felt by Mathers and Regio, who would have been pulled to the ground, had they not been gifted with preternatural strength.

"Behold!" exclaimed the Angel of the Dead, "With the seven gates opened, now this realm shall be visited by the three powers before Satan and their twenty-two[633] demonic incarnations!"

---

[633] Corresponding to the 22 letters of the Hebrew alphabet.

The final three swirling voids projected into manifestation three entities that were combined into one[634]. With this manifestation, the chill in the room became absolute. The air began to condense on the floor in swirling clouds, the first stages of the gases of oxygen and nitrogen separating into their liquid forms.

"Behold, the Satanic Trinity: Qemetial, Belial, and Othiel!" The dark angel bowed,

The three supreme devils had dark forms that appeared to be composed of red-stained ice, ash and charcoal. They had irregular misshapen faces with odd eyes, multiple horns and gaping holes at different places in their bodies filled with hideous asymmetrical fangs. From these deformed, multiple openings, they screamed endless obscenities against God.

Suddenly, at the end of the long temple, directly in front of the three Arch Devils, the shadowy outlines of three elderly people, hunched over in clearly advanced age, appeared. There were two males and one female. Although they faced certain destruction, they were focused on completing some ritual. Since they were only partially manifested, it was impossible to hear what they were invoking.

Mathers hissed in clear recognition and then screamed at the Dark Angel of the Dead, "No! Do not permit their intervention!"

At that precise moment, whether by the magical intervention of the elderly adepts or from the more mundane material intervention designed by the Scotsman,

---

[634] The supreme entities of many belief systems adopt a trinity. This is a symbolic representation of the universal esoteric law that three forces (the sacred Triangle of Pythagoras) are required for material manifestation.

Tavish Stewart, or a coincidental[635] mix of both influences, the electric lights in the temple ceiling flickered off, then returned, but were noticeably dimmer. The note from the turbines beneath them was also noticeably different. This process continued a few times before the lights finally extinguished. The vibration shaking the entire fortress faded as the electricity failed utterly, and the air became unnaturally still. As Mathers and Regio's vision adjusted to the lower light levels, they could see that the Demonic projections of the ten gates and the Satanic Trinity had gone.

Simultaneously with this recognition, they saw that the dark Angel of the Dead had moved with incredible speed and struck down the Meri-Maat adepts' projections before vanishing himself. The outline of the three elderly figures lay motionless as fading shadows on the temple floor, as they did on their temple floor back in Geneva. The ceremony was over.

Regio was elated,

"We have become the ultimate couple! Everything is now perfect!"

Mathers smiled, "Not *quite* perfect."

"Why? What is imperfect?" Regio looked momentarily perplexed, then added,

"Oh... you mean our *coupling.....*" Regio was looking forward to consummating their partnership.

Mathers approached closer, like a lover, but her right hand withdrew a concealed object from within her robes as she held the balding Cardinal in an embrace. She violently struck the ancient UG-ZI-ZU Assyrian adze into the crown of

---

[635] As any serious student of the esoteric will tell you this kind of uncertainty in causality is exactly how real magic manifests.

Regio's skull. As he fell to the floor, Regio's final thought was the recognition that Mathers had taken the Adze from him during their romantic embrace in the medical ward before the ceremony.

The French Adept laughed, "No, my dear Regio, two was one Ipsissimus too many! Now I am the ultimate evil!"

Moments afterwards, in the very highest realms of existence, three figures came slowly and unsteadily across a beam of light, high above the burning fires of karmic punishment blazing beneath the silver cord of the Chiviat Bridge[636]. The three elderly Meri-Maat adepts were surprised they were allowed to pass over unopposed. Their understanding of the ceremony they had just completed was that they would face terrible karmic consequences for calling forth an evil sufficient to banish whatever had been manifested through the opening of the Ten Qliphothic Gates. However, they had been permitted to pass over the Bridge of Souls instead of being cast into the fires. They now stood before a towering figure of such a size that it filled the visible universe. It had six wings that spread over the whole of creation. The surface of its body was covered in huge predatory eyes, filled with terrible intelligence and power[637]. In this entity's right hand was an enormous flaming sword, covered in Enochian symbols.

Before the three ancient adepts could say anything, Mathers' phrase echoed across the vast area before the mighty being,

---

[636] Chinvat Bridge (Bridge of the Requiter) is the sifting bridge for souls in Zoroastrianism.

[637] This fits the description of a Seraph, (plural Seraphim), in Jewish, Christian, and Islamic literature, these entities are described as the throne guardians of the unknowable God.

"Now I am the ultimate evil!"

The three veteran adepts realised their mortal sacrifice in performing the Claudendo Infernum had not been in vain. They saw the flaming sword carried in the mighty being's right-hand move and gesture down into the material realms far below, issuing an irresistible command upon the whole of creation.

Back in the refined Swiss Resort of Grindelwald, a violent storm raged, repeatedly striking lightning into the remains of ancient wooden churches and mountainside shrines. Inside a sealed boardroom deep within one of the peaks of the Bernese Alps, a group of corrupt men congratulated themselves. The hedging bets they had placed against the financial resources and reputation of the United Kingdom had paid off handsomely. They were now discussing ramping up their blackmail and extortion over the current leaders of the European Nations before they too were ousted from power.

These corrupt men who had gathered around what had been the Maelstrom boardroom were eagerly anticipating the advancement that would surely accompany their control over the continent of Europe. As they toasted each other with the finest Dom Pérignon champagne, vaporous clouds began to form in the room, and it became bitterly cold. Several champagne bottles and the fluted glasses shattered as the wine inside them froze, and the room was plunged into darkness.

The chairman of the meeting, Colonel Jaree, who had only recently taken over from Major General Smegett, announced,

"Gentlemen, please remain calm and seated. The emergency generator will come on momentarily."

Unseen by anyone, behind Jaree, the full-length picture of the late Dr Nissa Ad-Dajjal became increasingly lifelike. Thick, white ice tendrils formed around the edges of the image. Then slowly, like a butterfly emerges from a chrysalis, a perfect female form, with raven black hair and striking green hypnotic eyes, pulled itself slowly from the picture, finally stepping seductively from the portrait, unseen into the complete darkness of the board room.

After what felt like an eternity, the backup generators finally kicked in, and the red emergency lights came on from the ceiling. Jaree looked in shock as he saw the assembled men around the table all standing and looking aghast at something behind him before rushing in terror from the room.

Within seconds, he was the only person remaining. He wondered what could have caused such dread in these most ruthless men. As the icy cold air in the deserted board room became filled with the highly distinctive intoxicating musky scent of the Ghost flower of the Mojave Desert[638], he turned, saw that the canvas of the infamous portrait behind him was empty, and then, with a start, noticed that standing beside him was the tall, raven-haired, Dr Nissa Ad-Dajjal; involuntarily he exclaimed,

"Jesus Christ!"

A sultry voice corrected him, "Guess again...."

---

[638] This unique perfume was distilled exclusively by the Sultan of Oman's own perfume house, Amouage for only one person.

The story continues in:

THE NEW REPUBLIC: TWILIGHT OF THE GODS

Social Media

If you enjoyed reading this book, please leave a review on social media so others can also discover the adventures of Tavish Stewart.

ALSO BY K.R.M. Morgan

Bridge of Souls: Ancient Prophecy. Ultimate Evil.

An ancient esoteric object, once used by Elizabethan
Magician John Dee in his infamous occult rituals, attracts a
deadly interest from the clandestine world of outsourced
military operations and leads Antiquarian and former
Scottish Military hero, Tavish Stewart, to uncover a global
conspiracy to control world leaders and enslave the whole
of humanity.

Stewart's discovery leads him, and his friends, into a race
across the globe to locate ancient maps, mysterious lost
cities, magical relics and a forgotten civilisation so ancient
and advanced that it would rewrite human history. Stewart
must use all his Military and Martial Arts expertise to
overcome the elite warriors, weapons and technologies that
are set against him before a final apocalyptic confrontation
in the desolate wastes of Asia, to preserve the greatest
secret of all time!

ISBN: 978-1-5272-2595-4

What readers had to say:

"What an absolute cracker of a novel. Jam packed with action from start to finish. Well crafted with a cleverly woven plot, full of twists and turns.. K.R.M. Morgan is one heck of a storyteller. I loved it so much on Kindle, I bought the paperback to keep. Can't wait for the movie!" – 5 Star Review Amazon.co.uk

"Think James Bond versus The Omen. Fast cars, prophecy, gunplay, religion, martial arts, the occult, and an unlikely trio on a mission to avert the Apocalypse. If you liked Charlie Stross's "The Jennifer Morgue" you'll love this." – 5 Star Review Amazon.co.uk

"From the thoroughly gripping beginning this story takes you on a roller coaster of twists and turns, dark alleys and darker characters. Intelligently written its a must for anyone who likes a conspiracy. If you like James Bond, Indiana Jones, The Mummy, ancient history, or Dan Browne you'll LOVE this more! Why on earth isn't it a film yet?" – 5 Star Review Amazon.co.uk

About K.R.M. Morgan

After leaving school, Konrad worked to fund himself through several years of further and higher education. When he was not studying, he spent his free time practising various martial arts in his back garden, much to his neighbours' amusement. After finishing his studies, Konrad pursued an academic career that permitted him to work in several regions around the world.

During his travels, Konrad encountered some extraordinary individuals, including politicians, bureaucrats, mad professors, spies, ritual magicians, bankers and media moguls. Some were good, some were bad, and some were just bizarre. His experiences form the basis for his books' complex plots and characters.

Connect with K.R.M. Morgan:
Twitter: @KRM_Morgan

Lightning Source UK Ltd.
Milton Keynes UK
UKHW010820031022
409835UK00003B/557